WESTERN FRINGES

AMER ANWAR

D1080964

EDURUS
BOOKS

WESTERN FRINGES

EDURUS BOOKS

ISBN: 978-0-9957123-0-0

First published in Great Britain by Edurus Books 2017

1

Supported using public funding by the National Lottery through Arts Council England.

A catalogue record for this book
is available from the British Library.

Edurus Books
86-90 Paul Street
London EC2A 4NE
www.edurusbooks.com

Printed and bound in Great Britain by
Clays Ltd, St Ives plc

*For my mother, Shahnaz
and Lana,
with love, always.*

WESTERN FRINGES

CHAPTER ONE

Zaq had a bad feeling.

The most senior person he usually dealt with at the builders' yard where he worked was the manager or one of the supervisors, but this morning he'd been called in to see the owner, Mr Brar. That could only mean one thing – trouble.

The yard manager, Jatinder Singh Sidhu, known to everyone as Sid, had caught Zaq flicking through a newspaper before taking his deliveries out. '*Thu haleh aythay uh?*' Sid had said in Punjabi. '*Brar sahib thenu balanda.*' A short, squat man with a thick black moustache, he might have looked athletic if it weren't for the large potbelly straining the fabric of his polo shirt.

Zaq pushed the refugee crisis, the latest political scandal and the robbery of a plane at Heathrow from his mind and put the paper down. 'What's he want?'

'*Mehnu kee putha? Ja ke dekh la.*' Sid waved at the building behind him.

Zaq patted brick dust, plaster and wood chips from his clothing and headed inside through the warehouse, weaving his way between the high stacks of timber and building materials. Hindi music from the latest Bollywood blockbuster accompanied him as he tried to figure out what the boss wanted with him. He hadn't been there long enough to be getting a raise and there wasn't any scope for career advancement, so it couldn't be either of those things.

Then a thought struck him – maybe he was about to get sacked? Shit... He hadn't done anything to warrant it. As far as anyone knew, he worked hard, was good at his job and, unlike most of the guys that worked there, he spoke fluent English. But, as the only Muslim in a company owned and run by Sikhs, he knew if anyone was going to get the boot, it'd be him. It didn't even matter that he wasn't religious; just having a Muslim name and coming from a Pakistani family would be reason enough – and that was before you even mentioned his criminal record. Shit.

He climbed the dingy stairs up to the first-floor office and stopped outside the cheap wooden door. Mr Brar's name was spelled out on it in bold black capitals on gold stickers. *Sod it*, he thought, if I get sacked, maybe I'll find something better. His optimism faded as he remembered how hard it had been to land even this job. Five years inside and a record of violence weren't the sort of qualifications employers were looking for and there was no shortage of people looking for work. He'd only got this job driving deliveries for Brar Building Supplies because a friend of his dad's had put in a word.

He steeled himself and knocked on the door. Let's just get it over with, he told himself.

'*Haah? Ajaa*,' a deep bass voice called out. Zaq opened the door and went in.

Mr Brar sat behind a huge mahogany desk. He was a heavyset man in his late fifties, with a barrel chest and wide shoulders. His calloused, shovel-sized hands had clearly seen a lot of manual labour. His coarse skin was molasses brown, and his broad face was nailed in place by dark, deep-set eyes, which regarded Zaq with little warmth despite the tooth-filled smile that split his face. The teeth and eyes reminded Zaq of a documentary he'd seen recently about sharks. Thick black hair smoothed back from a large forehead only added to the impression.

'Zaqir,' Mr Brar said, using Zaq's given name. He gestured to a pair of cheap office chairs facing his desk. '*Ah ke behja.*'

Zaq took the seat on the right. He'd only been in the office once before, when he'd come about the job. It hadn't changed in the six months since. It didn't look as if it had changed much in the last few decades. It was done up like the set of a bad 1970s TV show. Some of the furniture might actually have been from the '70s. A garishly patterned threadbare carpet lay dying on the floor, and the walls were covered with faded cream and brown striped paper, peeling at the edges. Brightly coloured religious images, intended to bestow blessings and good fortune on the business, looked down from the wall on the right. On the left, windows let in a dull grey light which did little to brighten the gloom. 'You wanted to see me?' Zaq said.

'*Haah, haah!* How is everything?'

'Fine.'

'Your mum, dad? How are they?' He didn't really know them – it was just the sort of thing you asked.

'They're OK, thanks.'

'The rest of your family? You have a brother, *hena*?'

That was one of the things about living in a tight-knit community like Southall. Everyone knew everyone else, at least as far as the Asian community was concerned. Forget six degrees of separation, in Southall it was down to one or two.

'He's all right.' Zaq said.

'And how is the job? OK?'

This had to be his way of working up to it. 'Yeah, it's fine.'

A momentary silence hung between them like a bad smell. A sound from behind made Zaq look over his shoulder. Two men he hadn't noticed when he came in were sitting in the shadows against the back wall. They were bigger and bulkier than he was and were both staring right at him. There was something vaguely familiar about them...

'You know my sons?' Mr Brar said. 'Parminder and Rajinder.'

'No.' He didn't know them but it explained why they looked familiar. They were younger versions of their old man, with the same intimidating, shark-like presence. The Brar brothers had a reputation in and around Southall, and it wasn't a good one.

Zaq gave them a nod. They gave the slightest of nods in return but said nothing. Zaq turned back to face Mr Brar. 'What was it you wanted to see me about?'

The remnants of the smile faded from Mr Brar's face. 'OK, Zaqir, I will come straight to the point.'

Zaq let out a slow breath and waited.

'I want you to do something for me. I want you to find someone.'

It wasn't what he had expected. 'Who?'

Mr Brar's face was as impassive as a block of stone. 'My daughter.'

Zaq managed to contain his surprise. 'If she's missing, shouldn't you tell the police?'

'This is a family matter, not something for the police. She has just run away from home. All we want is to find her and bring her back – no police, no fuss.'

If word got round in the community that Mr Brar's daughter had run away from home, it would be the subject of gossip for months, possibly years, and would never be forgotten. The family's reputation would be tarnished forever – if you bought into old-fashioned crap like that.

'If it's a family matter,' Zaq said, 'maybe you'd be better off having your boys look for her...'

'I didn't ask for your opinion.' Mr Brar's eyes bored into him, any pretence of friendliness now gone. 'You are here to do what I tell you, and I'm telling you to find my daughter.'

'What if I can't?'

'Then you will go back to prison. We will arrange it.'

It hit Zaq like a punch in the stomach. He felt short of breath, like his lungs were being squeezed.

'*Haah*, now you have a good reason to make sure you find her.'

'Arrange, how?'

Mr Brar shrugged. 'A call to the police perhaps, to tell them you have been caught stealing from us.'

'I haven't though. There's no proof?'

'Proof? We can make proof, don't you worry. Everyone here will say whatever I tell them to. If I tell them you have been stealing, then that is what they will say to the police.'

Zaq knew it was true. The staff were shit scared of the Brars.

'And we will also say you attacked the staff when they caught you, beat them most viciously. The police will believe that, don't you think?'

What Zaq was thinking was how much he'd like to dive across the desk and punch the old fuck in the face – and then he realised exactly why Parminder and Rajinder Brar were there. If he made any move toward their old man they'd be on him like a pair of rabid Rottweilers. 'Why're you doing this?' he managed to rasp, his throat dry, a sick feeling taking hold of his stomach.

'Because I want my daughter found quickly and quietly and

I don't want people to know what has happened. This way I can be sure you will keep your mouth shut and do whatever you have to, to find her.'

'What if I just quit and walk out?'

Mr Brar gave him a cold smile. 'There is no quit, bastard. You do what I'm telling you or you go back to prison… for another five years, maybe more this time.'

Zaq's mind was spinning. He couldn't see any other choice but to agree to what Mr Brar wanted. 'How the hell am I supposed to find her?' he said. 'I don't know anything about her.'

Mr Brar signalled to his sons. One of them – Zaq wasn't sure which – came over and handed his dad an envelope, then took up position standing just behind Zaq. It was like being back in the prison governor's office with a guard hovering over him, a situation he was all too familiar with. Mr Brar took two items out of the envelope and looked at them, before placing one in front of Zaq.

'This is a photo of Surinder,' he said. 'Everyone calls her Rita.'

Zaq was surprised to see a portrait shot of a very attractive girl, who bore absolutely no resemblance to the men in the office. Lucky for her.

Next to the photograph Mr Brar placed a hand-scrawled list and tapped it with a meaty finger. 'These are the names and numbers of some of her friends and workmates. We managed to find them from things in her room. Maybe one of them will have some idea where she is.'

Zaq looked up from the list. 'Even if I manage to find her, how am I supposed to get her to come home? She don't know me. She ain't going to come with me.'

'You don't worry about that. You just find her and tell us where she is. We will sort out the rest.'

That didn't sound like a good thing – but then, there was

nothing good about any of it. It was bullshit, and if he didn't do what they wanted they'd drown him in it. Zaq looked at the big blocky son-of-a-bitch sitting opposite him then glanced at the son-of-the-son-of-a-bitch looming over him. These guys didn't believe in talking and negotiation; they got what they wanted faster with threats and intimidation. Whatever their reasons, Zaq didn't see he had a choice. He looked at Mr Brar again, hoping it was all some big wind-up, that they would start laughing and tell him he ought to see the look on his face. But when he looked into the older man's iron-black eyes, he saw he was serious as cancer. 'When do you want me to start?'

'*Huun*, right now. Ram will take the deliveries. This is your top priority.'

'How am I supposed to get around?'

Mr Brar's face clouded with annoyance. 'You don't have a car?' He thought for a moment, then said, '*Thu ja, aur* Sid *nu uthay bhej de.*' Zaq stood. 'You will need these.' Mr Brar pushed the photograph of Rita and the list of names and numbers towards him. Zaq slipped them into the back pocket of his jeans. 'And Zaqir,' Mr Brar said, 'find her quickly. I am not a patient man.'

Zaq turned to leave and found his way blocked by the son who'd been standing over him. He could have moved a chair aside and slipped past or gone around the other way, but he did neither. He stayed where he was and returned the big lump's stare, waiting for him to either let him pass or do something. It probably wasn't the best idea to get into a punch-up with the boss's son, but it sure as fuck might make him feel better.

Mr Brar tutted. 'Rajinder, *enu jaane de,*' he ordered.

Rajinder didn't move. The muscles in his jaw tightened and his eyes narrowed as he stayed where he was for a few more seconds... then moved before his father had to tell him again. He turned his body slightly but not enough to allow Zaq to get past. It was a tactic used by bullies in the playground, and in prison too. Rather than nudge a chair out of the way to make more room, he simply shouldered Rajinder aside. He felt him tense but was past him before he had time to react. Zaq's senses were fully jacked up, alert for even the slightest whisper of movement behind him, ready to turn and slug it out if he had to. He took a step, then another… but nothing happened.

Parminder Brar was still seated near the door, staring at him too. Zaq stared right back. If they wanted to intimidate him, they'd have to do a lot better. Zaq had learnt the rules of this sort of game the hard way, but he'd learnt them well. Faced with threats and intimidation, you never backed down. If you showed fear or weakness, your opponents would be all over you. It was the law of the jungle, a primal thing. In order to survive you had to confront anything like this head on – and anyway, he was too angry to be scared.

He met Parminder's gaze and forced it right back at him. His anger was a molten ball burning in his guts and blazing behind his eyes. Maybe Parminder sensed it or read it in his face; either way, he broke eye contact first. He didn't want to and was clearly pissed off that he had, but he was unsure about Zaq. They all knew what he'd been done for and other stories would have done the rounds, some true, some not… but if they made shitheads like these think twice, Zaq didn't care what the stories were or who believed them.

CHAPTER TWO

He went down the stairs, taking deep breaths and trying to keep his anger in check, rage bubbling away in his gut. They could've just asked him to find the girl – but no, they'd wanted to show their dominance, make it clear he had to do what they wanted. Arrogant fucks.

Bowling into Sid's office, he found the yard manager sat behind his shabby desk reading a newspaper. 'He wants you upstairs.'

Sid looked over the top of the paper, '*Kohn?*'

'Who d'you think?'

Sid's brows knitted in a frown. '*Kyoh?*'

'How should I know? Why don't you go and find out?'

Sid gave him an unpleasant look, then folded the paper on the desk and left to see the boss.

Zaq needed to calm down and clear his head, so he left the office to go out to the yard. On the way he saw Ram sorting wooden flooring in the warehouse, in preparation for a new delivery coming in. 'You're going to be taking the deliveries out in the white van today.'

'How come?'

'I've got to do something else for that wanker upstairs.'

'Who... Mr Brar? OK, cool.'

Ram would be happy just to get out of the yard for the day. It also meant someone else would have to sort out the flooring.

When Zaq had started work at the yard, he'd taken over from Ram as a delivery driver, which caused some friction between them. Things had blown over once it became clear Zaq hadn't got the position out of any sort of favouritism, but simply because he could drive and navigate at the same time. The company was too cheap to fit sat-nav in its vehicles, so the drivers had to rely on their own phones or tatty old copies of the A-Z. Ram could drive but he had a terrible sense of direction and couldn't read a map for shit.

Zaq strode out into the yard. Ram left what he'd been doing and went with him.

'Here,' Zaq said, handing Ram the keys to the van. 'You might as well take these now.' Zaq took a breath of the crisp morning air, breathing in the scents of timber, sawdust and diesel. The whine of wood being cut and voices shouting in Punjabi came from the saw room.

'Shits already gone out?' Ram asked. He was talking about the other van driver, Bits. The guy's family nickname was Bittu but he'd thought it sounded too childish and told everyone to call him Bits, reckoning it was more 'street'. Unfortunately, Bits soon became Shits and, like shit, it had stuck.

'Yeah.' Zaq mimed holding a roach and taking a drag.

'Ah, right.' Ram understood the action as meaning Bits had gone off to smoke a spliff.

'*Ay, kautha,*' came a shout. They turned and saw Sid coming towards them. '*Yeh leh.*' The manager threw something to Zaq that he caught and found was a set of keys.

'*Chauti van di eh,*' Sid said, pointing to a small Vauxhall Rascal van in the corner of the yard, a spare vehicle only used now and again for running errands. It was dark blue and orange. Zaq knew it was blue because he'd once seen the colour under the dirt. The orange was rust. Light reflected off the bodywork at odd angles, from prangs and dents that had never been repaired. It was a piece of junk… but at least it was a set of wheels.

'*Brar sahib vaste ki karnah?*' Sid asked. 'What you doing for him?' His English was mangled by his heavy Indian accent.

'A special job.'

'*Haah, haah, bouthi* special job *howga.* Blow job *tha nahi?*' Sid leered at him. 'Maybe you sucking his cock, huh?'

'Nah, your missus is already taking care of that,' Zaq said.

Ram tried not to laugh but couldn't help himself.

'*Theri bhen dhi…*' Sid pulled back a fist as if to throw a punch. Zaq didn't move. The manager stood poised for a second then let his arm fall to his side and forced a smile to show he could take a joke. '*Chal, duffa hoja.*' He waved Zaq away, encouraging him to piss off and do whatever it was he had to do.

'See you later,' Zaq said to Ram, who was still laughing, and he walked over to the van. It took three tries to get the engine started. When it finally coughed to life, Zaq let it idle. His anger had cooled a little and he tried to think objectively about the situation he was in. If the Brars made good on their threats he'd be in deep shit. All he had to do was find this Rita, tell her fat fuck of a dad where she was, and that would be the end of it – only he knew it wouldn't be. Once they had a hold over him, they wouldn't let go. People like that never did. They'd have him do any dirty little job that came up and if the shit ever hit the fan – well, who the fuck was he? Nobody. They'd deny any knowledge of whatever he was doing for them and let him take the fall.

He might not have any choice but to do what they wanted now but, once he was done with it, he'd tell them to stick their job and leave. They could find another mug to push around.

Right, so, find this girl – but how the hell was he meant to do it? Where did he even start?

He pulled out the photo and took a good look at it. She was certainly a looker. There was nothing remotely shark-like about Rita Brar. Her skin was the colour of milky tea, smooth and unblemished. She had a small straight nose and her eyes were the amber of warm caramel. Her smile showed off perfect white teeth and full lips. The hair that framed her face was fashionably cut and coloured, not tied back in the braided plait more traditional parents made their daughters wear. She could easily have been mistaken for Mediterranean or South American, instead of Indian. She'd certainly been lucky not to inherit her father's size or looks and must've taken after her mother. The photograph was only a head and shoulders shot and Zaq found himself wondering what the rest of her looked like.

He turned his attention to the list. The first name on it was Rita's, along with her mobile number. He didn't recognise any of the other names, so he took out his phone and tried calling her. No answer. Obvious, but he'd had to try. She was probably screening her calls, if she was still using the number at all.

Right, now what? The answer popped into his head. His phone still in his hand, he thumbed to his contacts, pressed 'J' and hit the first name on the screen to make the call.

'All right, Zaq?' a male voice answered.

'What you doing? You at work?'

'I'm working from home today.'

'Can I come round? I need to talk to you about something.'

'Ain't you supposed to be working too?'

'I am. I'll tell you about it when I see you. Be there in about

fifteen minutes. Oh, and Jags...'
    'What?'
    'Stick the kettle on.'

CHAPTER THREE

Zaq had been away for five years and though some things had changed, the sights, sounds and smells of Southall were essentially the same. The brightly coloured sari shops and glittering Indian jewellers were still there in all their spangly glory, even if some of the names were new. Music shops and street stalls continued to blare out the latest Punjabi and Hindi hits. Indian restaurants and supermarkets did a roaring trade, filling the air with the pungent aromas of spices and real Indian cooking that made the place smell like home. He had changed much more than the streets he moved through.

He rattled along Southall Broadway, heading toward Hayes. Road layouts and traffic controls might have been improved while he was away but the congestion hadn't. The chicanes for slowing down boy racers on the side streets had been replaced by batteries of speed bumps and now the roads were mostly one-way, alternately going towards the Broadway or away from it.

The slow grind of traffic had its plus points though. When he was growing up, the Broadway had been the place to cruise, up and down, by car or on foot. Going nowhere fast meant you had plenty of time to chat to your mates, check out girls and generally show off and be seen. Weekends were good but the summer holidays had always been the best time. It wasn't quite the same now, on a cold and overcast Monday morning.

He crossed Hayes Bridge, heading west over the Grand Union Canal, still thinking about what had happened in Mr Brar's office – and still pissed off about it. It was their sheer arrogance that really needled him; how they'd made their demands and enforced them with threats and blackmail. Zaq knew what a contrary sod he could be at the best of times but this situation really had him balking. If they thought he was just going to roll over and do what they wanted, they had another thing coming. He realised his jaw was clenched and he was grinding his teeth. He made exaggerated chewing motions to loosen the muscles and tried to relax.

Much as he hated to, he was going to have to go along with what they wanted – at least for the time being. He drove along the Uxbridge Road and thought about how he was supposed to find Rita Brar. What the hell did he know about looking for a missing person? He wasn't a bloody detective. What if he couldn't find her, even after trying everything he could think of? Would the Brars accept that and let him off the hook? 'Course they fucking wouldn't. They'd shop him out of spite and simply because they could.

He turned off near Hayes police station, drove along some residential streets, and pulled over outside a small mid-terrace house. He got out of the van and walked past a sleek black BMW in the driveway, to the front door, where he rang the bell.

Jags opened the door. '*Kidaah*?' he said and they shook hands.

Jagdev Kholi was Zaq's best friend and had been since they were about nine years old. Although he was a Sikh, he'd never worn a turban or a topknot and his dark hair was styled in trendy disarray. His neatly trimmed, stubbly beard lent his appearance a slightly rough edge. He was almost the same height as Zaq, though a little slimmer in build. His eyes were dark brown, sharp and intelligent. Laughter made them twinkle but Zaq had seen anger turn them hard and sharp as black diamonds.

He followed Jags into the L-shaped, open-plan living area. The lounge was to the right, at the front of the house, with a large kitchen and dining area at the back, forming the base of the L. French doors to the garden added to the natural light that filled the bright and airy interior. Zaq took a seat at the dining table.

'Kettle's just boiled,' Jags said. 'You want tea or coffee?'

'Tea.'

'Sugar?'

'Not any more.'

'You used to.'

'When I was about twelve.'

Jags brought their mugs over and set one down in front of Zaq. He took a seat opposite and pushed his laptop out of the way. 'So, what's up?'

Zaq took a breath. 'You know Mr Brar?' he said.

'No. Should I?'

'He owns the builders' yard where I work. I just got dragged into his office and told to do something for him.'

'It didn't involve his dick and your mouth, did it?'

'No, it fucking didn't.' Even though he'd been told to keep quiet about what he was doing, Zaq needed help and there was no one he trusted more than Jags. 'I've got to find his daughter. And he's blackmailing me to make sure I do it. I don't find her, he's going to have me banged up again.'

'For what?'

'Nicking stuff from the yard.'

'You haven't though... have you?'

''Course not. But he's got a story all worked out, how I been taking stuff and when I got caught, I beat up the guys who found out.'

Jags shook his head. 'That's fucked up, man. What you going to do?'

'What can I do? I ain't got a choice. I got to try and find this girl... least until I figure something else out.'

'Why don't you just quit and walk out?'

'I was going to but they'd have called the cops there and then and had me busted.'

'They?'

'His boys were in the office too.' Zaq saw the blank look on Jags' face. 'Parminder and Rajinder Brar.'

'Oh, shit. I forgot you worked for their old man. Those guys are bad news. They ain't joking about fucking you up. They'd do it.'

'I worked that out myself.'

'Damn...'

They drank their tea in silence for a while. Telling Jags hadn't made Zaq feel much better about what was going on; anger was still burning a hole in him. He put his mug down. 'Can I have the key to the garage?'

'What for?'

'I need to go and hit something.'

Zaq went out through the French doors into the garden and followed the path to the large brick-built double garage that took up the whole of the far end. He let himself in the side door, entering what Jags used as a home gym and storage area. Small windows near the ceiling allowed some daylight in but

Zaq turned on the overhead fluorescents anyway. They flickered to life and lit up the collection of fitness equipment set up on the floor.

There were barbell and dumbbell weights and a couple of benches, as well as a treadmill, a rowing machine and an exercise bike. It wasn't a bad little set-up. But what Zaq had come for was the punchbag hanging from one of the thick roof joists by a heavy duty chain and suspended in front of a large mirror. He took off his sweatshirt and draped it on the treadmill, so he was just in his T-shirt and got a set of boxing wraps from a shelf. He wound one round his left hand first, like a bandage, making sure it was nice and tight, then did the right.

He shook himself as loose as he could, and began hitting the bag. Left, right. Left, left, right. He was light on his feet, bouncing, sticking and moving. Jab, jab, straight right, hook. The blows were easy to start with but as his thoughts returned to Mr Brar, they became harder and faster, until he was unloading everything he had into them, making the heavy bag bounce around on its chain.

When he finally stopped, he was panting and sweaty. He realised it had been ages since he'd last trained. He'd meant to keep it up but his resolve had weakened gradually until he'd stopped altogether. His workout now had managed to burn off some of the anger and frustration he'd carried from the builder's yard and he felt better for it, calmer.

He took off the wraps, put on his sweatshirt, locked the garage and went back to the house.

'Feeling better?' Jags enquired.

'Yeah.' Zaq gave him back the keys.

'Your tea's gone cold.'

'I need some water.' He took his mug to the sink, emptied it, and filled it with cold water from the tap. He drank it down in one go, refilled it and sat back down at the table with Jags. 'Right, where were we?'

'You just got done telling me how you're being blackmailed,' Jags said. 'What's the score with the daughter?'

'She's done a legger from home and no one knows where she is. He wants me to track her down.'

'Why you? Ain't like you're Sherlock Holmes or anything.'

'Says he wants it done quietly, without anyone finding out.'

'I can believe that – *desi* family wanting to keep it all under wraps. So, what you going to do?'

Zaq shrugged. 'I don't know. You said it yourself, I ain't no Sherlock Holmes. Where do I even start?'

'They give you anything to go on?'

'Not much.' Zaq took out the photograph and the list and handed them to Jags.

'All right, let's see what we can do.'

Zaq smiled at Jags' use of the word 'we'. It was a small word but it carried a lot of weight. It meant Jags was going to help him, that they were in it together, just like the old days. It was also an affirmation of their friendship – and as Zaq knew only too well, sometimes your friends were all you had.

Jags looked at the photo. 'Bloody hell, she's well fit!'

'Lucky for her she don't take after her old man or her brothers.'

'You got that right. What's her name?'

'Surinder. But everyone calls her Rita.'

'That don't narrow it down much. You know how many Asian girls are called Rita?'

'Loads, but at least we got a picture.'

Jags turned his attention to the names and numbers. 'This her number at the top?'

'Yep. I tried it already but no answer.'

'If she don't want to be found, she'll have ditched the phone and got a new one.' Jags looked down the page, lips pursed in concentration. 'Some of these names seem familiar.'

'That's cool...'

'Don't mean I actually know any of them though. Like there's a Ranjit Singh here. You know how many Ranjit Singhs there are in Southall and Hounslow? Be like searching for a *gora* called John Smith.'

Zaq took a breath and let it out slowly. 'That list and the photo are all I've got.'

'Sorry, man.' Jags handed them back. 'Wish I could be more help.'

'Don't worry about it.' Zaq looked at the photo again and found himself studying Rita's eyes... her nose... her mouth...

'You're checking her out too, ain't you?' Jags said. 'Told you she was fit.'

'Just having a proper look.'

'Yeah, I'd like to have a proper look at her, all right.'

Zaq put the photograph face down on the table and took another look at the list. 'There's a number here says WORK.'

'Where's she work?'

'I didn't ask – had other stuff on my mind.'

'So call the number and find out. We ain't got nothing else to go on.'

He had a point. Zaq took out his phone and called the number.

'Hello, Speedwright Logistics,' a young-sounding woman said.

'Could I speak to Rita Brar please?'

'I'm sorry, she's not here today. Can I help you with anything?'

'No, I really need to speak to her.'

'I'm handling some of Rita's work while she's away; I might

be able to help.'

'What's your name?'

'Nina.'

'Is she on holiday, Nina? Any idea when she'll be back?'

'I'm not sure, but if you need to discuss anything to do with her work, you can talk to me. What was the name, sir?'

'Actually, it's nothing to do with work. I'm a friend of hers and I really need to talk to her but I can't get hold of her. You don't know where she is, do you? It's important.'

'I'm sorry, I don't.' Her voice had taken on a different tone, cautious, maybe even a little suspicious. 'Who are you?'

Zaq considered a couple of lies but quickly discounted them. He had nothing to lose by telling her who he was. His name wouldn't mean anything to her, or Rita either. 'My name's Zaq, Zaq Khan.'

Her voice took on an icy formality. 'I'm sorry, Mr Khan, but all I can tell you is Rita's away. If there's nothing else I can help you with…' She was getting ready to end the call.

'There is something…' he said. 'Can you pass my number on to her?'

'If you're a friend of hers, wouldn't she already have your number?'

'I just got a new one,' he lied.

She hesitated. 'I don't know when I'll talk to her next.'

'Well, whenever you do.' He wasn't sure she believed him but she took his number anyway. 'Tell her to call me, please. It's important.' He waited in case she said anything else. She didn't, so he thanked her and hung up.

'Well…?' Jags said.

'She works at a place called Speedwright Logistics. I just talked to someone called Nina and I got a feeling she knows more than she's letting on.'

'That your female intuition?'

'Nah, your mum's. She's letting me borrow hers.'

'Up yours,' Jags said, laughing. He opened his laptop and began typing.

Zaq studied the list again. 'Hey, there's a Nina on here, Nina Sanghar. I wonder if it was her I just spoke to. There's a number for her as well.'

'Here, check this out,' Jags said. He turned the laptop so Zaq could see the screen. On it was the website of Speedwright Logistics, in their corporate colours of red, white and grey. The blurb proclaimed them the dog's bollocks with all things logistical. Jags moved the cursor to the menu and clicked the Contact Us link. It opened another red, white and grey page, this time with an address. 'It's over near the airport. Half of Southall works round there. If we're lucky, we might know someone there that can help us. Maybe this detective shit ain't so hard after all.'

'Don't count your chickens just yet. We ain't exactly found out much. Her old man probably knows where she works.'

'It's a start. We know more than we did when you got here.'

'That's true.' Zaq stood up. 'Thanks for your help.'

'Where you going?'

'Speedwright Logistics. Might as well head over there, see if I can find out anything else.'

'Without me? You think I'm going to sit around wondering if you've got yourself into any more trouble? I'm coming with you.'

'You sure?'

'Does a Singh like a drink?'

'All right, come on then.' Zaq welcomed the help – and the company. Hanging out with Jags would stop him brooding over what was going on. He slipped the photo and the list into his pocket.

'I just need to set up the computer,' Jags said, picking up a small metal pig from the centre of the table and placing it carefully on the keyboard.

'What you doing?'

'I'm leaving Pigsy here, so it'll look like I'm still working.' Zaq frowned, so Jags explained further. 'If I leave the computer untouched for ten minutes, it automatically changes my status to AWAY FROM COMPUTER and everyone at work'll know I'm not here. If anyone notices how long I'm away for, it could drop me in it. But if I leave Pigsy pressing down the Control key, my status'll stay ACTIVE. I could be eating, sleeping, shitting or wanking and they'd think I was sitting right here.'

'You often do that stuff when you're supposed to be working?'

'Not all at the same time,' Jags said, with a grin.

'What if they email you, or instant message?'

'It's all pushed to my phone, so I can get it anywhere and reply. They'll still think I'm here.'

'You take slacking to a whole new level.'

'Thanks.'

'Can we go now?'

Jags picked up his jacket and keys, and they left the house. Zaq was halfway to the battered van at the kerb when Jags said, 'Hang on a minute... what the fuck's that?'

'It's the spare van from work. I'm using it while I look for Rita.'

'Whoop-dee-fucking-doo. You don't seriously want us to drive round in that, do you? It's worse than that van you usually drive. Why don't we take my wheels?'

Zaq looked at the van then at the gleaming black BMW in the drive, then at Jags. 'OK.'

CHAPTER FOUR

The interior of the car still had the smell of new leather and carpets, the surfaces all clean and shiny. Jags turned the ignition and the engine thrummed to life, then purred like a contented cat, a complete contrast to the coughing, spluttering van. The stereo kicked in and the sounds of Tinie Tempah and Jess Glynne came blasting from the speakers. Jags pressed a button on the steering wheel to turn the volume down. 'What we going to do when we get to this Speedwell place?' he asked, as he eased the car out of the drive.

'Speed*wright*,' Zaq corrected. 'Just check it out, I guess, see if we recognise anyone we can talk to. Apart from that, we'll just play it by ear.'

'We're going to be staking the place out, huh? Just like in the movies.'

'You'll be wanting coffee and donuts next.'

'No, this'll be a proper *desi* stakeout. It'd have to be *samosai*, *pakorai* and masala chai.'

'What about *jalebis* to go with the tea, instead of donuts?'

'No way. That stuff's way too sticky to eat in here, mess up my flippin' interior, man.'

Speedwright Logistics was based in an area made up mainly of businesses and services centred around the airport and aviation industries.

'Reminds me of old times, driving round here,' Jags said. A lot had happened since they'd worked there together after college. Those had been happier days, with no real responsibilities; their main concerns had been chasing girls and getting drunk.

The two of them had become friends at primary school and had lived just a couple of roads apart. They'd grown up together, playing in the streets and parks of Southall. While Zaq's family were from Pakistan and Jags' were from India, it had never been an issue for them. They were too young to worry about religious or political differences and as they grew older, they simply didn't care about that stuff. They went on to the same high school together and hung out most afternoons and evenings too, constantly in and out of each other's houses. They were practically part of each other's families. When they left school they goofed around for a year, playing football and tennis, watching movies and drinking. After that, they decided to go to college and enrolled on the same computing course. It had been the best time; hanging out with his best mate, learning something genuinely interesting, making new friends, meeting new girls and partying.

Despite not being the most conscientious students, they managed to pass with good grades and applied for university. Even when they wound up choosing different courses at different universities, they visited each other's campuses for parties, events and gigs, and hung out together during the holidays. After graduating, they both wound up with jobs in central London and, while lots of their friends seemed to drift away, they still met up at least once a week for a drink. They had been pretty much inseparable for most of their lives – right up until Zaq went to prison.

It had stretched their friendship but even so, the bond between them had remained strong – unlike Zaq's relationship with his brother Tariq, which had become increasingly strained and eventually fractured. Even when Jags didn't visit, he sent a steady stream of books, silly postcards and newspaper articles about Southall. When Zaq was finally released and came home, there'd been no awkwardness between them, no sense of readjustment like there was with his family. With Jags, things just picked up right where they'd left off, almost as if he'd never been away.

It didn't take long to find the business park they were looking for. They drove around amongst the nondescript industrial units until they found the three that housed Speedwright Logistics. Jags parked in an out-of-the-way spot with a good view of the buildings. 'Hope nobody thinks we're a couple out for a romantic drive,' he said.

'I doubt it. Anyone can see I could do better than you, if I was into guys.'

'Fuck you,' Jags said.

'No, you can't – not ever – so stop thinking about it.'

Jags started messing with the stereo.

'Don't be putting on any Village People,' Zaq said.

They listened to old skool tunes from an Eighties Soul Weekender CD, while they watched the comings and goings at Speedwright Logistics. The nearest of the units looked like it housed all the office and admin staff. It was also where the main entrance was, with a reception area inside a glass-fronted lobby. The other two units were lined with shuttered loading bays. Through those that were open they could see a cavernous interior, filled with aisles of racking that held shipments of all shapes and sizes, going to or coming from the airport. A steady stream of lorries, trucks and vans came and went.

They'd been there for about half an hour and Zaq was beginning to think maybe they were wasting their time, when something caught Jags' attention and made him sit up.

'That van over there,' he said. 'White Transit, reversing to the loading bay. I know the name on the side… Heathrow Computer Centre. I'm sure I know someone that works there.'

'Who?'

'That's just it – I can't remember.'

'Want me to help you?' Zaq brandished an open hand in front of Jags, threatening him with a slap – a favourite gesture of Asian mothers.

'Kiss my ass.'

'The one between your ears or the other one?'

'Hang on…' Jags got out his phone.

'I don't think directory enquiries can help,' Zaq said.

'I'm going to go through my contacts, see if a name'll jog my memory.' Jags scrolled through the list of names. 'Ah, ha,' he said after a little while. 'What'd I tell you? Anil Cheema!'

'You mean *Anal* Cheema?' Zaq hadn't seen the guy in years. Anil had gone to the same high school as them but had hung out with a different crowd, the geek squad. The main reason they were friendly with him was because Anil was the kid who could fix your Sega or Nintendo games console if anything went wrong with it. 'OK, but how's that help us?'

'I bumped into him at a wedding a few weeks ago. Man, he bored the shit out of me, going on about how he's some kind of big cheese at this Heathrow Computer place. I think he said he's in charge of their engineers or something and shipping whatever stuff they need all over the place.'

'So…?'

'If they use Speedwright to ship their stuff, chances are he'll know some people here – maybe someone that can help us.'

A smile spread over Zaq's face. 'You know, sometimes you ain't as dumb as you look.'

'Sitting next to you, I probably look like a genius. Shall I give him a call?'

'Yeah.' Zaq glanced at the car's digital clock. It was almost lunchtime. 'Does he work close by?'

'Er, the clue's in the company name.'

'All right, smartarse. Call and tell him we'll meet him for lunch.'

'What if he asks why?'

'I don't know, make something up. Talking bollocks has never been a problem for you.'

'I'll take that as a compliment.' Jags turned the music down and made the call. 'All right, Anil? It's Jags. How're they hanging?'

Zaq kept his eyes on the Speedwright buildings and listened to Jags' side of the conversation.

'Yeah, it's been a while… What's new? Any more kids on the way?' Jags laughed. 'Listen, me and Zaq are in the area, we're going to swing by to see you, go get something to eat. We need to talk to you about something.' He listened for a moment, looking over at Zaq and rolling his eyes. 'Nah, nothing like that, it's work-related… Yeah, 'course I'm sure. What's the address? OK, we'll meet you outside in about twenty minutes…' He ended the call and looked at Zaq.

'What?' Zaq said.

'He shat himself soon as I mentioned your name, thinks he's in some kind of trouble or something. Kept asking what's up, why we want to see him.'

Zaq shook his head. Since he'd gotten out of prison everyone seemed to think he was some kind of violent head-case. True, prison had been a violent and physical experience, but that was all done with now and he was trying to put it behind him. People thinking he was a psychotic nut job did have some advantages though. It had made Rajinder and Parminder Brar wary of him and most of the local rudeboys and hardmen thought better of messing with him now too. While that was no bad thing, everyone else tended to give him a wide berth as well; they were scared of him, the way they would be of a pit bull roaming loose.

'Don't worry about it,' Jags said, slapping Zaq on the shoulder. 'He don't know nothing – just believes whatever he hears.'

'I ain't worried. It's just... people who don't know what actually happened, making stuff up and spreading it around. I wouldn't give a shit, except it makes it harder to get a job and find a place to live.'

'Fuck them,' Jags said. 'You're doing OK now, ain't you?'

'What, renting a room in a house with five other guys and being blackmailed to look for a girl or else I get sent back to prison? That your idea of OK?'

'When you put it like that...' Jags started the car. 'Come on, you moody sod, let's go get some lunch.'

You're The One For Me by D Train played on the stereo as they drove.

'Why'd you tell him it was to do with work?' Zaq said.

'You told me to make something up, so I did.'

'He's got kids, huh? I didn't even know he was married.'

'Two boys. He got hitched about four years ago, I think.'

'How'd he manage that?'

'His parents, how else? They were on his case big time, so

he just let them sort it out. They hooked him up with a proper *freshie* from India, innit. Otherwise he'd still be single and pulling his own plonker.'

Zaq's own parents used to talk to him about an arranged marriage... but now they no longer brought the subject up, too embarrassed by their eldest son's stint in prison to face questions about it from any prospective in-laws. 'What about you?' Zaq asked.

'What? Am I still pulling my own plonker?'

'I mean, your parents still hassling you to get married?'

'They never give up. I tell them I'm too busy with work, sorting out my career and that. I'll settle down when I'm ready.'

'And they believe that?'

Jags shrugged. 'I don't live at home any more, so I don't get it that often. My brother's still there though, so they're on his case instead.'

'You want to get married?'

'You proposing?'

'It's just a question, shithead.'

'I ain't in no rush. Besides, there's enough fit gal out there for me to be checking.'

'That why you're single?'

'Just in between girlfriends right now.'

'Sure.' Zaq stretched the word out, making his disbelief clear.

'Why you so interested? Your folks on at you to get hitched?'

'Not any more. How would they explain what I been doing for the last five years? No one wants their daughter to marry an ex-con.'

'You never wanted any of that arranged business anyhow.'

'I know. It's just... I wonder how I'm ever going to meet anyone. I mean, I got a shit job, no money and no real prospects at the moment. I share a house with a load of *desis* and now I got all this stuff with the Brars to deal with. I ain't exactly got a lot going for me.'

'Yeah, that's true.'

'You don't have to agree.'

'Just give it time, man. Everything'll fall into place.'

'I wish it was that easy.'

'Who the fuck said it'd be easy?'

They pulled into the car park of Heathrow Computer Centre and waited for Anil Cheema to appear. After about ten minutes Zaq felt an elbow in his side.

'There he is.' Jags nodded at a figure coming out of the building.

'Bloody hell.' Zaq wouldn't have recognised him. In the five or six years since he'd last seen him, Anil had gone from a skinny young man to an overweight thirty-something with thinning hair, bad skin and a goatee beard that didn't suit him one bit. He was wearing a black V-neck jumper with a plain white shirt and black trousers. A tap of the horn got his attention. He saw them and hesitated before coming over.

Jags lowered the passenger window and leaned across Zaq to shout, 'Anal, man, how's it going?'

Anil winced at the nickname. 'All right,' he said, then 'All right, Zaq?' He extended his hand as if he thought it might get bitten off. 'How've you been?'

'Fine,' Zaq said. He shook the limp hand firmly and tried to drag a smile onto his face. Anil looked as if he would rather be anywhere else than there.

'Where can we go to eat round here?' Jags said as he reached across to shake Anil's hand too. 'I'm well hungry.'

'There's a pub just down the road. Food's OK.'

'That'll do. Jump in,' Jags said.

The BMW was a three door coupé, so Zaq had to get out to let Anil in the back. Five and a half years of training and conditioning had kept Zaq in good shape, whereas home comforts and easy living had softened Anil's body, causing it to expand. Even though it was a cool day, his forehead was shiny with sweat. Once Anil was seated Zaq got back in.

'Which way?' Jags asked.

'Out of the car park then left,' Anil said.

When they were moving Zaq turned to Anil. 'I just heard from Jags you got married. Congratulations. He said you got kids too.'

'Yeah.' Anil cracked a smile at last. 'Couple of boys. One's two, the other's three.' He got out his wallet and handed Zaq a photograph. It showed two of the ugliest children Zaq had ever seen.

'Lovely,' he said and handed it back. 'How's married life?'

'OK.' Anil shrugged. 'Bit up and down. Her being from India's got a lot to do with it.'

'No shit?' Jags said. 'What did you expect? Which way now?'

'Left at the lights. My parents said it'd be better getting married to someone from over there, more traditional, less stress and hassle than a girl from here.'

'And you believed that?'

'I thought they knew what they were talking about.'

Jags shook his head. 'You must've seen too many of them *desi* dramas with your mum.'

'Yeah well, it was all OK until she got over here. She must've thought she was coming to live some Bollywood bling lifestyle, with servants and all that. She weren't interested in making *rotis* and ironing my shirts.'

'You make it sound so romantic,' Jags said.

'Yeah, yeah. There's the pub, on the right.'

Inside, the pub was light airy, with fresh neutral colours and lots of pale wood. It catered for those working in the area and was set up for the lunchtime rush. They found an empty table and Jags went to the bar; he returned with three pints of lager. Anil took a hefty swig of his.

They looked at the menus and decided what they wanted. 'I'll get it,' Jags said and went back to the bar to order. He came back with another pint, which he placed in front of Anil. ''Cause you seem to be going through that one pretty fast,' he said.

Anil's glass was almost empty. Zaq and Jags had barely touched theirs. 'I'm just a bit thirsty.' He finished off the first pint and started on the second. 'So, uh, what did you want to see me about?'

'Remember that wedding we were at?' Jags said. 'You told me all about your job. What is it you do again?'

'Technical Services Manager. I organise our company's engineers, make sure all the hardware and software gets where it's needed.'

Zaq wondered where the hell Jags was going with this.

'You guys handle your own distribution, or you use couriers for that?'

'Neither. We use a logistics company.'

'No shit.' Jags glanced at Zaq. 'Which one?'

'Speedwright. They're based around here.'

'They any good? Would you recommend them?'

'Yeah, they're OK. We been using them for quite a while. Why're you asking?'

'Well...' Jags paused, working out his story. 'Company I work for are looking for someone to take over our distribution, national and international. They've got a firm but they're looking around for someone more competitive. You know anyone at this Speedwright place I could talk to?'

'Why don't you just call up their sales department?'

'If I can talk to someone on the inside, we might be able to work something out, know what I mean?' Anil didn't and neither did Zaq, so he had to spell it out. 'We're talking a big account here, worth a shitload of money. If I can get details of what we're currently paying and the proposals from the other companies pitching for the contract, I could give them to someone working with us at this Speedwright place, so they can put together a winning bid, you get me?'

Anil looked like he was still trying to get it.

'Thing is, that information ain't going to be easy to come by and I ain't going to do it for nothing. We'd need to sort things out with your contact so I get a nice commission – call it a consulting fee – when they win the account. Your contact can sort out a nice bonus for himself too, and if things work out you'll get a cut as well, for introducing us.' Jags smiled.

Zaq never ceased to be amazed at Jags' ability to bullshit.

'What sort of cut we talking about?' Anil asked.

'It's a big contract; be a few grand in it for you, at least.'

Anil thought for a moment, then said, 'I think I do know someone who could help. Dhanesh, he's the Operations Manager, good bloke.'

'Will he be able to talk to the right people, sort things out so we can all make some money?'

Anil nodded. 'He's your guy.'

The waitress arrived and set down their plates. When she had gone, Jags leaned across to Anil. 'Why don't you call him and tell him we're coming to see him after lunch?'

Anil stopped shaking salt over his sausage and mash. 'You want me to call him now?'

'No time like the present,' Jags said. 'And if you're quick, your food won't even get cold.'

CHAPTER FIVE

They got Anil back to work a little late. 'What're they going to say?' he asked as he got out of the car, 'I'm a flippin' manager.'

Zaq wondered if it had been such a good idea to get him those two pints. 'Later, Anil,' he said, getting back into the car.

'Give my love to your missus,' Jags called out. 'She says she can't get enough of it.' He took off before Anil could respond.

Zaq looked at him. 'What was all that rubbish about contracts and backhanders?'

'I had to tell him something and you said, make it up. He bought it, didn't he?'

Zaq couldn't argue with that. 'What're you going to tell this Dhanesh geezer?'

'Leave that to me.'

At Speedwright, they parked in the same place as before, got out of the car and walked over to the buildings. Instead of going to the main entrance, they made for one of the loading bays, where three guys were unloading a van.

'I help you?' one of them said. He was short, stocky and unshaven. Zaq caught a strong whiff of body odour from him.

The guy needed a wash even more than his grubby work clothes.

'We're here to see Dhanesh,' Zaq said.

'You mean Dan?'

'If he's the Operations Manager. He's expecting us.'

The guy directed them to where they might find him and went back to work.

'Phew, you smell that bloke?' Jags muttered and waved a hand in front of his nose. 'Geezer must be allergic to soap or something.'

The interior of the warehouse was huge and they had to ask someone else before they found Dhanesh. He was the same height as Zaq, with black hair cropped close and shot through with grey. He was clean-shaven, though the early shadow on his cheeks and jaw suggested a heavy growth. His thick eyebrows looked as if they'd been drawn on with a marker.

Zaq gave him their names. 'Anil told you we were coming?'

'Yeah, he said you had some sort of business proposition.'

'Don't believe everything that guy tells you,' Jags said. 'He don't half talk some shit at times.'

Dan frowned. 'What do you want then?'

'Somewhere we can talk?'

'Depends what you want to talk about.'

'You know someone called Rita Brar?' Zaq said, deciding to take the lead and not waste time. He saw Dan's expression change.

'Might do. Who wants to know?'

'We do. She ain't been home for a couple of days and her family have asked me to make sure she's OK. They're worried about her.'

'I don't know you, and besides, I can't discuss anything to do with company employees with anyone. Anil shouldn't have sent you.' He started to turn away.

'You know who her brothers are? You want to talk to them instead?'

He turned back and though he didn't respond, it was plain he knew who Raj and Parm were.

'I'll tell them you didn't want to help find their sister, that maybe you even called her a slag and said they could go fuck themselves. How you think they'd take that?'

'I never said any of that.' There was a note of alarm in his voice.

'Who you think they'll believe?' Dan was looking very uncomfortable. 'You know what they're like – quick with their fists or anything else they get hold of. Do you over first, ask questions afterwards.' Zaq saw his Adam's apple bob as he swallowed. 'You don't want to talk to me – fine, your choice. Expect a visit from them instead. They won't ask as nicely.' Zaq turned away. 'Come on,' he said to Jags, 'let's go.'

'Wait,' Dan said. 'OK. What do you want to know?'

'There somewhere we can talk, apart from out here?'

'My office.' Dan led the way between the towering racks, through the clamour and bustle of work going on all around them. His office was a rectangular box made of prefabricated panels, up against a side wall of the warehouse. The upper half of each panel was glass. Fluorescent lights hung from a suspended ceiling and lit the room. It was a functional space, all business, no frills. Dan closed the door behind them and took a seat. He didn't offer Zaq or Jags one but they sat down anyway.

'When did you last see Rita?' Zaq asked.

'Last week,' Dan said. 'She was here on Tuesday but hasn't been in since.'

'You know if she said anything to anyone, maybe mentioned she was going away?'

'I don't know. If she did it would've been to one of her friends

43

up in the offices.'

'Anyone notice anything out of the ordinary? Was she upset or anything?'

Dan hesitated. 'No.'

It was just a fraction of a second but Zaq caught it. 'If there *is* something, you better tell me now. If I find out from someone else, I won't know what else you haven't told me and I'll have to pass that on.'

'OK… some guy turned up to see her on the Tuesday. They left together and she hasn't been back to work since, hasn't called or anything.'

'You know who he was?'

Dan shook his head. 'I didn't see him, I just heard about it. Apparently, he was pretty beaten up. Then on Thursday, her brothers came looking for her. They were asking about the guy too.'

'You sure about that?' Zaq said.

'That's what I was told. They were asking about both of them. Everyone thinks…' He stopped himself.

'What?'

'It's just office gossip. I don't know if it's true or anything…'

Zaq waited.

'All right. Apparently, she was seeing someone – and the rumour is he's Muslim. Everyone thinks that was him that turned up here.'

The Brars hadn't said anything about a guy. Why not? If it was true, it was a massive reason for Rita to have run off. Of all the guys she could have picked to go out with, a Muslim would have been the very worst choice as far as her family were concerned. The reasons were historical, both recent and old, and the animosities they generated seemed to be impossible to forgive or forget. Zaq knew what it was like from personal experience. Growing up in Southall, he'd been out with a couple of Sikh girls and knew the score. All the time he'd been seeing them, the girls had been terrified of their families finding out; first, that they had a boyfriend but, even worse, that he was Muslim. It didn't make any difference that he wasn't religious, liked a drink and was partial to a bacon sandwich. Having a boyfriend could possibly be forgiven, but having a Muslim one would never be. As a result, none of the relationships had lasted very long. 'Any idea where she might've gone?' Zaq said.

'No.'

'Anyone who might?'

'I don't know.' He was a bad liar.

'Tell me or I'll let her brothers beat it out of you – up to you.'

Dan swore under his breath. 'Look, I don't want to drop anyone in it.'

'You won't. I just want to ask a few questions, that's all.'

Dan chewed his lip and squirmed in his seat. Finally, he said, 'I'm not saying she knows anything, but Rita's good friends with a girl here called Nina. If anyone might know something, it's her.'

'Where can I find her?'

'Up in the offices. But don't say I told you. I don't want her to know you got her name from me.'

While it had been relatively easy getting into the warehouse to talk to Dan, Zaq doubted it would be the same story with the offices. It didn't matter anyhow – he'd already talked to her on the phone and could do so again. 'What's Nina's surname?'

'Sanghar.'

'Thanks.' He looked at Jags. 'Come on, let's go.'

They left Dan in his office and made their way back through the warehouse the way they'd come.

'You never said anything about her running off with some

bloke,' Jags said.

'I didn't know. They never mentioned it.'

'Pretty big thing to forget.'

'I don't think they forgot.'

'Least now we know why they want to keep the whole thing quiet – her running off with a guy.'

'And if he's Muslim…' Zaq didn't need to finish the sentence.

Jags knew as well as he did what that meant. 'Yeah, could get a bit nasty for Rita and whoever the guy is.'

Things didn't usually end well for mixed Sikh and Muslim couples. If Rita was lucky, she'd be disowned by her family and ostracised by the community. If she was unlucky, she could wind up dead, along with her boyfriend.

'No wonder her old man and her brothers are so wound up,' Zaq said.

The Brars weren't the kind of people who'd be happy just simply disowning Rita and letting her carry on with a Muslim. She'd be doing their *besti*, shaming them in front of everyone. They'd have to restore their *izat* – their honour and self-respect.

They found the shutter they'd come in through and went out the same way. The three men had finished loading the van; they didn't say anything as Zaq and Jags walked past them and crossed the car park towards the BMW.

'Why didn't they just tell me?' Zaq said when they reached the car. 'They must've known I'd find out sooner or later.'

Jags shrugged. 'Maybe they were hoping you could find her without having to know the details.'

'I don't see how. If they're together, I find one, I find them both. Unless… they didn't tell me 'cause they're planning to do something to them.'

'Like what?'

Zaq looked at him and raised an eyebrow. 'She's run off with a Muslim geezer she's probably shagging. What d'you think they'll do to them?'

Jags' expression made it clear he knew it wouldn't be anything good.

'And if I'm the one who's been asking around about her, who do you think'll get the blame?'

'Shit. So, what you want to do?'

'I don't know. For now, maybe we should find out who the guy is.'

'How we going to do that?'

'We'll ask this Nina.'

Even though he had her mobile number on the list in his pocket, Zaq decided to call her work number again. The phone rang three times before it was picked up.

'Hello, Speedwright Logistics,' a woman answered.

'Can I speak to Nina Sanghar, please?'

'May I ask who's calling?'

'Mr Khan.'

'Just a moment, please.' He was put on hold, the woman came back on and said, 'I'll just transfer you now.'

'Hello. Mr Khan? This is Nina. How can I help you?'

'Who's the guy came to see Rita last week? Is she with him?'

There was a long pause before Nina responded. 'Who is this?'

'We spoke earlier. What's his name?'

'I'm sorry. As I explained before, I can't help you with that.' Her tone was rigidly formal. 'Goodbye.' She hung up.

Zaq frowned. 'She definitely knows something.'

'How d'you work that out? You hardly spoke to her.'

'Way she reacted. She didn't say she had no idea what I was talking about and she hesitated too long, like she was thinking something up – something that weren't the truth.'

'You got all that in ten seconds? You'll be wearing a

47

deerstalker and smoking a pipe next.'

'I need to talk to her properly. In the meanwhile, we still need to find out who this bloke is.'

'How you plan on doing that? She don't want to talk to you.'

'Guess I'll have to go ask the Brars.'

CHAPTER SIX

Zaq picked up the van from Jags' place and drove back to work. He parked in front of the builder's yard, which had originally been three shops that had been combined over time to make up the current premises of Brar Building Supplies. Zaq went in through the main entrance, which was in the left most building. The interior was an Aladdin's cave of electrical, building and plumbing supplies. Tools and equipment filled racks and bins, covered the walls and even hung from the ceiling. There was barely room for their customers. The place smelled of paint and sawdust, with undertones of plastic, new metal and Indian food.

It was a Monday and the place was busy with builders and plumbers buying what they needed for the week. The shop staff were busy serving customers, so Zaq didn't stop and chat with anyone. He nodded to Jeet, the shop manager, ducked behind the counter and went through a door marked STAFF ONLY. On the other side, a short corridor ran straight ahead between Sid's office and the staff kitchen and a small toilet. To his right another corridor led to the stairs up to the first floor. He went that way, climbed the stairs and knocked on Mr Brar's door.

'*Haah*?' came a voice.

Zaq went in. Mr Brar was hunched over his desk. '*Eni chethi lublaya*?'

He had to be joking. 'Not yet.' Zaq glanced around the room but there was no one else there this time.

'If you haven't found her, then why are you here?'

'Who's the guy she's with? The one Parminder and Rajinder have been looking for?' If her old man didn't know about him already, he was about to find out.

Mr Brar frowned, his whole demeanour hardening. 'You've learned about this already?'

'Yeah. Why didn't you just tell me she's run off with her boyfriend?'

'IS NOT HER BLOODY BOYFRIEND!' Mr Brar exploded, slamming a massive hand on the desk. 'Don't call him that.' His eyes blazed. 'She had a fight with her brothers, that is why she left the home. This *bhen chaud* has taken advantage of her situation.'

'All right, whatever, but you should've mentioned it.'

'Don't tell me what I should do. This is not for everyone to know. I want it kept quiet, no silly rumours or tittle-tattle.'

'Might be a bit late for that. How d'you think I heard about it?'

Mr Brar's eyes narrowed, the muscles in his face tightening. 'I don't want it going any further, so you better find her quickly before it does.'

'If I can find the guy, it might help me find Rita quicker. What do you know about him?'

'Nothing, except he's a… *Muslim*.'

That explained why he wanted her found so fast – so he could deal with it and cover it up. 'Would Rajinder or Parminder know any more?'

'Perhaps.'

'You know where I can find them?'

Mr Brar scowled at Zaq for a moment, then picked up his phone and made a call. 'Rajinder, *thu kithay uh*?' He spoke to his son in Punjabi briefly then asked him, 'Address *ki eh*?' He grabbed a pen and scribbled something on the back of an envelope. '*Au huuni aundah.*' He hung up and held out the envelope. 'They are there now.'

Zaq took it. 'You said Rita had a fight with her brothers and that's why she left home. You know what the fight was about?'

'No. They are brothers and sister, they always argue about something.'

If Rita's brothers had found out about her boyfriend it could've been the reason for the bust-up; it would certainly explain her running away. Dan had said the guy who came to see her looked as though he'd been badly beaten up. By Rajinder and Parminder? Very likely.

After Mr Brar's reaction at the mere mention of Rita being involved with the guy, Zaq figured it best to keep his thoughts to himself. 'I'll go and see Rajinder and Parminder now.'

'Zaqir,' Mr Brar said, his voice a low growl. 'Don't make a lot of noise finding her. Remember, I want it done quietly. Ask your questions, but don't start spreading any stories. If you do our *besti* in this, whether you find her or not, I will make sure you go to prison.'

The address was for a house on Park Avenue, near Southall Park. Zaq recognised the place – he'd made a couple of deliveries there. It was a standard 1930s semi with bay windows and a shabby garage at the side. A waist-high brick wall edged the paved driveway and a narrow alley with a gate ran between the garage and the neighbouring house. A skip full of builders debris sat in the drive.

Zaq drove past and turned onto Green Drive where he parked, then walked back to the house. It looked as though there had been a porch until recently; it was probably at the bottom of the skip now. If it had been anything like the windows, Zaq could see why it had been torn down. The rotten, peeling frames all needed replacing. Everything looked worn and aged. The house needed its guts ripped out, so everything could be done new. He knocked on the flaking wooden front door. The semi-circular pane of glass in it rattled with each impact. He heard voices from inside and heavy footsteps approaching. The door was pulled open by a heavy-set Indian man, with a large blue turban and dusty work clothes. His big pockmarked nose stuck out over a full black beard. '*Parminder aur Rajinder ethay heh gey?*' Zaq said.

'*Haah, heh gey eh,*' the man nodded. '*Pichay uh.*' He stood aside and gestured toward the back of the house. He was probably a *fauji* - Punjabi slang for an illegal worker – and didn't speak much English.

Zaq went down the bare stripped hallway to what had once been the kitchen. Everything had been removed, leaving ghostly shapes where the cupboards and fittings used to be. A man was in there, on his knees, yanking out old pipework and swearing in Punjabi. Zaq didn't see Parminder or Rajinder, so he went through a doorway to the right, into a rear reception room that had no back wall, allowing a stiff breeze to blow in through the opening. An exposed steel joist had been put in to support the floor above, The foundations for a rear extension were already laid and concrete block walls were being put up.

Rajinder was out there talking to a couple of builders. He saw Zaq step out onto the cement floor of the extension but carried on with his conversation. Zaq took the opportunity to look him over properly. He was big and burly, his body pumped up from pushing weights. He looked heavy and probably moved slowly, relying on size and strength over speed and agility. His thick black hair was cropped close, and dark stubble covered a blocky jaw. He wore a heavy black jacket over a grey hoodie, jogging pants and a pair of work boots. He didn't give a shit that Zaq was waiting.

It didn't bother Zaq. He had nowhere else to be and was getting paid by Rajinder's old man anyway. He could wait all day. It wouldn't come to that though. All he had to do was stand there, watching and not saying a word, and before long it would wind Rajinder up enough that he'd have to come over and ask him what he wanted.

Rajinder continued with his conversation, perhaps hoping Zaq would approach so he could make a display of ignoring him in front of an audience. But Zaq made no move to interrupt and Rajinder must have felt his eyes on him. It didn't help that the two builders kept looking in Zaq's direction. Pretty soon, Rajinder brought the conversation to an end, turned and, puffing himself up, strode towards Zaq. 'What the fuck d'you want?' he said, loud enough for everyone else to hear.

'I need to talk to you and your brother – about the guy your sister's with.'

Rajinder glanced around at the builders and then said, more quietly, 'What guy?'

'Next you'll be telling me it wasn't you that kicked the shit out of him.'

'Don't know what you're on about.'

'That right? Then how come you and your brother were over where Rita works asking about him?'

'Must've been someone else.'

'Not what I heard. Bit of a coincidence – guy supposed to be seeing your sister gets beaten up?'

He shrugged. 'Nothing to do with us.'

'So, who is he?'

'I told you, I don't know.'

'I think you do.'

Rajinder clenched his fists. 'You calling me a liar?'

'I didn't call you anything – but I don't think you're telling the truth.' Zaq was tensed, ready in case Rajinder took a swipe at him.

'What's going on?' Parminder Brar stepped from the garden into the concrete extension. He was taller and slimmer than his brother, though still solidly built. His features were sharper, his eyes too. He wore an expensive black leather jacket, jeans and work boots that were too new and clean to have ever seen any real work.

'He's asking about Rita and some guy,' Rajinder said.

'And why you didn't mention him in your dad's office this morning,' Zaq added.

Parminder stepped closer and dropped his voice. 'We didn't mention it 'cause our dad don't want anyone knowing she's run off with a *sullah*.' He looked Zaq squarely in the eye as he said it.

Zaq smothered any anger he might have had at the use of the insulting Punjabi term for a Muslim and stared right back at Parm.

'I said you'd probably find out anyway but he wanted you to try and find her without knowing.'

'So you do know something about the guy?' Zaq looked at Rajinder, who just sneered at him.

'We heard they're together.'

'That why you beat him up?'

'We never touched him. Only found out about him after she

ran off.'

'So who beat him up?'

'How the fuck should I know? Probably someone else he pissed off.'

'What *do* you know out about him?'

'Not much.'

Zaq waited. 'You going to tell me or do I have to guess?'

Parminder's eyes narrowed. He probably wasn't used to people talking to him like that. He gave Zaq a cold, hard stare. 'His name's Kasim.'

'Kasim what?'

'I don't fucking know.'

'You know his address?'

'No.'

'You know anything else?'

'I know you're pushing your luck.'

If it kicked off, Zaq was sure he could hit Parminder before Parminder hit him. He just had to hope Rajinder wasn't faster than he looked.

'I think he drives an RS 5...' Parminder said.

'What's that? A Ford or something?'

Parminder looked at him as if he were stupid. 'It's an Audi, black, with private plates.'

'Don't suppose you know the reg?'

'K-A-5-1-M-B.' Parm didn't add anything else.

Zaq didn't think he was going to get any more out of them, whether they knew or not, so there was no point asking. At least he had a name now, and the info about the car might be some use. 'All right,' he said. 'Thanks for your help.' He managed to keep most of the sarcasm from his voice.

'Hang on,' Parminder said. 'You find Rita or this Kasim motherfucker, make sure you tell *us* before you let our dad know.'

'Why?'

''Cause I said so.'

'I don't work for you. I work for your dad.'

'Listen, our old man's a proper old school *desi*, innit. Far as he's concerned, Rita's done our *besti*, big time. No telling what he'll do to them if he gets his hands on them, know what I'm saying? We get to them first, they might get off a bit lighter.'

'What's your idea of lighter? Putting them in the hospital?'

'Better than in the ground.'

There were plenty of stories about couples in similar situations who'd ended up that way. Still, Rita had to have known what she was getting into. Everyone in the Asian community knew the score. Though he didn't agree with those attitudes, it wasn't really his problem. All he had to do was find her and tell these two, then her old man, where she was. What happened after that was none of his business. 'OK,' he said. 'I'll tell you first, but I got to tell your old man straight after.'

Parminder nodded. 'Whatever.'

Zaq gave Rajinder a last look, then turned and left.

CHAPTER SEVEN

It was starting to get dark as Zaq made his way into Old Southall. He took a right at the Prince of Wales and drove down a couple of residential streets until he reached the Scotsman on the corner of Scotts Road. The old gas tower dominated the skyline, looming over the rooftops. A light flashed at its top, a warning to aircraft heading for Heathrow.

The pub was already lit up against the approaching darkness. The upper floor of the building was painted white though it had long since turned to grey. The ground floor exterior was clad in brown tile, with black trim. Signs advertised TRADITIONAL PUNJABI CUISINE alongside the FULL ENGLISH BREAKFAST that was served all day.

Its corner position meant the pub had two entrances. Zaq went in through the door on Caxton Road and found himself facing the central bar head on. To his left was a lounge with flat-screen TVs on the walls. To the right was the Games Room, with pool tables, arcade machines and a dartboard. Behind the bar was the kitchen, where proper *desi* chefs cooked real Indian food. The punters were a mix of workers from the nearby industrial estates and local residents, Asian and white. Zaq checked the lounge first but didn't see who he was looking for, so tried the Games Room.

Nine or ten young Asian men stood around drinking, chatting and watching a couple of pool players at a table. The game was being played by a white guy and an Asian. The Asian was about to take a shot and Zaq stopped, not wanting to distract him. The guy fired the cue ball the length of the table and potted a stripe, then straightened up and looked at Zaq. He was about five eight, lean and wiry. His shaved head was nicked by scars, mementos of a rough life. His eyes were quick and sharp. 'What the fuck you doing here?' he said.

Everyone in the Games Room stopped to look.

'Looking for a friend of mine,' Zaq said. 'Bald dude with a big mouth, always getting into trouble.'

The Asian guy came around the table, still holding his cue. He stopped in front of Zaq and looked him up and down. 'How long's it been?'

'About a year.'

'Shit…' The guy's hard expression changed to a grin. A gold tooth glinted in the light. Along with his gold earrings, it made him look like a bit like a pirate. 'How the fuck you doing, man?' He put down the cue, shook Zaq's hand, then pulled him close into a hug. 'Good to see you, bro.'

'You too, Biri.'

Biri turned to the others. 'Hey, yo, this is my mate Zaq. This geezer had my back more than once when we were inside. I owe him, big time. Nobody fucks with him, you get me?' He clapped Zaq on the shoulder. 'Jas,' he called, to one of the guys sitting at the bar, 'finish my game for me – and if you can't beat Punjabi Mike from that position, you're buying the next round.' There was laughter as Jas got off his stool and everyone seemed to relax. 'Let's get some drinks.' Biri led the way into the lounge and to the bar.

'Punjabi Mike?'

Biri laughed. 'Mikey grew up round here, innit. Geezer speaks better Punjabi than some *upnay*.'

'What're you having?' Zaq asked.

'Nah, man, I'll get these.'

They argued about buying the drinks in a typically Asian fashion. Eventually, Zaq gave in and let Biri get the round.

'I'll have a Diet Coke,' he said.

Biri shook his head. 'You ain't having no Diet Coke. We got to have a proper drink together.'

'I'm driving.'

'You can still have a pint, innit? Fucking Diet Coke.'

'All right, get me a half.'

Biri got him a full pint of Stella and one for himself. They grabbed a couple of seats and drank a toast to being on the outside. 'So, what you been up to, man?'

'Not much, just working and trying to stay out of trouble,' Zaq said.

'Working, huh? Doing what?'

'Delivering building supplies.'

'Shit, ain't you a bit over-qualified for that?'

Zaq shrugged. 'Beggars can't be choosers, you know how it is. How about you? What you been doing? Still into motors?'

'What can I say? It's my area of expertise.'

Biri was a professional car thief. He'd been doing a two stretch when they'd met inside. Word was he now ran a crew that specialised in stealing high-end motors to order. The vehicles were taken at night, delivered, paid for and immediately shipped overseas to end customers in India, Pakistan and Afghanistan. By the time the owners knew they were gone and called the police, the cars were probably already on their way out of the country.

'That's why I'm here,' Zaq said. 'I need a favour.' He felt bad – he hadn't seen the guy for a year and was here now just because he wanted something.

'Name it, man.'

Zaq leaned forward and lowered his voice. 'I'm looking for a car. A black Audi RS 5.'

'What you want with a hot motor? I thought you was trying to steer clear of trouble.'

'It's not the motor I'm after, it's the guy that owns it. It's got private plates. K-A-5-1-M-B.'

Biri took out his mobile phone, typed in the details and saved them. 'What should I do if I find it?'

'Let me know where it is and see if someone can keep an eye on it.'

Biri nodded. 'Shouldn't be a problem, *if* we find it.'

'The guy might be keeping a low profile.'

'He know you're looking for him?'

'Something like that.'

'I'll see what I can do.'

'Cheers, man.' They touched glasses and drank their beers.

'You want another?' Biri asked.

'No thanks, I better get going.'

'You just got here.'

Zaq stood up. 'There's some stuff I got to do but after that, in a few days, we should definitely get together, have a proper drink. Call me if you find out anything?'

'Will do.'

They shook hands and hugged again.

'Take it easy,' Zaq said.

'You know me,' Biri replied, 'I always do.'

* * *

It was fully dark when Zaq left the pub, daylight having long since fled the scene. The streetlights were weak and too far apart, leaving large areas of darkness between the pools of light. Vehicles parked on both sides of the road blocked what little light there was, creating deeper shadows around the van.

As he crossed the road towards it, he pulled out his keys and, along with them, the photograph of Rita Brar. He must have slipped it in his front pocket earlier. He was trying to look at it in the dim light, when a couple of figures stepped out from behind the van and stopped in front of him.

Two men. He couldn't see who they were, but he sensed trouble straight away. He heard footsteps from behind and threw a quick glance over his shoulder, to see a third man a few feet away. Zaq moved away from the van and backed up to the brick wall so he could see all three at the same time. He stuffed the keys and the photo back in his pocket.

'Is it him?' the third man, now to Zaq's right, asked.

'Can I help you guys with something?' Zaq's heart was thumping. He set his feet and shifted into a fighting stance, muscles tense, ready to fight if he had to.

'Yeah, it's him,' one on the left said.

'Look, I don't know what this is about...' He gauged the distance between himself and each of the three men.

'Well, you fucking should.' It was the guy on the left again. All three began to edge forward, probably hoping to attack together.

Zaq wasn't about to stand around and wait for them. If he'd learnt anything in prison, it was to strike first and strike hard – so he sprang left and smashed his elbow into the face of the man closest to him. It connected with a meaty smack that sent the guy reeling. Reflex brought Zaq back into a fighting stance as the guy on the right came at him. Zaq twisted from the hip and put his weight behind a wicked straight left. The guy ran into the punch, doubling the force of the impact, which put him flat on his back. Zaq spun to face the last attacker – but he wasn't fast enough. A fist caught him in the mouth and snapped his head back.

The blow stunned Zaq for a second. It had been a while since he'd taken a punch.

'FUCKING BASTARD!' the guy screamed, taking another swing.

Zaq threw up his left arm to block it and fired his right at the attacker's face. It didn't land solidly but the motion of throwing the right drew back his left hand, so it was cocked and ready to go. He took a step forward and let fly. He felt bone jar as his fist connected. He followed with a quick right then whipped his left elbow round and caught the guy on the temple, dropping him to the ground like a sack of shit.

Then something crashed into Zaq's left cheek causing spots to dance before his eyes. He shook his head to clear his vision. The first guy was back on his feet. Zaq backed up towards the wall. The guy's confidence was boosted, having landed a punch and seen Zaq back off, and he charged forward. Zaq judged the distance and thrust his right arm straight out, driving the heel of his palm into the man's face. There was a brittle crunch as his nose broke. Zaq pulled his arm back and used the torque to fire his knee into the guy's balls. He was about to finish him off when a blow from behind caught him just above the right ear, wrenching the muscles of his neck. A second punch landed, then another. Zaq brought his arms up to defend himself and managed to swat away another punch, flicking out a quick jab of his own, not hard but enough to distract the guy for a second. It was all Zaq needed. He ducked in close, grabbed the guy's head in both hands and pulled it down, right into the path of his knee. The force shot the guy's head up and back, in an arc that ended with him hitting the pavement, an unconscious heap, lights out.

Zaq spun round to meet the next attack, adrenalin surging through him – only to find all three assailants down, moaning and groaning. Time to get the fuck out of there. Zaq fumbled for his keys and got in the van. He gunned the engine and wheel spun away, not giving a shit about the speed bumps as he jounced over them. His heart was banging against his ribs, trying to break out of his chest. His head and face tingled, his neck was starting to stiffen and he could taste blood in his mouth. It would be worse once the adrenalin wore off.

He was still too keyed-up to think straight. Who the fuck were they? What did they jump him for? He took some deep breaths to calm himself. As his heart rate slowed, so did the van. He got to Western Road, turned left and promptly got stuck in traffic. 'Fuck.'

His only consolation was that if the guys who'd attacked him made it to a car and came after him, they'd be stuck a good way behind him. The problem was the junction up ahead and the sheer volume of traffic trying to get through it. He checked his mirrors and realised he had no idea what he was looking for. He didn't know what any of them looked like or what kind of car they might be in.

When he finally reached the lights, he went left onto King Street, which was just as choked with vehicles. By the time he got to Southall station, he was calm again, or as calm as he could be after being attacked. Snatches of the fight flashed through his mind and he tried to pick out anything that might help him identify his attackers, but came up with nothing.

Waiting at a set of traffic lights, he wondered where the hell he was going? He looked at the clock on the dashboard and decided that was it, he was going home. He'd had enough of playing detective for one day.

CHAPTER EIGHT

He didn't want to park the van outside the house, in case the guys who'd attacked him were driving around looking for it, so he decided to dump it at the yard and walk home. The rear gates were locked, so he parked on the small service road behind the shuttered shops, just past a skip piled high with rubbish from the builder's yard.

His body was starting to ache and his face was throbbing. He used his tongue to probe a cut inside his lower lip. Hands in his pockets, shoulders hunched, he started to walk home keeping to the shadows. Despite how he felt, he took a longer route, through quieter residential streets, warily checking any cars that passed by. It took about fifteen minutes. He checked the street in both directions as he crossed the road towards the house. Satisfied the coast was clear, he slipped between the two vans in the driveway and let himself in.

He was greeted by the pungent aroma of onions, ginger, garlic and chilli being fried with turmeric, coriander, cumin and cinnamon. It made him realise how hungry he was. He dragged himself upstairs to put his jacket in his room, otherwise it would reek of cooking and make him smell like a proper *freshie* next day.

Zaq had the double room at the front all to himself. He paid extra for the privilege but it was worth it. He'd spent too much time sharing a cell and was prepared to fork out a little extra for the space and privacy. There was a single bed against the wall, with a two-drawer bedside table next to it. A wooden chair stood over by the bay window. On the floor were some dumbbells, a rolled up yoga mat and a punchbag lying on its side like a giant cushion. Opposite the bed were a double wardrobe, a tall chest of drawers and a wheeled clothes rail. A full-length mirror was propped against the wall. The room was painted a neutral magnolia and the carpet was brown. It wasn't much but it was enough.

Zaq hung his jacket behind the door, grabbed a face towel and went to the bathroom. He looked at his face in the mirror. Shit. His cheeks were red and starting to puff up. There was a nick on the right one with blood smeared around it. His lower lip was split and swollen and there was more blood on his chin.

He cleaned his face with warm water, patted it dry, then filled the sink with cold water. He dipped the bunched up towel in the water and used it as a compress to try and reduce the swelling. It numbed the pain slightly but did nothing about the bruising. Finally, he dabbed some antiseptic on the cuts, effing and blinding as he did so.

When he was done, he went downstairs. The communal part of the house was at the back, a large space made up of the rear reception room and an extension combined to make an open plan lounge, kitchen and dining area.

'What the fuck happened to you?' Manjit Singh asked from the sofa when he saw Zaq. He was built like a heavyweight boxer, lean muscle on a big frame. His size, his black turban and his black beard all made him look like a traditional Sikh warrior; the faded jeans, purple polo shirt and beer in his hand didn't.

'I had a disagreement with some guys,' Zaq said.

'What about?'

'They wanted to beat me up. I wasn't so keen on the idea.'

'Where was this? You want to go back, see if they're still there?'

'Thanks but they've probably gone by now.'

'You sure? Bal will be back in a bit and we can all go look for them.'

'They're probably at a hospital. I managed to lay them out pretty good.'

'How many were there?'

'Three.'

Manjit raised an eyebrow. 'Three against one and you laid *them* out?'

'I caught them with a few shots, wasn't like Bruce Lee or anything.'

'They caught you with a few too, huh? You sure you don't want to go look for them, fuck them up properly?'

'Nah, it's all right. I just want to take it easy.'

'Suit yourself. You want a beer?'

'I could do with one.'

'They're in the fridge, help yourself. They ain't halal though.'

'No shit.'

It was a running joke in the house where, once again, Zaq was the only Muslim. When he'd first moved in his family background had been more of an issue than his criminal record. Growing up in Southall, Zaq hadn't known many other Muslims which, to his dad, who'd never exactly been religious himself, wasn't a big deal. The result was that Zaq was about as Muslim as the Archbishop of Canterbury. That didn't stop his housemates remarking on it though.

In the kitchen Pali was at the cooker, stirring a large pot. His heavy mop of unruly black hair had no discernible style and was simply pushed to one side of his head. He had on a pale blue work shirt, hanging out over black trousers, and a pair of flip-flops. He looked at Zaq's face but must have heard the conversation with Manjit as he didn't ask what had happened.

'What's cooking?' Zaq said. 'It smells good.'

'Lamb.'

Zaq went to the fridge and grabbed a can of beer. He pressed the cold tin to the swelling on his face. 'How long's it going to be?'

'About fifteen minutes. Bal should be back in a minute with some *naan*. Dips and Lax should be here by then too.'

'You need a hand with anything?'

'Nah, it's done. Go and sit down.'

Zaq got a glass and poured the lager into it. He went back to the lounge and joined Manjit on the sofa. The news was on TV, a report about some Islamic militant leader being killed in Pakistan.

'Was it anyone you know?' Manjit said.

'Just 'cause my family's from Pakistan, don't mean I know every fucking *jihadi* nut job out there.'

'I meant the guys that jumped you.'

'I know – I was just messing with you. Nope, ain't got a clue who they were.'

'What was it about?'

'They didn't say.'

'You think they'll try again?'

It hadn't occurred to Zaq. 'Fuckin' hope not.'

They drank their beer and the local news came on. Police were still appealing for witnesses who saw the two white men who carried out a robbery at the airport the week before.

'You want to be careful,' Manjit said. 'They come looking for payback you might not be so lucky next time.'

'You got a point,' Zaq said, 'and not just the one on your turban.'

'Now I get why someone would want to hit you.'

Zaq grinned. He got on real well with Manjit. Once they'd gotten to know each other they found they had more in common than not and shared the same sense of humour, otherwise Zaq would never have made a joke about his turban.

They heard the front door open and close, then Bal came into the lounge carrying two carrier bags of freshly made tandoori *naan*. Broad, squat and muscular, with bristly hair and thick stubble, he reminded Zaq of a wild boar. '*Kidaah*?' he greeted them. Then he saw Zaq's face and stopped. 'What the fuck happened to your *buthi*?'

The soft lamb in its thick spicy sauce went down well with the fresh *naan* and a red onion, cucumber and chilli salad. A second beer helped soften the edges of Zaq's pain. After dinner, it was his turn to do the dishes. He might have been in a fight but the others' sympathies didn't stretch to doing the washing up for him. By the time he finished, he felt his muscles stiffening and knew if he didn't do something about it, he'd feel worse the next day. He popped two ibuprofens and went up to his room. It was only as he was emptying his pockets that he realised something was missing. The photograph of Rita… shit, it wasn't there.

Where was it? Last time he'd seen it was just before the three guys had jumped him. He was sure he'd put it back in his pocket but… maybe he'd dropped it. Bollocks. He wasn't about to go back there now. If he was in the area tomorrow, he'd take a look, see if he could find it, otherwise it was lost and he'd have to make do without it.

He took off his jeans and sweatshirt. Then, in T-shirt, boxers and socks he started shadow boxing, to get his muscles moving. He replayed the attack over and over in his head, each time coming up with different ways to counter and attack. The speed and intensity of his punches increased as he loosened up and soon he was throwing elbows, knees and kicks into the mix. After ten minutes he had a light sweat on and felt warmed up enough to go through a deep stretch routine. He held each stretch for thirty seconds, until the burn became a buzz. The combination of alcohol, painkillers and stretching seemed to do the trick. When he finished, he didn't feel too bad.

It was too early to go to sleep but he didn't want to go back downstairs and get into another conversation about what had happened. Instead, he changed, got into bed and picked up the book he was reading, The Anubis Gates by Tim Powers.

If nothing else, prison had afforded him plenty of time and opportunity to read. He used to prefer crime and thrillers but in prison he read whatever was available and found he particularly enjoyed science fiction, fantasy and historical adventures. When the world around you was so shit, it was good to escape somewhere else for a while, even if it was only in your imagination.

He'd been reading for half an hour when his phone rang. The caller's number was withheld but he answered anyway.

'It was you, wasn't it?' a woman accused him. 'You came to work, snooping around, asking about Rita.'

It took Zaq a moment figure out who it was. 'Nina?'

'It *was* you, wasn't it? Why don't you just leave her alone? What's it got to do with you anyway?'

'I said, I'm a friend of hers and –'

'No, you're not. I know you're not.'

'You talked to her.' How else could she be so certain?

'No.' The denial was too forced.

'Did you give her my message?'

'I told you, I haven't spoken to her.'

'OK, if you say so. I'll just find her some other way.'

'Why're you looking for her?'

''Cause her family have told me to.'

'You mean her brothers?'

'No, her dad, actually.'

'Same thing. Did he say why she left home?'

'Something about an argument with her brothers.'

She gave a derisive laugh. 'With her whole family, more like. Did he mention the wedding? She's supposed to marry some guy they've got lined up for her. She doesn't have a say in the matter.'

That was something else they'd neglected to mention. Not that it made much difference to Zaq – he might not like the idea of arranged marriages, but it was their business, nothing to do with him. All he had to do was find her. Whatever problems she had at home, she'd have to sort them out herself once she was back there. 'So, the guy she's run off with, this Kasim, he her boyfriend?'

'No, he's not. Who told you that?'

'It's what I heard, what her dad and her brothers think too.'

'Raj and Parm...' There was anger in her voice now. 'They *know* he's not her boyfriend. There's nothing going on between them; they're just friends.'

'Right.' Zaq's tone made his doubt plain.

'It's true. They went out a couple of times, but that's all.'

'Maybe they been seeing each other on the sly.'

'Not the way her brothers keep an eye on her. Anyway, they knew he was taking her out and they were OK with it, at first anyway. Rita thought it was because he's a friend of theirs, but then things got weird.'

'Hang on… what do you mean, he's a friend of theirs? They told me they didn't know him.'

'Who do you think introduced them? They obviously don't want their dad to know about it – but they couldn't wait to drop Rita in it by telling him about *her* and Kasim.'

'Why?'

'It's obvious. Because it was a set-up. They let her go out with Kasim just so they could turn it around and use it against her. Kasim found out what they were going to do and came to warn her –'

'I heard he'd been beaten up.'

'Yes, by Raj and Parm – to show what happens to any guy who goes near their sister. He came straight from the hospital to let her know they were going to her dad, to tell him she'd been going out with a Muslim.'

'Why would they do that?'

'To wind him up so much he'd get her married off straight away, no chance of her getting out of it. Their idea of a proper Punjabi girl is one that's married at sixteen, having kids at seventeen and who spends the rest of her life at home, cooking and cleaning. They think it looks bad that she's isn't married already.'

'That's a bit *pindoofied*.'

'That's how they are. It's all right for them to do whatever the hell they want – smoking, drinking, sleeping around – but Rita has to be all traditional and uphold the family's honour.'

'But then why run off with Kasim? It just makes what her brothers have said look true.'

'What choice did she have? She couldn't have gone home – there's no telling what her dad might've done. At the very least, she wouldn't have been allowed out of the house, not until after the wedding. She was getting ready to leave home anyway. There was no way she was going through with the wedding – then all this happened.'

'Why didn't she just tell her dad the truth, that there was nothing going on with her and Kasim?'

'It'd be her word against her brothers'. And he wouldn't believe her anyway.'

'Why not?'

Nina paused, then said, 'Because of what happened last year…'

'Which was what…?'

'They found out about the guy she was *really* seeing.'

'He a Muslim too?'

'No, he was Sikh.'

'So what was the problem?'

'Just that she had a boyfriend. It didn't matter that he was Sikh. As far as they were concerned she should have been married, not going out with anyone.'

'What happened?'

'Things were serious between them – they'd been seeing each other for about three years and managed to keep it quiet all that time. They wanted to get married and Rita was just waiting for the right time to tell her mum and dad – but then her brothers found out and ruined everything. They put her boyfriend in hospital and dragged Rita in front of their dad, told him all sorts of stuff, made it sound really cheap and sordid, when it wasn't anything like that. They loved each other.'

'How'd her dad react?'

'He totally lost it. He didn't hit her but he was rough with her. She showed me the bruises. He had a go at Raj and Parm too, for letting it happen. When she said she wanted to marry the guy, it only made things worse.'

'I thought they wanted her to get married?'

'Not to just anyone though. They want her to marry into a family with money and status – it's all about money and status with them. As far as they were concerned her boyfriend didn't have either – and to top it off, he wasn't a *Jatt*.'

'I thought Sikhs don't believe in the whole caste thing.'

'We're not meant to, but it still matters to some people.'

'So, what happened then?'

'She wasn't allowed to see him again, not even to visit him in hospital. Her dad starting looking for a husband for her, while her brothers and their friends kept an eye on her wherever she went. Rita's never forgiven them. It's been really tense at home for her ever since.'

'Running off with Kasim ain't going to make things any better.'

'What else was she supposed to do? Her brothers set her up, only now it's all backfired on them. They never expected her to just up and leave.'

'Serves them right then,' Zaq said. He couldn't blame her for running away – but it didn't change the fact he still had to find her. 'Look, I'm sorry she's had such a hard time of it and all – but I still need to know where she is.'

'Why? So her family can drag her back and force her into an arranged marriage she doesn't want – or maybe worse? If her dad believes all the lies Raj and Parm have told him, who knows what he might do to her?'

She had a point. Zaq had heard plenty of stories about Asian girls who'd had boyfriends, refused arranged marriages or become too '*Westernised*' or 'modern' and been killed by their families. In some instances they were whisked off to India or Pakistan and killed there, where it was easier to murder someone and dispose of the body after. It wasn't just confined to Sikh families either – it happened with Hindus as well and especially with Muslims. A Sikh girl shacking up with a Muslim bloke would be the ultimate shame for her family. To some, the only way to restore their honour was by shedding the blood of the guilty.

Zaq didn't like the thought of being involved in something like that – but then, he didn't like anything about the whole goddam situation. He tried telling himself Nina was just focusing on the worst case scenario – but deep down he knew better. With her brothers' reputation for violence and her dad's temper, a bad outcome for Rita was highly probable. He tried to push the thought out of his mind. What he needed to do was concentrate on finding her. Whatever happened after that wasn't his concern. 'You got any idea where they might be?'

'You think I'd tell you even if I did?'

'I've got to find her, with or without your help.'

'It'll have to be without then. Why don't you just tell them you couldn't find her?'

'I can't.'

'Why not?'

'It's complicated.' He sensed the conversation was coming to an end. 'If you speak to Rita again,' he said, 'tell her I'm looking for her. Pass on my number too, in case she wants to talk.'

'About what?'

'Trying to sort things out with her dad. If I can talk to her, maybe we can figure out a way.'

'She won't talk to you.'

'How do you know?'

'Because you're working for her dad and that means her brothers too. She'd trust you about as far as she could throw you.'

'*You* talk to her then, see if you can convince her to call me.'

'And why would I do that?'

'Because you're her friend and you want to help her.'

'How would that be helping her?'

'Put it this way – who would you rather found her first, me or her brothers?'

'Neither.' After a moment, she said, 'If I talk to her, I'll tell her what you've said – but it'll be up to her if she calls you.'

It was the best he could hope for.

CHAPTER NINE

When he reached to turn off his alarm clock the next morning, Zaq instantly regretted moving. Stretching had helped but lying still all night had caused his body to seize up like a set of rusty gears. The last time he'd ached so much was probably after his first training session with the small group of serious fighters back in prison, when he'd had to undergo an initiation of sorts to see if he had what it took to join them. Only after he kept returning, despite being constantly battered and bruised, had he eventually been accepted into the tight-knit group.

He eased himself back, flat on the mattress, until the pain subsided to a dull but constant ache. His neck was stiff, so it was difficult to turn his head. It had been a big mistake to neglect his training; he was paying the price for it now. Memory and reflexes meant he'd remembered the moves, but his body had been nowhere near as quick as his mind. It was only the hours he'd spent training in the prison gym with the hardcore fighters that had saved him from a more severe beating last night. He'd learned techniques and practised moves from a variety of styles; Karate, boxing, Tae Kwon Do, Jiu-Jitsu, and Krav Maga amongst others – along with every dirty trick any of them knew. Sparring sessions had been brutal, resulting in regular visits to the prison infirmary. Stick the Marquis of Queensbury and his rules; they weren't interested in going twelve rounds; their aim was to put down an opponent in under twelve seconds, any way they could.

At last, Zaq forced himself up – it was either that or wet the bed. He lumbered to the bathroom like Frankenstein's monster, only to find it occupied. There was another toilet under the stairs, but he didn't fancy dragging himself all the way down and back up again. He knocked on the door. 'Hurry up, I got to take a leak.'

'Yeah, yeah,' came a muffled response.

He had to wait a minute or so before he heard the toilet flush, followed by the sound of a tap running and finally the click of the lock. 'You took your time,' he said, as the door opened.

'Can't even take a shit in peace round here,' Bal said, coming out of the bathroom. He wore a pair of red briefs and a black T-shirt stretched tight across his upper body. His stocky arms and legs were visible and covered in dark hair that made him look like a werewolf in mid-transition. 'Talking of shit, you seen the state of your face?'

Zaq pushed past him but was stopped in his tracks. 'Bloody hell, it stinks in there.' The odour was almost a physical barrier and waving his hand in front of his face wasn't helping. 'You need to see a doctor, mate. I think something crawled up your arse and died.'

'It's all right, I just shat it out again.' Bal laughed and sauntered back to the room he shared with Lax. Zaq took a deep breath, went into the bathroom, grabbed the can of air freshener and gave the bathroom a good long blast before finally taking a piss and then washing his hands. A quick look in the mirror confirmed what Bal had said – he did look like shit.

Back in his room, he pulled back the curtains. The day outside was bleak and grey. He went to the middle of the room and shook his arms and legs loose, doing his best to ignore his body's complaints. When he felt limber enough, he began to shadow box again, moving around slowly to get himself warmed up. The effect was like WD40 being applied to squeaky hinges. His movements became less leaden and the pain and stiffness lessened. After ten minutes, he felt a sheen of sweat on his face and back. He pulled on a heavy hooded top and repeated the stretches he'd done the night before. When he was finished, there was still some tightness in his muscles but he could move easier.

He grabbed his wash bag and towel and went to the bathroom only to find it occupied again. He heard the shower turn off though and decided to wait. A few moments later the lock was pulled back and the door opened.

'Bloody hell,' Manjit said, when he saw Zaq. 'I didn't know it was Halloween.' He stood in the doorway, a bright orange towel wrapped around his waist and steam curling around his big frame. His long hair was tied up on top of his head and water glinted on his beard and chest. 'You look like shit.'

'So I been told,' Zaq said.

'Does your face hurt?'

'A bit.'

'Yeah, well it's killing me.' Manjit laughed and his teeth flashed white in his black beard.

'That joke's so old.'

'Don't matter how old it is, it's what you do with it.'

'Bet you say that to all the girls.'

'They ain't worried how old it is,' Manjit said, ''cause I know exactly what to do with it.' He demonstrated with some pelvic thrusts and a big grin.

Zaq held up a hand to block the sight. 'Please, I don't need to see that first thing in the morning – no wait, make that *ever.*'

'What the fuck're you two doing?' Lax, in a pair of stripy pyjama bottoms and a white vest, with a towel slung over his shoulder, was standing watching them. His hair stood out at odd angles like an exploded firework. In his mid-twenties, he talked too much and thought too little. 'Actually, your *buthi* is pretty messed up. Looks worse than it did last night.'

'Thanks, that makes me feel a lot better.' Zaq stepped around Manjit to get to the bathroom. 'Now if you two *luloos* don't mind, I'm going to take a shower.'

The hot water did little for the bruising on his face, which had started to turn a bluish purple, but it did soothe away some of his aches. He stood under the driving spray and replayed the attack in his head – but still came away clueless as to the identity of his attackers or their motive. He was pretty sure they'd be feeling as bad as he was, if not worse. Then a thought struck him – what if they went to the police and said *he* attacked *them*? Shit. With his record, he'd be screwed. Maybe he should report it himself, give his own version of events – after all, he was the one who'd actually been attacked. He had the cuts and bruises to prove it and, with it having been three against one, the numbers would be in his favour.

Back in his room he pulled on a pair of jeans and a navy blue sweatshirt, stuffed his phone, keys and money into his pockets along with the list of Rita's contacts, then grabbed his jacket from a hook on the door and went downstairs. He had a bowl of microwave porridge before leaving the house.

Outside, he was wary as he crossed the empty drive. The two vans were already gone. One was Bal's, the other Manjit's – both of them builders. Zaq scanned the street, on the lookout for anyone who might be waiting for him. He didn't expect there to be; if the guys last night had known where he lived, they would've jumped him here, not at the Scotsman as he hardly ever went there. They must've seen him there by chance; either that or they'd followed him there. Whoever they were, they could come at him again so he had to be on his guard.

It took him a quarter of an hour to get to work. The van was still where he'd left it, on the service road behind the yard. He'd intended to just take it and go but decided he better see Sid, let him know he'd come in and then gone out.

'*Heh*?' Sid looked up, his scowl changing to a look of surprise when he saw Zaq's face. '*Their buthi nu ki hoya*?' he said, unable to keep from grinning.

'Your missus got a bit rough while I was giving her one.'

The grin disappeared from Sid's face. '*Arrey, kutha, haramzada!*' he shouted, slamming his mug onto the desk and spilling tea.

'All right, calm down,' Zaq said. 'I had a bit of trouble last night.'

'Trouble? I give you the fucking trouble.' Sid was breathing heavily through his nose, his nostrils flaring. 'Where you bloody going with van?'

'I still got things to do for Mr Brar.'

'You no finish this yesterday? What you do for him?'

'You want to know, go ask him.'

Sid waved toward the vans parked outside. 'What about *bhen chaud* delivery?'

'Ram'll have to go out again.'

'*Phudi da. Ohnu* map *e purdh nay ahn da.*'

'Get him sat-nav then.'

'Who buying bloody sat-nav? You?'

'Nothing to do with me. If Ram can't find the drops, tell

Mr Brar.' If enough customers complained about their late deliveries, Zaq might get put back on normal duties instead of having to search for Rita. That would be fine with him.

'*Mera sir na kah. Jaa,* fuck off *hoja.*' Sid waved him off.

Zaq found Ram and Bits talking outside.

'Boy, looks like someone give you a good thump, innit?' Bits spoke like the rudeboy he thought he was.

'Not as good as I gave them,' Zaq said, unsmiling. Bits nodded and shut up. Zaq turned to Ram, 'I'm going out for Mr Brar again today, so you'll be taking the deliveries.'

'Wicked.'

'Oh, and Ram...'

'Yeah?'

He was going to tell him to take more time studying the maps... then stopped himself. If he wanted to get put back on deliveries, the best thing to do was let Ram carry on being as shit as he was. 'Take it easy,' he said instead.

Zaq pulled over near the Plough and parked. He got a ticket from the parking machine and left it on the dashboard. It was only a short walk from there.

Southall police station is a blocky, angular, four-storey brick building with small windows, standing guard at the corner of North Road and Uxbridge Road.

An automatic glass door opened and let him into the grey waiting area. Both of the two enclosed counters, staffed by civilian police support assistants, were busy, so Zaq sat down and waited.

A bearded man with matted hair was at the nearer counter. The assistant was talking on the phone, which she then handed to the man, who spoke into it loudly in what sounded to Zaq like Polish. At the other counter was a middle-aged Asian woman wearing a heavy black coat. The woman was the first to finish and come out. Zaq went in through the open door.

'Can you wait outside until you're called,' the woman behind the counter told him. She was about fifty, her blond hair as faded and tired as she seemed. She had on a dark blue jumper with a blue and white checked neckerchief, intended to make her civilian outfit look as similar as possible to a real police uniform.

'Sorry.' Zaq went back out and sat down.

'Next,' the woman called, after a few minutes. The door slid open with a *whoosh* that reminded Zaq of the Starship Enterprise; it whooshed shut behind him. He took a seat in front of the counter. The woman inspected him through rectangular framed glasses, with a look that said she'd heard it all before. 'How can I help you?'

'I'd like to report an assault.'

'Who was assaulted?'

Was she having a laugh? 'I was.'

She cast her eyes over the bruises on his face. 'When did the assault take place?'

'Last night.' Zaq told her what had happened outside the Scotsman, though he downplayed his own part. He gave her the when, where and what, but he didn't know the who or the why. The woman entered the information on a computer. He didn't expect the cops to do much about it but it was good to have his version of events officially documented, hopefully before his three assailants tried to make any complaint against him. If they came after him again, he'd be able to show a pattern of attacks, which could work in his favour later on.

When he'd told her everything he remembered, the woman said, 'We'll need a record of your injuries for the report.' With a digital camera, she took several pictures of his face from different angles and, when she was satisfied, went over the report with him, to check everything was correct. She then had him sign a printout and gave him a copy to keep. 'If you think of anything else that might help, just call us and give the reference number on the top there and we can add the information to the report.'

Zaq thanked her, shoved the crime report in his jacket pocket and left the police station. He returned to the van. Park Avenue was nearby... and he had a few more questions for Raj and Parm Brar.

The front door was opened by the same Indian builder who'd answered the day before.

'*Parminder aur Rajinder heh gey eh*?' Zaq asked him again.

The man took a good look at Zaq's face. Maybe he recognised him, maybe not. '*Raj heh ga.*' He nodded his turbaned head toward the back of the house.

Zaq went down the hall, and through to the extension. The concrete block walls were up now and the builders were working on the exterior brickwork. Rajinder was sitting on a white plastic chair in the middle of the concrete floor, talking on his phone. When he saw Zaq, he frowned, turned away and continued his conversation. Zaq could wait, that didn't bother him; what did needle him though was the lack of basic manners. It wouldn't have cost him anything to be civil – a simple acknowledgement, a nod, a hand in the air to say just a minute. Dissing someone like that in prison could get a man shanked.

A train rattled by on the tracks beyond the end of the garden. Zaq watched the *faujis* working away. They seemed to be doing a good job but he knew if you used them you had to be on top of them. You needed to tell them *exactly* what you wanted, *how* you wanted it done and you'd better explain it all in Punjabi just to be sure, and even then they could still fuck it up. He'd seen it happen more than once. But they worked cheap and at the end of the day, that was the overriding factor that got them work.

'What the fuck you want now?' Raj had finished his phone call. 'What happened to your face?'

'Nothing,' Zaq said. 'Your brother here?'

'No.'

'You want to call him, so I can talk to him?'

'You can talk to me.'

'I would but you don't seem to know anything.'

Plastic screeched against concrete as Rajinder pushed himself up out of his chair and came over to him. 'What did you say?'

Zaq didn't move. Rajinder stood right in front of him, glaring. The guy was big and no doubt strong, but Zaq was sure he'd be quicker and that would make all the difference. Hit him fast and hard, with a few well-timed, well-placed blows and put him on the floor. 'If you're going to bullshit me like yesterday, I'd rather talk to Parminder,' he said.

'No wonder someone smacked you up – you got a big fucking mouth. You got anything to say, say it to me.'

'OK, I just wanted to double-check a couple of things. This bloke your sister's run off with – Kasim – he's her boyfriend, right?'

'Yeah.'

'Anything else you can tell me about him?'

'No. We told you already, we don't know him.'

'I'm just making sure I got it straight. How'd Rita meet him?'

'How the fuck should I know?'

'Any idea how long they been seeing each other?'

'No.'

'And you and Parminder didn't beat him up?'

'We never touched him.'

'What about Rita's ex?'

The question took him by surprise. 'What?'

'You remember him, right? You put him in hospital, about a year ago.'

'What the fuck's that got to do with anything?'

'I don't know, maybe nothing. What was his name?'

'How should I know?'

'You must know his name. How'd you know who to beat up?'

'I don't remember.'

'See? That's what I thought you'd say. Let me talk to your brother.'

'What if he don't know either?'

'Then I'll have to go ask your dad. 'Course, I'll have to tell him why I'm bothering him – 'cause you and Parm ain't helping me find Rita. What you think he'd say to that?'

Raj's mouth compressed into a tight thin line. There was nothing friendly in the look he was giving Zaq. 'Why you asking about him? What's he got to do with any of this?'

'Nothing, far as I know. I might talk to him though, see if he knows anything that could help. You remember his name now? Or should I go talk to your dad?'

Raj's brow knotted into a frown. When he finally spoke, it seemed like the words were leaving a bad taste in his mouth. 'Davinder Panesar.'

'You know where I can find him?' Zaq knew what the answer was going to be but asked anyway.

'No.'

'You think your dad might?'

Raj fixed him with a baleful stare. It might've scared little kids but to Zaq he just looked constipated. 'All I remember is he lived in Hounslow.'

'That's not much to go on.'

'Ain't my problem. You want to talk to him, find him yourself.'

'All right. Anything else you can think of that might help me?'

'Yeah, get the fuck out of my face and stay out my way!'

CHAPTER TEN

Sitting in the van, Zaq thought about the conversation he'd just had. If Nina had told him the truth last night, then Rajinder had lied again about not knowing Kasim. Why though? He might not have wanted to mention that they knew Kasim in front of their old man, but he could've come clean to Zaq just now. Knowing more about Kasim would definitely help in trying to find Rita. Perhaps Parminder would've been more forthcoming. Zaq would bet money that Rajinder was on the phone to his brother right now.

Two names – that was all Zaq had to go on – Kasim and Davinder Panesar. Maybe he should talk to the ex-boyfriend, see if he did know anything. He was wondering how to track him down when he saw Rajinder come rushing out of the house and get into a silver Mercedes. He didn't see Zaq. Where was he off to in such a hurry? Having no other plans just then, Zaq decided to follow him and see.

The Mercedes pulled out and sped away. Zaq waited a couple of seconds then went after it. He let another car get between them as they drove along Park Avenue and by the time they joined the queue for the lights at South Road, Zaq was two cars behind. The big Gurdwara was on his left while, across the road, was where the old Glassy Junction pub had been, a Southall landmark Zaq still couldn't believe was gone.

The lights turned green and Rajinder took a left up past the station and on into Old Southall. Zaq hung back but kept him in sight. At Western International the road widened to four lanes approaching the big roundabout. Zaq kept a close watch, in case he had to jump lanes. He only hoped Rajinder wasn't heading for the M4; there was no way the van could keep up with the Mercedes on the motorway. Fortunately, Rajinder indicated right and moved into that lane. Zaq did the same. They took the third exit off the roundabout, for Hayes and Yeading.

The road was a fast stretch of dual carriageway that rose up over railway lines and the Grand Union Canal. Zaq had to stamp hard on the accelerator to keep pace with Rajinder on the gradient. The Mercedes crested the rise and disappeared. Zaq floored the pedal, rocking back and forth in his seat, urging the van to go faster. He reached the point where he'd lost sight of the Rajinder and was so focused on gaining speed he almost missed seeing the Mercedes, on the short exit slip to the left.

Zaq had to brake suddenly and swerve hard to make the exit. A horn blared behind him. Rajinder had already gone around the sharp turn at the end. Zaq took it faster than was sensible and felt two wheels leave the ground as the van careered round the bend. Sweat slicked his forehead and a drop snaked down his back. The road made a tight curve left, almost 180°, and then straightened. He came out of the bend just in time to see Rajinder turning right, into an industrial estate. Zaq eased off the accelerator and allowed a car to pass in the opposite direction before making the same turn into the estate.

A big tyre and auto place welcomed him in; the rest of the

buildings were a mix of industrial and commercial premises. He was on Pasadena Close, though what it had to do with Pasadena, California was anyone's guess. Up ahead, Rajinder turned left. Zaq drifted after him, onto a shorter road flanked by a chain link fence on one side and a two-storey brick building on the other. He didn't see the Mercedes, so sped up to the next corner, turned right onto a one-way road and cruised along, checking the parking spaces in front of each industrial unit for any sign of Rajinder or his car. Then he spotted it, outside the last unit, number 12, parked next to a black but otherwise identical Mercedes.

Zaq found a space between two other vans outside unit 9 and pulled over. He had a good line of sight to unit 12, through gaps in some trees and shrubbery. Units 11 and 12 together formed a U around a shared parking area. All the units were paired the same way. Each unit took up half of the U. The main entrance and what looked to be offices extended out from the main buildings to form the uprights of the U.

Zaq sat and watched even though nothing seemed to be happening. Rajinder must have gone inside. No one else was coming or going. The only cars outside unit 12 were the two Mercs. He figured the black one had to be Parminder's. There was no signage to indicate what went on inside. Did the brothers actually have a proper business? If so, it was news to Zaq; as far as he knew most of the Brar brothers' money came from less than legal sources. He turned on the crappy radio to help pass the time.

Some time later, as he was beginning to think he should be doing something more constructive, he saw the shutter jerk then begin to rise. It stopped halfway up and Rajinder came out, pushing a blue metal sack truck with two sacks on it.

Parminder followed him and together they went over to the black Mercedes, where Parminder pulled out a key fob and opened the boot. Zaq watched as they took a sack each and put it in the boot. Maybe he was mistaken but they looked very much like bags of cement. But why would the Brars be carting around bags of cement in a Merc when they could've had it delivered from their dad's yard? What was this place anyway and what else did they have in there?

Rajinder went back inside with the sack truck, while Parminder closed the boot and got in the car. The shutter came down and a moment later Raj came out through the front door, which he locked, and then got in the car with his brother. They drove out of the car park and away along the one-way road. Zaq waited until they were around the corner then started the van and followed after them.

He kept his distance as they took a right out of the estate and then sped up so he wouldn't lose them. Their route took them past the big Tarmac works and under the flyover, the road looping around to join the Parkway on the other side, going back the way Rajinder had come. At the big roundabout they went left, toward Southall. Zaq figured they were returning to the house on Park Avenue. The only thing he'd learned was that they had some cement stored in an industrial unit – big deal.

They passed Tesco and Toys-R-Us, and continued on to a mini-roundabout. Zaq expected them to go straight but the Merc's indicator flashed right and they turned towards Cranford. Some other vehicles made the turn before he managed to but the road ran in a straight line, so he could still see the black Mercedes up ahead.

The loading docks of Western International Park flashed by on the right, giving way to an expanse of undeveloped land covered with wild grass. Similar tracts of land were dotted all around this area of west London, probably owned by the airport, Zaq reckoned, and kept empty in case a plane ever needed to crash land in an emergency. The road crossed a bridge over the M4 – six lanes of traffic hurtling by beneath them – then dipped to go through a residential area with a school, a college and a lot of speed bumps.

The Brars slowed at another mini-roundabout. Still a few cars behind, Zaq watched to see which way they'd go. They went straight. Zaq cursed the drivers in front of him, not wanting to lose the Mercedes, but then saw it signal and turn into the car park of a pub, the Queen's Head.

Zaq hadn't expected that; it was too early to go to a pub. No way he could follow them into the car park – it was practically empty so they'd spot him straight away. What the hell should he do? He was at the roundabout now and had to decide fast. Then he spotted an access road running between blocks of flats on the right. It probably led to a car park at the back of the buildings. That would do. He whizzed around the roundabout and took the access road. He'd been right about the parking area and made a quick U-turn there, then crept back toward the main road. He pulled up onto the pavement, from where he was able to observe the pub car park.

The Mercedes was parked over by a fence, away from the pub itself. Although there were plenty of empty spaces, the Brars had pulled in next to a big black 4x4 truck. Zaq watched Rajinder and Parminder get out of the car as two other heavyset guys got out of the truck. The four shook hands and, after a brief exchange, went to the back of the Mercedes where Parminder opened the boot. The two new guys took a bag each and hefted them into their truck, after which all four stood around, discussing something. From their body language it was clear they weren't telling each other jokes. Even from across the road, Zaq could see none of them was smiling. Parminder did most of the talking, Rajinder contributing now and again.

What was going on? Why were the Brars delivering cement in a pub car park? Could it be hooky gear, ripped off from somewhere, that they were trying to get rid of on the sly? They'd have to shift a lot of bloody cement to make any money out of it. Something didn't add up.

One of the heavyset guys took out a mobile phone and made a call. When he finished, they all shook hands again and got back in their vehicles. The truck reversed out and turned toward the exit, followed by the Brars.

Now what? He knew how to find the Brars, so decided to follow the other two to see what they did with the cement. The truck took a right at the roundabout. Zaq ducked down so the Brars wouldn't see him as they passed by. He waited a few seconds then sat up to see which way they had gone. He could see the truck driving away ahead of him but no sign of the Mercedes following after it. Rajinder and Parminder must have gone the other way, back towards Southall.

Zaq started his engine and forced his way into the traffic, pissing off several other drivers in the process. Now he saw Parminder's car in the distance briefly, as he took the right exit and went after the truck. He had to go around a bus at a stop, then stomp on the accelerator to make up the gap to the 4x4. It was easier following the truck; they didn't know him or the van, so he could stay fairly close behind them.

He tailed them along Cranford Lane, past housing estates and yet another fenced-off plot of vacant land, then on through Heston and into Hounslow. The roads were busier there but Zaq managed to stick with them. His phone vibrated in his pocket but he couldn't answer it while driving. He'd call whoever it was back when he got a chance.

The Bath Road curved left just before Hounslow High Street and became Lampton Road. Up ahead he saw Hounslow Central tube station and the bridge that carried the Piccadilly Line over the road. In front of him, the truck indicated left and turned into a road opposite the Bulstrode pub. Several seconds after them, Zaq took the same turn.

Small three-bedroom terraced houses lined both sides of the street, most worn and shabby, packed tight together. Nearly all the front gardens had been paved or concreted, which gave the street a bleak, barren look. Apart from the odd tree or bush, the only other greenery was the weeds sprouting from cracks in the pavements.

The truck pulled over on the left. Zaq continued past and saw it in the driveway of a house. The drive wasn't deep enough so it was parked at an angle. Both men were out of the vehicle, one wearing a dark green jacket, the other dark blue. Green was at the tailgate, hoisting a bag of cement onto his shoulder; Blue was opening the front door to the house. Zaq didn't get a look at their faces. Further along, he turned around and came back to park where he could see the house. Neither of the men was outside now. They'd probably taken the cement inside. Maybe they were just doing the place up – it definitely looked like it needed some work.

He remembered the missed call and took out his phone. Biri's name was on the screen. Zaq was about to call him when both guys came out of the house and started walking towards the main road. He was there anyway… might as well see where they were going; couldn't be far in any case if they were walking. He overtook them in the van and nabbed a parking space close to the shops. They were still a way off as he got a ticket from the pay-and-display machine and put it on the dashboard. He locked the van and went to lean against some railings and call

Biri back.

'I was driving when you called. What's up?'

'That thing you asked about... I got something. Swing by and I'll give you the details.'

'Where?'

Blue and Green came around the corner. They looked like a couple of villains from a PEGI 18 computer game – big boned, heavy limbed, steroid pumped – walking with a swagger that said, *'Don't fuck with us'*. Blue's hair was cropped close at the back and sides but longer on the top and gelled back. He had angular, well-defined features and a gold hoop earring in each ear. Green was darker and uglier, his features rough-cut and blunt like an unfinished statue's, his thick shaggy hair long at the back. Black stubble covered his jaw, dark, like it had been painted on. Zaq didn't know them.

'The *office*,' Biri said – which meant the Scotsman.

Zaq wasn't keen to go back after what had happened the previous night – but what were the chances he'd get jumped in the same place again, in broad daylight? 'All right,' he said. 'Be there in a bit.'

'Cool.'

He put his phone away and watched Blue and Green walk into a shop. The sign over the front read Prewal & Son Butchers. Zaq pushed himself away from the railings and walked past the shop to get a look inside. The window displayed cuts of meat and poultry in a refrigerated counter, which ran the full width of the window, then up the middle of the shop and across the back. Blue and Green were talking to a young man, maybe late twenties, who was wearing a white coat and a red apron. Zaq carried on walking to the zebra crossing, where he crossed the road to the station and doubled back so he could see into the shop again. He joined people waiting at the bus stop outside the Bulstrode, from where he could still see into the butcher's.

The trio were still talking, huddled together like they were discussing something private. Whatever it was, it didn't look like it was anything to do with chicken or lamb. The young butcher didn't look happy. They seemed to reach an agreement and then Blue and Green left the shop. If they'd gone in to buy some meat, they'd forgotten it.

Zaq left the bus stop and walked with other pedestrians until he reached a point where he could see the two men walking down the side road, back towards the house. He might as well head over and see what Biri had for him. He crossed over to the van with the keys in his hand when his phone rang.

'What's happening?' This time it was Jags.

'Nothing much.'

'Where are you?'

'Hounslow.'

'What you doing there?'

'Long story. I'll tell you later. What you up to?'

'Fuck all. How'd it go with the Brar's yesterday?'

'They weren't much help – but I did learn a couple of things.' He could still make out Blue and Green in the distance.

'Like what?'

'If you're home I'll come and tell you. I just need to do something on the way.'

'All right. See you in a bit.'

Zaq got in the van and decided to make some notes so he wouldn't forget anything – not that there was much to forget. He found a pen in the glove compartment and looked around for something to write on, eventually pulling a crumpled piece of paper from is pocket. He smoothed it out on the dashboard and saw it was the list of names and numbers Mr Brar had given him. As he was looking at it, one name in particular caught his eye.

DAVINDER.

There was a phone number next to it. Studying the list more closely, he saw there was another DAVINDER on it too. It was a pretty common Indian name, so it wasn't unusual Rita would know more than one. Hopefully one was the ex-boyfriend. He'd try calling them later on.

It was the first bit of luck he'd had since starting his search. In putting together a list of any names and numbers they had found amongst Rita's things, it seemed the Brars had unwittingly given Zaq something that was actually of use.

He turned the list over and jotted down his own notes.

RAJ + PARM BRAR – WAREHOUSE, UNIT 12
OFF PASADENA CLOSE, HAYES
CEMENT ???
BLUE + GREEN, BLACK NISSAN TRUCK
BULSTRODE AVE, HOUNSLOW
PREWAL + SONS, BUTCHERS, LAMPTON ROAD.

It wasn't much and none of it seemed to have anything to do with Rita or where she might be. He turned the paper over and looked at the Davinders on the list. Had one of them spoken to Rita recently or, better still, know where she was? Even if they'd split up a year ago, they might still have kept in touch. It was definitely worth chasing up. First though, he'd go see Biri.

CHAPTER ELEVEN

He didn't want to park in the same place, so drove past the pub onto Johnson Street and parked outside the industrial estate. There was something vaguely comforting in the sight of the huge gas tower in the distance, pale blue against the dark grey sky. A Southall landmark, it was visible from miles around and Zaq always felt close to home if he could see it. His eyes swept left and right as he approached the Scotsman, even though he wasn't expecting the guys from the night before to be there now. He wasn't sure what he was looking for in any case – he didn't know what they looked like or what kind of car they'd be in.

He was almost at the pub door when he remembered the photo of Rita Brar he'd dropped the night before. He went over to where he'd been parked and searched for it but there was no sign. He swore, crossed back to the pub and went inside.

'Yo,' Biri called and beckoned him over to a table in the lounge. The place was busy, doing a good lunchtime trade, workers coming in from nearby for food and maybe even a cheeky pint. Zaq made his way over to the table and saw there was someone with Biri.

'What the fuck happened to you?' Biri asked.

'I got jumped when I left here last night.'

'Shit… who by?'

'Don't know, didn't get a look at them.'

'Them?'

'Were three of them.'

'Three against one? Must've felt like old times. Looks pretty bad.'

'I been worse. You notice anyone hanging around here yesterday?'

Biri frowned. 'Nah, but I'll ask around, see if anyone else did.'

'Thanks.' Zaq glanced sideways at Biri's companion.

'This is Rav,' Biri said. 'Rav, meet Zaq.'

Rav was about twenty, clean cut and fresh faced. He looked like he belonged in a boy band, with his carefully crafted hair and designer casual wear. 'All right,' he said.

Zaq nodded back.

'Sit down,' Biri said. 'What you drinking?' There were a couple of pints on the table and some empty crisp packets.

'Not today, mate, not even a half. I got to drive. Next time.'

'OK,' Biri said. 'Let's go outside so I can have a snout. Back in a bit, Rav.'

Biri led the way to the patio at the side of the pub. A group of smokers stood just outside the doors, so Biri walked to the small beer garden at the back, really just a patch of worn grass with some picnic tables, chose one and sat down.

'Who's the kid?' Zaq asked.

'Rav? Call him my *protégé*.' Biri took out a pack of cigarettes, put one in his mouth and lit it with a plastic lighter.

'*Protégé*? Didn't know you spoke French.'

Biri took a drag and blew out smoke. 'I heard it on TV, had to look up what it meant.'

'You used a dictionary? I'm even more impressed.'

'Fuck that, I Googled it on my phone.'

'Right,' Zaq said. 'So, what's with the *protégé*?'

'He's into cars – especially ones that ain't his. I'm showing him the ropes, teaching him how to *not* get collared, so we can both make some money.'

'He seemed a bit nervous.'

'Probably 'cause of you. I was just telling him about the time you saved my ass from those Muslim brothers inside, and then you turned up.'

Zaq and Biri had met in prison. They knew each other from Southall but not to talk to. By chance they ended up sharing a cell and became friends. Both being from Southall gave them plenty to talk about and it was good to have a connection to home. Even before Biri's arrival though, Zaq had been having problems with a group of Muslim inmates. They called him a *kafir* because he wasn't religious, he didn't pray, his friends were mostly non-Muslims and, most offensive of all, he ate pork.

Things only got worse when Biri became his cellmate. They focused some of their anger on him too, accusing him of polluting Zaq's mind, leading him astray and as a result, targeted him as well.

One day five of them cornered Biri on his own and attacked him. Someone got word to Zaq and he'd rushed from the gym to help. Luckily, he got there before Biri suffered any major injuries and piled into the attackers, laying out all five before they knew what was happening. He managed to drag Biri to the prison doctor but their problems with the brothers had only escalated after that.

'He probably didn't believe you when he saw the state of my face.'

'You kidding? You just told us you took on three dudes last

night. You's a bad motherfucker, man.'

'I'm aching like a motherfucker, that's for sure.'

Biri laughed. 'Ain't training every day like you used to inside, huh?'

'Real life gets in the way. What did you want to see me about?'

Biri blew a long plume of smoke. 'That car you asked about, the Audi... I talked to some of the guys, told them to keep an eye out for it. One of them knew it already – that exact one. He'd been scoping it out, in case we got an order for one like it.'

'You're joking!'

Biri shook his head. 'He followed it to see where it was kept so he could figure out where and when would be best to swipe it.'

'And...?'

'Dude that owns it lives on Tollgate Drive, off Delamere Road.'

'By Hayes Bridge? He know the house number?'

'Yep.' Biri told him. 'It ain't there no more though. My man says he ain't seen it for about a week. If any of the others do, they'll let me know. Soon as I hear anything, I'll give you a bell.' Biri took a last drag on his cigarette and put it out in the ashtray. 'Geezer that owns it must be on holiday or something, 'cause he ain't been at work either.'

'How d'you know that?'

'I told you, my guy followed the car to find out where it was kept. Guy who owns it works at the airport. No chance of taking it from there, too much security and shit. What's the deal with this dude anyway?'

'I got to find him for my boss,' Zaq said.

'He owe him money?'

'Something like that.'

Biri nodded. 'Safe. I hear anything else, I'll let you know. And I'll see if I can find out anything about who jumped you too.'

CHAPTER TWELVE

Lightning *could* strike twice in the same place, so Zaq was doubly wary when he left the pub. He scanned the street and, even though he didn't see anything untoward, remained tense all the way to the van. He still had no idea who the three guys were or why they'd attacked him, so there was no telling when or where they might come at him again.

He drove to Hayes and turned off the Uxbridge Road at the Angel pub, driving around Jags' block and looking in his mirrors to make sure no one was tailing him. He found a wide corner with a lot of space on the pavement and parked the van. It meant that when he came back he'd be able to see if anyone was hanging around it.

He walked to Jags', looking up and down the street both ways before going up the driveway and ringing the doorbell. He sucked at the cut to his lower lip as he waited, his eyes on the corner he'd just come around.

Jags opened the door. 'What kept –? Jeez, what the fuck happened to you?'

'Let me in and I'll tell you.'

Jags ushered him inside and shut the door. 'It weren't the Brars, was it?'

'No. Got anything to eat? I'm starving.'

'I look like your cook?'

'I wouldn't mind a cup of tea too.'

'You ever think that attitude could be what got you them bruises?' They went through to the living area and Zaq sat down at the dining table while Jags put the kettle on. 'Ham and cheese sandwich all right?'

'Yeah, thanks.'

As Jags made the sandwich, Zaq told him about the attack outside the Scotsman. '*Damn*. You know who they were?' Jags asked.

'No, I didn't get a look at them.'

'Too bad, otherwise we could go after them, fuck them up. Tomato and onion?'

'Cool.'

'What was it about?'

'I don't know. Didn't hang about to find out either. It's just...'

'What?'

'Day I start looking for Rita Brar is the same day I get jumped.'

'You think it's something to do with that?'

Zaq shrugged. 'Bit of a coincidence though.'

'What were you doing at the Scotsman anyway?'

'Went to see a mate, guy I know from Bullingdon. About a car.'

'What car?'

'I ain't told you what happened with the Brars yesterday, have I?'

The kettle clicked off. Jags made the tea while Zaq told him about seeing Mr Brar, then going to see Rajinder and Parminder.

'So they *do* know something about this Kasim guy?'

'Apparently only his first name and what car he drives – though I think they're lying.'

'How come?'

'I got a call from Nina last night.'

Jags looked blank.

'The girl I talked to at Speedwright, Rita's mate. She had a right go at me for snooping around there yesterday.'

'How'd she know it was us?'

'She figured it out. Anyway, once she calmed down she told me what's really going on with Rita and her family. Seems like she's supposed to be having an arranged marriage.' Zaq filled him in on the details.

'Sounds like a good reason to run away.'

'Well, however good it is, I still got to find her.'

'If this Kasim's a mate of theirs, why are her brothers saying they don't know him?'

'I can see why they wouldn't want their old man to know but they kept on denying it, even when I saw them afterwards. I went to see them again this morning after talking to Nina last night.'

'And...?'

'I only saw Raj but he was still sticking to their story, saying they don't know him – but he was way too touchy about it. Besides, why would Nina lie?'

'Er... because she's Rita's mate? Maybe she was just giving you a sob story so you'd stop looking for her.'

'I don't know... what she said fits. The stuff about Rita's ex was true. You should've seen Raj's reaction when I mentioned him. I had to push just to get a name out of him. Way they're acting, you'd think they didn't want me to find her.'

Jags brought over the sandwich on a plate, then got two mugs of tea. Zaq started to eat.

'So what's his name?' Jags said. 'The ex-boyfriend.'

'Davinder Panesar – ring any bells?'

'Nope. You find out anything else?'

'Just his name and that he lives in Hounslow, least he used to. Thing is… I think his number's on the list they gave me.'

'That's a result.'

'Yeah. I don't think they knew whose numbers they were writing down, they just gave me whatever they found. Oh, and I've got an address for this Kasim bloke.'

'How d'you manage that?'

'Biri – guy I went to see at the Scotsman – he tracked down the car for me.'

'He work for the DVLA or something?'

'Don't ask. He also told me Kasim works at the airport.' Zaq took another bite of his sandwich and drank some tea. 'I'll try calling this Davinder geezer after I've eaten, see if he knows anything.'

Zaq finished the sandwich and his tea, then got out his phone. He was pulling the list of numbers from his pocket when he remembered the photograph. 'Shit! I lost that photo of Rita. I had it in my hand when I got jumped last night, thought I put it in my pocket but must've dropped it. Tried looking for it today but it weren't there.'

'You remember what she looks like?'

'Yeah, I think so.'

'I know I do. She's kind of hard to forget.'

Zaq looked at the list, found the first Davinder and keyed in the number.

'Hello,' a woman who answered.

'Hi, can I speak to Davinder, please?'

'Yes, speaking.'

Damn. It hadn't occurred to Zaq that either of the names on the list could belong to a woman. A lot of Sikh names were unisex, the same for both male and female, like Balwinder, Kuldip and Manjit – same with Davinder. Supposed to be something to do with gender equality, in theory at least. If their full names had been written down, he would have known the difference. Sikh men all had the middle name *Singh*, while for women it was *Kaur*. 'Oh, I was looking for a guy.'

'Aren't we all?' she said. 'You've got the wrong number, then.'

'Sorry.' He hung up.

'Looking for a guy, huh?' Jags said. 'Prison can be rough on a young man.'

'Shut up.'

Further down the list was the other Davinder. He hoped this one was a bloke. He made the call and this time it was a male voice that answered.

'You don't know me,' Zaq said, 'but I'm hoping you can help me out. I'm looking for someone you know.'

'Who's that?'

'Rita.'

'Rita who?'

How many did he know? 'Rita Brar.'

'Rita Brar? I haven't seen her in ages.'

'When did you last hear from her?'

'I don't know, a year ago, maybe more. Sorry, who're you?'

'I'm a friend of the family's. She's gone missing and we're trying to find her. Have you spoken to her recently?'

'No. Not for about a year, like I said.'

'Since you split up, you mean?'

'*Split up*? What're you talking about?'

'It's all right, I know about the two of you.'

'Know what? I don't know who you are or how you got my

number but I haven't got a clue what you're on about.'

'You went out with Rita, didn't you?'

'No. I went to university with her. I never went out with her. I had a girlfriend – who I'm married to now. For God's sake, my wife knows Rita too.'

'Your name's Davinder, right?'

'Yeah.'

'Davinder Panesar?'

'No, Davinder *Gill*.' There was a second's silence, then he said, 'You've got the wrong number, you arsehole.' The line went dead.

'Shit.'

'Another wrong number, huh?' Jags said.

'Fuck. Two Davinders but neither of them the right one.' Zaq threw the list on the table.

Jags picked it up. 'Was always going to be a long shot with no surnames to help you. What about this one – Davy?'

'Davy? Don't sound too Indian.'

'So…? Maybe it's what his mates call him, or Rita's nickname for him. I can think of worse.'

'I don't know…'

'What you got to lose by trying it?'

What the hell – Jags was right, he might as well give it a go. The number next to DAVY was for a mobile. He keyed it in and waited.

'Hello.'

'Is that Davinder?'

'Yes.'

Zaq glanced at Jags, who was listening with interest. 'Davinder Panesar?'

'Yes, that's right. Who's calling?'

'You don't know me – my name's Zaq.'

Jags sat back in his chair with a satisfied look on his face that said, *'See, told you.'*

'What's this about? I'm at work.' Davinder said.

'I need to talk to you about Rita Brar.'

There was a moment of silence. 'Who did you say you were?'

'Zaq Khan. Have you heard from her recently?'

'No, I haven't. How did you get my number?'

'A friend of hers gave it to me.'

'Which friend?'

'It doesn't matter.' Zaq said. 'Look, Rita's in trouble, she's disappeared from home.'

There was another pause, then Davinder said, 'Why are you calling me?'

'She been in touch with you?'

'Who are you? What's this got to do with you?'

After what Nina had told him last night, Zaq thought it best not to say he was working for Rita's dad and brothers. 'I'm a friend, trying to help her out.'

'OK...' He didn't sound convinced. 'I haven't heard from Rita in about a year and I've got no idea where she might be.'

'You ain't talked to her in the last few weeks?'

'No.'

Zaq swore just loud enough for Davinder to hear. 'If her dad or her brothers find her first, she's had it. Can you think of anything that could help me find her?'

'What's going on?'

It was Zaq's turn to pause, then put on a pretence of reluctance. 'Look, I don't want to be spreading gossip. I probably shouldn't say anything...'

'Come on, you called me, remember?' There was concern in his voice. 'I want to know.'

Zaq had him hooked. Now he just had to reel him in. He

waited, as if deciding what to do, then said, 'All right, listen, you want to know what's going on? Meet me later and I'll tell you. Then maybe you'll be able to think of something that can help.'

'I don't know...'

'I thought you'd want to help her, but if you don't....'

'I do,' he said. 'All right, when?'

'How about tonight?'

'OK. Where?'

'Where d'you work?'

'Canary Wharf.'

That was too far. 'Where d'you live?'

'Hounslow.'

'Hounslow's good. Give me a time and a place.'

'You know the Black Horse? I can meet you there, about six-thirty.'

'All right, see you then.' Zaq hung up.

Jags was grinning. 'Was I right, or was I right?'

'You were right.'

'You're meeting up with him then? If he does know something, why's he going to tell you?'

'To help Rita.'

'You ain't really helping her though, are you?'

'He don't know that.'

Jags pulled a face. 'Man, that's pretty cold. Sounds like she had good reason to run away. You find her and tell her old man or her brothers where she is, she's going to be in deep shit.'

'I don't like it any more than you do, but what choice have I got?'

After a moments uneasy silence Jags picked up the plate and mugs and took them to the sink.

He was right – Rita did have a perfectly valid reason to leave home. If it was up to him, Zaq would've wish her luck and let her get on with it. But it wasn't up to him. Mr-fucking-Brar and his thuggish sons were calling the shots and, like it or not, he had to do what they wanted. It might be wrong but if it kept him out of prison it was right for him.

Jags finished washing up. 'I better check my emails.' He sat down, pulled his laptop over and started tapping keys. Zaq sat in silence. When Jags was done, he closed the laptop. 'You ain't meeting Davinder until six-thirty – what you want to do till then?'

Zaq hadn't thought about it. 'I don't know.'

'Didn't you say something about having Kasim's address?'

'Yeah, I did... might as well go check it out.'

'I'll come with you. I've done what I needed for work, just waiting on people to get back to me now. I can check that on my phone. Did most of my documentation last night. Got till next week to finish it anyway, so I can pretty much do what I want for now.'

'They pay you good money for that?'

'Yep.'

'Man, I'm in the wrong job. Come on then, let's go.'

Kasim's house was a small, boxy, two-storey affair, one of a pair sandwiched in the middle of a terrace of four. Everything about it was small; the door, the windows, probably the rooms inside too. The ground floor was bare brick, the upper rendered and painted white; the roof and porch were covered in sombre grey tiles. It was part of a modern development, the houses all stunted compared to the older properties on neighbouring streets. They did, however, overlook the canal and no doubt fetched inflated prices because of their *"waterfront views"*. It wasn't exactly Henley-on-Thames though.

Jags parked beside a low metal railing that separated the road from the canal. 'Were here,' he said. 'What now?'

Zaq shrugged. 'We might as well knock, see if anyone's in.'

'If he's done a runner with Rita, I doubt he's hiding out at home.'

'I know, but maybe he shares the place. Whoever else lives there might know something.'

They crossed the road and walked up to the front door. Zaq tried the bell a couple of times, then used the letterbox as a knocker and finally hammered on the door with his fist. There was no answer and no sound or movement from inside.

'Now what?' Jags said.

'If we could get inside and have a look round, there might be something to tell us where they've gone.'

'You ain't saying what I think you're saying are you?' Jags dropped his voice to a whisper. 'You want to break in.'

'Not in broad daylight.'

'You want to come back tonight?'

'No. Maybe there's a spare key somewhere. If we find it, we won't be breaking in.'

'You sure you didn't get concussed last night?'

'Let's just have a quick look around.' Zaq started checking the weedy flowerbed below the ground floor window. It wasn't really a flowerbed, as there were no flowers in it, just dry dirt, some weeds and a couple of loose bricks. He rooted around in the soil then inspected the wall for anywhere that might conceal a key and moved on to examine the area around the front door. He could hear Jags grumbling as he searched the larger flowerbed that separated the house from its neighbour.

'Don't look now,' Jags said, 'but we're being watched. Curtains twitching next door.'

'Shit.' Last thing they needed was someone calling the cops. His first thought was to leave... but then he had another idea.

'Let's go ask if they know anything.'

'You serious?'

'Yeah. We'll say we're friends of Kasim's, ain't seen him for a few days, and we're worried something's happened to him.'

'They ain't going to believe that.'

'Fine, I'll go on my own.'

'Wait,' Jags said. 'You can't go knocking on people's doors looking like that – your face'll scare the pants off them. I got a better chance of making it work. You go wait in the car, I'll talk to them.'

'All right, see what you can find out.'

Zaq got in the car and waited. After several minutes Jags came back and got behind the wheel.

'Well...?'

'Let's get out of here first.' Jags turned the car around and drove back the way they'd come, until they were around the corner, where he pulled over. 'She don't know where he's gone but she saw him leave in a hurry – with a girl.'

'She?'

'The old biddy lives next door. I told her we were friends of Kasim's, like you said, and she just started rabbiting away.'

'She say when they left?'

'Last Thursday, late. She heard a car outside, about ten o'clock. It had a noisy engine so she got up to see who it was. Says she saw a girl get out of a car, probably a cab, 'cause it drove off. The girl had a suitcase with her and knocked on Kasim's door. Then she heard them clattering about next door, before they came out, loaded up Kasim's motor and drove off in a hurry. Ain't been back since.'

'She say anything else about the girl?'

'Nope.'

Zaq could sense there was more though. 'You get any more

from her?'

'Yeah, check this out – two blokes turned up next day, banging on the door, shouting for Kasim. Scared the hell out of the old dear. She said they were well pissed off.'

'She said, "pissed off"?'

'She said they were very angry – same thing. Anyway, she called the cops but the guys left before the Old Bill arrived. She thought we were them again, was going to call the cops, only we were better behaved and we've got a different car.'

'She noticed their car?'

'Yeah, said it was a Mercedes, big two-door model, silver.'

'She sure it was a Merc?'

'That's what I said. She told me Mercedes-Benz was around before I was born and she used to fucking own one.'

'She actually said, "fucking"?'

'Nah, too polite, but I think she wanted to.'

'Raj Brar drives a silver Merc,' Zaq said.

'Yeah? Well, get this... she said they were a couple of big Asian guys, scary looking. She thinks they might've been related 'cause they looked alike.'

'Bloody hell, she don't miss much!' To be fair, a couple of scary looking Asian guys could have described half the blokes in Southall but the fact they looked similar and drove a silver Merc was enough to convince Zaq it had to have been Raj and Parm Brar.

'That ain't all,' Jags said. 'She'd seen them before, said they were friends of Kasim's, around here a lot, least up until a couple of weeks ago.'

So, Nina had been telling the truth; Raj and Parm *were* friends with Kasim. They'd lied about knowing him. But why? And even though he was now sure they were lying, it didn't put him any closer to finding Rita.

CHAPTER THIRTEEN

Zaq left Jags' place in plenty of time to meet Davinder, which was just as well because traffic was all backed up on the Parkway. It took him half an hour to reach the Great West Road, only to find that bumper to bumper as well. It required some aggressive driving but he made it to Hounslow East with ten minutes to spare and found a spot to park at the far end of Taunton Avenue. It was after six o'clock so he didn't have to pay to park either.

He started walking to the pub then changed his mind. What if he was waiting there and Davinder had second thoughts and decided not to meet him? If he was coming from Canary Wharf, he'd probably be travelling by tube, so Zaq went to the station instead. If he met him there as he came out, it'd be harder for him to simply blow off their meeting.

It was only when he got there that Zaq realised he didn't know what Davinder looked like. Swearing, he took out his phone and tried calling him. Fortunately, he got through. 'I'm at the station,' he said. 'I'll meet you outside.'

There was a lot of noise in the background. 'I've just passed

Boston Manor, so I'll be there in a bit.'

'How will I recognise you?'

'I'm wearing a black coat and carrying a blue and brown laptop bag. How about you?'

'I've got cuts and bruises on my face, look like I've been in a fight, should be easy to spot.'

Trains rumbled across the bridge overhead. It might be called the Underground but here it was fifteen feet above the ground. The station itself was sleek and modern, all curved steel and glass, its green roof slanted at a jaunty angle, in stark contrast to all the buildings around it.

Zaq leaned against some railings and watched the tide of commuters ebb and flow with the comings and goings of the tube trains. A lot of Asian guys came out, and a lot of them were wearing black coats. Zaq wouldn't have known the right one if Davinder hadn't come up to him.

He was slim and compact, a welterweight, possibly a middleweight, an inch or so shorter than Zaq. His coat was expensive, as was the charcoal grey suit underneath it. His shoes were as shiny as black glass and the light blue strap of his bag crossed his chest like a sash. Zaq offered his hand and the two of them shook.

'What happened?' Davinder said, looking at the marks on Zaq's face.

'Nothing. Let's go get a drink.'

They walked under the bridge as another train trundled overhead.

'What do you do at Canary Wharf?' Zaq thought some small talk might help put Davinder at ease.

'I work in banking, corporate side.'

'You one of those fat cat bankers with the silly bonuses?'

'I wish,' Davinder said. 'Not everyone gets paid that much.

What about you?'

'I ain't no fat cat and I definitely don't get no bonuses. I'm a driver.'

'Oh.' They walked on. Then Davinder asked, 'How do you know Rita?'

Zaq had been hoping to avoid that question for as long as he could. How to answer? If he maintained he was a friend of Rita's and Davinder talked to her, he'd find out it was a lie. If he said he knew her through Nina or worked with her and Davinder asked Nina, he'd also be found out. But if he told the truth – that he was working for Rita's dad and brothers – Davinder would probably tell him to go fuck himself. The best lies were those that stuck close to the truth, so that's what he tried to do. 'I know her through work.'

'You work with her?'

'No, at her dad's place in Southall.'

'Her dad's?' There was accusation in his tone.

'Yeah. I've seen her there now and again and we got chatting. When I've seen her out and about, we've talked, had a laugh. She's a nice girl, not like her arsehole brothers. When I heard what was going on, I wanted to try and help her.'

'Why? What *is* going on? You said something about her being in trouble.'

'That's why I'm here. Let's get that drink and I'll tell you.'

The Black Horse stood at the corner of Spring Grove Road and Lampton Road. The ground floor was brick with thick stone trim painted dark crimson or purple. Zaq wondered if the paint was piss and puke resistant. The first floor was mock Tudor; black timber and once-white render, now turned grubby grey by years of CO_2 emissions. Traffic queued back from the roundabout outside the pub, filling the cold evening with engine noise and exhaust fumes.

The place was a lot nicer inside. The double doors opened onto a large room with a couple of pool tables, which they crossed to get into the old-fashioned wood-panelled bar, where a large LCD TV mounted on the wall was showing a European football match with the sound turned down. 'What're you having?' Zaq said.

'Fosters, please.'

Zaq ordered a Fosters and a shandy for himself, – 'I'm driving,' he explained. He paid for the drinks and followed Davinder around the bar and into a spacious lounge area with bold red and deep purple walls. Tables and chairs were arranged all around, along with a couple of small sofas and some armchairs. The room was empty and they settled on a couple of armchairs away from the bar.

Davinder slipped his bag off and put it on the floor beside the table. It was a funky looking courier bag, pale blue around the zips and pockets, the rest of it a rich chocolate brown. 'So, what's all this about Rita being in trouble?'

Zaq took a drink, giving himself time to get his story set. 'She's being forced into an arranged marriage. And, if that ain't bad enough, her brothers set her up to make sure she can't get out of it. That's why she's run away.'

'What d'you mean, set her up?'

'They let a friend of theirs take her out, encouraged him even – only then they beat the shit out of him and told their old man they'd caught them sleeping together.'

'She didn't though?'

'No.'

'Fucking bastards.'

'To make things worse, the guy was Muslim.'

'Shit.' Like every other Asian, Davinder knew what that

meant.

'Apparently, the guy found out what her brothers were planning to do and warned her. After they beat him up he went straight from the hospital to tell her. She knew she couldn't go home. I think he helped her get away.'

'Is she still with him?'

Zaq shrugged. 'They left together but it don't mean they still are. Thing is though, now she's run off, it makes it look as if she *is* guilty of what her brothers accused her of. Her old man's livid. No telling what he'll do when he finds her.'

Davinder stared at the table, probably trying to process what he'd been told. 'Her fuckin' family…' he said after a while. 'What is it with them? They've always been on her case, never let her do anything, always trying to control her. Telling her what to do, how to dress, who to see. Not that she listens to them. That just winds them up even more.' He looked at Zaq. 'You know we used to go out together? 'Course you do, that's why you're here, right? You know what her brothers did to me?'

'I heard they put you in hospital too.'

'Yeah. Who told you?'

'Rita,' Zaq lied.

'She told you about *me*?' He was surprised.

'Yeah. I told you, we used to talk. I told her stuff about me too, shit I'm dealing with. Like getting out of prison and trying to adjust to being back home. Looking for a job, month after month, and being turned down all the time 'cause of my record. Only thing I could get was working as a skivvy at her old man's yard.' It was the truth, except he hadn't told any of it to Rita. The bitterness in his voice was genuine and gave his lies the ring of truth. It seemed to do the trick.

Davinder looked at him like he was seeing him for the first time. 'I didn't know about any of that.'

'No reason you should.'

'What... er, what were you in prison for? If you don't mind me asking?'

'Manslaughter.' Zaq said. Davinder didn't know what to say to that, how to react – it was the usual response. It wasn't exactly the sort of thing that encouraged light-hearted conversation 'You were saying...' Zaq tried to get him back on topic, 'something about what her brothers did to you.'

'Yeah...' Davinder said. Though he might have been relieved at the change of subject, his eyes narrowed and the muscles round his mouth tightened at the memory of what had happened to him. 'Bastards really did me over. They found out where I lived and laid into me one night as I was walking home. Fuckers broke my jaw, a couple of ribs, fractured my wrist, not to mention all the bruises and swelling they left me with. I was in hospital for a week, off work for three. Then they went round and told my parents, said I better keep away from Rita, or else. My dad went mental, but what could he do? She was their sister. They had a right to protect their family's reputation, their honour.'

'You tell the police?'

'How would that've helped? It would've set her whole family against me and just made things worse for her. Even if I had, what would've happened? A month or two inside? A suspended sentence? Community service? You think they'd have just let it go afterwards? Besides, more than a few people thought they were justified in doing what they did.

'I wanted to get them back my own way but Rita begged me not to. She said things would get out of hand and she was worried what might happen to me. We had to stop seeing each other, so we did but... we kept in touch, despite...' His voice trailed off and his brow creased into a frown. 'Do you know all this already?'

'Only the broad strokes. It's different hearing your side of it.'

'Yeah, well, that's about it really.'

'You said you kept in touch...'

'Yeah. It was risky... but we'd been together for three years; we couldn't just end it like that.'

'You still in touch with her now?'

'No.'

His answer was too abrupt and, to Zaq's mind, missing that certain note of sadness or regret you expected in someone's voice when they shared a painful memory. Davinder's tone had been defensive, more like a denial. Zaq mentally filed it away. 'When did you last hear from her?'

Davinder thought about it. When he responded though, it was with a question of his own. 'How do I know you're not trying to find her for her family?'

Zaq had thought he might ask something like that. 'Why would they send me? If her brothers wanted to talk to you they'd have come themselves? I doubt they'd have bought you a drink either.' It seemed to allay Davinder's doubts a little. 'So...' Zaq said, getting the conversation back on track, 'when *was* the last time you heard from her?'

'A few months ago.'

'She mention anything about leaving home?'

'She was always talking about it. She was totally pissed off with how things were there. We used to chat about running off together, going somewhere hot and sunny.'

'This ain't all part of some plan of yours, is it? Something the two of you cooked up together? She runs away and you meet up with her somewhere when the heat's died down?'

'No.' His expression changed and this time his denial seemed genuine. 'We talked about it but we knew we couldn't actually *do it*. We'd have had to leave everything behind and start over from scratch – new home, new jobs, new names, new friends, new lives, new everything – and some place no one would find us. You got to have money for that and we didn't have any. If one of us had won the lottery, then maybe. If Rita had left home back then, her brothers would've come straight after me.' He frowned. 'Come to think of it, I'm surprised they haven't now.'

'I guess they know it's nothing to do with you this time.' Zaq remembered Rajinder's reaction when he'd asked about Rita's ex-boyfriend. 'To be honest, I don't even think your name crossed their minds in connection with what's happened.'

'I suppose I should be glad about that.'

'You haven't heard from Rita in the last few weeks then?'

'No. Last time I saw her –'

'*Saw her?*'

Davinder swore, knowing he'd just slipped up.

'When you said you kept in touch, I thought you just meant by phone or email, not that you were still *seeing* her.'

'Shit. Look, this is just between us, right? You're not going to tell anyone?'

'I ain't interested in dropping you in it. I'm just here 'cause I want to help her.'

Davinder took a drink of his beer. 'OK,' he said, 'we kept in touch… and saw each other now and then, when we could. No one else knew, we didn't tell anyone and always met well away from here or Southall, where we wouldn't bump into anyone we knew.'

'What happened the last time you saw her?'

'She said it was getting too risky. Her brothers were acting funny, more suspicious and keeping a closer eye on her. She wanted to try and talk to her dad about us, see if she could bring him around to the idea of us getting married – but if we got caught together, it would ruin any chance of that. So we decided to cool it for a while. That was about three months ago. Apart from some texts and the odd call, I haven't heard from her since.'

'You got any way of getting in touch with her?'

'I got her mobile number, email, Facebook, the usual stuff.'

None of that was going to be of any use. What Zaq needed was a something more real world. He'd hoped to get something useful from Davinder but he didn't seem to know anything. Or did he? Zaq thought about his denial earlier. It was only down to a mistake on his part that he'd told Zaq about them still seeing each other, otherwise he'd never have mentioned it.

Zaq's gut told him there was a strong possibility she might try and contact him now, maybe even arrange to meet him. Who else would she trust? If he could keep tabs on Davinder, the guy might just lead him straight to her.

'Why're you looking for her?' Davinder said, breaking his train of thought. 'I mean, how exactly can you help her?'

Zaq shrugged. 'I don't know, but I want to do whatever I can. I may not know her brothers that well but everyone knows what they're like – couple of right fuckers. I hate how they've stitched her up and I don't agree with her being forced to get married. She don't deserve any of that.'

Davinder seemed to buy it. Zaq knew he could be convincing when he had to be – he'd had enough practise in front of prison officers. He might have felt a little bad about lying to Davinder and using him to get to Rita, but it was a means to an end. Anyone in his situation would do the same. 'If you hear from her, just get her to call me. We'll see what we can work out. You've got my number on your phone now.'

'OK,' Davinder said and finished the last of his drink. 'I better be going.' He stood, picked up his bag and slipped the strap over his head, onto his shoulder.

'Me too.'

They walked back through the pub and out into the cold.

'Which way you headed?' Zaq said

'Way we came.'

'I'm parked down that way too.'

They walked down Kingsley Road, chit-chatting awkwardly about the weather and football, the two of them not really having much to talk about apart from Rita. They agreed the weather was shit and not likely to get better for a while and each thought their team was in with a chance of winning the Premiership this season: Liverpool for Davinder, Arsenal for Zaq.

They crossed over the road at a zebra crossing and continued on the other side. Houses gave way to shops. There was still some traffic, but less than earlier, and a chill breeze made the night feel colder than it was. Davinder stopped at the corner of Taunton Avenue. 'This is my road.'

'My van's at the far end.' They turned down the street together. It was darker than the main road, the streetlights dimmer, more spaced out. Only a couple of cars passed them.

About halfway along the street Davinder stopped. 'This is my house.'

'Thanks for meeting me and hearing me out,' Zaq said.

'I only met you 'cause you said Rita was in trouble.'

'Still. If you hear from her or think of anything I can do to help...' Zaq stepped aside to let two men pass on the pavement. 'Get in touch, yeah?'

'*Davinder?*' one of the passing men said. Davinder turned towards him.

Zaq was turning too when he was hit in the face, hard. A second blow smashed into his cheek. Stunned and off balance, he was hit again, even harder. Then he was falling and had to use his hands to stop himself crashing onto his face. He landed with a jolt, scraping his palms on the rough paving. When he tried to get up, he was kicked twice, once in the side and once in the thigh, and went down again.

Instinct screamed at him to cover up and he did, his arms protecting his head and face as more kicks slammed into him. The kicks stopped. He hoped it was over. But then his attacker was stamping down on him, sending bolts of pain through his hip, his thigh and the arm and shoulder shielding his head.

Zaq tensed for more but nothing came. The smell of damp concrete filled his nostrils; his heart was thumping, and something warm trickled across his face; he didn't know if it was blood, sweat or tears. When he opened his eyes, spots danced and popped before them. There was a buzzing in his ears but, over that, he heard other sounds – primal grunts, the smack of flesh on flesh, the scuffle of feet.

He forced himself up onto an elbow and blinked several times, clearing his vision enough that he could see two bulky figures silhouetted by the weak streetlight. They were standing over something. It took Zaq a second to work out it was Davinder.

He gritted his teeth and got to his hands and knees. Pain gripped him, restricting his breathing to short sharp bursts. He tensed and started to push himself to his feet. '*Bhen chaud.*' A voice, coming towards him. 'Stay the fuck down!' The order reinforced by another barrage of kicks and punches until he was flat on the ground again, numb with pain.

He tried to focus on the sounds around him and heard the distinctive rumble of a diesel engine getting louder, until it was right there, beside them. The vehicle skidded to a halt. Zaq moved his head and saw a white van in the middle of the road.

He waited, expecting the driver to shout, 'Hey, what's going on?' or something like that – but it didn't happen. Was he just sitting there watching?

Cautiously, Zaq lifted his head. Dark shapes were moving toward the van. The two bulky figures were shuffling along, carrying something. He saw an arm dangling and realised it was Davinder – they were taking him to the van. It was there to *pick them up*. He could only watch as they reached it and one of them slid the side door open.

He had to get up and do something, but when he tried to rise he felt as if he'd been trampled by an elephant. He grabbed hold of a nearby signpost and used it to haul himself to his feet.

The van's harsh interior light was on. The first guy was still in silhouette but as he backed into the van holding Davinder under the arms, Zaq caught sight of his face and his dark blue jacket. The second attacker shoved Davinder's legs in and jumped up into the van. Zaq pushed away from the signpost and started lurching toward them. As the second guy turned around to close the door, Zaq recognised him too and his green jacket. Then the door slammed shut and all Zaq could do was breathe exhaust fumes and watch the van speed away.

CHAPTER FOURTEEN

'What the fuck's happened to you now?' Jags said.

Zaq was getting fed up of hearing that question all the time. 'I got jumped again.' He stepped inside and Jags closed the door behind him.

'Same guys as yesterday?'

'No, some other guys.'

'You know who it was? Let's go sort them out!'

'Right now I just want to use your bathroom and get cleaned up.'

Jags led the way upstairs. 'Man, you sure know how to make friends. Seems like everyone wants to beat you up.'

'Must be my winning personality.' Zaq climbed the stairs like a man three times his age. He felt as if he'd had a truckload of bricks dropped on him. His right leg throbbed, the pain deep inside the muscle of his thigh. His ribs and sides ached from the kicks he'd taken, his face felt like it was buzzing and he had the kind of headache he'd normally associate with a hangover. 'Can I borrow a towel?'

Jags got him one. 'Here,' he said. 'It's an old one so don't worry about getting blood on it.'

'Thanks. You got any Dettol or TCP, some cotton buds?

'Look in the cabinet.'

'How about some painkillers?'

'In the kitchen. I'll go get some.'

Zaq's face, reflected in the mirrored doors of the bathroom cabinet, wasn't a pretty sight. The left side was grazed and bloody where it had scraped against the pavement, and blood from the cut below his left eye was smeared across his cheek and nose. The right side of his face was red and swollen from the punches he'd taken. Both palms and the knuckles of his right hand were grazed, from protecting his head while being kicked and stamped on.

He eased off his jacket and hung it on the back of the door, then slowly pulled off his sweatshirt and T-shirt. His side was red and tender, some areas already deepening to purple. He prodded his ribs but, though they hurt, he didn't think any were broken.

Jags returned with a couple of painkillers and a glass of water. He looked at the marks on Zaq's torso. 'Ow, that must hurt.'

Zaq swallowed the tablets with some water and handed the glass back to Jags. 'Thanks.'

'Need anything else?'

'How about a lottery win and a long holiday.'

'I was thinking more like a cup of tea.'

'I could do with something stronger.'

'You planning on driving home?'

'OK, tea it is then.'

Zaq cleaned dirt and grit from his cuts and scrapes. '*Fuck, fuck, fuck,*' he hissed through clenched teeth. The hot water stung like a motherfucker, worse still when he splashed it on his face. He kept dousing the cuts in hot water until the pain eased, then used soap to wash away the blood.

After patting his hands and face dry, he soaked some cotton buds in TCP and dabbed the wounds, wincing and grimacing against the sharp burning sensation of the antiseptic. There was nothing he could do about the bruising and tenderness on the rest of his body. He sat on the edge of the bath for a few minutes to recoup then put on his T-shirt and sweatshirt again.

Downstairs, Jags handed him a mug of strong tea and took a seat on the sofa opposite. 'You look like one of the Walking Dead.'

'Thanks. I feel like one.' He told Jags what had happened outside Davinder's house.

'They fucking *kidnapped* him?'

'They weren't taking him on a date.'

'You sure it wasn't the guys from last night?'

'I'm sure. I saw these two this morning, with Raj and Parm Brar, in a pub car park in Cranford.'

'What were you doing there?'

'Following Raj and Parm.' He filled Jags in on his meeting with Raj and how he'd followed him to Hayes and then afterwards, to the pub in Cranford.

'You think Raj and Parm had something to do with them taking Davinder?'

'It's too big a fucking coincidence otherwise. Thing is, I think I might've put them on to him. I don't think he was even on their radar in connection with what's going on until I asked about him this morning. Then, next thing you know, he's getting battered and dragged off by a couple of Raj and Parm's mates.'

'When you put it like that…'

Zaq remembered something. 'I think I know where they live. I followed them there after they left the Queen's Head, to see what was going on with the cement.'

'And…?'

'They went to a house in Hounslow, near the Bulstrode. I was there when you called this afternoon. Maybe that's where they've taken him.'

'Call the cops then.'

Zaq had thought about it on the drive over. 'I can't. I was told not to get the cops involved in anything to do with this Rita business. I do and I'm fucked. Plus, I was the last person seen with him.'

'So? It was nothing to do with you.'

'Yeah, but soon as they pull up my record, they'll haul me in for questioning – and until he turns up, I'll be in the frame.'

'We supposed to just leave it then?'

Zaq knew they had to do something, even of they couldn't go to the police. He couldn't just leave Davinder to his fate, especially as it was probably his fault the Brars had taken him. 'All right, we'll go over there ourselves.'

'What the fuck we going to do there?'

'I don't know. See what's going on, *maybe* call the cops.'

'I thought you said –'

'I know what I said. We'll just give them the address, tell them someone's being held there against their will, they can take it from there. We can make sure he's OK and everything'll be sorted without my name getting mentioned.'

'OK, it's better than doing nothing. Let's go.'

They took Jags' car. Zaq was glad he didn't have to drive; also the ride was a lot more comfortable in the BMW than it would've been in the van. He got out his phone when they were in Hounslow. 'What do you dial to withhold your number?'

'1-4-1.'

Zaq looked up the number for Crimestoppers. He didn't

trust that a call to 999 or the police couldn't be traced, even if you did withhold your number. Crimestoppers guaranteed anonymity. He added 141 in front of their number and made the call. He told the woman who answered that he'd seen two men drag someone into a house and believed they were holding him there against his will. He gave the address and a description of Blue and Green but declined to give his own name or any other details. He had to repeat it all again for a supervisor.

When he'd done that, he said, 'I've told you everything, just send someone round to check it out,' and hung up, hoping his frustration had been mistaken for fear.

They were on Lampton Road, approaching the Bulstrode pub. Zaq told Jags where to turn and pointed out the house as they drove past it. The 4x4 truck was parked in the drive though the house itself was completely dark. They carried on up the road, turned around and pulled over a safe distance away but from where they could still see anything that happened. Jags turned off the engine and the headlights but kept the electrics on. The dashboard lights glowed red and the radio was on, low. 'What now?' he asked.

'We wait.'

Zaq was glad of the opportunity to sit and do nothing, even though he knew he should try to keep moving and stretch.

'You sure they're in there?' Jags said.

'Maybe they're in the back.'

Jags used his phone to tune into an internet radio station that only played '80s soul and R&B, and connected it wirelessly to the car's sound system so they could listen over that. The old skool music kept them occupied until the police finally showed up, almost forty-five minutes later.

'About fucking time,' Jags said.

Two policemen got out of their patrol car and went and

knocked on the front door. When there was no answer they tried again. One of them looked in through the window. Then, while the one at the door was either looking or calling through the letterbox, the other one walked up and down the pavement, probably looking for a way round to the back. Failing to find anything, he went back and conferred with his colleague.

Zaq and Jags watched as one of the policemen called in on his radio. Following a brief exchange, both went and knocked at the door of the house on the right.

'Now what're they doing?' Jags said.

'Probably asking the neighbours if they saw or heard anything.'

The policemen repeated the procedure at the house on the left, then did the same at a couple of houses directly opposite, all without any apparent confirmation that anything untoward had happened. After that, they got back in their car.

'Don't tell me they're leaving?' Jags said.

'Looks like it. Maybe they ain't here after all.'

The police car turned around and drove away.

'Fat lot of good they were. What now?'

'It's been a couple of hours since they took him. Maybe they got what they wanted and let him go. I can try calling him, see if he answers.' Zaq took out his phone and looked up Davinder's number. Just to be safe, he added 141 and made the call. He listened to it ring for some time then, just as he expected it to go to voicemail, the ringing stopped and someone picked up. Whoever it was didn't say anything.

'Davinder?' Zaq finally said.

'Yeah.'

Though he'd only spoken to Davinder twice on the phone, Zaq knew it wasn't him. This voice was heavier, rougher. 'No, you ain't. Where is he?'

'He can't come to the phone right now, told me to answer it.'

'I need to talk to him; put him on.'

'I told you,' the voice on the phone said, 'he can't talk now. He's busy.'

'Doing what?'

'What's the fuck's it got to do with you? Who are you anyway?'

'I'm a mate of his. Who the fuck are you?'

'I'm a friend of his too.'

'That why you beat him up and dragged him off in that van?'

There was a moment of silence at the other end, then something that sounded like a laugh, only more unpleasant. 'You're the cunt what was with him.'

Zaq tried to keep cool. 'And you're one of the cunts that jumped us.'

'And...? What you going to do about it?'

'What d'you want with him?'

'None of your fucking business.'

'What if I make it my business?'

'Then you're going to get fucking hurt, more than you did already.'

Zaq forced a laugh. 'I been hit harder by little girls.'

'I'll make sure to hurt you good and proper next time then, innit?'

'Let me talk to him. You've got his phone, so he must be there.'

'He your boyfriend or something?'

'You must've got what you wanted from him by now – let him go.'

'You know what's good for you, fuck off and keep your nose out of it.'

'I ain't talked to Davinder yet.'

'And you ain't going to. Now fuck off and don't call back.' The guy hung up.

'Fucking arsehole.' Zaq slammed the phone on his thigh – and immediately regretted it; pain flared through his injured leg. 'Shit,' he said, through clenched teeth.

'That went well, then,' Jags said.

'They've got his phone, so they've probably still got him.'

'What did they say?'

'Just told me to fuck off.'

'What do we do now?'

Zaq was still keyed up after the phone call. 'That's their house, they'll come back sooner or later. We're here... might as well wait for them, see what happens.'

'Flippin' hell, if I'd known we were going to sit here all night, I'd've gotten something to eat.'

'There's a kebab shop near the station. You can go get us both something.'

Jags frowned. 'How come I got to go?'

''Cause those arseholes only beat me up a little while ago. They might recognise me limping down their street. Besides, one of us has to stay here in the car in case they come back.'

'What d'you mean, *stay here in the car*? You saying I got to *walk* to the shops?'

'I can't just stand around watching the place. Someone might think I'm casing the joint and call the Old Bill back.'

'Well, if I got to walk, you're buying the fucking kebabs.'

The chicken kebabs and chips went down a treat, washed down with ice cold cans of Coke Zero. They both felt better after eating. The '80s tracks were still playing on the stereo, stirring up memories, and the two of them chatted about things they'd gotten up to back when their lives were full of possibilities and very little regret.

Two hours later they were fidgeting in their seats and still watching the house. The smell of chicken and chips lingered in the car, even though they'd put the bag with their rubbish outside for the time being. It was a cold night and Jags had the engine running so they could keep warm. Zaq was glad the expensive German motor was so quiet.

'How much longer we going to wait?' Jags wanted to know.

'We been here this long, might as well wait a little longer, till they turn up.'

'I could be at home watching TV.'

'Yeah, but then you'd be missing out on all the excitement.'

'What bloody excitement?' Jags grumbled.

Movement at the end of the street caught Zaq's eye. 'Turn everything off.'

Jags turned the key, killing the dashboard lights and silencing Luther Vandross in the middle of Never Too Much. They sat cloaked in darkness. 'Is that them?'

Zaq watched as two figures passed under streetlights and through shadows, coming towards them. Even from a distance, it was clear they were both big and moved with an arrogant confidence that Zaq recognised. 'Yeah, it's them.' As they got closer, he was able to see them better.

So was Jags. 'Oh, shit,' he said, sliding further down in his seat. 'You know who the fuck they are?'

'Yeah, the fuckers that jumped me and Davinder.'

'That's Dev Jhutti and Gurps Chadha. Don't you remember them? They were two years above us at school. Thick as shit but mean as hell. Even the teachers didn't mess with them.'

'So?'

'They're a couple of psychos, like to fuck people up.'

'Which one's which?'

Jags peeped over the top of the dashboard. 'One with short hair is Jhutti. One carrying the bag's Chadha.'

As the two men reached the house Zaq saw the bag. The other one, Jhutti, opened the door and they both disappeared inside. Lights came on in the hallway and downstairs windows.

'That bag Chadha was carrying – it's Davinder's. He had his laptop in it when we met. They've got his stuff... but where's he?'

'Maybe they took his laptop and let him go.'

It was possible. 'I'll try calling him again.' Zaq tried Davinder's number, withholding his own number once more. It rang several times before being picked up. There was the faint hiss of electronic static but no one spoke. This time Zaq decided to wait.

Then a voice said, 'That you, Rita?' It was a different voice to the one he'd heard before, not as deep but just as cold. Zaq stayed silent. 'Surprised?' the voice said. 'That's right, we been talking to your boyfriend. You want him to stay in one piece, you better get your pretty little arse back home and sort shit out, else you'll fucking regret it. We won't stop looking till we find you and when we do, that *sullah* you're with... he's dead. But you... I'm going to sort you out good and proper.'

Zaq hung up.

Jags must've seen the look on his face. 'What?'

'It wasn't Davinder. It was one of them.' Zaq nodded at the house. 'Not the one I spoke to before.'

'So they've got his phone and his computer. They still might've let him go.'

'No, they ain't. When I didn't say anything, he thought it was Rita calling, said if she wants to keep Davinder in one piece, she better get back home.'

'You think he was serious?'

'You're the one just told me they're a couple of psychos. What d'you reckon?'

'Shit.'

'He also said, when they find her and Kasim, Kasim's dead and they're going to sort her out *good and proper*.'

'You think he means –?'

'That's what it sounded like.'

'Dirty bastards.' Jags shook his head. 'What the fuck's going on? Beatings, a kidnapping, now a hostage and death threats – I thought we were just looking for a runaway girl.'

'So did I but this shit's getting way more complicated.'

They sat in silence. After a while, Jags said, 'Maybe we're in over our heads. Should we just let the police handle it?'

Zaq had been wondering the same thing. 'We can't, not yet. I was told no cops. I get them involved and the fucking Brars'll make sure I go down for the bullshit theft and assault charges they're threatening me with.'

'But this is something else – *kidnapping*.'

'It's all linked to Rita though.'

'I'll report it then.'

'You think Jhutti and Chadha'll just own up to it? They'll deny it and we ain't exactly got any proof.'

'They've got his stuff.'

Zaq shook his head. 'That ain't proof. They could say they found it. It don't tie them to a kidnapping. And if the cops go looking for any suspects, who d'you think they'll find? *Me*. I was the last person seen with him before he was taken. There's probably CCTV from the station, maybe the pub too – and I look like I've been in a scrap. With my record, they probably won't bother looking for anyone else.'

'Shit.'

'Yeah. If either of us goes to the police, I'll be screwed. But, if *we* find Davinder and get him out, then, as long as he keeps my name out of it, *he* can go to the police and fuck those wankers up to his heart's content.'

Jags considered it. 'All right,' he said, eventually, 'but how the hell do we find him?'

It was late. Zaq doubted Jhutti and Chadha would go anywhere else that night, so Jags started the car and they went back to his place. Zaq said he'd call him the next day and drove back to Southall in the van. The journey didn't take long at that time of night but the ride was uncomfortable. Every turn of the steering wheel, every gear change and every speed bump and pothole caused him pain.

He made sure no one was following him and when he got to the builder's yard, he went round the back and parked on the service road again. He checked the cars parked around, in case anyone was waiting in one for him. When he finally eased himself out of the van, he felt like he'd just spent an hour being thrown around inside an industrial cement mixer.

He zipped up his jacket against the cold and started for home on foot, hoping the walk would do him good after having sat on his arse for several hours. It took twice as long as normal but he made it back without any further incident.

Once home, he went to the kitchen to find some Ibuprofen, took two with a glass of water, turned off the lights and dragged himself upstairs. In his room, he peeled off his jacket, reawakening the aches all over his body. He just wanted to crawl into bed but knew if he did that, he'd pay for it in the morning. So, he made himself strip down to his boxers and go through his stretching routine. Each exercise made him scrunch his face in a grimace to start with, until eventually the fuzzy warm feeling of endorphins kicking in took over. It wasn't exactly pleasant but afterwards, as he crawled into bed, he did feel a tiny bit better.

CHAPTER FIFTEEN

He didn't feel good at all the next morning when his alarm clock pulled him out of the depths of a deep sleep. It was as though someone had filled his body with concrete during the night then taken a sledgehammer to it. Several deep breaths and a lot of willpower were required to get himself into a sitting position – only to wish he'd stayed as he was. Then, when he felt ready, he planted his hands on his knees and levered himself up onto his feet.

He repeated the stretches from the night before, focusing on pulling the bunched muscle fibres apart, until he felt the familiar tingling burn. After that, he grabbed his towel and went to take a shower. He checked his face in the bathroom mirror; it was worse now than last night. His eyes and cheeks were more discoloured with bruises – red, purple and yellow, with smudges of grey and green – new bruises next to older ones. The cuts and scrapes had dried to dark crusty patches and swelling made his face look lumpy and uneven. Short of a paper bag over his head, there was no way to hide the fact he'd taken another pasting.

He brushed his teeth, trying to ignore his aching jaw. Then he stood under the shower for a long time, allowing the heat to seep into his muscles and bones. Back in his room, he dabbed aftershave on his cuts. It felt like red-hot needles being stuck in his face but took his mind off his other complaints for a few moments.

He dressed in jeans, trainers and a long-sleeved T-shirt with a short-sleeved one over the top. Then he grabbed his stuff from the bedside table, shoved it in his pockets, picked up his jacket and left the room.

The sound of voices and the clatter of dishes drifted up from downstairs. Zaq could've done without seeing his housemates, but he needed to eat something and take some more painkillers. He walked into the kitchen hoping no one would notice the new marks on his face. Fat chance.

Lax was the first to say something. 'Bloody hell, what happened to you?'

The others looked up, Manjit turning from the cooker.

'You get in another fight?' Dips enquired.

'Something like that.'

'Same fuckers from the other day?'

'No, some other fuckers this time.'

'You know who?' Bal said round a mouthful of cereal. 'We'll go sort them out tonight.' The others agreed with differing levels of enthusiasm.

'Thanks, but I'll take care of it.'

'Don't look like you done too well so far,' Bal said. 'You need some back-up, we'll come with you.'

'I'll let you know if I need any help.'

'Seems you could do with all the help you can get.' Bal took his bowl to the sink and came over to scrutinise Zaq's face. He grabbed him by the chin and jerked his head from side to side

141

to get a better look.

'What the fuck you doing?' Zaq yelled, slapping Bal's hand away.

'They done you over pretty good. I thought you could take care of yourself.'

'They took me by surprise.'

Bal sucked his teeth loudly. 'We should go surprise them then, innit? They fight dirty, you got to be dirtier.'

'I'll try and remember that,' Zaq said, through the pain in his face and neck.

'You better. Way you're going, you'll end up in fucking hospital. Just be ready for the *ma chauds* next time.'

Zaq went to make himself some toast. Manjit was watching him and shaking his head. 'What?' Zaq said.

Manjit turned back to the eggs he was scrambling. 'That's twice in two days you been jumped. Different guys?'

'Yeah.'

'Hope you ain't going for three out of three.'

'Not if I can help it.' Zaq took two slices of brown bread from a loaf on the worktop, only to find the toaster was already being used.

'They're mine,' Manjit said. 'Should be done in a bit. You know who it was this time?'

'Yeah. Wasn't me they were after, though. I was just in the wrong place at the wrong time.'

'Happens to you a lot, huh? How many of them this time?'

'Two… and a third in a van.'

Manjit stirred his eggs with a wooden spatula. 'Ain't been your week, has it? What you going to do about it?'

'I'm thinking about it.'

'What's to think about? Either you're going to fuck them up or you ain't.'

'It's a bit more complicated than that.'

'Complicated? Shit, that means there's either money or a girl involved. So which is it?'

All Zaq said was, 'Make sure your eggs don't burn.'

'That's what I thought.' Manjit said, giving him a knowing look. 'I hope she's worth it.'

'How d'you know it ain't money?'

Manjit shrugged. 'Just a hunch. When you decide what you're going to do, let me know if you need a hand.'

'I will, thanks.'

The toaster mechanism sprang and ejected two well-done slices. 'In the meantime,' Manjit said, 'butter those for me. My eggs are nearly done.'

A mug of tea and two slices of toast with Marmite and peanut butter later, Zaq was on his way to work. Manjit had offered him a lift but Zaq decided the walk would do him good. He left the house, scanning the street both ways to make sure the coast was clear and started on his way.

He arrived at the yard twenty minutes later and went round to the back, where the other guys were waiting by the rear gates. They were all looking at something, pointing and commenting on it. The van. It was right where he'd had parked it – only now Zaq saw that all the tyres were flat, every single one. '*Oh, teri phouk nickle gaye,*' Sukh called out and got a laugh from the others.

'Sid'll shit a brick when he sees that,' Bits said.

Zaq walked around the van. A short, straight slash mark was clearly visible on each tyre. '*Moth-er-fuck-er,*' he swore, one syllable for each tyre. Then he noticed a small white square of folded paper under one of the wipers. He pulled it out and opened it. Most of the A4 sheet was taken up by a rough black and white photocopy of the picture of Rita Brar, the one he'd lost. Underneath that, there was a message scrawled in black marker.

YOUR SO FUCKING TUFF LETS SEE HOW TUFF YOUR GIRLFRIEND IS!

It had to have been left by the guys that had jumped him outside the Scotsman. They must've picked up the photo and assumed it was his girlfriend. Now they were threatening *her* because they hadn't been able to do *him* over – bunch of arseholes. Good luck if they thought they could find her – Zaq had been looking for two days and hadn't managed it. He doubted they'd do any better.

An old Mercedes, the colour of clotted blood, turned into the service road, accompanied by the sweet sounds of Lata Mangeshkar. Zaq slipped the note into his pocket as the car cruised up and stopped. The passenger window slid down with an electric hum and Sid leaned across from the driver's seat. '*Van nu ki hoyah?*'

'What's it look like?'

Sid saw the state of Zaq's face and frowned. '*Theri buthi nu ki hoyah?*' He didn't wait for an answer, but straightened up and drove on, the window humming closed as he moved off.

'*Oh, bhen dee…,*' Sukh said, in his guttural Punjabi as Zaq joined the others at the gates. '*Hor maar kah ke ayah.*'

'You look worse than you did yesterday,' Bits said.

Sid parked his car and came sauntering over, carrying his lunch in a carrier bag and a copy of the Sun. 'I hope you get bruises fighting with fuckers who do this to van,' he said to

Zaq. 'What happening?'

'I left it there last night and this morning it was like that. Probably just some kids.'

'*Bhen chaud haramzadei.*' Sid threw a bunch of keys to Hari. '*Hari, kohl de.*' Hari caught the keys and started unlocking the six heavy-duty padlocks that secured the small shutter next to the gates. Sid always got Hari to do it. If he asked any of the others they'd just tell him to piss off and he knew if he bent over to open the lower locks himself, he'd get kicked in the arse.

When Hari got the last lock off, Sukh squatted down to throw up the shutter – and let rip with a massive fart. Everyone cracked up laughing and swore at him in English and Punjabi. Sid waved his newspaper like a fan. The shutter clattered up and the group walked into the saw room. Every flat surface was covered in a layer of sawdust and the room smelled of cut timber. A large circular saw bench stood in the middle of the floor.

Hari dropped the padlocks into a plastic box just inside the shutter and followed the others through a heavy partition of thick plastic strips, into a storage area. Most of the guys headed for the kitchen to make themselves tea. Sid went into his office. Zaq followed him, as did Hari who still had his keys.

'*Hari, thu* gate *be* open *kardeh,*' Sid said, as he eased himself into the chair behind his desk. Hari sighed and trudged off to open the gates to the yard. Sid looked at Zaq. '*Haah, thenu kee chaida?*'

'I need to get the tyres on the van fixed.'

'Bloody hell, why you always bring me the headache?'

'I still got stuff to do for Mr Brar, so they need sorting.'

'I must to check with Brar *sahib*, see what he saying.'

'Go on then,' Zaq said.

'You his little *chumcha* now, why you not call him?'

'You're the manager, ain't you? The vehicles are your

responsibility.'

'*Fitay moo thera.*' Sid picked up the phone and tapped in the number. Zaq could tell it was Mr Brar on the other end by how meek and polite he became. Then Sid held the handset out to him. 'He want talk with you.'

'What is going on?' Mr Brar's voice was like two breeze blocks being ground together.

'I think it was just kids messing about – '

'Van *de bond mar*,' Mr Brar said. 'I'm asking about Rita. Have you found her yet?'

Zaq glanced at Sid, who was pretending not to listen, then turned his back and lowered his voice. 'I'm still working on it,' he said.

'Then you need to work *harder*. Understand? Let me talk to Sid again.'

Zaq handed the phone back to Sid, who nodded and agreed with whatever Mr Brar said, then hung up and gave Zaq a sour look. 'OK, you go get fucking van fixed.' Then he looked past Zaq and called out, 'RAM! OH, RAM!'

Ram came into the office. 'What?'

'Help him to sort out van – and be quick, or deliveries will be late.'

'We'll need to take the wheels off and take them to the tyre place to get them done,' Zaq said. 'Ram'll have to drive me.'

'Fucking the hell. *Chethi kar phir.*' Sid waved them out.

'What happened to your face?' Ram said, as they walked out to the yard.

Zaq was getting really cheesed off with having to answer the same question all the time. 'I walked into a door.'

'Yeah? How many times?'

'Go grab the jack from your van,' Zaq said.

'Ain't there one in yours?'

'Be quicker with two.'

Ram got the jack and they went over to the blue van, slumped there on its slashed tyres. Zaq got his jack out of the back and a wheel wrench and handed the wrench to Ram. 'Loosen all the nuts first, then we'll jack it up.'

'Why do I have to loosen them?'

''Cause I'm fucking aching all over and you'll be doing me a favour.' Ram took the wrench. 'Once it's up, we can shove some concrete blocks underneath.'

'What for?'

Zaq looked at him. 'How else is it going to stay up without any wheels?'

Once Ram had loosened the nuts on each wheel, they took a side each and began to crank the small jacks to lift the front of the van first. Zaq felt the effort in every muscle.

When the front of the van was high enough, they placed some concrete blocks from the yard underneath and lowered the van onto them. Then they took the wheels off and repeated the procedure for the rear ones. When all four were off, Ram fetched the other van and loaded the wheels into the back.

'Wait here a minute,' Zaq said and went back to Sid's office.

'*Huun kee chaidah*?'

'Cash for the tyres.'

'How much?'

Zaq shrugged.

'Phone *kar ke puch la*.' Sid pushed the phone across the desk. 'You got the number?'

Sid muttered to himself and fished around in a drawer. He pulled out a card for a tyre place on Lady Margaret Road and flicked it down next to the phone. Zaq found out that reconditioned tyres were twenty quid a pop. Sid counted out a hundred in well-used tens and twenties from the petty cash box. 'Receipt *be le ke ah*. And don't be getting beaten by any more girls, huh.'

'Don't worry, I'll tell your missus to take it easy next time I'm giving her one.'

'Bloody bastard!'

But Zaq was already out the door.

When they returned from the tyre place, Ram helped Zaq put the wheels back on the van. He was tightening the last of the wheel nuts when Sid came over.

'Ram, *bhen chaud, thu haley ethay uh?*'

'I'm helping Zaq, like you told me to.'

'He bloody do himself now. *Chal*, delivery *chethey kar ke le ja, kautha.*'

Ram handed the wrench to Zaq, picked up his jack and got in his van. He started the engine and backed away down the service road.

'You make the *bhen chaud* deliveries late,' Sid said.

'Here's the receipt and the change for the tyres.'

'Delivery is coming. You help to take in.'

'No way, I got stuff to do.' Zaq chucked the jack and the wrench into the back of the van and shut the door.

'What you do is so important, heh? You no doing the real work.'

'You don't know what I'm doing.' He got into the driver's seat.

'*Thu dus phir.*'

'I can't, it's confidential.'

'Confidential, *da bucha!*' Sid was clearly desperate to know what was going on. It was really bugging him that Zaq was working on something important for Mr Brar, that he was in the dark about.

Zaq turned the key in the ignition and the engine rattled to life, the mechanical equivalent of a wheezy old bloke getting out of bed. 'Sorry, Sid, can't sit around chatting to you all day, I got to get going.' The manager had to jump out of the way as Zaq pulled the door shut. The service road was too tight for a three-point turn, so Zaq backed along it as Ram had done. When he looked back, Sid was still standing there muttering to himself.

CHAPTER SIXTEEN

He drove to an Indian restaurant that doubled as a *desi* café during the day. Sorting out the van had re-awakened his aches and pains; it had also made him hungry. He ordered two *aloo parathas* with yogurt on the side and a mug of *masala chai*. The place wasn't busy, so he sat at a table at the back, facing the entrance and the big window looking out on the street, and tried to get his thoughts in order.

So much was going on it was all getting jumbled up in his head. First, the shit with the Brars and being blackmailed into finding Rita. Then the fight outside the Scotsman – who the hell were those guys? The news about the arranged marriage and that Rita had run off with this Kasim guy only complicated matters further, as did the fact Raj and Parm were lying about knowing him. If that wasn't enough to deal with, there was also Davinder's abduction, getting beaten up *again*, and now the stuff with the van and the note to deal with too. Just contemplating it all made his head hurt.

The food arrived and Zaq was glad of the distraction. He tore off a piece of hot *aloo paratha* and dipped it in the yogurt.

It wasn't quite as good as his mum's but he made short work of both *parathas* anyway, finished off the yogurt with a spoon and swallowed the last of his tea. The food had revived him; it also seemed to have alleviated some of his stiffness, though that was probably only imaginary.

The police station was just up the road. He decided he'd go and report last night's assault too – though he wouldn't mention Davinder or the abduction, not yet anyway. He'd simply say he'd been attacked again, by persons unknown. He could give Jhutti and Chadha's names later on, after he had a chance to convince Davinder he'd had no part in the kidnap. He'd already reported the assault outside the Scotsman; this second one would show a pattern, that someone was out to get him. It might be useful later on.

Whatever else was going on, finding Rita was still his top priority – but what was his next step? The information on Kasim had been a dead end, and he had no idea where Davinder might be. What should he do after the police station? Stuck for an answer, he took the list of names and numbers from his pocket and looked it over. His eyes stopped at a name.

Yeah, that was it… that was who he should talk to.

Zaq left the van where it was and walked to the police station. He'd make the phone call afterwards. At the station, he was called into one of the two Perspex-enclosed rooms and found himself in front of the same woman he'd seen the day before.

'How can I help you?' Her face gave nothing away.

'I'd like to report an assault.'

'Who was assaulted?'

Was there something wrong with her eyesight? 'I was.'

'Didn't I see you yesterday?'

'Yeah. I got jumped again.'

'Unlucky, aren't you?'

Zaq couldn't tell if she was being sarcastic or trying to be funny.

'Can you tell me what happened?' she said. Zaq told her the attack had happened near his own house instead of in Hounslow, and he didn't say anything about Davinder. 'Did you recognise any of the attackers?'

'No.'

'Could you describe them?'

'I didn't really get a look at them.'

'Could it have been the same people who attacked you on Monday?'

'Maybe. I'm not sure.'

She took more photographs of his injuries for the report, printed out two copies, had him sign one and gave him the other. 'I hope you're not back again tomorrow,' she said.

Back in the van Zaq locked the doors, took out his phone and the list, keyed in the number he wanted and listened to the ringing at the other end. Someone picked up.

'Nina, it's Zaq. Zaq Khan – you called me the other night, about Rita.'

'What do you want?'

'I *really* need to get in touch with her – it's urgent.'

'She doesn't want to talk to you.' Her voice was low but firm. 'Whatever you've got to say, she's not interested.'

'They've got Davinder.'

Silence... followed by, 'What?'

'Rita's ex, the one you told me about, her brothers took him.'

'What do you mean, *took him*? Hold on...' Zaq heard movement and then, a moment later she came back on the line. 'What the hell are you talking about?' Her voice was louder now, firmer.

'Couple of her brothers' mates grabbed him last night. They beat him up, bundled him in the back of a van and took him away.'

'Why?'

''Cause they think he might know where Rita is. Does he?'

'No.'

'You sure? If he does, he might've told them already.'

'How do I know you're telling the truth?'

'Try calling him, or get Rita to. See who answers and listen to what they say.'

'How do you know he was taken?'

'You've got a lot of questions. If you want answers, meet me later.' When she didn't respond, he said, 'If Rita won't talk to me, *you* come and hear me out, decide if you think she should talk to me. You don't have to trust me – all I'm asking is that you to listen to what I've got to say, then do whatever you think is best. Look, I could've just given Rita's brothers your name, let them come and talk to you. But I didn't… and I don't want to.' He paused. 'If I can talk to her, she might be able to help me find Davinder, so I can help him.'

'Why do you want to help him?'

'I've got my reasons.'

'Aren't you trying to find Rita?'

'Yeah. I told you, I ain't got a choice about that – but whatever happens, I won't make her go home.' That much was true, at least. Her brothers would be the ones who'd drag her home, once Zaq told them where she was. If Nina didn't agree to meet him, he'd be back to square one – with no idea how to get to square two.

'I finish work at five-thirty,' she said. 'I can meet you around six. Just to hear what you've got to say.'

'That's all I'm asking. Where shall we meet? Pick somewhere you'll feel comfortable.'

'Do you know the Hare & Hounds?' He did. He'd spent many evenings there in his late teens and early twenties, though it was ages since he'd last been. 'I'll meet you there, around six,' she said.

'OK. How will I recognise you?'

'I've got shoulder-length hair, I wear glasses and I'll have a red coat. What about you?'

'That's easy. I look like I've just been twelve rounds with Amir Khan.'

The sky was a flat watery grey with not a break or a cloud to be seen. All colour was muted, as if the world was being viewed through smoked glass. It had started to rain as he left Southall and was now pelting down. Though it was only mid-morning, all the vehicles on the road had their lights on.

Arranging the meeting with Nina had been a right result. He sensed she was in touch with Rita and possibly knew more about her whereabouts than she was letting on. He'd tell her about Davinder and anything else he could think of that would get her to trust him enough that she'd convince Rita to talk to him. If that failed, there was always a chance she might let something slip during their conversation, a tiny detail that could help him find Rita.

He passed Hounslow Central tube station and turned onto Bulstrode Avenue. The 4x4 truck was still outside Jhutti and Chadha's place. Zaq drove past, turned back and pulled over where he could see the house. He'd had another idea. It was time to shake the tree, so to speak.

Rain pattered on the roof of the van as he took out his phone and called Davinder's phone again. It was picked up, but whoever answered said nothing. Zaq waited.

'Rita?' a voice finally said. 'I know it's you.'

'Who's Rita?' Zaq said.

'Who the fuck're *you*?'

'Never mind. Where's Davinder?' Zaq didn't know if he was speaking to Jhutti or Chadha but he was happy to wind up either one.

'He can't come to the phone.'

'Bullshit. What you done with him?'

The penny dropped. 'You're the fucker that called yesterday.'

'You must be the smart one. I want to know where Davinder is.'

'None of your fucking business.'

'What if I make it my business?'

'You stick your nose where it ain't wanted, I'll break it off.'

'How about I tell the Old Bill you kidnapped him? You'll do serious time for that.'

He laughed. 'Someone already blabbed. The cops were here this morning, about a report of something. We let them in, showed them round. They asked where we were last night; we told them we was drinking in the Bulstrode – and there's plenty of people who'll say we were.'

'What if I tell them about the evidence?'

'What fucking evidence?'

Now to take a chance and see what they'd do. 'I know you've got Davinder's phone and his laptop; that'll be proof enough – especially if the cops check and find out he didn't go home last night.'

The guy was quiet for a moment, then said, 'We'll get rid of them, then you got jack shit.'

Zaq was gambling on the fact they wouldn't dump it, that they'd move the stuff somewhere else, like wherever they had

Davinder. 'I can always give them your descriptions, as the kidnappers, maybe even your names – which one are you, Jhutti or Chadha?' Silence. 'Tell me where Davinder is or I'm calling the cops right now.'

'You do and you're a dead man.'

'I'll tell them you threatened to kill me too. Might add some time to your sentence.'

'Tell them whatever the fuck you want, they ain't going to find nothing – but you... when I find you, you're fucking dead.'

'You got to find me first. You going to tell me where he is?'

'Fuck you.' The guy hung up.

'Wanker.' Zaq smiled and put his phone away. All he could do now was sit and wait and see what they'd do.

Five minutes later they both came rushing out of the house, Chadha carrying Davinder's bag. Zaq ducked down in his seat. They were moving the stuff, as he'd hoped, but what exactly were they going to do with it? Maybe he'd rattled them enough that they'd let Davinder go. He'd follow them, see what they did. If they released Davinder, he'd talk to him, explain he had nothing to do with what happened to him. And if they didn't let him go? They might still lead the way to where they were holding him.

The 4x4 pulled out of the drive. Zaq waited then started after it. They turned left at the main road. He followed, remaining a car or two back all the way to the M4 roundabout. If they got on the motorway his plan would probably fail – once again, the shitty van's inability to keep up with a more powerful vehicle was a major drawback. Fortunately, they went under the motorway and carried on towards Southall and Hayes.

At the Bulls Bridge roundabout they carried straight on and then took the same exit Zaq had almost missed the day before. He remembered the tight bend, took it slower this time, and saw them turn into the industrial estate. He trailed after them. At the corner of the one-way road he waited and watched them turn in at unit 12.

He found a spot outside unit 8 and parked behind a blue Ford Mondeo. Trees, shrubs and other vehicles provided some cover. The van blended in perfectly; no one gave it a second look. It was good for something after all.

Jhutti and Chadha stalked across the car park to the front door of the Brar's unit, where Jhutti pressed the bell. Zaq could see the blue and brown of Davinder's laptop bag in Chadha's hands. Parminder Brar opened the door and they all disappeared inside.

Was this where they had Davinder? It made sense; it was an out-of-the-way place, in the middle of an industrial estate, noisy during the day, probably dead at night, and with no nosy neighbours. The more he thought about it, the more likely it seemed. Turning the screws on Jhutti and Chadha felt good. He just hoped they wouldn't get his name from Davinder and come looking for him. What he needed to do now, was figure a way to get inside the warehouse and take a look around.

A dark grey BMW turned into the car park and stopped near the shutter. A young Asian guy, a bit short, a bit fat, got out, went to the door and pressed the bell. Chadha let him in.

A few minutes later the shutter started to rise. It went up halfway then stopped. Chadha emerged with something on his shoulder – a bag of cement. The driver of the BMW opened the boot and Chadha put the bag into it, then went back inside and returned with another bag.

Parminder and Jhutti came out as the driver closed the boot and Chadha dusted off his shoulder. The driver shook hands with all three then got in his car and drove away. Parminder, Jhutti and Chadha stood in the car park having what looked like a heated debate. Finally, Parminder said something the other two agreed with and they shook hands. Parminder went inside and brought the shutter down. Jhutti and Chadha got in their truck. They didn't have Davinder's bag, which meant it they'd left it inside. The truck reversed, turned and drove away. Zaq let them go. He didn't need to follow them now.

He was finally starting to piece things together. He might have just tracked Davinder down and his meeting with Nina later might put him a step closer to finding Rita too. Not a bad morning's work, even if he did say so himself.

Movement drew his attention back to the warehouse. Parminder came out. He locked the door behind him, got in his car and drove away. Zaq sank down in his seat and watched him go.

CHAPTER SEVENTEEN

It didn't take long to get to where he was going. The closer Zaq got to his destination though, the more wary he became; every parked car and pedestrian a possible threat. He parked on Johnson Street, as he had the day before, and walked to the Scotsman, on the lookout for any hint of trouble. The rain had stopped and everything seemed a little fresher, a little less grey. He found Biri inside, sitting at a table with two young men in hooded sweat tops. It looked like he was just finishing a full English breakfast, even though it was lunchtime.

'Fuck, man, what happened? You get jumped again or something?'

'It's nothing,' Zaq said. 'Bit late for breakfast, ain't it?'

Biri pushed his plate away and picked up his mug of tea. 'You know me, don't keep no regular office hours. Sit down, man, relax yourself. You remember Rav? And this is Aakil.'

Zaq nodded a greeting to Biri's young *protégé* and the other youth and took the last seat at the table. 'I need a word, Biri.'

Biri looked at the other two. 'Go have a doob or something.'

When they had gone, Zaq said, 'Another student? You'll be

handing out degrees next.'

Biri laughed. 'Only degree you get round here is the third degree from the cops.'

'You got that right.'

'They ain't got nothing else to do, so they hang around here. Better than loafing on street corners. Rav's got skills, like I told you. Too soon to say about the other one. Anyway, what's going on? I don't see you for six months and now I seen you three times in three days. If it's about that motor, it ain't turned up yet.'

Zaq looked around to make sure no one could hear them, then leaned forward. 'You know anyone that can break into a building for me? I need to get inside somewhere.'

'Just 'cause I deal in dodgy motors, don't mean I know every dodgy geezer in Southall. I thought you was on the straight and narrow anyhow.'

'I am – but something's come up.'

Biri sat back and drank some tea. 'I might know someone, as it happens. What kind of place we talking about? House, shop, what?'

'A warehouse, on an industrial estate.'

Biri raised an eyebrow. 'You know if it's got an alarm?'

Zaq hadn't thought about it. 'I don't know. I guess so, yeah.'

'What you jacking?'

'Nothing, I just want to take a look inside. In and out – ten, fifteen minutes tops. I ain't looking to boost anything '

'Lot of trouble just for a look. What's so special about the place?'

'Nothing, as far as I know.'

Biri shook his head. 'Bruv, I don't know what you're up to – it's your business, that's cool.'

'Probably better that way. You think your guy can handle

an alarm, if there is one?'

Biri rubbed his chin. 'Yeah, but he won't do it for free. It'll cost you.'

Paying hadn't even crossed Zaq's mind. 'How much?'

Biri shrugged. 'I don't know – two, maybe three hundred. That's if it's a simple set-up. Anything complicated, he'll probably want more.'

'I'll sort the money.' It was two or three hundred Zaq didn't have. 'Will he do it, though?'

'When you thinking of?'

'Tonight.'

'Bit short notice but I can call him, see what he says.'

'If he can't do it, is there anyone else?'

'Maybe – but this geezer's good. Let's see what he says first.'

'Cheers, Biri.'

'Can't see why you'd want to break into somewhere just to have a look around though, unless you're scoping it out to knock over later.'

'Nothing like that.'

'Then you're taking a big risk for nothing.'

'If this bloke's as good as you say, there shouldn't be much risk. I'll be in and out and no one'll be the wiser.'

'I'll call him now, if you want to wait.'

'I got to get going, but thanks, Biri. I really appreciate it. Let me know what he says, yeah?'

They shook hands and Zaq hurried back to the van. He had a phone call to make himself but wanted to put some distance between himself and the pub, in case anyone was driving around hoping to catch him there again. He drove a couple of streets away, pulled over and called Jags. 'Where are you?'

'Driving home from the gym. Why, what's up?'

'How long you going to be?'

'About ten minutes.'

'I'm on my way.'

'Holy shit,' Jags said. 'You seen the state of your face? It's even worse than usual.'

'You never seen a bruise before?'

'Not so many in one place.'

'I'm going to take a leak. Why don't you do something useful and put the kettle on?'

'You just come round for a cuppa?'

'No, I need to talk to you about something.'

Zaq went upstairs and used the bathroom. He looked at his face in the mirror as he washed his hands. His skin was mottled a variety of colours, none of them healthy, the cuts and scrapes crusting over with scabs.

He had just walked into the lounge when his phone rang. 'I got to take this,' he told Jags.

It was Biri. 'I just spoke to that guy, about the thing you needed. He said he'll do it.'

'Cool.'

'I had to talk him into it, seeing as he don't know you. But I told him you were OK and he'd be doing me a favour. I was right about the price; it'll be three cents.' *Three hundred pounds*.

'All right, fine.'

'He can do it when you said but he wants to meet here, so I can do the intros and everything.'

Zaq was OK with that. He worked out how long his meeting with Nina might take and allowed time in case she was late and also for him to get to Old Southall. 'Let's meet about nine.'

'I'll tell him. See you later.'

'What was that about?' Jags asked, bringing two mugs of tea from the kitchen.

'First, let me tell you what happened this morning...' Zaq told him about the van's wheels being slashed and handed him the note. 'This was on the windscreen.'

Jags frowned. 'They think she's your girlfriend? They must be dumber than we thought.'

'Dumb or not, now they're after Rita too. Anything happens to her 'cause of me, I'm screwed.'

'You sure you ain't got any idea who these guys are?' Zaq shook his head. 'You pissed anyone off recently?'

'Not that I can think of.' Since getting out of prison he'd done his best to keep his head down and steer clear of trouble. He hadn't been doing too badly either – until this whole Rita Brar thing had been dropped on him. 'I wonder if it could have anything to do with Biri. Maybe they targeted me 'cause they saw me with him?'

'Why do your tyres, and leave this?' Jags held up the note.

'To get me back for decking all three of them, making them feel stupid. Maybe they want to show they ain't a bunch of pussies.'

'By vandalising your van and threatening a girl? Sounds pretty pussy to me.'

'Yeah but I have to take it seriously. They might really go after her.' He went on to tell Jags about the meeting he'd arranged with Nina and how he'd followed Jhutti and Chadha to the Brars' warehouse. 'I think it might be where they're holding Davinder. Good a place as any, better than most.'

'So call the Old Bill then.'

'I got to talk to Davinder first, remember? So he knows I didn't have anything to do with it. Make sure he keeps my name out of it.'

'How you going to talk to him?'

'That's sort of what I came to see you about. Can you lend

me three hundred quid?'

'What for?'

'Might be better if you didn't know.'

'Sod that! If I'm lending you the money, and it's to do with what's going on, I want to know.'

He knew he'd tell Jags eventually anyway. 'It's to get me inside the warehouse, so I can look around. I need to pay a guy Biri knows to take care of the locks and the alarm and let me in. I'll be in and out in no time, no mess, no fuss.'

'Sounds like you're talking about a hooker. I'd lend you three hundred for that. You sure you can trust this guy?'

'I trust Biri, so yeah.'

'I thought you was trying to stay out of trouble. This could land you in deep shit.'

'Only if I get caught,' Zaq said. 'We get Davinder out of there and straighten things out with him, the Brars are the ones that'll have to worry about getting in shit. And if we do manage to spring him, it could help us with Rita.'

'You reckon?'

''Course – we'll have rescued her ex and shafted her brothers at the same time – that's bound to put us in her good books. What d'you say? You going to lend me the money or what?'

'What d'you think?'

Zaq started to smile but it hurt and he ended up grimacing instead. 'Shit, you got any ibuprofen?'

'Your face hurting you?'

'Yeah.'

'It's killing me, too.'

He should have seen that one coming a mile off.

Jags heated up some *keema* and *dahl* his mum had made, for their lunch, along with some garlic and coriander *naans*. Zaq felt better after eating, the food and the painkillers combining to ease the throbbing and soreness he'd felt. Jags had a hundred and twenty pounds in cash at home and said he'd draw the rest out from a cash machine.

Zaq was taking his dishes to the sink when his phone rang again.

'*Thu kitheh unh*?' Sid didn't bother with a greeting.

'Hayes.'

'Hayes *da bucha*. You come back to here.'

'What for? I'm busy.'

'*Meh thenu* busy *dhendah*. Brar *sahib* want see you.'

He couldn't refuse to go see the boss. 'OK, I'll be there soon.' Maybe Ram had been so bad with the deliveries they had no choice but to put Zaq back on them. 'I got to go back to the yard,' he told Jags.

'What about the money?'

'Get it. I'll pick it up later.'

He made good time driving back to Southall, at least until he hit traffic on the Broadway. A bright confusion of sights, smells and sounds assailed him; the vibrant colours of silks and fabrics, fruits and vegetables; the glint of Indian gold in jewellers' windows; the powerful aromas of spices and incense; the mash-up of English, Punjabi, Hindi, Urdu, Somali and Polish; the blare of music. Absence was supposed to make the heart grow fonder and it was true, it did. He'd never thought he'd miss Southall but he had. Though things had changed while he'd been away, it still felt like home.

He found Sid sitting behind his desk reading a newspaper as usual. '*Aahgeya, saala*? What taking you so long?'

'Traffic,' Zaq said. 'The van don't fly, you know.'

Sid tutted loudly. '*Chal, utheh ja, chetty kar ke.*'

Zaq left the office, went upstairs and knocked on Mr Brar's door.

'Come in.'

Zaq entered the room – and saw it wasn't Mr Brar waiting for him, at least, not the one he'd been expecting anyway. Parminder Brar was sitting in his father's chair, Rajinder next to him in one of the chairs that usually faced the desk. Both glowered at Zaq from under their heavy brows. Zaq checked the seats behind him where Raj and Parm had been the other day – and found Jhutti and Chadha hunched there, staring at him with hard eyes. *Fuck, had Davinder given them his name?* The office suddenly felt too small... and he was trapped in it. It took a real effort not to react, though his stomach flipped a somersault. Forcing himself to feign indifference, Zaq faced Parminder, 'I thought it was your old man wanted to see me.'

'Well, it ain't.'

'What d'you want?'

'What happened to your face?' Parm's eyes were dark and hard as frozen puddles.

'I got jumped.'

'When?'

'Monday night, outside the Scotsman. I told your brother yesterday.'

Parm glanced at his brother.

Rajinder gave a reluctant nod. 'His face was like that when he came to the house yesterday.'

Parm looked back at Zaq. 'Where were you last night?'

'Why?'

"Cause I want to know.'

Zaq shrugged. 'Depends. What time?'

'Between seven and eight.'

'At a mate's.'

'In Hounslow?'

'No.'

'You sure about that? You didn't go talk to Davinder Panesar?'

'Who?'

'Guy you were asking me about yesterday,' Raj said.

'Was I? Who is he?'

Raj was too busy glaring at Zaq to respond, so Parm did instead. 'The guy Rita used to see.'

'Oh yeah,' Zaq said. 'I did ask about him but Raj didn't know anything, apart from the guy's name and that he used to live in Hounslow. Weren't much to go on, so I left it. You manage to find him?'

'No.' Parm looked over at Jhutti and Chadha. 'Well?'

Zaq turned to look at them too. They were still staring at him. He nodded to them, acting like it was the first time he'd ever laid eyes on the pair. Jhutti, he remembered, was the one with short hair. Under his jacket, his T-shirt was stretched tight over slab-like pecs. Chadha was similarly large, his blunt face heavily scarred, suggesting he was prone to either accidents or violence, most probably the latter. Zaq had to suppress the urge to smash their faces in while they weren't expecting it. With four of them in the room, it would be suicide.

Jhutti shrugged. 'I don't know,' he said. 'I can't tell. We didn't really look at the other guy.'

'What about you?' Parm asked Chadha.

'It was dark and I was busy.'

'What about his voice?'

'Hard to say. Guy on the phone sounded different.'

Zaq turned back to Parm. 'What's going on?'

'Nothing,' Parm said. 'You sure you weren't in Hounslow last night?'

'I just told you I wasn't.'

'And you got those cuts and bruises on Monday?'

'Yeah, I even reported it to the police yesterday, got a Crime Reference Number and everything. I got a copy of the report here if you –'

'What the fuck? My dad told you not to get the cops involved!'

'It ain't nothing to do with your sister.'

'Don't matter. We don't want the cops sniffing around 'cause of whatever shit you got going on, understand? You found out where she is yet?'

'I'm working on it.'

'Best work harder then, innit? We want her found – and soon.'

'Might help if I didn't have to waste time finding out things you could've just told me.'

'Like what?'

'Like where Rita works, like she's run off with some guy and like there's an ex I can talk to.'

'You know now, so what's the problem?'

The problem was they still weren't telling him everything.

'What you waiting for?' Parm said. 'You ain't going to find her standing there.'

Zaq turned to leave and looked at Jhutti and Chadha with a neutral expression, giving no hint that he knew them.

'One more thing,' Parm called. 'When you find her, don't forget to let me or Raj know *before* you tell our dad. Got that?'

'Yeah, I got it.'

Zaq was glad to get out of the office. He wondered what they would've done if they'd recognised him as the guy with Davinder, or if they'd known he was the one who'd called Jhutti and Chadha? Given him a bloody good pasting or shopped him to the cops – or probably both. Keeping his mouth shut and acting dumb had been the best thing to do.

He didn't bother going to see Sid before leaving. Instead, he crossed the yard and walked out the rear gates. Dusk was fast approaching and the streetlights were already on. So far, his week had gone from bad to worse to shit. He told himself things couldn't get any worse – but he had a horrible feeling that if they could, they probably would.

CHAPTER EIGHTEEN

He still had time before he had to meet Nina at the Hare & Hounds, so Zaq decided to go and pick up the money from Jags. He drove away from the builders' yard and had just turned onto the main road when, checking his mirror, he saw a vehicle pull out and come after him. It could have been purely coincidental – except when he sped up, the vehicle behind did the same and stayed right on his tail.

Its lights were on full beam, so when Zaq looked in his mirror again, he couldn't see past their blinding glare. He took a right and as he did so, managed to glimpse the vehicle side on before it turned after him. It was a 4x4 truck – and he knew whose; Jhutti and Chadha's.

So they were keeping tabs on him. He thought they'd bought his story about not knowing what had happened to Davinder – but maybe not. Or they just want to keep an eye on him, see what he was up to. Zaq checked his mirror only to be dazzled by the high beams. They weren't exactly being subtle back there. But then, they had no idea Zaq knew their truck or that he was on the lookout for anyone tailing him.

At the mini-roundabout on Lady Margaret Road, Zaq carried straight on. Jhutti and Chadha followed. There was no way he was going to lead them to Jags' place or to his meeting with Nina. But how was he meant to shake them off? It was rush hour, and traffic was crawling.

He glanced at his parents' house as he passed it. The lights were on; his mum would be watching her Pakistani dramas on TV. At the end of the road, Zaq took a left towards the Broadway and got stuck in a long queue of cars. Jhutti and Chadha loomed up behind him. He wasn't going to outrun them, so he had to think of something else. The cars edged forward slowly until eventually, Zaq reached the top of the road.

He waited for a gap in the traffic or someone to let him out. When a car flashed its lights to give him way, he pulled forward to turn right, into the far lane – only no one let him in. He had wanted to make the manoeuvre quickly and leave Jhutti and Chadha behind, still waiting to pull out, but instead found himself blocking traffic. Jhutti and Chadha nosed forward and stayed bumper to bumper with him. When at last someone did let him in, the truck pushed its way in too, right behind him.

Great, now what? He'd wanted to lose Jhutti and Chadha without it looking as though he'd done it on purpose. He could try and shake them on the way to Jags' but that would mean taking a convoluted route, which would only raise their suspicion and make it seem like he was trying to hide something. There was no guarantee he'd be able to lose them anyway. So he ditched the idea of going to Jags' – he'd have to get the money later.

Approaching the big roundabout by Sainsbury's, an idea came to him. He wasn't sure it would work, but it was all he could come up with. Instead of going to Hayes, he took the first exit at the roundabout, onto the Parkway. A river of brake lights stretched in front of him into the distance. The speed limit was 50 miles an hour but no one was going much more than 10. Jhutti and Chadha were still right behind him, but that was OK; he wasn't trying to outrun them now – he had something else in mind.

On the elevated section of the road, Zaq glanced right. That was where the Brars' warehouse was – maybe Davinder as well. If things went to plan later, he would be there too.

At the Bull's Bridge roundabout he went left again, past Tesco and into Old Southall. Jhutti and Chadha were probably wondering why he'd gone such a long way round to get there. Zaq led them down some residential streets, until he finally turned onto a road and pulled into the first parking space he found, facing away from the Scotsman. The truck had to pass him and find a spot to park further on. Zaq watched to see where they stopped then got out of the van and started towards the pub. He heard vehicle doors slam and knew Jhutti and Chadha were coming after him.

The pub was busy. It was Wednesday evening and the TV screens were showing Sky Sports News in the build-up to another big Champions League game. Many of the punters were there to eat before the match. The smell of tandoori mixed grills and fried onions filled the air. Zaq could see the Indian chefs hard at work through the window to the kitchen. He didn't see Biri inside anywhere, so went to check the patio in case he was out there having a cigarette. Two smokers were standing in the shadows.

'You stalking me or what?' one said.

'Biri! I hate to keep bugging you, man, but I need a favour.'

'Another one?' Biri sounded amused. It was Rav with him. Didn't he ever go home?

'I wouldn't ask, but it's important. There's a couple of guys following me. I need to get rid of them.'

As if on cue, Jhutti and Chadha appeared in the doorway. They saw Zaq and stopped. Jhutti gave Chadha a nudge and they went back inside.

'Shit, they the ones following you?' Biri said. 'You know who they are? You want to steer well clear of them, mate, they're fucking psychos.'

'So I've heard. That's why I need your help.' Zaq told Biri what he had in mind. 'Reckon you can do it?'

Biri turned to Rav. 'What d'you think?'

The young man nodded. ''Course.'

'You got balls,' Biri said. 'You want to keep them, make sure they don't know it was you.'

'I ain't exactly going to advertise it.'

'Go in and get yourself a drink,' Biri told him, 'then hang around the pool tables. They might clock you as you walk in, but once you're over the other side, they'll forget about you. Ain't you they're here for. Wait a minute or two, then slip out. When you're done, come back in, pick up your drink and make out you been there the whole time.'

'OK.'

'Thanks Rav, I appreciate it.' Zaq stuck out his hand and they shook. Rav took a final drag on his cigarette and dropped it the large flower pot that served as an ashtray.

'You need anything?' Biri asked him.

'Nah, I got what I need on me.'

'Text us when it's done.'

Zaq and Biri waited a few minutes, then went inside. Zaq got them a couple of drinks and they managed to find a table near the door to the street. Jhutti and Chadha were on the other side of the lounge, watching them. If they were trying to be covert about it, they weren't succeeding.

'How long you think it'll take?' Zaq said.

'Not long. I told you, kid's got skills.'

'In that case, this beer's for him,' Zaq nodded at the pint he hadn't touched. 'I got to shoot soon as he gets back.'

'You still coming later?'

'Yeah, I'll be here for nine, like we said.'

'Cool.' They watched TV and talked football until Biri's phone chimed. He checked it. 'It's done.'

'Brilliant. Thanks, Biri.'

'Weren't me, it was Rav.'

'He only did it 'cause you asked him to.'

'And 'cause he wants to impress you. He knows who you are. You got a rep, and you know how it is round here – all about who you know, who you hang with. Won't do him no harm to say he knows you.'

'Won't do him much good, either.'

'That's what I told him,' Biri said, with a grin, 'but he thinks you're a hard case and that makes you someone worth knowing.'

Zaq shook his head. 'Tell him I said thanks and I'll buy him another drink next time I see him.' They waited until they saw Rav slip back into the pub, pick up his drink and act like he'd never left. 'See you later,' Zaq told Biri, then, without looking in Jhutti and Chadha's direction, he got up and walked out.

It would have taken them by surprise. They'd probably expected him to finish his drink before he left. Well, tough shit – he wasn't about to wait for them. He'd only have a couple of seconds head start, but that should be enough. He hurried to the van and heard what must've been Jhutti and Chadha come barging out of the pub some way behind him. He got in and started the engine. Jhutti and Chadha rushed past, heading for the 4x4 they'd parked further on.

Zaq pulled away from the kerb. As he drove past them, he saw the pair standing at the side of the road, arguing and looking around at the empty space where their truck should have been.

CHAPTER NINETEEN

Windmill Lane was more like a country road than a busy urban one. Barely wide enough in places for two cars to pass each other, it was bordered by tall hedges on the left and a high brick wall on the right. Further on, they gave way to trees on either side. At night you couldn't see anything but woods and darkness, nothing to hint that Southall was behind you, Hounslow in front. In daylight, you could see the open field on the right, part of the Osterley Park estate but at night it turned into a featureless black expanse.

The Hare & Hounds was set back from the road, a large brick building painted white, with a high pitched roof. Black timbers lent it a rustic *olde worlde* look and lights glowing in the windows gave the place a warm, inviting feel. Inside, it was light and bright, with cream walls, blond wood and dark red leather. It was so warm Zaq had to take his jacket off as soon as he entered. He looked around and saw a couple, a group of guys, and a larger party at some tables by the windows – but no one that fitted Nina's description.

Beyond the bar was a separate lounge, so he walked over

to see if she might be there. A woman was sitting alone at an alcove table in the corner by the window. She was looking down at something so he couldn't see her face. Then he spotted a red coat draped over the back of her chair and walked over. 'Nina?'

She looked up and put on the glasses she had been cleaning with a lens cloth. 'You're Zaq?'

She was in her early twenties, pretty and slender – at least she was from the waist up, which was all he could see. She had a fine, delicately featured face. Her lips weren't too full or too thin and the bright red lipstick she wore drew attention to them. She put her glasses on; the stylish rectangular frames made her look intelligent and sexy at the same time.

He suddenly felt awkward, conscious of his own appearance; his work clothes and rough demeanour. She was looking at his face a little too intently. 'You're wondering how I got these,' he said, gesturing at the marks there. 'That's what I'm here to tell you about.' There was a half-full glass in front of her. It looked like Coke, though it could have been mixed with something else. 'I'm going to get a drink – can I get you another?'

'No thanks, I'm fine. I wasn't planning on staying long.' Her tone was several degrees below friendly.

Zaq went to the bar, returned with a lager shandy and took a seat opposite her. 'Thanks for meeting me.'

'Can you just say whatever it is you came to say, so I can go?'

Zaq leaned forward. 'I was with Davinder when Raj and Parm's mates jumped us. That's how I got these.' He waved a hand at his face again. 'They dragged him into a van and took him away.'

'How do you know they were Raj and Parm's friends?'

''Cause I saw them all together, yesterday morning. I think Parminder got them to do it.'

'Why?'

'To find out if he knows where Rita is – same reason I was talking to him.'

'He doesn't. Rita didn't tell him.'

'How do you know?'

'I just do.'

'OK, but they've got him and now they're keeping him hostage, to force Rita to come back home.'

'A hostage? You're joking.'

'Does my face look like this is all a joke? I tried calling Davinder afterwards; he didn't answer but one of the guys that took him did. I kept quiet and he thought it was Rita, said if she wanted Davinder to stay in one piece she'd better get herself back home.'

Now she seemed concerned. 'Did you go to the police?'

'Kind of.'

'What does that mean?'

'I told the police where I thought they'd taken him – only he wasn't there.'

'That was a lot of good.'

'They must've taken him somewhere else.'

Nina bit her lip. 'I better let Rita know.'

So she *was* in contact with her. 'You think it'll make her come back?' If it did, he'd happily escort her to her dad's office. 'If you're going to talk to her you better tell her I'm not the only one looking for her. Her brothers and these mates of theirs are after her too, maybe some other people as well. If Davinder knows where she is, she better move, *fast*.'

Nina frowned. 'Why're you telling me all this? Aren't you working for her dad?'

'I might have to do what he wants, that don't mean I agree with what they want to do to her.'

She considered for a moment. 'I'll call her and tell her about

Davinder and the other stuff.'

'When? I think you better do it now. I don't mind waiting. And remember, if Davinder knows where she is, she needs to get out of there.'

Nina was a little hesitant but then agreed. She stood, slipped into her coat and picked up her handbag. 'I'm going to go outside to call her.'

Zaq switched seats as soon as she walked away. He'd been uncomfortable with his back to the rest of the pub; he preferred to see what was going on behind him, a habit he'd developed in prison. Now he had a good view of the lounge and the bar and was able to watch Nina walk towards the exit. Her coat was well cut and outlined her slim body well. Her dark wavy hair bounced with each step. She moved with a confidence and self-assurance that he found particularly attractive.

He could see her through a window, her red coat clearly visible under the outside lights. She had her phone to her ear, listening. He hoped he'd done enough to convince her. He just needed them to trust him enough that one of them might let slip some clue to Rita's location. Then he could tell her dad, and that would be the end of it. He might not feel good about it but it was better than the alternative.

A sudden flurry of motion caught his eye, a blur of red and then it vanished. It was too fast for him to see what had happened but the movements had been very abrupt and unnatural. Something was wrong. He grabbed his jacket and ran outside. There was no sign of Nina.

Where was she? Did Rita tell her to leave? He was listening for the sound of a car starting, thinking he might stop her before she drove away, when he heard a muffled scream.

It was silenced quickly but he was sure it had come from the car park. He went that way as quickly as he could, using hedges and parked cars for cover. He spotted a small group heading towards the far corner of the car park. Zaq counted three of them... no, four – one was ahead of the others – all making for a car. The trio were moving in jerky, shuffling motions that seemed odd – until Zaq saw a flash of red fabric.

He moved fast, crouching and darting over to the next row of cars. When he reached the last one, he broke from cover and rushed at the group. He moved quietly for his size and, with Nina's desperate struggling keeping them occupied, the men dragging her were oblivious to his approach.

One was trying to grab hold of Nina's legs so he could carry them but she was thrashing and kicking so wildly he was having real difficulty. Zaq grabbed him first, pulled him back and kneed him hard in the lower back and kidneys, twice. The guy fell to the ground and Zaq kicked him in the balls and head.

His partner was too busy restraining Nina, with one arm round her waist and his other hand clamped over her mouth. He had his hands full, so Zaq went for the guy nearing the car. As he tore towards him, the one holding Nina shouted some kind of warning – 'Mash' or 'Mesh' – Zaq wasn't sure what, but it came too late; Zaq was close enough. He jumped at the guy, extending his right leg in a kick that hit the driver in his solar plexus and dropping him to his knees as he desperately tried to suck air into his lungs. Zaq hit him with an uppercut that snapped his head back, then rabbit-punched him in the face. There was a brittle crack as something – probably his nose – broke. His vision would be fucked, so Zaq wouldn't have to worry about him for a while. The car keys were on the ground. Zaq picked them up and hurled them into the trees behind the car park, leaving the man slumped in the open door of the car.

The guy who'd been trying to grab Nina's legs was still curled up on the ground, clutching his balls. He wasn't getting up in a hurry. Heart thumping, Zaq turned to face the last man, who still had hold of Nina. He didn't know what to do. His friends were down and their car wasn't going anywhere. Nina had stopped struggling, eyes wide, the whites clearly visible. The guy holding her was trying to use her as a shield.

Zaq came forward. 'Let her go, or you'll be shitting teeth for a week.'

The guy looked at him, then at his friends on the ground, and finally pushed Nina away, towards Zaq and stepped back, hands up, like a footballer denying a foul. 'It wasn't my idea.'

Nina spun round to face him. 'You bastard!'

'Hit him,' Zaq told her. 'Go on, it'll make you feel better.'

'Fuck you,' the guy said.

'Either she hits you or I do – your choice.' The guy looked around as if looking for an escape route. 'Where you going to run? I'll get to you before you reach the pub.'

The guy's eyes moved from Zaq to Nina, weighing the options. 'Go on then.'

He was bigger than Nina but she squared up to him, looked him straight in the eye and slapped him so hard the sound echoed around the car park. It must've hurt. Light glinted off water in his eyes.

'And again,' Zaq said.

'What the fuck…?'

'Shut up,' Zaq told him. 'Go on, Nina, get it out of your system.'

The guy clenched his jaw, ready for another slap, only this time Nina threw a solid punch that cracked him hard in the mouth.

'Bitch,' he snarled, going to hit her back.

Zaq stepped in front of her, blocked the blow with his left arm, grabbing the guy's wrist and yanking him forward. As he did so, he rammed the heel of his right palm forward into the guy's right clavicle. There was a snap like a twig breaking. The guy screamed and fell to his knees, holding his right arm close to his body.

Zaq squatted down in front of him. 'That was your collar bone,' he said. 'It'll be all right in about six weeks.' The guy was swearing rapidly to cope with the shock of the injury. 'You come near me or her again,' Zaq said, 'and I'll break both your arms, you understand?' The guy didn't respond. 'I said, do you understand?' Zaq reached for his right shoulder.

'I understand, I understand.'

'Good. Make sure you tell those two idiots as well.' Zaq stood up, took Nina's arm and led her away. 'Did you come by car?'

'Yes.' She sounded unsure, distracted.

'Where you parked?'

'Over there. The red Golf.'

'You OK to drive?'

'I think so. Who were they?'

'I don't know,' he said. 'Maybe friends of Raj and Parm's, after Rita.'

'What did they want with me?'

'Same thing they wanted with Davinder, probably. Did you tell Rita?'

'They grabbed me before I had a chance.'

'You better call her back. Not here though. You know anywhere else we can go?'

She thought for a second. 'The London Apprentice, by the river?'

'OK. I'll follow you. I'm in the blue van over there.' She looked at it, then at him. 'Yeah, I know... my Porsche is getting serviced. Let's go.'

CHAPTER TWENTY

As Zaq followed Nina's Golf out of the car park, he saw the first guy helping the one with the busted collarbone to their car. He didn't think they'd come looking for them again tonight. They'd have to find their car keys before they could go anywhere and then it'd probably be to a hospital.

Nina drove towards Gillette Corner and into Isleworth. The adrenalin had worn off and Zaq felt tiredness pressing down on him. He was annoyed at himself. He'd been so concerned with Jhutti and Chadha, he hadn't been looking out for anyone else. He would've recognised either of the Brars' Mercedes if they'd shown up, but not seeing them, he'd let his guard down. Those arseholes could have followed him from Southall for all he knew. He was lucky things hadn't turned out a lot worse.

Something about the guys was bugging him... the driver in particular. Had he seen him somewhere before? He couldn't think where though? Southall? Prison? Or was it connected to Rita somehow? Mates of Raj and Parm's looking for her? If that was the case, why did they try to take Nina? Maybe the same reason they'd abducted Davinder.

Then he remembered the note on the van. What had it said? LETS SEE HOW TUFF YOUR GIRLFRIEND IS. Was it the same guys who'd attacked him Monday night? Had they followed him to the pub, seen him with Nina and thought she was the girl in the photo? Maybe. But if they'd tried to take her as a way to get to *him*, it meant they weren't really after Nina or Rita. *He* was their real target – and the fuckers were prepared to do anything to get to him.

What the hell was going on? His life had been turned on its head since in the last few days. He tried to make a mental list of everything that had happened, in an attempt to make sense of the chaos, get it all straight in his head;

Monday – he'd been forced into looking for Rita.
Monday night – he'd been jumped by the three blokes outside the Scotsman.
Tuesday – found out about Davinder. Saw Jhutti and Chadha with the Brars. Arranged to meet Davinder.
Tuesday night – Davinder taken by Jhutti and Chadha.
Wednesday – followed Jhutti and Chadha to the Warehouse, where they might be holding Davinder.
Wednesday night – Met Nina.
Just now – Nina grabbed, possibly by the same three assholes from Monday.

The night wasn't even done yet. Who knew what else could happen? Or what shit tomorrow might bring?

Nina went left at a sign for Syon House & Park and Zaq followed her. They passed a development of flats that gave way to a cemetery, on the far side of which were the lights of West Middlesex Hospital – not exactly an encouraging view for the patients. Planes passed low overhead, landing lights on, ready to touch down at nearby Heathrow Airport.

The road was quiet, so it was easy for Zaq to now make sure they weren't being followed. They passed the gates to the park, barely discernible in the dark, and a short distance further the road seemed to come to a dead end. Nina's headlights picked out cars parked there ahead of them and Zaq knew the road veered sharply to the right. Two orange lights shone in the distance, the smudged streaks below them their reflections on water. Nina's brake lights flashed and she disappeared around the bend. Zaq followed, the river now on his left, a church on the right, its ancient square tower brightly lit.

The London Apprentice was a quaint old boozer that emanated warmth and light. They found parking spaces near the pub, close to a slip that ran down to the water. Zaq walked over to Nina's car and found her staring through the windscreen, gripping the steering wheel so tight her knuckles showed white through her skin. He let her have a minute. The church bells began to peal as if the ringers were practicing for a wedding. Nina seemed to compose herself and got out of the car.

'You OK?'

'Yes, I think so.' She locked the car. 'Thanks… for what you did back there.' Some of her earlier confidence had left her. 'What made you come out?'

'You disappeared all of a sudden. I just came out to check you were OK.'

'I'm glad you did.'

'Me too.'

She pulled her coat tight about her. 'I thought I could defend myself in a situation like that – I do karate, you know – but they grabbed me from behind, took me by surprise.'

'It happens. That's how I got all these.' He pointed to his face.

'But you… just took on all three of them.'

'I've had a bit of practise, plus I surprised them too. Why don't we go inside? We could both use a drink.'

They were walking towards the pub when Nina's phone rang. She looked at the screen. 'It's Rita. Oh, my God, I was talking to her when they grabbed me. She must have heard it happen.'

'Answer it,' he said. 'I'll stay out here with you this time.'

Nina moved off a short distance to talk in private. Zaq leaned back against the railings at the edge of the embankment and kept an eye on the road. He scrutinised every car that passed and particular attention to any that stopped, but no one showed any interest in them. Whenever there were no vehicles going by, he would look over at Nina; she was busy on the phone and didn't notice. The church bells were still ringing and planes continued to rumble overhead in steady procession. Swans and geese called up from the darkness of the river behind him. He could hear Nina's voice as she spoke, the urgency in it, but not the actual words.

Then she came over and held out her phone. 'It's Rita, she wants to talk to you.'

He hadn't been expecting that but took the phone and put it to his ear.

'What's happened to Davinder?' Rita Brar was well spoken, her voice free of that particular Southall twang many of the area's inhabitants seemed to acquire.

'A couple of your brothers' mates grabbed him.'

'Did they hurt him?'

'Yeah, they did. They took him to make you come back.'

She swore under her breath. 'Why didn't you tell the police?'

'I did… Well, I told them as much as I could, where I thought they'd taken him, only he wasn't there. I think I know where he is now though. I'm going to check it out later on.'

'He doesn't have anything to do with of this. Why did they go after him?'

Zaq thought it best not to mention he was the one who'd brought up Davinder's name in connection with finding her. 'They probably thought he'd know where you are.'

'He doesn't. I didn't tell him, on purpose. He's not part of this.'

'They must've figured that out, so now they're using him as a hostage, to make you come back.'

Rita didn't speak for a moment. When she did, she said, 'And if I don't...? They'll have to let him go eventually, won't they?'

'Maybe... I don't know what sort of shape he'll be in though, when they do.'

'If he doesn't know where I am, there's no reason for them to do anything to him, is there? They'll just keep him until it's obvious I'm not coming back, then they'll release him, right?'

'I don't know...'

'But you know where he is?'

'I think so, yeah. At your brothers' warehouse.'

'What warehouse?'

'The one in Hayes.'

'I don't know anything about that. You're going to go look for Davinder there though? What'll you do if you find him?'

'Get him out, of course.'

'OK, good. I'd really appreciate that.'

'Enough to let me take you home?'

'No. It's too late for that. If my dad wants to believe whatever bullshit my brothers tell him, that's his business. I'm not going to be forced into a marriage I don't want, just to please them. I've had enough. I'm not going back.'

He didn't blame her, even had sympathy for her situation – but he had to push all that to one side. *He still had to find her.*

'Your dad's well pissed off about you running away with this Kasim bloke. He's real mad.'

'He can blame my brothers then. It's all their doing. They didn't leave me any choice.'

'Nina said Kasim warned you what was going to happen and helped you get away. What if you told your dad that's all there was between you?'

'It won't make any difference. He won't believe me and he'll still be angry because I've left home. It won't change his mind about the marriage either.'

'But if he knows the stuff about you and Kasim was just made up, it might calm him down a bit.'

'I doubt it. Even if he believes my brothers lied about it – which he won't because it'll just be my word against theirs – it would only make him angrier, at them as well as me.'

'Better at them than at me.'

'What's any of this got to do with you?'

'Nothing, except he's told me to find you. If I don't, I'm in deep shit.'

'Does it have anything to do with you being in prison?' *So she knew about that.* 'Has he threatened you, so you'll do what he wants? You're not the first person he's done that to.'

'Listen, what if *I* go see your dad, tell him about your brothers and Kasim?'

'He'll never believe you – that's if he even *listens* to you.'

'What if you tell him too? You could phone him…' She didn't respond. 'It might be better for both of us if your dad's angry at someone else, like your brothers.'

'Will you stop looking for me then?'

'I doubt it. Even if he's pissed off at your brothers, he'll still want you found.'

'Then what difference will it make?'

'You want me to help Davinder, don't you?' He kept quiet about wanting to find Davinder for his own reasons anyway.

'How do I know you're really going to help him?'

'You can ask him yourself after I get him out.'

She seemed to consider for a moment, then said, 'All right, I'll talk to my dad – for all the good it'll do.'

'Might be better if I talk to him first, then I'll call you and you can talk to him too.'

'If he hasn't thrown you out of his office by then,' she said. 'And how're you planning to call me? You don't have my number.'

'You better let me have it.'

'And why would I do that?'

'I ain't asking you to tell me where you are. Getting in touch with you will at least look like I've made some progress, which'll help me out with your dad. And if I'm helping Davinder, I want something in return.'

'All right, I'll give you the number – but just so you know, it's a pay-as-you-go phone. If anyone else calls me, I'll get rid of it and I won't talk to you again.'

He took out his own phone and entered the number she gave him. He saved it under the name BARNEY RUBBLE – cockney rhyming slang for TROUBLE, which is what she was proving to be. 'Has Davinder got this number?'

'No. Why?

''Cause if he has, he'll have given it to your brothers by now. Any of those guys call you, it's nothing to do with me. Just so you know. OK, I'm ringing you now so you can save my number to your phone.' Once that was done, he put his phone away and continued talking to her on Nina's.

'What exactly am I supposed to say to my dad when I talk to him?' she asked.

'Tell him the truth – that Kasim's a mate of Raj and Parm's, that they let him see you and didn't try to stop him, just so they could use it against you. Mention they beat the shit out of him too and you were scared they were going to do the same to you.'

'I'm not scared of –'

''Course you're not, but it'll sound better if you say you were.'

She gave it some thought, then said, 'Fine. You help Davinder, I'll help you – but what happens after?

'What d'you mean?'

'You'll still be looking for me, won't you?'

'If that's what your dad wants, I ain't got a choice.'

'Because he's threatening you? What if I made it worth your while *not* to look for me? How about ten thousand pounds to tell him you couldn't find me?'

Was she serious? 'Where would you get that sort of money?'

'You think I left home without any money? I've been saving to leave for ages.'

It was a lot of money. But weighed against five years in prison it wasn't so much. He could always take the money and *still* grass her up to her old man when he found out where she was. But no, he knew he'd never do anything that low. He did have *some* principles, after all. 'No, I can't…'

'All right, how about twenty thousand?'

Twenty grand? It was almost a year's take home pay for him. But what good would it be if he was banged up? Selling his freedom for four grand a year just wasn't worth it. 'I can't take your money and I don't want it.'

'Can't blame me for trying,' she said.

'I don't.' Someone with less to lose might well have taken up on her offer.

'All right, so… about Davinder? When will I be able to talk to him?'

'Later on tonight – *if* he's there and I get him out.'

'And what if he isn't?'

'I know who took him. I'll just have to watch them till they lead me to him.'

'But you still want me to talk to my dad tomorrow?'

He could hear the sarcasm in her voice. 'I can always leave him where he is and let them carry on doing whatever they're doing to him.'

'All right, fine, I'll talk to him – but I'm going to call you later to find out about Davinder.'

'OK.'

'Can you hand me back to Nina?'

He handed Nina her phone back. 'She wants to talk to you again.'

Nina took the phone and listened for a moment. She glanced at Zaq then turned away to talk in private. It was a short conversation and when it was over she had an odd look on her face. 'She's worried.'

'She should be, with that lot after her.'

'Davinder getting taken, what happened to me tonight – she didn't expect any of that.'

'I bet.' Zaq gestured toward the pub. 'Come on, I'll buy you that drink.' Nina seemed unsure, nervous. 'You look like you could do with one.'

CHAPTER TWENTY-ONE

The pub interior was low-ceilinged and dark-panelled, but had a burnished glow that made even the shadows seem warm and inviting. Zaq bought Nina a white wine and decided against anything stronger than a lager shandy for himself. They took their drinks over to a table by one of the windows. Zaq noticed that Nina was stealing glances at him and averting her eyes whenever he looked in her direction.

'Something wrong?' he asked.

'No. It's just... something Rita mentioned...' She looked at him. 'She told me you just got out of prison.'

'About nine months ago.'

'And you were in for...' she hesitated, 'murder.'

Zaq shook his head. 'It wasn't murder. Murder's when you set out to kill someone on purpose. I didn't. I was in for manslaughter.'

'But you did... kill someone?'

'He died, yeah... but I never meant for that to happen. It was totally unintentional.'

'How did it happen? Sorry, I understand if you don't want

to talk about...'

'It's fine.' He'd talked about it plenty when he first got out. Everyone had wanted to know what happened, about getting sent down and what prison had been like. Most guys saw him as some kind of hard case, an Asian anti-hero, who didn't take no shit, stood his ground and did his time. They had a romanticised view of the whole thing, taken from too many movies and TV shows. They didn't want to know about the reality of it, how a single act of violence had totally fucked up his life. They just wanted the action scenes without any boring or emotional bits. Eventually, he got fed up with telling people who weren't really listening, who only wanted the edited highlights. There were no highlights though – the whole episode had been the lowest point in his life. And so, he hadn't spoken about it for a long time. But now, if Nina was interested, he would tell her...

'I was at a pub in Ealing one night with some friends when this guy started an argument. He was drunk. I was trying to calm things down and all of a sudden he tells me to fuck off and smacks me in the face. His mates steamed in and it all kicked off. He went to hit me again. I didn't think about it, I just hit him back. He went down and then the doormen were there breaking it all up.'

'Sounds like you were just defending yourself.'

'I was. But, turns out the guy I hit had what's called an intracranial aneurysm.' It was a medical term Zaq would never forget. 'It's a swelling of a blood vessel in the brain. He could've had it for a while. I hit him, he went down, bumped his head and the aneurysm burst. That's what killed him.'

'It burst because you hit him, or because he bumped his head?'

'That's the thing, no one knows for sure. It could even have burst on its own. It was just waiting to happen. But I hit him and the prosecution said *that's* what led to everything else.'

Zaq's own barrister had argued that the victim, Suresh Dutta, 24, could have died at any time from a rupture of the aneurysm and that anything might have caused it – bumping into a door, heading a football, banging his head under a table. It could even have burst under its own pressure. 'If he hadn't had the aneurysm he would've been OK. The punch, the fall, the bump to his head, none of them would've killed him. Only he did have it. Even if I hadn't hit him, he would probably still have died, maybe not that night but the next, or the one after that.'

'But you did hit him.'

'Yeah, and that changed everything. It was bad luck.'

'Someone *died* and you just see it as bad luck?'

'I've had a lot of time to think about it. I didn't start the fight, it was self-defence. If he hadn't been drunk and looking for trouble, none of it would have happened and I wouldn't have had to spend five years behind bars.'

'But if it wasn't your fault, why did you go to prison for it?'

'There was a lot of drunken violence and gang trouble in the news at the time and the judge wanted to set an example. So, even though I claimed self-defence and pled guilty, and it was my first offence, he gave me the maximum sentence he could – five years.'

Everything had changed in that moment, when he'd heard the sentence pronounced. It had been a gut-wrenching experience, one he'd never forget. 'The guy's family didn't help matters,' he went on. 'Yeah, they were upset and understandably so, but they wouldn't accept he was even partly to blame for starting what happened. I wrote to them, to explain it all and tell them I was sorry he died, but they didn't give a toss about any of that, or for the facts of the case either – or even the medical evidence. He was dead and they wanted me done for murder and given a life sentence.

'I never wanted him dead though. He was the instigator. I was defending myself. It was an instinctive reaction. I've been over it again and again and in that same situation, someone attacking me, there's nothing I would've done any differently.'

'You could've just walked away.'

Zaq shook his head. 'Easy to say in hindsight. But I would've had to think about it to make that decision and it all happened too fast. I just reacted the most natural way I knew. Besides, it'd take a bigger man than me to just walk away from something like that. I don't think I could.'

'Violence never solves anything.'

'It seemed to solve what happened earlier – or should I have just walked away and let them bundle you into that car?'

'That's different…'

'How?'

She didn't answer.

Zaq saw her cheeks redden. 'So, what you're saying is, when some drunk guy smacks me in the mouth, I should just walk away, but when someone grabs you, it's OK to lay them out, is that it? Sounds a bit hypocritical to me.'

Nina was still blushing. 'You're right. I'm sorry.'

'Don't worry about it.' They sipped their drinks. 'I don't know what sort of impression you've got of me,' Zaq said, 'but I don't go round looking for trouble.' Her eyes moved over the cuts and bruises on his face and her eyebrows rose a fraction. 'What can I say? Trouble's finding me at the moment.'

'OK…'

They worked on their drinks for a while. It was Nina who eventually broke the silence. 'How long were you in prison for?'

'Five years.'

'I thought they let people out a bit earlier, for good behaviour or that sort of thing?'

He nodded. 'They do, only...' He shrugged. 'My behaviour wasn't that good.'

'Oh...?' There was a question there, even though she didn't ask it.

'I had trouble with some guys while I was inside.'

'More trouble?'

'Yeah. There was one bunch, didn't agree with my religious views – or rather, my lack of them.'

'But aren't you a –'

'Muslim? No. I'm an atheist.'

'That explains you being in a pub having a drink. I did wonder. It's not very Islamic.'

'Yeah, that's me and it's what they had a problem with. I ain't got any issue with anyone practising their religion, I just don't believe in it myself. They weren't exactly live and let live types, more do or die – as in, *do* what we say or *die*. They made it their mission to rectify my thinking or make me pay for it. I wasn't up for either.'

'Couldn't you have told someone about it?'

'No. There are rules in prison, unofficial ones. Main one being, you never grass. It's one of the worst things you can do. You ever watch any of those nature documentaries on TV? David Attenborough, that sort of stuff? You know when there's a group of lions, the males fight to show the others who's boss, who not to mess with. Well, it's like that in prison too – law of the jungle. If you're pushed, you have to fight, to show that no one messes with you, then you get left alone, for the most part at least, until some other guy wants to try it on.'

'That's why you got in trouble?'

'Yeah. It's what happens when you got a couple of hundred guys all banged up together – anger, frustration, testosterone, it all boils over. Tempers flare, guys fight. Just how it is.'

'Was that your problem? Anger, frustration and testosterone?'

'I guess, at first. I soon realised it wouldn't change anything though – wouldn't do me any good either. I was lucky, I managed to find a way to deal with it.'

'How?'

'I started training with a group of guys in the prison gym. Mixed martial arts, street fighting, that kind of thing.'

'Wait, you dealt with your anger and frustration by fighting? How is that any different?'

'It wasn't just about fighting, there was more to it than that. The training, the discipline, the perfecting of technique… it was about mental toughness as much as it was physical, maybe even more so. I'd walk out of that gym leaving my anger and frustration there, on the mats and bags. Trouble is, place like that, there's always someone looking for a fight, wanting to prove themselves, show how tough they are.'

'But if you left your aggression in the gym, why were you still getting into fights?'

'Prison's a bit like being in Southall – you back out of a fight, everyone knows about it and then they think they can push you round too, give you shit. Same thing inside. It was usually other Asian guys, some Middle Eastern, who wanted to make an impression. They'd start something, so I'd have to fight them. With all the training I was doing, I could usually keep it short and sweet, but sometimes the other guy would know how to fight too and things would get out of hand. We'd both end up hurt and the screws would have to break it up. No matter what happened, no one grassed. We'd both get punishment for fighting. I just happened to get done for it a lot, so I was tagged an unruly prisoner and had time added onto my sentence.'

Nina was fascinated. 'Wouldn't you rather have avoided

trouble and got out sooner?' she said.

''Course I would – but time's strange inside. If you're taking shit from everyone, five years can seem like a life sentence; but if you're left alone and can make the best of it, the same five years can end up feeling like less. I didn't fight because I enjoyed it. I did it because I had to, to survive and make the time more bearable. Same way I didn't fight those guys tonight because I wanted to or because I liked it, I did it because it was the only thing I could do. Though if I'm honest, I don't feel too bad about what happened to them.'

'Neither do I,' Nina said, with just the hint of a smile.

His openness and honesty seemed to have put her at ease and talking about his time inside had taken her mind off what had happened earlier. The wine had probably helped too. It was nice, sitting with her and talking, despite the circumstances that had brought them there.

They finished their drinks. Zaq would have been happy to get another round and stay longer but he still had things to do and somewhere else to be. He wondered if she'd stay if he asked, or make an excuse and leave? Should he see if she'd like to meet up again sometime? He thought about it but in the end chickened out. With everything that was going on, maybe it wasn't such a good idea. They got ready to leave.

'I'll take a look outside first,' Zaq said, 'make sure no one's waiting for us.'

When he was sure there was nothing to worry about, he signalled to Nina and walked her to her car. She opened the door, then turned to him. 'Thanks again for what you did earlier. I don't know what would've happened if you didn't come out when you did.'

'Try not to think about it. We got out of there and you're OK, that's the main thing. Focus on that. Be careful if you're out on your own, at least until this whole Rita thing's sorted out.'

She got into the car and was about to close the door when Zaq said, 'Listen, if anything happens or you're worried about something, just give me a call OK? Any time. You've got my number.'

'Thanks.' She gave him a smile.

'See you round,' he said.

She hesitated, as if about to say something, then seemed to change her mind and pulled the door shut. She started the engine, turned the car around and gave him wave as she drove off.

He watched her car disappear round the bend, wondering if she'd call... hoping that she would.

CHAPTER TWENTY-TWO

It was almost eight o'clock. Zaq called Jags to make sure he had the three hundred pounds. He did, so Zaq drove to his place to pick it up. After the fight at the Hare & Hounds, he was even more paranoid about being followed and kept a sharp lookout for anyone on his tail. He parked a street away and walked from there to Jags' house.

'What happened?' Jags said. 'I thought you'd be back ages ago.'

Zaq told him about the meeting with Parm and the others at the builders' yard, and how Jhutti and Chadha had followed him afterwards. He also told him how he managed to get rid of them.

Jags laughed, then got worried. 'You think they'll know it was down to you?'

Zaq shrugged. 'Doubt it. And even if they do suspect something, I was right there the whole time. Anyone could've taken their truck.'

'That's too funny, man,' Jags said. 'So...? How was your date with Nina?'

'It wasn't a date – and it went a bit off the rails.' Zaq explained how he'd met Nina and told her about Davinder's abduction. 'She went outside to call Rita… and that's when she got grabbed by some guys. I think it was the same ones that jumped me on Monday. They tried to drag her into a car.' Zaq described the fight in the car park.

'Bloody hell, who the fuck're you, Rambo? Ain't you got enough lumps and bumps already?'

'What was I supposed to do? Let them take her?'

'You at least get a better look at them this time? Recognise any of them?'

'I'm not sure. I might've seen one of them before but I don't know where.'

'What did you do after that?'

'Got the fuck out of there. We went to the London Apprentice. Nina called Rita back when we got there – those fuckers grabbed her while she was on the phone to her – and I spoke to her too.'

'You talked to Rita? You find out where she is?'

'Yeah, she gave me the address, told me to pop over for tea and crumpets. What d'you think?'

'I didn't know you liked crumpets. So, what did you talk about?'

'Just general stuff about what's going on. I was trying to get her to trust me, enough that I might learn something about where she is.' Jags didn't look convinced. 'And then she tried to buy me off.' He told Jags about the money Rita had offered.

'Maybe you should've taken it.'

'And done what with it? Won't do me a lot of good if I get banged up again, will it? Plus, if her brothers find her and she tells them about the money, you think they'd let me keep it? Forget the money. I couldn't take it, then tell her old man where she is – it wouldn't be right.'

'But making her go back to a forced marriage is?'

'Come on, man, what else can I do? I have to do what her old man wants, otherwise I'm fucked. I don't like it any more than you do.'

'Yeah, it's a shitty situation,' Jags conceded.

'I got her number though. Going to call her tomorrow, get her to talk to her old man. Least it'll show the old git I've made some progress, hopefully buy me some more time to find her.'

'You reckon?'

Zaq shrugged. 'You know anyone that can track a phone signal?'

'I don't work for the CIA, you know.'

'Just a thought. Can you grab me a couple of painkillers? I don't think all that effort in the car park's done me any good.' Jags went to the kitchen for some ibuprofen and a glass of water. Zaq took the tablets and put the glass down on the coffee table. 'Thanks. You got the cash? I better make a move.'

'Yep.' Jags left the lounge and came back with his jacket on and a wad of twenties in his hand. 'Here you go.'

'Thanks.' Zaq put the money in his pocket. 'Where are you going?'

'I'm coming with you.'

'No, you ain't. You're better off staying here.'

'You're the one who's supposed to be keeping out of trouble. And as I'm funding this little outing, I'm coming, whether you like it or not. Besides, you might need some help.'

'Looking around a warehouse?'

'A warehouse you're paying someone to break into for you.'

Zaq could see Jags was serious about coming and he didn't have time to argue. 'OK, let's go, else we'll be late.'

Jags locked the front door and deactivated the alarm on his BMW.

'What you doing?' Zaq said.

'How else we going to get there?'

'In the van.'

'Shut up.'

'We ain't going shopping at Harrods. We're going to break into a warehouse on an industrial estate. Someone might notice your motor but no one'll look twice at the van.'

Jags gave him a sullen look and reactivated the alarm. 'Where d'you park that piece of junk anyway?'

'Next street over.' Zaq fished the keys from his pocket and jangled them in front of Jags. 'If it makes you feel better, I'll let you drive.'

The majority of customers in the Scotsman were young, Asian and male. A few turned to look Zaq and Jags over as they entered, but then went back to what they were doing. It was still busy; the second half of the football was on. Zaq spotted Biri at a table with a white guy.

'All right?' Biri greeted them. His companion was in his early thirties, trim, with short sandy hair and blue eyes. 'This is Mark.'

'How you doing?' Zaq stuck out his hand and they shook. 'And this is Jags, he's coming along.'

Jags exchanged greetings with Mark and Biri, then asked if anyone wanted a drink.

'Nice one, I'll have a Stella, please,' Biri said.

'Mark?'

'I'm OK, thanks.' He had an almost full pint in front of him. 'Zaq?'

'I'll have a Diet Coke. I'm driving.'

'Well, I ain't, so I'm having a pint too.' He went to the bar.

Zaq sat down. 'What happened after I left?' he asked Biri.

'Jhutti and Chadha came charging back in, well pissed off.

They didn't have a clue who'd moved the truck, or even if it was anyone from here. They just gave everyone dirty looks then fucked off again.'

'Where'd Rav leave it?'

'Up the street, facing the other way. He had a look later and it was gone, so I guess they found it.'

'Must've confused the shit out of them.' Zaq turned to Mark. 'Sorry, just something that happened earlier. Biri's told you what I need?'

Mark nodded. 'I should be able to get you in, no problem. What you do after that's your business.'

'What about once we're done? Any way we can lock up and reset everything?'

Mark shook his head. 'I'll get you in, but I ain't going to hang about. I can give you the code to reset the alarm yourself but without keys it'll be a pain in the arse to re-lock the door. And it'll cost extra.'

Resetting the alarm would have to do. It might just look as though someone had forgotten to lock the door behind them. If Davinder was there and they managed to get him out, they wouldn't even have to bother resetting the alarm. It would look as if Davinder had somehow managed to disable it himself and escaped.

Jags came back with the drinks, set them down on the table and took the seat next to Mark.

'And you want to do it tonight?' Mark said to Zaq.

'I thought we'd go after we finish these.'

Mark looked at his watch. 'We should wait. Biri told me it's on an industrial estate.'

'That's right.'

'With other factories and businesses around it?' Zaq nodded. 'If we leave in a bit, it'll be coming up to ten o'clock. That's when most night shifts start. If there's anywhere round there that works nights, there'll be people coming and going. We don't want an audience, so we're better off waiting till about ten thirty when everything should've quietened down.'

It made sense. 'OK.'

'You got the money?' Zaq nodded and put his hand in his pocket. 'Not here. Outside, when we leave.'

'Cool.'

'Just so we're straight, all I'm doing is getting you in, then I'm gone. Anything happens after that, we've never met.'

With time to kill, they watched the end of the match and got another round in. Mark switched to Diet Coke, Biri and Jags stuck with lager. Just after half past ten Mark said, 'Should be all right to go now.' The three of them shook hands with Biri and left the pub.

'Where you parked?' Mark asked.

Zaq pointed out the blue van.

'I'm over there, white Astra van.' Mark jerked his thumb in the opposite direction. 'Come over with me. I'll drop you to your van.'

Zaq gave his keys to Jags. 'You might as well go wait in it.'

'Lucky me.'

In Mark's van, Zaq took out the money. 'Two sixty... two eighty... three hundred.'

'OK, thanks.' Mark folded the notes and stuffed them in his pocket, then drove over to the blue van. 'I'll follow you,' he said as Zaq got out, 'so make sure you don't lose me.'

'Don't worry, ain't much chance in that thing.'

Mark looked at the van. 'I see what you mean.'

They pulled up a short distance from the Brars' unit. There were no cars outside unit 12 and no lights on inside. Zaq got out and asked Mark if they should leave their vehicles where they were or drive up to the unit.

'No. Let's park by the entrance, give ourselves some cover. Anyone asks, there's a problem with the alarm and you've called me out to fix it. We'll attract less attention if we act like we're meant to be here.'

Zaq drove over to the main entrance. The security light over the shutter came on. Zaq parked close enough to the front door that the van would cast its shadow over them. He and Jags got out.

Mark joined them, carrying a small canvas tool bag. 'Might be an idea to put some gloves on,' he said. He was wearing black latex surgical gloves himself.

Jags pulled out a pair of leather driving gloves. 'I brought some, just in case.'

It hadn't even crossed Zaq's mind. He recalled seeing a pair of old work gloves in the van somewhere and found them jammed behind the driver's seat. Mark was kneeling in front of the door with the bag open beside him. 'Let me know if anyone's coming,' he said.

The lock picking equipment looked familiar from TV shows Zaq had seen, but he had no idea what the electronic device with wires and clips was. He watched what Mark was doing but it looked like he was just wiggling the picks around. Then he heard a click, followed by the sound of Mark letting out a breath.

'That's the first one done.' Mark selected a couple of different picks and moved on to the second lock. He got it open just as fast. 'We're in.' They heard a beeping sound from inside. 'Wait here.' Mark grabbed his tools and hurried in to deal with the alarm. The door swung closed and muffled the sound of the beeping.

'What if he can't do it?' Jags said.

'Then we get the fuck out of here.'

Zaq wondered how long they had to enter the code before the alarm went off. Seconds seemed like minutes as they stood there. He was so tense, waiting, that it took him a moment to realise the beeping had stopped.

Mark opened the door and held it for them. 'The code's 1664,' he said, 'like the beer.'

'Huh?'

'Kronenbourg 1664. Right, I'm off.' And with a quick nod, he went to his van, got in and drove away.

Zaq and Jags went inside. The locks weren't damaged. It didn't even look as if they'd been tampered with. Zaq shut the door and heard the upper mortice lock engage. 'OK, let's look around.'

There was enough light coming in through the windows for them to see they were in a short corridor. The alarm panel was on the wall to the right. It didn't look like it had been touched either. On the left was an office. Zaq ducked his head in and saw a desk, a few chairs and some filing cabinets, the usual stuff – but no sign of Davinder. Next to the office was a kitchenette, and then some toilets. At the far end of the corridor there was another door. They went and looked through the window in it and saw nothing, only complete darkness. There was no lock so Zaq pulled it open and went through, Jags right behind him.

'Find the light switches,' Zaq said. They ran their hands over the walls on either side of the door.

'I think I've got them,' Jags said. 'Shall I turn them on?'

'That's the idea.'

Rows of fluorescent lights blinked on, high above their heads. There were pallets everywhere, bags of plaster and cement piled on them. Zaq also saw there was paint, timber and plasterboard stacked there too. Further back there were some cement mixers, along with some heavy duty rollers and rammers. Away to the left, against the wall, a metal staircase ran up to a mezzanine level that housed what looked like another, larger office enclosed by partition walls. A large window looked down on the warehouse but all Zaq could see in it was the reflection of the warehouse lights. 'What the hell is all this?' he said, moving between the pallets, searching for any sign of Davinder.

Jags was walking parallel to him, one pallet over. 'Looks like building materials.'

'I can see that – but what's it all doing here? Don't make sense when their old man's got a yard full of the stuff back in Southall.'

'Maybe it's overstock.'

'I've never been asked to pick up anything from here.'

'Maybe it fell off the back of a lorry –'

'Fucking big lorry.'

'– and they don't want their old man to know about it? Who cares? How much you reckon this lot's worth anyway?' He slapped a bag of cement on top of the nearest pallet – only to be engulfed by a cloud of grey powder that exploded from it. 'Fucking hell, it's only bloody open.'

'You twat.' It would have been funny any other time but not then. The powder began to settle and Jags gradually became visible again, covered in a fine grey dust. 'You look like a fucking ghost.'

'Bollocks.' There was a soft hissing sound as cement powder poured from the open bag onto the floor. There were several large clumps in the spill.

'Look at the fucking mess you've made!'

Jags moved away from the pallet and began to pat himself down. It only raised more clouds of dust and made him cough.

'You're spreading the shit all over the place. Wait there. I'll see if I can find anything to clear it up with.' Zaq went back to the front door and looked out the window. There was nobody around, so he went into the kitchenette and turned on the light. He found a broom and a dustpan and brush. 'Here,' he said, back in the warehouse, holding them out to Jags.

'Ain't you going to help? My jacket's fucked.'

'I'm going to check upstairs. Get as much of that cement off you as you can, then tidy this crap up and have a look round down here. And try not to touch anything else. You better hope it ain't raining when we get outside.'

Jags sneezed, the sound echoing in the large open space of the warehouse. 'This powder's getting right up my bloody nose.'

'Like you're getting up mine.'

Jags showed him a dust-covered middle finger.

Zaq left him to it and made his way up the metal staircase. At the top, he found a door set in a plain white partition wall. He tried it and found it unlocked. It opened onto a small hallway. He crossed to another door and that was unlocked too. The Brars must've been pretty confident in their alarm system. He walked into a large office, the fluorescents from the warehouse shone through the big window and lit up the room. There was a sofa to the right under the window, a coffee table in front of it. Opposite, against the left wall there was a large flatscreen TV. The far end of the room was dominated by a mahogany shelving unit, in front of which stood a massive mahogany desk, with a padded leather office chair. A computer and a printer sat on the desk, along with a phone and some paper trays. Two armchairs faced the desk, the type you saw in offices rather than homes. Zaq took a look around, but there was no sign of Davinder here either.

He went back downstairs. There was still a pile of cement on the floor but no sign of Jags. He heard movement and saw him coming his way between the pallets in just his sweatshirt. 'Where's your jacket?'

'Cement dust kept making me sneeze, so I took it off. It's by the door.'

'Make sure you don't forget it.'

'Don't worry, I won't.'

'I thought you were clearing this shit up.' Zaq nodded at the mess on the floor.

'I was – till I found this.' Jags picked up what looked like a large clump of cement powder. Zaq expected it to break up and pour through his fingers like fine sand but it didn't. It was solid. 'Here.' Jags tossed it to him.

Zaq caught it in a puff of dust. He wiped the surface with a gloved hand. It was a package, about the size of a bag of flour, wrapped in thick clear plastic and secured with packing tape. Under the grey dust and the cloudiness of the plastic, the contents looked brown. He had a bad feeling. 'What is it?'

'It sure as fuck ain't sugar. I had a sniff. I think it's heroin.'

'How d'you know what heroin smells like?'

'That shit's everywhere in Southall. You get to know the smell. Besides, if it ain't heroin, why's it hidden in a bag of cement?' Jags pulled two more packages out of the bag. 'Look, there's loads of it.'

Zaq recalled the bag of cement the Brars had given Jhutti and Chadha in the pub car park and the two the guy in the grey BMW had picked up. Suddenly, the warehouse made sense – they were using it as a drug stash and dealing smack right out the door – and here he and Jags were, standing slap bang in the middle of it.

'That ain't all,' Jags continued. 'After I found this stuff, I started looking around and came across something else. Over here.' Jags led the way to a smaller pallet, off to one side. Instead of cement, it was stacked with bags of plaster. There were a couple of bags on the floor, opened but with the tops scrunched and rolled closed. Jags unrolled one and held it open.

Inside, covered in the reddish brown powder, Zaq saw more plastic-wrapped bundles. 'More gear?'

'Look closer.'

Zaq pulled one out. It was wrapped in plastic, same as the heroin, only the contents weren't brown. They were blue and purple and had the Queen's face on them. 'Bloody hell. How much is in here?'

'You're holding about five grand. That bag was already open; there's about thirty grand in there.' Zaq dropped the money back in. 'But there's close to a hundred grand in this other one.'

'A hundred grand?' There were six bags on the pallet and another two on the floor. 'There could be over three-quarters of a million pounds here.'

'The other bags are properly stitched shut though. They look totally legit. I think one of those machines back there is to stitch them closed.'

'That'd make sense. You check the rest of the place?'

'I'd just got this far when I heard you coming down.'

'OK, put the money back–'

'*Put it back?*'

'Yeah.'

'Why don't we take some? It's just sitting here. Don't tell me you couldn't use a little.'

'They'll notice it's gone. Then they'll wonder who took it.'

'So? They won't know it was us.'

'Don't matter. They're already suspicious of me. I don't want to give them any more reason to watch me closer.'

'I can't believe you're going to pass up all this cash.'

'What I'm passing up is trouble. I got enough of that to worry about as it is. Now let's finish looking for Davinder so we can get the fuck out of here.'

Jags looked thoughtful for a moment but didn't say anything. He put the money back in the bag and they continued searching amongst the pallets, boxes and machinery – but there was no sign of Davinder.

'*Fuck*. He ain't here,' Zaq said. 'All right, let's go.' He started walking but only got as far as the cement piled on the floor. 'Shit, we still got to clear this mess up.'

He grabbed the broom and started sweeping the cement into a pile. Jags scooped it up in the dustpan and poured it back into the bag. They shoved the bricks of heroin in and covered them, then lifted the bag carefully on top of the pallet.

'Don't forget your jacket.'

'I wasn't about to.'

They turned out the lights, put away the dustpan and broom, and were about to leave when Zaq stopped.

'What?' Jags said.

'We were only looking for Davinder but his stuff's here somewhere. I should've checked upstairs properly.' He fished out the van keys and gave them to Jags. 'You go wait in the van. I'm going to go back up and see if I can find anything. Call me if anyone comes.'

Zaq didn't want to be in the warehouse any longer than he had to but at least now Jags was outside acting as lookout.

CHAPTER TWENTY-THREE

Zaq made his way up to the office again. Jhutti and Chadha had brought Davinder's stuff here and hadn't take it away, so chances were it was still here somewhere. Maybe there'd be a clue with his things as to where they had him, or else he might find some other scrap of information up here that would tell him.

He searched the shelf unit against the far wall, then sat in the padded chair behind the desk and looked at the paperwork in the trays. It was mainly invoices and delivery notes for building supplies, addressed to a company called PJD ENTERPRISES. It looked like they were buying the stuff legit. So they were probably opening the bags, hiding the drugs inside then sealing them up again. A warehouse full of building supplies and people moving bags of cement wouldn't raise much suspicion. Zaq wondered if surrounding the bricks of heroin in cement dust would help mask its scent from sniffer dogs?

He searched through the papers for anything addressed to Rajinder or Parminder Brar, any physical proof that could link them to the warehouse and what was in it, but the only name that cropped up was Subash Prewal, whoever the fuck that was. The Brars were being careful. Zaq decided to take a couple of the invoices anyway, in case they came in handy for anything later, and stuffed them in a pocket. If nothing else, they had the address of the place.

The drawers on the left of the desk were unlocked, but there was nothing of interest in them. The ones on the right though were locked. He looked around for a key, checking under the large blotter on the desk but there was nothing there. The desk tidy was full of bits and pieces but no key. The only other things on the desk were the printer and the computer. He lifted up the keyboard... and discovered a small metal key. When he tried it in the lock, it slid right in.

The top drawer was full of the usual junk – pens, paperclips, rubber bands, notepads. The second drawer contained a small white box and a grubby grey cloth. The name WINCHESTER was emblazoned on the box in red. The first thing that popped into Zaq's head was an image of a Winchester rifle, familiar from TV westerns. Above the name was a logo, a cowboy on a galloping horse, with the words 'MADE IN USA', surrounded by a circle and some stars. On the side of the box he read, '9MM LUGER' and '50 ROUNDS'. He noticed that the grey cloth was wrapped around something, its ends tucked underneath. Zaq peeled the cloth away and sat staring at the dull black metal of a handgun. What the hell were the Brars doing with a gun? Had they ever used the thing?

He wanted to be there even less now. If the cops turned up and caught him – with a handgun on the premises – he'd be totally screwed. He re-wrapped it, careful not to touch the gun even though he had gloves on, and put it back the way he'd found it. He closed the drawer and took a deep breath to steady himself. He just had to look around a little bit more and then he could get the fuck out of there. He tried to put the gun out of his mind and opened the bottom drawer.

And there was Davinder's brown and blue laptop bag. There were dark patches where something had been spilled on it, staining the light blue areas a rusty brown. He unzipped the main compartment and took out a laptop computer. There was a yellow Post-it note stuck on the top, on which was written:

DPanesar

L1verpOOlfc

It looked like a username and password. Davinder must have given them up.

Zaq opened the laptop and turned it on. When the log-in screen appeared, he typed in the details from the Post-it. It wasn't easy to type with work gloves on but he didn't want to leave any prints in the warehouse, especially after finding the gun. Once he was in, he searched the icons at the bottom of the screen for an email program. There was one for Gmail. He double clicked it and a browser window opened that by-passed the Gmail log-in, and took him right to Davinder's email account.

There was a list of folders on the left. One was marked PERSONAL. He clicked on the arrow beside it and a list of sub folders dropped down, among them FAMILY, FOOTBALL and MATES. The one that really grabbed Zaq's attention was titled RITA.

He clicked on the folder and saw a long list of messages – the most recent only a few days old. So Davinder had lied when he said he hadn't heard from Rita in three months. He'd been in regular contact with her up until a few days ago. There were hundreds of messages from her. It wasn't a huge surprise. Why should Davinder have told him the truth?

He didn't have time to go through every message and decided to focus on the latest ones, to see if there was anything useful in them. Raj and Parm had surely done the same. The most recent read:

```
Subject: A Little Trouble
Hi hon,
Things have gotten messed up. I'm trying to get
everything sorted out. Will be in touch v. soon.
Just be ready.
Love you,
Rita xxx
```

Ready for what? It didn't really tell him anything. Zaq clicked on the next message, which had been sent a couple of days earlier.

```
Subject: Leaving Home
Hi hon,
I've had to leave home. A friend is helping me.
I just need to sort out a few things then we
can leave together and not have to worry about
anything anymore. I might not be able to email
you for a little while. Please just trust me and
be patient. I'm doing this for us.
See you soon.
Lots of love,
Rita xxx
```

Leave together? Zaq read the message again. So, Rita and Davinder *had* been planning to go off with each other all along. He noticed she'd been very vague about the friend who was helping her. Davinder probably wouldn't have been thrilled about her being with Kasim, whatever the reason.

The next mail was from a few days before:

```
Subject: Good News
Hon,
I have to be quick - but good news! I think things
are going to work out. I should be able to get
it in a few days and then we can get away from
here, just the two of us. Can't wait to see you.
Lots of love,
Rita xxxx
```

What was the '*it*' she was referring to? A passport? A visa? A plane ticket? One thing was clear – she and Davinder had been planning a getaway for some time. She hadn't told him where she was because of Kasim, but once she'd sorted out whatever she needed to, she and Davinder would have been off.

A sudden jolt made Zaq jump. It took him a second to realise his phone was vibrating in his pocket. It was Jags calling. He answered. 'Is someone here?'

'No. I was wondering what's keeping you. You found him?'

'No.'

'Then what you doing up there?'

'I found his laptop, with his log-in details. I'm looking through his emails. There's loads from Rita.'

'She say where she is?'

'No...'

'Then what's the point? Leave it and let's go.'

Jags was right. How much longer did he want to stay there, with a gun in the drawer and a warehouse full of heroin and cash?

'All right, just let me put this stuff away and I'll be out.' He hung up and started shutting down the laptop. He doubted he'd have found out much more from the emails anyway – Rita had been very guarded about what she wrote, not giving anything away.

Waiting for the computer to shut down, he opened the side pocket of the laptop bag and found a mobile phone. It had to be Davinder's. The battery and SIM card had been taken out but were there with it. He also pulled out a power adaptor, some computer cables, a few letters and a security pass with Davinder's name and photo on it.

He kept the pass and the letters and shoved the rest of the stuff back in the pocket. The laptop finished shutting down and he slipped it back in the bag, which he returned to the drawer. He locked it and replaced the key under the keyboard where he'd found it. Then he got up from the chair and looked around the office for a likely spot...

The *sofa* – that would do. He went over and jammed Davinder's pass down between the seats, then slid the letters as far under the sofa as he could. There was hardly any space between the sofa and the floor, so they wouldn't be seen – not unless someone decided to rearrange the furniture. Satisfied, he turned off the lights and made his way down the stairs.

He turned off the warehouse lights too and went through to the corridor that led to the front door. He keyed in 1-6-6-4 on the control panel to reset the alarm. The system began to beep a warning tone. He probably had about 30 seconds to get out, which he did, pulling the door firmly shut behind him. The spring latch engaged but he had no way to turn the dead bolt. Hopefully, the Brars would think they'd forgotten to lock it themselves. He got in the van.

'About time,' Jags said. 'It's bloody freezing out here.'

'Why don't you put your jacket on?'

'And choke on cement dust? Let's just go.'

Zaq started the van and they drove away. He watched the warehouse recede in his rear-view mirror and thought about what they'd found inside; *heroin, cash and a gun*. Not a good mix. He thought about the emails too, about Rita and Davinder – and he wondered whether the stains on the laptop bag could have been blood.

CHAPTER TWENTY-FOUR

They didn't talk as they drove through Hayes. Zaq was thinking about what they'd found in the warehouse and Jags was trying to keep warm as he didn't have his jacket on. The van's heater wasn't was cranked up to full. At last Zaq said, 'He wasn't there. It was a waste of time and money. I'll pay you back the three hundred.'

'Don't worry about it.'

'But it's three hundred quid.'

'Forget it. '

'You sure? At least let me pay to get your jacket cleaned.'

'What, this thing?' It was bundled up on Jags' lap. 'I was thinking of getting a new one anyway.'

'Sorry.'

'Don't be. It was my own fault. What we going to do now?'

'I'll drop you off then head home.'

'I meant about Davinder and the stuff we found at the warehouse. We could tell the cops.'

'There was nothing there to tie the place to the Brars. All the paperwork's in someone else's name. That's who'll get nicked.

Raj and Parm'll deny all knowledge. Then they'll wonder how the Old Bill found out.'

'What if we make the call when they're in the place?'

Zaq shrugged. 'They'll just say they were there to buy some cement. There's nothing to prove they know anything about the smack, the money or the gun.'

'The *gun*?'

'Yeah, I found it in the office when I was looking around.'

'Great,' Jags said. 'First they're kidnappers, then drug-dealing kidnappers, now they're armed, drug-dealing kidnappers. What next?'

'We're not going up against them. We just need to find Davinder. Once I straighten things out with him, he can go to the cops and tell them all about it – the assault, the kidnapping, the false imprisonment and anything else he wants to throw in. Maybe he can tie them to the warehouse too.'

'He wasn't there though, might not know anything about it.'

'He will if we tell him. His laptop and phone were there and other stuff in his bag too. I hid some of it in the office. Even if they get rid of the bag, his things'll still be there for the cops to find if they search the place. All he has to say is that they took him there.'

'We don't know that they did.'

'So what? After what they've done to him, he'll jump at a chance to stitch them up. Ain't like we'll be making the shit up. They did kidnap him and we know the gear in the warehouse is theirs. They get done for all of that, they'll be looking at some serious time.'

'All we got to do is find Davinder.'

'Yeah.' Zaq checked his mirrors. Sure no one was following them, he turned off the Uxbridge Road and drove towards Jags' house. 'I'll drop you on the corner, just in case.'

'What you going to tell Rita when she calls?'

'The truth – what else? He weren't there. I doubt she'll be happy. I just hope she'll still talk to her old man tomorrow.'

'You reckon it'll do any good?'

'Might do *me* some good. If we can convince him, could even do her some good too.'

Zaq drove around the block to make doubly sure they weren't being followed, then stopped at the corner and let Jags out.

'You want to come in, have something to eat?' Jags said.

'I'll grab something on the way home. I'm knackered. I just want to get back, eat and go to sleep.'

'Cool.' Jags shut the door and walked away, his jacket bundled under his arm.

Zaq stopped at a KFC and bought a Wicked Zinger box meal. The smell of chicken and fries made his stomach rumble. He drove past the yard to make sure the coast was clear, before coming back and turning onto the service road. This time he parked at the very far end, in one of the residents' spaces belonging to the low-rise flats that bordered the green behind the shops. Access to the spaces was a real hassle during the day because of all the commercial vehicles using the service road, so most of the residents parked out on the street. As a result, the builders' yard's 7.5 tonne lorry was usually parked in one of the spaces, as it was now. Zaq squeezed the van in between it and the high brick wall where the road ended so it was hidden by the bulk of the lorry. The closest streetlight wasn't working, which meant the van was shrouded in shadow and safely out of sight.

He locked it and started walking home. Holding his takeaway box in one hand, he took out his phone and made a call, hoping it wasn't too late.

'Hello.'

'Nina, it's me, Zaq. I was just calling to make sure you got home OK.'

'I did, thanks.'

'How're you doing, after... you know.'

'Still a little shaky but I'll be all right. Did you manage to find Davinder?'

'No. He wasn't there. I'll have to tell Rita when she calls.' He couldn't think what else to say. 'Well... I just wanted to see how you were.'

'Thank you.'

'If you're worried about anything, just call me.'

'I will.'

He put his phone away and hoped she didn't think he was a complete idiot. He had a chicken wing as he walked, then another but saved the rest for when he got in.

He made it back without incident and was thankful his housemates had all gone to bed. He went to the lounge, threw his jacket over the back of a sofa, turned on the TV with the volume low and sat down to eat. He'd just started on the Zinger Burger when his phone rang. It was Rita.

She didn't bother with hello. 'Was he there?'

'No.'

'Then where is he?'

'I don't know.'

'Didn't you find out?'

'There was nothing there to say where he might be.'

'What now?'

'Your brothers and their mates have got him somewhere. I'll watch them till they lead me to him. In the meantime, I know what they're using the warehouse for.'

'I don't care.'

'You might, once you know what it is.'

'What, then?'

'They're dealing heroin out of it.'

It silenced her for a moment. 'Are you sure?'

'I saw it, hidden inside bags of cement – money too, lots of it.'

'How much?'

'I don't know… over half a million.'

'*Pounds*?' She sounded astonished.

'Yeah, what else?'

'Just lying around?'

'No, the money was hidden inside bags of plaster. What would your dad do if he knew what they were up to?'

'Go ballistic. He'd make them get rid of the drugs for sure… but he'd definitely keep the money.'

'What if you tell your dad you found out what they were doing and they threatened you, that's why you ran? He sees the drugs and cash at the warehouse, it'll back up your story.'

'It still won't get me out of the marriage though.'

Zaq tried to think of another angle. 'What if you say that's why they set you up, with the whole Kasim thing? So your dad wouldn't listen to anything you said and they'd get you out of the way. The proof will be right there.'

'Maybe…' she said, sounding thoughtful. 'Where is this warehouse exactly?'

He gave her the directions.

'How did *you* manage to get inside?'

'Don't ask. They've got a gun there too.'

'What?'

'Yeah.' He told her where it was. 'The only problem is, the place ain't registered to your brothers, so they'll say they don't know anything about it.'

'Who is it registered to?'

'Hang on.' Zaq reached for his jacket and pulled out the

paperwork he'd taken from the office. 'Some guy called Subash Prewal.'

'*Him*? He's a friend of theirs, more of a *chumcha* really. My dad knows his family; they've got a butcher's shop in Hounslow. Even if the warehouse is in his name, my dad'll know Raj and Parm are involved. Subash does whatever they tell him to.'

'Hang on, did you say a butcher's shop in Hounslow? Does he work there?'

'As far as I know.'

Zaq dug out the list of names and numbers from his pocket and looked at the notes he'd made on the back. The last thing he'd written was PREWAL + SON, BUTCHERS, LAMPTON ROAD. 'I saw Jhutti and Chadha in his shop yesterday.'

'That's not surprising; they all hang round together.'

'If you mention the warehouse to your dad, keep my name out of it. Don't tell him I told you about it.'

'All right,' she said. 'You still want me to talk to him tomorrow?'

'Perfect time to tell him about the warehouse.' Would it be enough to defuse the whole Rita situation and get him off the hook?

'What about Davinder?'

'I'll keep looking. Oh, yeah...' he'd almost forgotten, 'they had his laptop and phone there, with his username and password. Any emails and texts between the two of you, they've seen them.'

'*Shit*,' she said.

'I thought you better know.' He didn't mention he'd looked at them too.

'What did you do with the stuff? Have you got it?'

'No, I left it there. It was too risky to take it.'

She swore again. 'Can you find him quickly?' There was

worry in her voice.

'I'll do my best.' What else could he say? 'I'll call you tomorrow when I'm at your dad's office.'

The call ended and Zaq finished off his chicken burger and fries, followed by the beans, just because they were there, and washed it all down with the cola. When he was finished, he sat back and yawned. It had been a hell of a day. He turned off the TV and went into the kitchen to throw his rubbish away. Then he rummaged in a drawer for some painkillers, took two, grabbed his jacket, and went upstairs to collapse into bed.

CHAPTER TWENTY-FIVE

Just before eight the next morning, Zaq was in the lounge finishing some toast and downing the last of his tea when the BBC local news bulletin came on the TV. The lead story was about the previous week's robbery at Heathrow, where a cargo plane had been robbed. They showed E-Fits again of the two white men wanted in connection with the robbery and also reported that the security guard attacked during the hold-up had gone missing.

It was the next item though that really grabbed his attention:

'Parts of a body were found yesterday in Cranford Park, near Heathrow Airport in West London...'

The female reporter was surrounded by greenery and standing in front of a cordon of blue and white police tape.

'The dismembered remains were found at the edge of the River Crane by a man walking his dog. Police search teams will carry out an intensive search of the river and the surrounding area today to try and find the remainder of the body. Detective Superintendent Angela Drury, leading the investigation, has confirmed that the body is that of a male, of Asian origin.

Further identification will have to be determined by forensic investigations which could take several days to complete. In the meantime, she said, police are treating the death as suspicious.'

No shit? Of course it was suspicious, unless they thought the guy had chopped himself up. Male, of Asian origin… there couldn't be a link, surely. What would the Brars have got out of killing Davinder? It didn't make sense. Then he remembered the stains on the laptop bag… but that didn't prove anything. He'd probably bled over it after Jhutti and Chadha beat him up and dragged him into the van. Zaq told himself he was letting his imagination run away with him – that was what came of reading too many crime novels.

He walked to work. He arrived at the yard about 8.30 and found the others waiting by the rear gate for Sid to show up and let them in. Mr Brar usually turned up around ten, which meant Zaq would have an hour and a half to wait. He didn't fancy hanging around and decided he'd go to Jags' instead. He would come back when Mr Brar was there.

'You'll have to take the deliveries out again today,' he told Ram.

'Sweet,' Ram said.

'Tell Sid I was here and I'll be back in a while.'

The van was still where he'd left it, thankfully with all its tyres intact. He gave it a once-over anyway. Satisfied it was OK, he got in. He honked his horn as he drove past the guys waiting by the gates and was almost at the end of the road when Sid's Mercedes turned in. Sid pulled over and started to lower his window but Zaq had no intention of stopping. He tapped his horn twice at the yard manager, sped past him, and was gone.

Jags' car was in the drive, so he was home. Zaq rang the bell three times, until Jags came and opened the door. 'Oh, it's you. What're you doing here? If you were hoping to catch me in the shower, you're out of luck.'

'Why, 'cause you don't shower?' Zaq stepped inside.

'No, 'cause I already had one.' Jags shut the door. 'What's up?'

'You see the news this morning?'

'No, why?'

Zaq was about to tell him about the body parts in the park but then thought better of it. 'Nothing, it don't matter. What you doing today?'

'Was going to go to the gym a bit later. Otherwise, not much. Some work...'

'I need a favour.'

'Again?'

'It's important, to do with what's going on.'

'OK, what?'

'I need you to watch the Brars' warehouse for me. There's a chance they might try and get rid of Davinder's stuff today.'

'How do you know that? Your female intuition again?'

'Something like that. I want to know what they do with it, if they dump it or take it somewhere else.'

'Like maybe where they've got Davinder?'

'Yeah. Will you do it?'

Jags let out a long slow breath, like he'd just made a tough decision. 'All right.'

'Thanks, man. I knew you wouldn't let me down.'

'How long will I have to watch them for?'

'Couple of hours, tops, just while I go see Rita's old man and get them to talk to each other, hopefully straighten some stuff out. Then I'll come and take over from you.'

'OK.'

'Might need you to do another stint later on though, if I'm still there and need a break.'

'Great.'

'Might not come to that, if they move the stuff this morning. How soon can you get over there?'

'You want me to go right now?'

'We don't want to miss them.'

'Let me grab a few things and I'll head over there.'

'Cheers, Jags, I owe you one.'

'Must be more than that by now.'

Zaq parked on the service road and called Rita before going in to see her dad. He wondered if she'd seen the news about the body in the park and whether she thought it could have anything to do with Davinder? But she didn't sound upset or distressed when she answered, so he didn't mention it. No point getting her worked up over nothing. 'I'm at the yard,' he said. 'Just about to go see your dad. You're still going to talk to him, right? Haven't changed your mind?'

'I'll talk to him, for all the good it'll do.'

'I'll go in and tell him what I've found out first, then I'll call you.'

'Will my number show up on your screen?'

He hadn't thought about it. 'I saved your number under a different name.'

'It doesn't matter whose name it's under, he'll know it's my number. I'll have to get rid of this phone afterwards.'

Zaq thought fast. 'I'll text you, then delete the message so there'll be no record who I sent it to. You call me back and put 1-4-1 in front of my number, that way yours will be withheld.'

'All right, let's do that.'

He got out of the van and went through the yard to Sid's

office. The yard manager was at his desk, reading a newspaper. 'Working hard, I see,' Zaq said.

'*Thenu kum da ki putha?*'

'I know it don't involve sitting on your arse reading the paper all day.'

'You want work? Plenty to do here.'

'No thanks. The boss in?'

'*Meh thera* boss *hain*.'

'I mean the *real* boss.'

'Real *da bucha. Meh ki uh?*'

'You really want me to answer that? He in or not?'

Sid made a tutting sound and motioned upstairs with a tilt of his head. 'Office *vich hai*.'

'Can you tell him I need to see him?'

'*Meh thera bhen chaud* secretary *lug da?*'

'No way. She'd be much better looking than you.'

'*Bhen di...*' Sid picked up the phone, hit the button for Mr Brar's office and explained in Punjabi that Zaq wanted to see him. Then he hung up and said, '*Ja utheh*,' gesturing toward the stairs.

Zaq went up to the first-floor office and knocked on the door. '*Ajaa*,' rumbled the voice from inside.

Mr Brar pointed to one of the chairs facing him. '*Behja*.' Zaq sat down. Mr Brar's dark eyes glinted like polished stones. There was no smile today; instead his mouth was a hard line gouged across his face. He wore a shirt and tie, the shirt tight over his massive chest and arms. 'You've found Rita?'

'Not exactly.'

'Then why are bothering me?'

'You said to tell you whatever I found out.'

'And... what have you found out?'

'She didn't run off to be with that Muslim guy. She left for other reasons; one is because of the arranged marriage she's being forced into, the other is because of Raj and Parm.'

'What about the boy?'

'What about him? He just helped her get away, that's all.'

Mr Brar's brow creased into a frown. 'I was told she ran away with him.'

'Who told you that?'

'Rajinder and Parminder.'

'That's what they want you to think. Did they mention the guy's a friend of theirs? That they know him?'

Mr Brar's frown deepened. 'What are you talking about?'

'They're the ones that introduced him and Rita. They *let* him take her out, even encouraged it. They knew all about it and didn't try to stop it.'

'They would never do that.'

'Well, they did... to set Rita up, so they could come and tell you all about it. They knew how you'd react. That's what they wanted, so you wouldn't listen to anything she had to say and you'd make her get married. They didn't want there to be any way out for her.'

'*Eh kee bukwaas uh?*'

'Even though there was nothing going on, Raj and Parm still beat the guy up and put him in hospital, to make it all look real. Soon as he got out though, Kasim warned Rita they were coming to tell you a pack of lies. She knew what would happen, so she ran.'

'How do you know all this?'

'I talked to people, asked around... the rest, she told me herself.'

'You've spoken to Rita?'

'Only on the phone. She doesn't trust me.'

'You have her phone number? Give it to me.'

'I ain't got it,' Zaq said. 'I told you, she don't trust me.'

'Then how did you contact her?'

'Through a friend of hers.'

'Which friend?'

'I can't say. I promised not to get them involved.'

Mr Brar's face clouded with the fury of an impending storm. 'I DON'T CARE WHAT YOU PROMISED. WHO IS THIS FRIEND?'

'All they have is a phone number,' Zaq said, keeping calm. 'Rita was real clear. If anyone else calls her, she'll chuck the phone and won't talk to me again. Then there'll be no way of contacting her. I'm trying to do what you want and find her, but I have to do it my way.'

Mr Brar eyed Zaq with undisguised malice. 'Then bloody do it, whatever way you like but do it quickly, like I told you, before everyone finds out she has run away with this... Muslim.'

'She hasn't though, that's the point. He just helped her 'cause of what Raj and Parm were doing.'

'I don't care. She went with this Muslim and I want her back.'

'Maybe if you heard it from Rita yourself...?'

'If she comes home, I can listen to what she has to say.'

'She won't come home until it's all been sorted out.'

Mr Brar's whole body seemed to clench. It was clear he had anger management issues. 'SHE SHOULD COME HOME AND TALK TO ME FACE-TO-FACE,' he shouted, stabbing the desk with a meaty finger, as though trying to drive it through the wood.

'That's what I told her,' Zaq fibbed, 'but she'll only talk to you on the phone, for now.'

Mr Brar breathed heavily and tried, visibly, to regain his calm. Finally, he said, 'All right, let me talk to her.'

'I have to text her friend and they'll get Rita to call.'

'Hurry up and do it.' He looked ready to rip something apart.

Zaq was glad there was a desk between them. He took out his phone and sent the blank text to Rita, then deleted it from his SENT messages. He had already deleted any record of calls to and from her number, so there was nothing in his call logs. 'She should call soon.'

They waited in uncomfortable silence. Sitting in the office with Mr Brar was like being stuck in a cage with a grizzly bear – a really pissed off grizzly bear. He hoped talking to Rita would cool him down. His phone rang, the caller's number withheld. 'It's me,' Rita said.

'I'll pass you to your dad.' Zaq handed the phone to Mr Brar, who took it and then sat looking at him, waiting. 'What?' Zaq said.

'*Bhar ja ke*, wait *kar*.'

For some reason Zaq had expected to stay where he was and listen in to the conversation, or at least Mr Brar's side of it. But he was telling him to leave. Zaq had no choice but to go outside. He closed the door behind him but leaned in close, so he could at least hear some of what was going on.

'They didn't tell me this,' Mr Brar said. 'I said NO and that's the end of it… Of course I care, we all care… Don't you care about any of us? This is not acceptable… I am your father, you will do as I say.' It didn't sound like it was going well. What the hell was she saying to him? Mr Brar's voice rose during the conversation, until finally he was shouting. 'I AM TELLING YOU TO COME HOME, RIGHT NOW. Rita? RITA…?' It was followed by a series of crashes. Zaq stepped away from the door. 'ZAQIR!,' Mr Brar called, '*undher ah*.' Zaq went back in.

Everything that had been on the desk was now on the floor. Mr Brar was on his feet, hands planted on the desk, breathing through his nose like an enraged bull; anger radiated from him like heat.

'*Le.*' He threw Zaq's phone across the desk and it fell to the floor with the rest of the things.

Zaq bent to retrieve it.

'Pick up the rest of those things and put them back on the desk.' Zaq's instinctive reaction was to refuse but he stopped himself and took a breath. *Just think of it as work.* He got paid to pick things up, put them on the van and take them off again, so what was the big deal about picking this lot up? He knelt down and began gathering everything and putting it on the desk.

'Talking was a waste of time,' Mr Brar said.

'I thought you might've been able to sort things out.'

'I DON'T PAY YOU TO BLOODY THINK,' Mr Brar raged. 'I pay you to *do what I tell you* – and I'm telling you to find my fucking daughter, you understand? Maybe you need a reminder of what will happen if you don't. Give me the phone.' Zaq picked it up from the floor and handed it to him. He lifted the receiver and punched a button. 'Sid, Hari *nuh utthey bhej deh.*'

What the hell did he want with Hari?

A few minutes later Hari came in. Mr Brar pointed to one of the chairs in front of the desk. '*Behja.*' Hari looked at Zaq and sat down. Mr Brar came around from behind the desk to stand in front of him. 'Hari, you have seen Zaqir stealing from the shop, *hena?*'

Hari looked up, confused. 'No, I – '

Mr Brar slapped him.

'You have seen him stealing from the shop, *hena?*'

'I don't – '

Mr Brar slapped him again, harder.

'You have seen him stealing from the shop!' It wasn't a question now; it was more like an order.

The penny dropped. Hari looked at Zaq, eyes watering, the

side of his face smarting red.

'Don't look at him,' Mr Brar said, and slapped him yet again. 'You have seen him stealing from the shop, yes?'

Hari looked down at the floor. 'Yes.'

Mr Brar slapped him again. 'I didn't hear you.'

'Yes,' Hari said, louder, his voice breaking.

'And when you were going to tell someone, he attacked you.'

'What…?' It slipped out before Hari realised he'd said it.

The slap almost knocked him out of the chair. Mr Brar grabbed him by the shirt. 'When you tried to tell someone, he attacked you, right?'

'Yes,' Hari said, tears visible on his cheeks.

'Who did you see stealing?' Mr Brar said.

Hari knew what was expected of him now. 'Zaq,' he said, only he said it too quietly, clearly embarrassed with Zaq standing right there.

He was slapped again, his face burning red by now.

'Who?' Mr Brar said.

'Zaq.' Louder this time.

'And what did he do then?'

'Hit me.'

'Who gave you these marks on your face?'

'Zaq.'

Mr Brar stepped back. '*Ja*,' he told Hari.

Hari got up out of the chair, put a hand to his face and rushed out of the office, head down, not looking at Zaq.

Mr Brar glared at Zaq. 'Do we understand each other?' he said.

'Yeah.'

'Good. Then get out of my fucking office and find my daughter.'

CHAPTER TWENTY-SIX

It hadn't gone anything like he'd expected. His plan to show Mr Brar that he was making progress and buy himself some time had gone right down the shitter.

He looked for Hari to apologise for what had happened, but couldn't find him. In the end, he just got out of there and drove a few streets away before pulling over to call Rita.

'I told you it wouldn't do any good,' she said. 'He didn't want to listen, just shouted at me to come home, no discussion, nothing.'

'You must've said something to get him that pissed off.'

'All I said was, if he's not going to listen, I'm not coming home. He can forget about the wedding and should stop looking for me.'

It sounded like they'd had more of an argument than a conversation. 'Did you tell him about Raj and Parm lying?'

'What do you think I was trying to do? He just brushed it aside, said if there was a problem I should've talked to him, even though he totally believed what they told him without a second thought. Didn't even occur to him that it might not be true. How do you think that makes me feel? No, if he won't listen to me now, he won't when I'm back home. I know him, he'll want to lock me up like some Disney princess, keep me prisoner until the wedding.'

'You told him there's nothing going on between you and Kasim?'

'I *tried*. He was too busy ranting and raving to take any notice. He's more worried about what people will say if word gets out I left home with a Muslim. Everyone will think the worst anyway, no matter what the truth is – just like he has. Nothing I say will change his mind now.'

So much for that idea. 'What about the warehouse and the drugs? You mention those?'

'I didn't get a chance.'

'That was one of the main things you were supposed to tell him.'

'I'm sorry... I told him about them kidnapping Davinder though.'

'What? We never said anything about telling him *that*.' Shit, would her brothers wonder how she knew about the abduction? No, they wouldn't. He remembered the call he'd made to Jhutti or Chadha; they'd thought it was Rita on the line and said they had Davinder hostage. They thought she knew. It wouldn't point to him. 'What did he say?'

She gave a bitter laugh. 'He said he'd ask them about it. As if they'd admit it. Without proof, it's just my word against theirs.'

'Couldn't you try talking to him again? To tell him about the drugs and your brothers threatening you?'

'Not right now. Maybe tomorrow, after he's had time to calm down. I can call him myself. You've done your bit. He thinks you made contact.'

Fat lot of good it had done. The way things had gone, he

wasn't sure she'd have any more success second time around.

'What are you going to do now?' she said.

'Carry on looking for you.'

'Good luck with that. What about Davinder?'

'I don't know…' From the emails he'd seen, it was clear there was still something going on between them. With Rita's obvious concern for him, the best way to get to her might well be through him. Maybe her brothers were right about that, though not in the way they'd chosen to exploit it. 'I guess I'll carry on looking for him too.'

'Thanks.'

'We'll have to see what happens. I mean, if your dad goes and asks them about Davinder. He does, it might shake your brothers up, make them let him go, or else do something that'll let us know where they've got him.' If that happened, he'd keep it to himself, at least till after he talked to Davinder first. He didn't want Rita calling the cops before he'd had a chance to straighten things out.

'If you can help him, I'd really appreciate it,' she said.

Not enough to come home and get her old man off his back though. 'Sure,' he said. Fat lot of good her appreciation would do him when he was being thrown in the back of a police van and carted off to prison. 'I'll let you know if I find out anything.'

He ended the call and dialled Jags' number next, to see how he was getting on at the warehouse.

'Nothing doing so far,' Jags said. 'Not a fucking sausage.'

'All right. Sit tight, I'm on my way.'

Zaq parked out of sight of the warehouse and approached the car on foot, acting natural so as not to attract any attention. He opened the passenger door and put the seat forward so he could get in the back, where Jags was already. 'What're *you* doing there? I'm getting in the back 'cause one of those fuckers might recognise me sitting in the front.'

'I get clocked sitting in the front seat for a couple of hours, someone might wonder what I'm doing. No one'll see me back here.'

It made sense. 'Anything happen?'

'Raj and Parm were here earlier. Went inside for a bit, then left.'

'They take anything with them?'

'Nope, came out empty handed.'

'Anything else?'

'Yeah, my arse is aching. How did it go with Rita and her old man?'

'Not good.' He told Jags about the call and what had happened afterwards with Hari.

'Fuckin' hell,' Jags said, 'that's a bit harsh. What you going to do?'

'What can I do? I got to find Rita sharpish, and the only way I can think to do that is through Davinder. So, I have to sit here and hope one of those arseholes will eventually lead me to him. And if they just dump his stuff, least I'll see where.'

'That won't lead you to him though.'

Zaq shrugged. 'I know but it might be useful. Might have their prints on it, tie them to him.'

'I guess,' Jags said.

'I'll take over here for now but can you come back for a while later on, so I can have a break?'

Jags didn't seem very keen on the idea but agreed all the same. 'Where did you park the van?'

'Back around the corner,' Zaq said.

'Bring it up and take this space. Good view of the unit from here.'

'I can't sit out here in the van, they know it. Jhutti and Chadha followed me in it last night. They'll spot it a mile off.'

'What you going to do then? You can't just stand around.'

'I thought I'd stay in here.'

'In my car? What the fuck am I supposed to do?'

'Take the van.'

'You're having a laugh, right?'

'You're only going home and coming back later.'

'No way. I ain't swapping this for that piece of shit.'

'It's only for a little while. Ain't like we're swapping for good.' Jags would have continued arguing but Zaq held up his hand and stopped him. His phone was ringing. He didn't recognise the number but answered anyway.

'That Zaq?' a heavy male voice said. 'It's Parminder... Brar. Where are you?'

'Hillingdon,' Zaq lied.

'What you doing there?'

'Looking for your sister.'

'Yeah, well, get back to Southall. Now. I want to talk to you.'

'What about?'

'You'll find out.'

'Where? The yard?'

'No, the place on Park Avenue, one you came to before. And get a fucking move on.' He hung up.

'Parm Brar wants to see me.'

'What for?'

'He didn't say.'

'When?'

'Now.'

'Now? Who's going to watch this place?'

'Sorry, mate,' Zaq said, 'looks like you'll have to stay a bit longer.'

'*What?*'

'Look on the bright side, though. Least you don't have to drive the van.'

Both the black and the silver Mercedes were parked in front of the house. The front door was open and Zaq walked straight in and into the front reception room, where three *desi* builders were busy putting up a new ceiling. They were chatting away in Punjabi but stopped when they saw Zaq in the doorway.

'*Paji*, Parminder *hega*?' Zaq said. It was only three words but they were in Punjabi and he spoke them in a *pukka* accent, which put the men at ease.

'*Au uthay eh*,' one of them said, gesturing upstairs.

Zaq nodded his thanks, crossed the hall and went up the stripped wooden stairs to the first floor. He could hear Parm's voice when he was halfway up. Four doors opened off the landing; his voice was coming from the one on the left.

He was standing with his back to the door, talking to a stocky bloke with salt and pepper stubble. They guy was wearing a beanie hat, an old Man United football shirt, grubby jeans and a pair of old work boots. He must have been the builder in charge because Parminder was talking to him in English, explaining what he wanted.

'...the bath over there, under the window. Toilet over here and the sink opposite, on that wall there. These tiles are for the walls and those ones for the floor.' He swept his arm around and saw Zaq. 'Go check how they're getting on downstairs,' he told the builder, 'and send Raj up.'

The builder glanced at Zaq on his way out and then tromped away down the stairs.

'When did you get here?' Parm said.

'Just now.'

'You found Rita yet?'

'No.'

'What the fuck you been doing, then?'

'Looking for her. If it was that easy, you'd have found her yourself.'

'I heard you talked to her. Give me her number.'

'I ain't got it.'

'How did you get in touch with her then?'

'Through a friend.'

'What friend?'

'No one you know. I said I'd leave them out of it.'

Parm's eyes narrowed. 'I don't give a fuck what you said. Who was it?'

Zaq returned Parm's stare. 'I can't say.'

'We might have to see about that.'

Zaq shrugged. They scowled at each other across the room.

'You were supposed to tell me if you found anything out,' Parm said, '*before* you went to my dad.'

'I haven't found out anything yet – not that you don't know already.'

'You know how to get in touch with her.'

'She won't talk to you. Was all I could do to get her to talk to your dad.'

'You shouldn't have done that. She's been chatting some right shit to him and now he's vexed with us. She told him that *sullah* she's run off with is a mate of ours, that we introduced them. Said we beat him up too and were going to do the same to her. What a load of bollocks. She also told him we kidnapped her fucking ex.'

'Who? The guy I asked Raj about? Did you?'

'Fuck off. No, we didn't. She made it all up, trying to blame us for her running off with that Paki. Our dad was well pissed off after talking to her, had a right go at me and Raj. That's down to *you*, not doing what I fucking told you to.'

'How was I supposed to know what she'd say?' Zaq heard heavy footsteps coming up the stairs.

'I don't give a shit. I told you to come to me first and you didn't.'

'Don't take this the wrong way but I don't work for you, I work for your old man.'

Raj appeared in the doorway. Zaq moved into the room and backed up against the wall, so he could see them both. It would have been a tight squeeze in the bathroom if all the fixtures and fittings had been in place.

'Shut the door,' Parm told Raj, then turned to Zaq again. 'You might work for him but if you want to stay out of prison and keep your shitty little job, you'll do what I tell you, right? One word from me and we'll have the fucking *mammai* down on you before you know what's going on. You get me?'

'Yeah, I get you.'

'Ain't so tough now, are you?' Parm said. 'In fact, you look like you've had a good arse kicking. You might have a rep but I ain't seen nothing to make me believe it.'

Zaq shrugged. 'Believe what you want.'

'Tell the truth, you seem like a bit of a pussy to me, doing what you're told, scared what might happen to you.'

'If you say so.'

'Yeah, I do. What you going to do about it?'

Zaq could think of a few things... but all he said was, 'Nothing.' The last thing he needed right now was to get into a fight with these arseholes. Another time maybe. For now, all he had to do was keep his cool, listen to their bullshit and get out of there.

Parm's lip curled into a sneer. 'That's what I thought. Where did you go last night, after you left the yard?'

'Why?'

''Cause I'm fucking asking, that's why.'

Zaq looked at him for a moment before replying. 'I went to see a mate.'

'Where?'

'At the Scotsman, in Old Southall.' Jhutti and Chadha had followed him there anyway, so Parm must've already known that.

'You get someone to move Jhutti's motor?'

Zaq frowned. 'What you talking about?'

'Someone moved his truck.'

'What the fuck's that got to do with me?'

Parm looked at him for a moment, then said, 'Where did you go when you left there?'

'What's with all the questions?'

'Just tell me where you fucking went.'

Zaq pretended to think. 'I went to see the person who put me in touch with Rita.'

'What person?' Raj said, from the doorway.

Zaq nodded toward Parm. 'Ask him.'

'He ain't saying.'

Raj puffed out his chest, making himself even bigger. 'I can make him,' he said.

'You can try.' Zaq shifted slightly, into a loose fighting stance, feet apart, fists ready. True, last thing he wanted was to get into a fight – but that didn't mean he was just going to stand there and take a beating.

Parm waved his brother back. Raj stood blocking the doorway and glaring at Zaq.

'Where did you meet them?' Parm said.

There was no reason not to say now. 'The Hare & Hounds.'

'I want to know who it was.'

'There's no point. They don't know where Rita is anyway. All they've got is a mobile number for her, pay-as-you-go. Anyone else calls her on it, she'll chuck it and get a new one. That happens, she won't talk to me again and we're back to square one. You want me to find your sister, you need to back off and let me do it. I told your dad the same thing.'

Parm stared at him for a long moment. 'Fine...,' he said eventually, though it sounded anything but. 'I'll tell you one thing right now though – you find out anything else, you better come to me first. Otherwise, no matter what my dad says, you're fucked. Got that?'

'Yeah, I got it.' What difference would it make who he told first? Once he found out where she was, he could tell Parm, then tell their dad straight after and be done with the whole thing.

'What did you do after the Hare & Hounds?' Parm asked.

'I went to see a friend.'

'Where?'

'Hillingdon.'

'You go to Hayes at all?'

'I went through it to get to Hillingdon.'

'You stop off anywhere on the way, like an industrial estate, maybe?'

'What for? I wasn't working.'

'You didn't go to our warehouse?'

Zaq frowned again. 'What warehouse? What're you on about?' He hoped he looked suitably confused. Parm was looking at him closely, searching his face for any hint he was lying. Zaq maintained his slightly puzzled expression, one he'd perfected on prison guards, and continued to feign ignorance.

'All right, never mind,' Parm finally said. 'Let's get back to Rita.'

It wasn't much of an interrogation but it told Zaq that they knew someone had been inside the warehouse. They might have had their suspicions about him but, as far as they knew, he had absolutely no knowledge of the place. They had never mentioned it to him or taken him there, so there was no reason he would know of it. That was probably why they didn't push him harder on the subject.

'She say anything to you?' Parm demanded.

'She told me the same thing she told your dad, that this Kasim bloke's a friend of yours –'

'I told you, we don't know him.'

'You asked me what she said and I'm telling you. She also said she only went out with him a couple of times and you both knew all about it and didn't say anything. Then you beat him up and went straight to your old man and told him she was fucking around with a Muslim. Kasim told her what you were up to and helped her get away... least, that's the way she tells it. Apparently, she was planning to leave home anyway. Then she mentioned something about you kidnapping her ex-boyfriend.'

'You believe her?' Parm said.

'I couldn't care less either way. Ain't none of my business. All I'm interested in is finding her, telling you and your dad where she is and then forgetting the whole thing.'

That seemed to satisfy Parm. 'That all?'

Zaq thought for a moment. 'She offered me money not to look for her.' He saw Parm glance at his brother.

'How much?'

'Ten grand, then twenty. I told her, if I'm going to go down for five years, I'd want a lot more than twenty grand.'

'Ha, you're dumber than I thought,' Raj said, from the doorway. 'You could've taken the money and still told us where she is.'

Zaq looked at him. 'If you found out about the money, would you let me keep it?' No one said anything – they all knew the answer to that.

'She say where she got the money from?' Parm asked.

'She saved it.'

'*Saved it*?' Raj said. 'Stupid cow.'

'She *stole* it.' Parm told Zaq. 'From *us*. That's our money she's run off with.'

All at once the situation became clear. Zaq thought of the bricks of cash in the warehouse. Whoever was telling the truth about why she'd run away – and he found himself leaning more toward her version of things than her brothers' – Rita probably *had* taken their money. Drug money, most likely. She hadn't known about the warehouse but that didn't matter; they probably kept cash in more than one location. It explained why they were so hell bent on finding her and why they wanted to get to her before their old man did. They wanted the money back and they wanted to make sure she kept her mouth shut. Davinder was their way of ensuring they got both. He wasn't supposed to know about any of it, so he kept a blank look on his face and said nothing.

'Make sure you remember that, if she offers you any more,' Parm said. 'We want it back. All of it.'

'OK.'

'Well, what you waiting for? Fuck off and find that silly bitch before we get pissed off with waiting and have you slung back inside. And don't fuck up this time. You tell us whatever you find out before going to my dad.' Parm looked at his brother. 'Anything else?'

'No.'

Zaq turned to leave. Let them act tough and say what they wanted. At the end of the day, it didn't mean shit. It was just hot air out of a couple of arseholes. What did it matter, as long as he could get out of there without having to fight? But Raj didn't move out of the doorway. His piggy eyes glinted with malice from under his heavy brows.

Zaq sized him up. Raj was bigger but his size and weight would make him slower. He might be able to fight a bit, but was probably more used to pub brawls and strong-arming people smaller than himself. Zaq had spent five years training in a prison gym, with guys who really knew how to fight. If it came down to it, he reckoned he could take him.

'Let him go,' Parm said, waving his brother back.

Raj frowned at Zaq a moment longer, then moved aside.

Zaq opened the door and walked out. He didn't look at Raj but made sure he could see him from the corner of his eye, just in case he tried anything. He felt his hackles rise, the skin prickling on the back of his neck. On the landing, he listened out for the sound of anyone coming behind him. No one did, but he did hear Raj say: 'I don't like that cunt. I don't think we should trust him.'

The feeling was mutual.

It was only when he'd put some distance between himself and the house that Zaq finally allowed himself to relax.

CHAPTER TWENTY-SEVEN

'You took your time,' Jags said, as Zaq climbed into the back seat again.

'Figured I might be here a while, so I picked up my book and some food on the way.'

'You get me anything?'

'Didn't think you'd be sticking around.'

'Thanks. What did Brar want?'

'He wanted to know if I was here last night. I played dumb, acted like I didn't know what he was on about.'

'He believe you?'

'I think so – but they know someone was here and they're suspicious of me anyway after what happened to Jhutti and Chadha's truck, even if they can't prove I had anything to do with it.' He explained how they'd asked about his contact with Rita and had been pissed off by what Rita had told their old man. 'I think I know what's *really* going on with Rita and her brothers though. It's to do with money. Remember that twenty grand she offered me? She never saved it – she *took it*, from them. Probably a chunk of their drug money.'

'Damn,' Jags said. 'You think she got it from here?'

'No. She didn't know anything about this place when I mentioned it to her. Besides, I doubt they keep all their cash in one place. She probably found another stash.'

'How much she take?'

'They didn't say and I didn't ask but, judging by how much was in there,' he nodded at the warehouse, 'it's probably a *lot*.'

'Everyone knows what those guys do to people that fuck with them. No wonder she don't want to be found.'

The radio was on, playing at low volume. Perhaps it was the sound waves or the rhythmic pulse of the music, whatever it was, something helped an idea to form in his head. 'I wonder...'

'What?'

'I wonder what would happen if she gave the money to her dad?'

'Why would she do that?'

'What's that saying? *Money talks and bullshit walks*? Well, that money would definitely talk to him, grab his attention, especially if she dumped it on his desk. Might make him sit up and take notice of what else she's saying.'

'And what would that be?'

'Same as she told him already, only this time the money'll show she ain't making it all up. She can tell him about this place and he can come see for himself. He does that, he might *start* believing her about Kasim and Davinder.'

'Still might not change his mind about the whole marriage thing hanging over her.'

'It could get called off. If, say, the guy's family were to find out her brothers are a couple of drug dealers.'

'How would they find that out?'

'I don't know... maybe Rita could tell them.'

'It might work,' Jags said. 'Just one problem though.'

'What's that?'

'You think Rita will go for it?'

'Only other option I can see is she gives the money back to her brothers – after they tell their dad they made up the whole Kasim thing and there was never anything going on between them. And they let Davinder go too.'

'You think Raj and Parm would agree to that?'

'No. I can't see them going to their old man and admitting they lied about it.' He shrugged. 'But they'd get their money back, which is what they want. They get off Rita's case and Davinder gets freed. It works out for all of them. OK, there might still be the marriage to worry about but Rita would be in a better position to get out of it. Maybe I should run it by her, see what she thinks.'

'Worth a go, I guess,' Jags said. 'Right, I might as well head off then.'

Zaq took out the van keys and held them up.

'You ain't serious?' Jags said. 'You're not really going to make me drive that thing?'

'It's only to your house and then back later.'

'Even that's too far.'

'Park it away from your house, just to be safe.'

'I can't even drive all the way home? I got to walk too?'

'Quit moaning. It's not like you were going to park it in front of your house, anyway.'

Zaq watched the warehouse and wondered how to explain to Rita that giving the money to her dad or back to her brothers might be a good idea. He doubted she'd like either option. He was trying to come up with a way to convince her when his phone rang. It was her calling.

'I've been thinking,' she said. 'I should've told my dad about the warehouse straight away and what Raj and Parm are doing there.'

'I can't believe you didn't. That was the main reason you called him.'

'He wouldn't listen though, that's why we started arguing. Things got heated and I said whatever popped into my head.'

'I don't know if mentioning Davinder was such a good idea. He asked Raj and Parm about it afterwards.'

'How do you know?'

'I saw them a little while ago. Parm wanted to talk to me. They weren't happy about it. I don't know how much your dad believed of what you told him but he had a right go at them all the same.'

'Good.'

'They denied everything, just like you said. If you'd told him about the drugs and stuff, he could've gone and seen it all for himself. Then whatever else you tell him will seem more believable.'

'I know, I know, I should've done it. That why I'm calling. I think I should try and talk to him again – and this time I'll definitely tell him. Only...'

'What?'

'If I do and he wants to go have a look, how will he get in?'

'He'll have to force the front door but I can give you the code for the alarm, so at least he can turn that off.'

'Won't breaking in bring the police straight away?'

'I doubt your brothers have got it hooked up to the police, not with what they've got inside. They'll probably get a call from a private security company and then go check it out themselves. They find your dad there, are they going to call the cops on him?'

'No. And my dad won't call them either, no matter what Raj and Parm have been doing. Last thing he'll want is the police involved.'

'OK, the code's 1-6-6-4.'

She made a note of it. 'How did you find that out?'

'Never mind.'

'Fine. Where's Davinder's stuff? It'll prove I was telling the truth about them kidnapping him.'

'Maybe, but… look, I really need to talk to Davinder before he goes the police, to make sure he knows I didn't have anything to do with them taking him.'

'I can do that. Once they let him go, I'll tell him you weren't part of it and that you helped me get him out.'

That would work. It might even be better coming from her. Davinder would be much more likely to believe it if she was the one who told him. 'OK,' Zaq said. 'His phone and laptop are in the office above the warehouse, locked in a desk drawer. The key's under the computer keyboard.'

'I'll let my dad know. I don't know when I'll talk to him. Maybe this evening once he's had time to cool down, or else tomorrow morning. I'll let you know how it goes.'

'Cool,' Zaq said. 'Actually, there's something I wanted to talk to you about. When I saw Parm… he told me you've got their money.' Rita didn't say anything to that, so he carried on. 'He didn't say how much but he said you took it.'

It was a moment before she said, 'OK, I did. So what?'

'They want it back.'

'That's their tough luck. I need it.'

'It's probably from the heroin, maybe tied into a drug deal or something…'

'So?'

'So, that's why they took Davinder. They want their money back. I wondered why they'd go as far as kidnapping someone. Now I know. How much did you take?'

She didn't answer straight away. When she did, she said, 'A hundred thousand pounds.'

'A hundred thou...' He didn't know what he'd been expecting, a few grand maybe but not that much. 'No wonder they're after you. If the warehouse thing doesn't work, I had another idea... how about giving the money back –'

'No way,' she said, cutting him off. 'Absolutely not. You must be mad if you think –'

'On condition they tell your dad the truth about how they made up all that stuff to do with you and Kasim *and* they let Davinder go.'

'They won't do it. How can they? They've already denied it to my dad's face. They're not going to turn around now and admit they lied about it – then lied again when he asked about it today. My dad will go through the roof and they won't want to risk that. They'd never agree to it and they'll keep Davinder to get to me.'

'The other option is you give it to your dad. You whack the hundred grand in front of him. He'll definitely take notice of that. Then you tell him there's more at the warehouse, a *lot more*. He'll be round there like a shot. Explain your brothers didn't want anyone knowing what they were up to, they threatened you and all the rest of it – that's why you ran. The whole Kasim story was their way of trying to cover it up.' It sounded pretty good, even to Zaq. 'When he finds Davinder's stuff, he'll know that's true too.'

He let her mull it over. Eventually she said, 'Even if he believes all that and things go the way you say, I still won't be able to go home. My brothers won't just forgive and forget me telling my dad about their drug business. They might leave it for a while, but they'll get me back – and I mean, really get me back. I won't be safe.'

'Your dad won't let them do anything.'

'They'll do it in a way that won't be linked to them, or they'll get someone else to do it. I know them, what they do to people.'

'Then explain all that to your dad too, tell him that's why you left home. He might not like it, but it makes sense. Blame Raj and Parm for all of it.'

'Let me think about it.'

'All right, but don't take too long. The sooner we can get this sorted, the better.'

'OK, I'll let you know.'

The call left Zaq feeling positive. If she did agree to give the money to her dad, then maybe everything could be resolved soon. The other pieces would hopefully fall into place the way he imagined. Sure, Rita would still have to convince her dad about why she didn't want to come home but that was for them to sort out. And if the old man bought it, he might drop the threats of arrest and imprisonment he'd been holding over Zaq. Then he would be free to quit the yard and leave.

If things *did* work out that way, it would drop Raj and Parm right in the shit. Once they found out about the deal between Rita and her dad – a deal Zaq would've arranged and which involved their money being handed over to their dad – they'd come after him for sure. As long as their old man was no longer interested in sending Zaq to prison, he figured he could deal with his sons.

They'd most likely want to inflict some physical harm on him, make their vengeance bloody and painful. It was what they did, what their reputation was built on. One way or the other though, he could cope with that. He'd had five years of dealing with that sort of crap. It was only if they decided to be more calculating and came after him the way their old man had intended to, using the law and his own past against him, that he'd be truly fucked.

He watched the warehouse for hours without anything happening. He'd thought time would drag but by reading his book, The Anubis Gates, and listening to the Robert Elms show on BBC Radio London, it passed a lot quicker than he expected. He eventually called Jags to come and take over for a while because he needed a toilet break. What did cops do when they were on surveillance and needed to go?

Jags arrived about 4.30pm and got into the back with Zaq. 'Anything happen?'

'No.'

'How long you going to be?'

'Not long. I'll be back in a while to carry on.'

Zaq went and got in the van, which Jags had parked out of sight of the warehouse. He drove to the other side of Parkway and to the Tesco at Bulls Bridge. He used the customer toilets there and then bought some more food and water. It was the start of the evening rush and the return trip took longer, so when he got back to the industrial estate most people were leaving. He parked the van in the same spot Jags had.

'I miss anything?'

'Nope.'

'All right. Thanks. You can shoot off, if you want.'

'Now I got to drive that heap of junk back through rush hour. So embarrassing.'

'You can always walk. Anyway, you've only got to do it once or twice more. It won't kill you.'

'It might – I could die of shame.'

'If shame was going to kill you, you'd be dead already. Lucky for you, you're totally *besharam*.'

Jags smiled at that. 'What time shall I come back?'

'Around dinner time. I'll give you a call.'

Jags left. Zaq sat in the front for a while as it might have looked odd for him get in the rear. He pretended to be on the phone and kept his face obscured then, when the coast was clear, he slipped into the back again.

As night fell, his eyes got tired from reading in the glow of the streetlights and he put his book away. He turned on the radio and ended up listening to a drive time show for a while, then a sports show, followed by dance music and later on some classical.

Between them, he and Jags had been there the whole day and nothing had happened. Maybe he'd let his imagination get the better of him and the body in the park had been nothing to do with the Brars. If it had been, he felt sure they would've come and disposed of any evidence that could link them to it. So it probably wasn't related. Unless... what if they hadn't wanted to move the stuff during the day and were going to do it tonight? Did he really believe that or was it just wishful thinking on his part? Well, he was here anyway, so he might as well keep an eye on the place till morning, just to be absolutely sure. He'd take the night shift himself, so he wouldn't feel bad about making Jags do it.

At 8.30pm, he called Jags – having waited till then to give him time to have his dinner – and asked him to come take over for another spell. Zaq made sure the interior light was turned off, so it wouldn't come on when Jags got in. He showed up twenty minutes later, carrying a rucksack.

'Don't tell me you brought your pyjamas.'

'No, just my laptop and a flask of tea. How long you going to be?'

'Two hours, tops. I just want to go home, eat and change,

then I'll be back.'

'Cool. Long enough for me to watch a film.'

Zaq parked in a quiet cul-de-sac not too far from the house. Being a dead end, it was less likely anyone looking for him would just happen to turn in and spot the van there, tucked in between the other vehicles. As he was about to get out, his phone rang.

'Hi,' Rita said. 'Where are you?'

'At home.' He was as good as there.

'OK, I've thought about it and I'll give the money to my dad. Not all of it though – I need some.'

'How much you thinking of keeping?'

'Half.'

'It's too much. I don't think fifty thousand will make enough of an impression on your dad.'

'I'll keep forty then.'

'Twenty-five. That'll last you for a while and seventy-five should make your dad sit up and take notice.'

'All right,' she said, after a moment, though it was clear from her tone she wasn't over the moon about it.

'When will you take it to him?'

'*Me*? I'm not taking it. It's too risky. You can do it.'

'You trust me to take it to him?'

'I don't have a choice. Besides, it belongs to my brothers. I don't think you want to rip them off.'

'How you going to get the money to me?'

'You'll have to pick it up from somewhere. I'll let you know when I've figured it out.'

She was being careful. He didn't blame her. 'OK, but make it soon.'

'I will. That's all I called about. What are you doing?'

'I was about to eat.'

'I'll let you go then.'

She was certainly determined – and she had guts, Zaq had to give her that. Seventy-five thousand pounds. He hoped it would do the trick and convince her old man to take their story seriously. If it didn't, then he had to trust that seventy-five grand would at least buy him some more time to find Rita.

CHAPTER TWENTY-EIGHT

His housemates had already eaten and were sat around drinking beer, chatting rubbish and watching TV.

'All right?' Manjit greeted him. 'No one tried to beat you up today?'

'Not so far. You guys cook anything?' He nodded in the direction of the kitchen.

'Yeah, chicken curry and *aloo gobi*. There's some left.'

There were also a couple of fresh *naans*. Zaq got himself a plate and warmed everything up. After he'd eaten, he put the kettle on while he went upstairs and changed into some warmer clothes.

'Anyone want tea?' he asked, but they were all happy drinking beer. Zaq had just made himself a nice strong mugful when Jags rang.

'You better get over here,' he said. 'I think someone's trying to break into the place.'

'You sure?'

'There's a geezer outside, messing about at the main entrance. I can see him right there.'

'I mean, you sure he's trying to break in?'

'Either that or he's taking a really long piss on their door. He's been there since before I called you. If he had a key, he'd have been in by now.'

Had Rita called her dad already and told him? 'It might be their old man?'

'No way, this bloke looks about our age.'

'How can you tell?'

'I got a look at him as he walked past.'

'Walked? He didn't drive?'

'If he did, he parked somewhere else.'

'You recognise him?'

'No – hold on, he's got the door open. Now he's gone inside.'

'Wait, there's the alarm. He'll probably come straight back out when he can't switch it off.'

They waited. After a while, Jags said, 'He's still in there.'

Zaq took a gulp of tea and poured the rest down the sink. 'All right, stay there, I'm on my way.'

He left the house and kept a lookout as he hurried along the street to the cul-de-sac. He got in the van, started the engine and had just pulled out when Jags rang again.

'You better hurry – a car's just pulled in.'

'What sort of car?'

'A black Merc.'

'Shit. It's probably Parminder.'

'Yeah, you're right – him and his brother just got out.'

'Where's the guy that broke in?'

'He ain't come out yet.'

'Shit. OK, make sure no one sees you. I'll be there quick as I can.'

'What if they leave?'

'Follow them. Let me know where you end up and I'll meet

you there.'

'What if they leave separately?'

'If Raj or Parm are carrying anything, stick with them. If not, follow the other guy.' He hung up, put the van in gear and screeched off.

Zaq broke the speed limit, slowing only for speed cameras. On the Parkway he even got the van up to a juddering seventy miles an hour. He took the exit for Hayes and looped down under the dual carriageway and around, towards the industrial estate.

He left the van and snuck the rest of the way to the car, keeping to the shadows, slipping into the back when he reached it. The Mercedes was still parked outside unit 12. 'Anything happened since they got here?'

'Some lights went on inside but nothing else.'

They watched and waited. A few minutes passed and then headlights turned onto the one-way road behind them. They ducked out of sight as two vehicles came past. When they had gone by, Zaq and Jags raised their heads just enough to see out the windows. A 4x4 truck and a large white van had just pulled up outside the unit.

'Jhutti and Chadha,' Zaq said. 'And I swear that's same the van they bundled Davinder into.'

The van turned around and backed up to the shutter. The driver got out. Jhutti and Chadha joined him and all three went to the front door, where they stopped and looked around for a second before disappearing inside.

'What're *they* doing here?' Jags said.

'Search me.'

They continued watching until finally there was some movement. A small group came out the front door. The van driver hurried to his vehicle and opened the rear doors, while Jhutti and Chadha half-carried, half-dragged something to it.

That was when Zaq spotted a pair of legs hanging limply between them. 'Shit, look. That must be the guy that was in there.'

Jhutti and Chadha disappeared round the back of the van. Raj and Parm Brar appeared and stood talking by the front door. Parm was holding something.

'He's got Davinder's bag,' Zaq said. 'So they *are* moving it or they're going to dump it.'

Parm went to his car but Raj stayed where he was. The van doors slammed shut and the driver got behind the wheel. He started the engine and turned on his lights.

'Where are Jhutti and Chadha?' Jags said.

'Must be in the back, with the guy.' Just as they had been the other night, with Davinder.

The van moved off first, then Parm right behind them. Zaq and Jags ducked again as the vehicles turned onto the road and drove away.

'Wait for Raj to go inside, then let's follow them,' Zaq said.

Raj stood and watched until the vehicles were out of sight, then disappeared back into the warehouse. As soon as he was gone, Zaq and Jags clambered into the front seats and Jags started the engine.

'Leave your lights off for now,' Zaq said.

Jags drove slowly past the warehouse to minimise the engine noise, then on around the bend. 'Why didn't Raj go with them?'

'If you had three-quarters of a million pounds stashed somewhere with a busted door, would you just leave it? He's probably staying there till they get the door sorted.'

They saw the tail lights of Parm's car and the van in front of it, as they slowed to exit the estate. Both vehicles turned right, onto the main road.

'Keep your lights off till we hit the road,' Zaq said. 'There'll be other cars there, so then we won't have to worry.' Jags put his foot down and they shot to the exit in time to see Parm disappear from view round a bend. 'OK, stick your lights on and let's get after them but not too close.'

'I've seen car chases on TV as well, you know.' Jags got onto the road and sped in pursuit. They caught sight of the two vehicles ahead, at the junction by the Tarmac works, signalling left. Jags eased back a touch now he had them in sight. The van and the Mercedes drove under the dual carriageway and followed the road in a wide arc, joining the Parkway on the other side. Traffic was heavier there, so they didn't stand out. They stayed behind them over the canal and the railway lines, and down to the traffic lights – which started to change as they approached.

'Put your foot down, 'Zaq said. 'Don't lose –'

Jags didn't need to be told. He stamped on the accelerator, launching the car forward and pressing Zaq into his seat. The van and the Mercedes went through the lights a second or two before they turned red. Jags didn't even think about stopping. He shot through the signal just as the cars from the right started moving. Zaq's hands gripped the sides of his seat. It was nothing like driving his van.

Jags slowed down and they trailed the vehicles all the way to the Great West Road and into Hounslow. Zaq saw the Black Horse up ahead, where he'd met Davinder only a couple of days ago. Jags hung back as they made their way down Lampton Road towards the High Street.

'Jhutti and Chadha's place is this way,' Zaq said. 'I wonder if that's where they're going.' Up ahead, both vehicles started indicating right. 'That's their road, so it must be.'

'Shall I follow them?'

'Yeah, but take your time.'

Jags slowed as he approached the turn, so they wouldn't be too close behind – but as they drew level with the street, they saw the Mercedes stopped in the middle of the road, the van blocking the way as it made a U-turn.

'Shit,' Zaq said. '*Keep going, keep going.*' Jags accelerated. 'Take the left, here.' Jags turned down the road beside the pub. 'Go down there, turn around and come back. Stop where we can see them.'

They sped out of sight of the vehicles across the road, swung the car around and crept back.

'Turn your lights off and move up slowly.'

Jags did as he said and eased the BMW up the road, stopping once they had a good view across the road.

The van was had parked and the driver was standing beside the Mercedes, talking to Parm through the open passenger window. After a brief exchange, the guy stepped back and Parm drove away up the road.

'He can't be going far,' Zaq said. 'The road's blocked off halfway up. Maybe he's going to Jhutti and Chadha's.'

'They in there with him?'

'How should I know?'

'What's he doing now?' Jags nodded towards the driver, who had gone to the back of the van. They saw one of the rear doors open.

'Letting them out,' Zaq said.

The driver came out from behind the vehicle and looked around, checking the coast was clear. He signalled the others and they came shambling out, crossing the side street. Jhutti and Chadha were on either side of their limp captive, supporting his weight between them. If he didn't know better, Zaq would have said the guy was drunk.

The driver closed the doors and the van's indicators flashed as the alarm went on. He overtook the slow-moving trio – and promptly disappeared from view.

'Where'd he go?' Jags said.

Zaq looked hard at the spot where the driver had vanished. It took a moment for him to make out a deeper slash of blackness in the shadows between the rear of the corner shop and the first house on the street. 'There's an alley there, must run behind the shops.'

Jhutti and Chadha reached it and shuffled sideways into the narrow space, still supporting the man between them.

'The *butcher's*,' Zaq said. 'They must be going to the butcher's shop. Jhutti and Chadha were there the other day, before they grabbed Davinder. So the driver must be Subash Prewal – it's his van. His family own the shop.' Zaq remembered something else. 'The Brars' warehouse is registered in *his* name.'

'All right – but why the fuck have they brought that other guy here?'

'I don't know.' Zaq made a snap decision. 'But I'm going to go find out.' He opened his door.

'What the fuck you doing?'

'If Parm went to their house, it gives me enough time to get down that alley to try and see what's going on.'

'What if he comes back before you get out?'

'I'll hide somewhere. They won't be expecting anyone down there this time of night.' He slammed the car door and sprinted for the alley.

CHAPTER TWENTY-NINE

Zaq ran diagonally across the main road, to the mouth of the alley. He looked down it but there wasn't much to see, just a paved walkway that disappeared into pitch dark, where no light reached, high walls on either side and a narrow strip of night sky above. He ducked into the alley and picked his way along it as quickly and quietly as he could.

The wall to his left belonged to a house and then its garden, a featureless expanse of red brick that seemed to run the entire length of the alley. On the right, the wall was split into sections, each one the rear of one of the shops that looked onto the main road. There was a door in each section, most of them solid steel. He remembered the butcher's was toward the far end of the parade, so would be near the end of the alley. Moving along, he came to a door that was slightly ajar, roughly where he expected the butcher's to be. A sliver of light showed through the gap. Zaq heard sounds from within but not well enough to make out what they were. His heart was thumping against the inside of his chest, like it was trying to beat its way out and sweat was cooling on his brow in the night air.

What now? He wasn't going to find anything out by standing there in the dark. *Fuck it, he'd come this far...*

Carefully, he pushed the heavy steel door open a little further, desperately hoping the hinges wouldn't squeal. They didn't and he slipped inside, into an unlit storage room crowded with large rectangular objects, silhouetted by light from further inside. He worked out they were big industrial bins. Plastic crates and piles of flattened cardboard boxes were stacked around the room too; the air was thick with the smell of blood, raw meat and sawdust, undercut with a faint whiff of disinfectant.

On the far side of the room was another door. It had been left open too and what little light there was came through it. If he could get close enough to see or hear what was going on through there, maybe he'd learn something useful. Besides, if he went back out now, he might run into Parminder.

His mouth felt dry as dust, as he ducked low and moved over to the wall on his right. He pressed his back against it and started forwards. A drop of sweat snaked down his back, leaving a thin trail of moisture. He got behind one of the bins and was pushing it away from the wall so he could slip past, when he heard footsteps approaching from the alley.

He shoved the bin aside enough that he could slip between it and the wall and crouched down, making himself as small as possible. The smell of blood and old meat was stronger here. Peering between the bins he saw Parm enter and shut the door behind him with a solid clunk. Then he crossed the room and went through the other door.

Zaq moved further forward.

'He awake yet?' Parminder's voice.

Zaq was close enough to hear what was being said.

'Nah, fucker's still out. We went through his pockets though and found these.'

It sounded like Jhutti or Chadha, he didn't know which or what they had found. There were a couple of bins still between him and the inner door, which had been left open. Zaq manoeuvred his way between them until he was behind the last bin, from where he could see through the doorway, as well as hear what was going on.

'Wake him up,' Parm said. 'I don't want to be here all night.'

Peering past the bin, Zaq saw a short corridor lit by fluorescent tubes. It was lined with a series of stainless steel worktops and sinks, with cupboards above and more storage below. The place had a harsh, sterile feel. The walls were panelled in stainless steel to about chest height, above which they were painted white, as was the ceiling. At its far end, the corridor opened into a wider space. It was there that Zaq saw a man, hanging, suspended by his hands, which were tied together and hitched onto a meathook, one of several on a rail fixed to the ceiling. The man looked unconscious, body limp, head on his chest, feet dangling above the floor. His clothes were a mess and his pockets had been turned inside out.

Chadha stepped forward, whipped a meaty hand round and slapped the hanging man hard across the face. The sudden sound made Zaq flinch. Parminder Brar, Jhutti, Chadha and the one who had to be Subash Prewal, all stood watching.

'*Bhen de…*,' Jhutti laughed at Chadha. 'He didn't even feel that.'

The captive was spinning from the force of the blow. As he spun back, Chadha slapped him again, harder. Zaq winced, involuntarily. The man stirred but didn't wake. He spun faster.

'Want *me* to do it?' Jhutti asked.

'Fuck you, I'll wake him up,' Chadha said. He hit him twice more, once with his left hand, then with his right, his feet almost leaving the ground with the effort. The man raised his head for a second – just long enough for Zaq to see that his mouth was covered with duct tape, his face all bruised and bloody – before he let it slump down again.

'My mum can slap harder than that,' Jhutti said.

'That's 'cause she's a slapper, innit?'

'Up yours!'

'Stop fucking about and get on with it,' Parm snapped at them.

This time Chadha delivered three forceful slaps, a right, a left and a final resounding right. The man's head jerked up, eyes wide, legs thrashing around for something solid to stand on.

'Rise and shine, Kasim, you cunt.' Chadha said, then punched him in the stomach. The captive jack-knifed in the air, his face screwed up in pain.

Kasim? Had he just heard that right? *What the fuck would Kasim have been doing breaking into the Brars' warehouse?*

'Take the tape off,' Parm said. Chadha ripped the duct tape away from Kasim's mouth, causing him to cry out.

'Where's the money?' Parm said, his voice devoid of any emotion.

Would Kasim know about the hundred grand Rita had taken? He would *if* she'd told him about it.

'Fuck you,' Kasim wheezed.

Parm nodded to Chadha who hit Kasim twice in the ribs – mean, powerful blows that twisted Kasim's face in agony with each impact. Zaq heard him gasping for breath, unable to speak, his body trying to curl in on itself. Parm nodded again. This time Chadha raised his hands like a boxer and hit Kasim with three vicious hooks to the body. Kasim could only screw his eyes shut and grit his teeth against the pain.

'Remember that bit in Rocky?' Chadha said. 'Where he uses the slab of meat as a punchbag?' He was grinning and trying to bounce around on his feet.

When Kasim was finally able to speak, he said, 'If you were going to kill me, you should've done it properly the first time.'

'What the fuck you on about?'

'That was your plan, wasn't it? But you fucked up.'

'If we wanted you dead, you'd be dead.' Parm said.

'Rita told me.'

'Told you *what*?'

'She heard you, saying it'd be better to get rid of me and split my share.'

'You what? We never said that. *She fucking lied to you.*'

'Why would she do that?'

'Why the fuck d'you think? For the *money*.'

'Way you beat me up…'

'What the fuck did you expect? It had to look real.'

'Yeah, but if she hadn't called the ambulance, I might not have made it.'

'What you on about? How'd she know to call you an ambulance?'

'She was there,' Kasim said. 'In case you tried to fuck me over.'

'*You fucking told her about it?*'

'After she told me what you were going to do. She said she'd help me.'

'She fucking used you to get the money.'

'She didn't try to kill me to get it.'

Zaq saw Parm frowning. 'We weren't trying to kill you, you fucking idiot. I wish we had now though.'

'The fuck you weren't. Doctors said I was lucky not to have any permanent injuries.'

'It weren't luck. We knew what we were doing. But I'll tell you this right now – you don't tell us where the money is, this time we will fucking kill you. Now, where is it?'

'Safe.'

'Well, you ain't, not until we get it back.' Parm looked at Chadha. 'Hit him till I tell you to stop.'

Chadha went to work, pummelling the undefended face and body. Kasim tried to squirm away from the blows but hanging as he was, there was no escape. He took the full impact of every punch. It was hard for Zaq to watch. He knew what such punishment felt like.

'OK, that's enough,' Parm said after a while. 'Now, where's the fucking money?'

Kasim's breath came in ragged gasps. Fresh blood streamed from his face, onto his T-shirt. Parm and the others had to wait until he could talk. He coughed and spat on the floor.

'Hey, that's well unhygienic!' It was the first time Zaq had heard Subash Prewal speak.

Kasim looked at Parm. 'Fuck you.' He spat again.

This time Parm looked at Jhutti, who was standing with his arms crossed. 'Your turn,' he said.

Grinning, Jhutti picked up a long-bladed filleting knife from the butcher's block he'd been leaning against and pushed himself towards Kasim. 'All right, Gurps,' he said to Chadha, 'out the way. Let me show you how it's done.'

'Like last time?' Chadha said.

'That weren't my fault. How was I supposed to know he'd bleed to death? What am I, a fucking doctor?'

What did he mean by that?

'Just be careful this time,' Parm said. 'We don't want another accident before we find out what we want.'

'I ain't telling you shit.' Kasim said, though his tough talk wasn't fooling anyone. Even from where he was, Zaq could hear the quaver of fear in his voice. It was only a matter of time before he told them whatever they wanted to know.

'We'll see,' Parm said. 'Tape his mouth again.'

Chadha used a rag to wipe the blood away from Kasim's mouth and stuck the duct tape back over it. Meanwhile, Jhutti cut all of Kasim's clothing off with the knife. When he was hanging naked and totally exposed, Jhutti held the knife up in front of his eyes. 'Now let's see how tough you really are.' He stepped back and, with a quick flick of his wrist, slashed Kasim across the chest. Everything was still for a moment – then a thin red line appeared, thickening until tendrils of blood began running down his body.

'You probably didn't even feel that,' Jhutti said. 'Don't worry, you will.' He brought the knife up in an angled stroke across the ribs. Kasim flinched, and blood began to well from the cut. Jhutti cut him several more times. There was a lot more blood. Then Jhutti either miscalculated or got carried away because he sliced deep into an arm, around the triceps. The wound gaped open like a mouth. '*Shit*,' Jhutti said.

Kasim began to buck and thrash like a panicked animal. Jhutti stood back and laughed. 'Fucking hell.' He looked at Subash Prewal. 'Subs, get some lemon juice and salt, and some chilli powder. We'll marinate the fucker, see if that gets him talking.'

Fuck this. Zaq felt sick at the thought of what they were going to do. It was barbaric.

Prewal didn't move at first but when the others all looked at him, he pushed himself away from the worktop and disappeared. He didn't look happy.

Chadha walked all the way around Kasim until he was standing in front of him again. 'We're going to make you scream, bitch.'

A moment later Prewal came back carrying what Jhutti

had asked for. Kasim began to struggle but it didn't make any difference.

Jhutti opened the plastic squeezy bottle of concentrated lemon juice. 'Let's see how you like this...' He aimed at the wound across Kasim's ribs and squeezed off a good squirt. Kasim's reaction was instant. He began to convulse violently, as if he was being electrocuted, his screams muffled by the duct tape. 'Ooh, that's got to sting,' Jhutti said, laughing.

Zaq was wincing. He could only imagine what it must have felt like.

Jhutti waited until the convulsions stopped. Kasim's eyes were wild and tears glistened on his face. Jhutti made Kasim wait... then squeezed a burst of lemon juice right into the gaping wound on his arm. His screams were loud, even through the duct tape.

Zaq started forward without thinking, his natural instinct – to stop what was happening... but his head overrode his heart, halting his motion, knowing that it would be suicide. He stopped, but swore at himself anyway, for not being able to do anything.

The stifled cries ceased and Kasim went limp.

'He's fucking fainted,' Jhutti said.

'Wake him up, then,' Parm said.

'Subs, get some water,' Jhutti ordered.

Prewal went to one of the sinks, filled a plastic container with water and handed it to Jhutti, who threw it over Kasim. The shock brought Kasim round. The water washed much of the blood from him but more seeped from his wounds and began to run down his body again, mixing with the water. Zaq could hear him sobbing.

'Take the tape off,' Parm said. Jhutti ripped it away. Kasim barely registered it. His head was down and he was breathing hard. 'Let's try again,' Parm said. 'Where's the money?'

Kasim looked up. 'What're you going to do to me if I tell you?' His voice was hoarse and weak.

'Nothing. We'll let you go. We just want the money. You can go get yourself fixed up. Then you pack your bags and leave. We'll give you a couple of days. We see you after that, you're dead.'

'You're just going to let me go?'

'Why not?' Parm said. 'All we want's the money. Tell us where it is and you can fuck off. What did you think we were going to do?'

'Kill me... whether I tell you or not.'

'You don't tell us, we'll definitely kill you. You do and you got a chance of walking out of here alive. So, the sooner you tell us, sooner this'll all be over and you can get yourself looked at.'

'I don't... I don't believe you.'

Parm shrugged. 'Suit yourself. But you're going to tell us one way or another. Why not make it easy on yourself?'

'Fuck you. If you're going to kill me, go ahead – at least I'll know you ain't got the money.'

'I told you, we ain't going to kill you – though by the time we're done with you, you'll wish we had.' Parm looked at Jhutti. 'Make him talk.'

Jhutti slapped the tape back over Kasim's mouth, then took a pair of blue polythene gloves from a box on the worktop and put them on.

'I don't think the money's up his arse, if that's where you're going to look,' Chadha said.

'You're so interested in his arse, you go ahead and take a look up there.' Jhutti took the pack of chilli powder from Prewal, ripped off a corner and shook some onto a gloved hand. Then he slapped it against a deep slash in Kasim's side, working the chilli right into the wound.

Kasim went berserk, kicking and twisting. His eyes bulged and his face flushed red with strain. He screamed against the gag and threw his head around as if he were having a fit.

Zaq looked away in disgust. He'd seen people slashed and stabbed before, on the street and in prison, but this was something else; *torture*, pure and simple. *And these motherfuckers were enjoying it.*

'Woo hoo!' Jhutti yelled. Zaq looked back and saw him shake a mass of chilli powder right into the big wound on Kasim's arm. Kasim promptly passed out again.

Silent rage swept through Zaq; rage at the bastards in front of him and what they were doing – but also at himself, for only being able to sit and watch. Outnumbered and unarmed, if he tried anything he'd end up hanging right next to Kasim – but knowing that didn't lessen the shame he felt for not acting.

What the fuck had Kasim been doing at the warehouse anyway? From what he'd overheard, it was plain to Zaq there was something going on he didn't understand. The way Kasim had talked… it was like he *knew* the Brars would beat him up… but that didn't make any sense. Was he helping Rita or working with her brothers in some way? Or was he just out for himself?

'Bring him round,' Parm said.

'More water,' Jhutti told Subs, who did as he was told. Jhutti threw the water over Kasim and slapped him until he came to.

'Take the tape off.'

Jhutti pulled it off. Kasim's breathing was panicky and erratic.

'You want more of that?'

Just fucking tell them what they want, Zaq willed him. It's only money.

'Fuck yourself,' Kasim said, through gritted teeth.

Zaq couldn't believe his stubbornness.

'No, *fuck you*,' Parm said. 'I've had enough of this shit.' He grabbed a pair of gloves from the butcher's block and pulled them on, then stalked over to Kasim and punched him in the face, once, twice, three times.

'You take our fucking money...' Parm punched him again.

'Fuck us over...' Another punch.

'Then you come back...' Punch.

'and steal more...' Punch.

'of our money...' Punch.

'You fucking...' Punch.

'piece...' Punch.

'of...' Punch.

'shit!' Punch.

Kasim hung limp and groaning, hitching his breath.

'Give me the knife,' Parm said. Jhutti handed him the filleting knife. 'Bad enough you and that silly bitch sister of mine ran off together – but you should never have taken the money.' Parm moved in front of Kasim, the knife in his right hand. 'You fucking her?' Kasim didn't respond. 'Dirty whore. If she was here, she'd get what's coming to her too. What is it you Muslims do when someone gets caught sticking their dick where they shouldn't?'

'They fucking chop it off,' Chadha said.

'That what we should do with you?'

Zaq could hear Kasim sobbing.

Parm brought the knife up and touched the flat of the blade to the head of Kasim's flaccid penis. 'You been sticking this in my sister?'

Kasim flinched involuntarily and tried to twist away. 'Please,' he croaked. 'Don't....' Blood, snot and tears ran down his face.

'Don't what? *This*?' Parm put the sharp edge of the blade against the head of Kasim's penis and sliced upward. There were sharp intakes of breath as everyone flinched, tensing their own dicks, including Zaq. Kasim screamed – but the sound came out like sandpaper rubbing on brick. The strange sound continued for a while and then he fainted. A trail of red ran from the cut, making it look like he was pissing blood.

Zaq felt his gorge rise.

'Fucking hell, Parm, that was nasty,' Jhutti said.

Parm glared at him. 'You want to kiss it better, go ahead.'

Jhutti threw more water over Kasim, then slapped him awake again. 'No more... please...' Kasim begged in a thin, cracked voice.

Parm ignored him and pointed to Kasim's penis with the knife. 'Rub some chilli powder on it,' he ordered Jhutti.

'*What*?' Jhutti said. 'I ain't touching his cock.'

'Then fucking *sprinkle* it on!'

'No, *please*...' Kasim said. 'I'll tell you... I'll tell you where the money is.'

Thank fuck for that. Zaq was relieved for him. Hopefully, once he told them where the money was they'd dump him at a hospital somewhere. He'd held out for as long as he could – much longer than most – but in the end, he didn't really have any choice. He might have wanted Rita and the money, but he wanted his dick and his life more.

'About fucking time,' Parm said. 'Well...?'

Zaq fought down the disgust and loathing he felt for Parm at that moment and listened hard.

'It's in a self-storage place in Hanger Lane.' There was no fight left in his voice. He was broken.

'Where exactly?'

'Off the gyratory system, going towards Alperton. There's a drive-thru McDonald's, it's behind that.'

'What's it called?'

'West London Storage.'

'Must be in a unit there? What's the number?'

'232.'

Parm looked at Jhutti. 'Where are those keys you found on him?'

Jhutti threw a bunch of keys to Parm, who held them up in front of Kasim. 'Which one of these is for the unit?'

'None of them.'

'You want to dip your dick in the chilli powder?'

'I don't have it on me. It's at the flat.'

'What flat?'

'In Kensington. Where we're staying.'

'You and *Rita*? She there now?' Kasim gave a weak nod. 'What's the address?'

'Apartment 1, Campden Hill Court, in Kensington.'

Zaq repeated the address in his head till he was sure he had it. He didn't have to worry about telling Parm where Rita was any more; he already knew. All he had to do now was sit back and let them go get her, then everything would be sorted. Right?

Wrong.

Could he really just sit back and do nothing after what he'd just witnessed? Was he going to leave Rita to a similar fate and then carry on as if nothing had happened? The answer was simple; *no, he wasn't.*

He knew where she was now too and needed to get over there as fast as he could, before any of this lot did. He could worry about taking her to her dad after he got her away from the flat. But he'd have to leave now and get a head start. He'd call the cops on the way, tell them what had happened here. He couldn't let it slide. This was *way more* than he'd bargained for. These psychos had to be stopped.

He started to back away between the bins. The hardest part was going to be getting out of the back door without being seen or heard.

'Two nights in a row…' Parm was saying. 'You might've got away with it, if you hadn't been so fucking greedy.'

'What you talking about?' Kasim said.

'The fucking warehouse. No point denying it now.'

'I told you what you wanted. Just let me go. I need a fucking hospital.'

'Oh, yeah. Right, no problem.' Parm walked around behind Kasim, pulled his head back… and cut his throat.

Kasim's eyes went wide with shock. His mouth moved but no sound came out; he kicked his legs in a desperate panic. Blood poured from the wound and ran down his body in thick red waves, joining the dark pool already on the floor, a stark contrast to the white tiles. Parm stepped back. They all stood and watched as the life drained out of Kasim. Zaq watched too, stunned – he couldn't believe it. But then the voice in his head was shouting at him to GO, telling him this would be his best chance of getting out of there, while everyone's attention was on Kasim. He started moving backwards again, slipping between the bins towards the exit. Kasim was still now, hanging there. The blood slowed to a trickle, dripping from his feet.

Parm was the first to move. 'Here,' he said, handing the knife to Prewal. 'Get this cleaned up.'

'Fucking hell,' Prewal complained. 'That's *twice* in one week.'

Zaq frowned. *Twice? What the fuck did that mean?* Then it hit him. *Davinder.* Holy shit! Had they done the same to him?

'You got a problem with that?' Parm's voice had an edge as sharp as the blade he'd just used. 'You're getting paid enough, so just get on with it.'

'Fuck, Parm, I didn't know you was going to do him like that,' Jhutti said.

'What the fuck did you expect? What else were we going to

do with him?'

'It was just a bit sudden, that's all. I thought you'd have made him suffer a bit more, for all the shit he's caused us.'

'We ain't got time for that. We know where the money is, and the key we'll need. All we got to do is go pick them up.'

Zaq moved away faster.

'What about Rita?'

'What about her?' Parm said. 'Once we've got the key I don't give a shit. She's shamed my family by fucking this *sullah*. I don't even want to look at her. Who the fuck's going to marry her now? We're getting rid of him… might as well get rid of her too, make it look like they disappeared together.'

'Me and Chadha'll take care of her for you.'

'Whatever. Just make sure she ain't found.'

Zaq was so focused on getting to the door unheard, it took him a couple of seconds to register what they were saying – that they were going to *kill Rita*.

He was almost at the back door – but there was a problem. The door had been open when he'd snuck in but Parm had closed it after him and now it was firmly shut. It was a fire door, the type where you had to push down on a metal bar and then shove it open. It didn't look like there was any chance of it opening without making a sound.

'Take care of this fucker properly,' Parm was saying, 'not like the last one. Don't just chop him up into pieces. We don't want his arms and legs getting found this time.'

'That weren't my fault,' Prewal said. 'Them two should've disposed of the bits properly.'

Hang on. What? Chop him up? Dispose of… properly? Zaq felt as if a lead weight had dropped through him and taken his stomach with it. They had to be talking about Davinder – who else could it be? *That meant the body parts in the park were his.*

'Just do it right this time,' Parm said. Then, 'Come on, let's go.' He must've been talking to Jhutti and Chadha.

'How am I supposed to get rid of him then?' It was Prewal again.

'I don't know. You're a fucking *butcher* – take the meat off him and grind it up in that big fucking mincer you got over there. Saw up the bones and chuck them away with the animal ones. No one'll know the difference.'

'Are you serious?'

'I look like I'm fucking joking?'

'What am I meant to do with the meat?'

'Fucking sell it, for all I care – you can say it's *halal*.'

All the while he'd been listening Zaq had been psyching himself up to go for the door. He knew his time was almost up. Fuck caution, he had to go now. He bolted for the door, smashed the bar down and threw it open. The clash of metal on metal and the scrape of metal on stone shrieked his presence for all to hear.

'*OI!*' he heard behind him – but he didn't care, he was already flying down the alley.

CHAPTER THIRTY

His escape must have taken them by surprise giving him a few seconds head start. He burst out of the alley as he heard them barging their way out of the back door after him.

He'd never make it back to Jags' car without them seeing him and he didn't want them to see Jags, so he went right and sprinted up Bulstrode Avenue. He just hoped Jags would see what was happening and stay out of sight. His heart was hammering away in his chest, pushing him on, driving him to run harder and faster.

Behind him, he could hear the sounds of pursuit; up ahead, a turning to the right. He took it and fled along a narrow path between houses. It led to a subway under the tube tracks and into the pitch black expanse of Lampton Park beyond. If he could make it into the darkness on the other side of the subway, he might have a chance at losing them.

He shot through the short subway, into the park and kept going, across the grass. Lungs burning, he had to slow down – no way could he keep sprinting full tilt – but continued on, jogging, angling left towards an exit he knew was there from having made deliveries in the area. There were shouts behind him – they must've just entered the park. They were confused, would have difficulty spotting him in the darkness of the middle of the park, away from the lit paths. He upped his pace as much as he could, heading for some trees at the edge of the park, outlined against the fractionally less dark sky. Then he was on the path and saw streetlights outside the park, ahead of him. He came to a waist-high metal gate, leapt over it, and emerged onto a residential street, houses either side.

He couldn't stop here. They were still behind him somewhere. Then a thought hit him; what if Parm had got his car and was driving this way right now, to check this exit? He had to get away from the park. He tried to speed up but his energy was almost spent; it was all he could do just to keep going.

He got to the end of the street. Across the road in front of him was a primary school. Zaq crossed to it and clambered over the perimeter wall. Using it as cover, he moved along to the right, past the school buildings, across a playground and to a large fenced-in area of grass, where he finally dropped to the ground under a tree to get his breath back.

He took out his phone, turned it to silent – last thing he needed was for his ringtone to go off and give him away. Then he called Jags.

'*What the fuck happened?*'

'Never mind that,' Zaq said, in a hoarse whisper. 'Where are you?'

'On Bath Road. I saw you leg it and that lot chasing after you. Soon as they disappeared I got out of there. Been trying to work out where you might've gone.'

'I cut through the park. There's a school on the other side, on Sutton Lane. I'm in the grounds.'

'I'm on my way.'

* * *

The memory of Kasim's throat being cut played over and over in his head; he couldn't shake it. He told himself it was shock but rationalising it did nothing to help. It had been totally unexpected. What they'd already done to him was bad enough – he thought they would have stopped at that – but they hadn't.

And all he'd done was sit and watch.

But, even if he'd known what Parm was going to do, what could he have done about it? Should he even have done anything? What was Kasim to him, that he should've risked his life to help him? It was no good though; no matter how much he tried to justify his inaction, he couldn't escape the weight of the guilt he felt, pressing down on his conscience.

And not just for Kasim. He was now sure that Davinder was dead too. *Twice in one week*, Prewal had said. Then they'd mentioned chopping someone up and parts being discovered. That was why Parm had been so insistent they were more thorough getting rid of Kasim. Who else could they have been talking about? It had to be Davinder. Had they tortured him too, before killing him? Pretty fucking likely.

What the hell was going on? What was he mixed up in? Whatever it was, he was in way over his head. He had no choice now; he had to call the police. He couldn't let the fuckers get away with two murders – maybe even three, if they got to Rita first… Shit – *Rita!* He had to warn her.

He tried her number but there was no answer. *Fuck.* Where was Jags? They'd have to try and get to the flat before Parm and the others. With any luck, they were still searching for him in the park, which might give him and Jags just enough time to get there and get Rita out ahead of them. Maybe it was better that way. If he'd warned her over the phone, she'd have run.

As he sat there thinking, it dawned on him that he didn't only have to get her out for her own sake. If those guys got to her first and made her disappear, he wouldn't find her, which meant Mr Brar would have him sent back to prison. Not that Raj and Parm would give a fuck about that. As if that wasn't enough, he was the last person with Davinder before he disappeared and he'd been asking around about Kasim – *both of whom were now dead*. If Rita disappeared too, what was there to stop her brothers trying to pin all three on him?

He had to get to Rita first. She was his best bet for getting out of this whole shitty mess. She could tell the police the truth about her brothers and their search for her, if it came down to it – and he'd also have the option of simply handing her over to her old man and walking away from the whole thing.

He needed to move *now*, get going, not waste time sitting under a fucking tree. The waiting was driving him nuts.

Then he heard a car turning off the main road, onto the street that ran along the side of the school grounds. It stopped part way down. Zaq watched it and waited. Then his phone began to vibrate.

'I'm parked by the side of the school. Where are you?'

'That you on the street, next to the grass area?'

'Yeah.'

'You see anyone else about?'

'No.'

'I'm coming out.'

He ran in a crouch across the grass, keeping his eyes and ears open. Making sure the coast was clear, he vaulted over the low hedge and railings that bordered that side of the school, ran to the car and clambered into the back. Jags took off before the door was even closed. 'What the fuck happened back there?'

'Get on the A4, as quick as you can. We've got to go get Kensington.'

'What for?'

'That's where Rita is.'

'How d'you know that?'

'The geezer they dragged into the shop... that was Kasim. He told them where to find her.'

'*Shit*. So what happened in there? How come they were chasing you?'

'*They fucking killed him*. I saw it happen – and then I ran.'

Jags slammed on the brakes. '*What the* –?'

'DRIVE!' Zaq shouted. When they were moving again he said, 'I just got the hell out of there. Only way out was through the back door. I had to barge my way through it and they came after me.'

'*Fuckin' hell!* What we going to do?'

'*You're* going to get on the A4 and take us to Kensington. *I'm* going to call the cops.'

'I thought you didn't want to do that.'

'That was before I saw someone get murdered.' He took out his phone and found the Crimestoppers number, checked that 1-4-1 was in front of it from the last time, and made the call. He might be reporting what he'd seen but he wasn't about to leave his own details.

'Would you like to report a crime?' asked the elderly sounding man who answered.

'Yes,' Zaq said. 'I've just seen a murder.'

There was a moment's silence, then the man said, 'You need to talk to the emergency operator. I'll put you through to 999.'

'No, I'm not talking to them. I'll tell you and you can tell them.'

And Zaq told him.

He made the information he gave as detailed as he could while leaving out names, giving only descriptions of Parm and the others. By the time the call ended Jags knew the details of how Kasim had been killed. He'd also heard Zaq mention talk of another body, possibly connected to the body parts found in Cranford Park.

They drove on in silence for while, and then Jags said, 'The body in the park...? You never said anything about it before.'

'I didn't know for sure it was anything to do with all this. But after what I heard back there...'

'You think it was Davinder?'

'Yeah... I'm pretty sure.'

There was another brief spell of silence.

'What you going to tell Rita?' Jags asked.

That was a good question. 'I don't know. Let's get to her first.'

CHAPTER THIRTY-ONE

It was late and the roads were fairly clear, so they were making good time.

'Why didn't you give their names?' Jags asked after a while.

Now Zaq thought about it, the reason sounded kind of dumb, especially given the circumstances. 'I ain't a grass,' he said. All his life, growing up in Southall – and even more so in prison – he'd been conditioned never to name names. You could tell the rozzers what happened, even where and when, sometimes even why, but you never told them who. It hadn't felt right to do it, even now. Besides, he'd given them enough to go on. They'd find out their names soon enough once they nicked them.

There was another reason too. 'Besides, this way it'll look like whoever called didn't know who they were – unlike me, who could've named the whole lot of them. Cops get there quick enough they could even catch them red-handed, in which case a witness might not even matter.'

Jags' driving shaved several minutes off their journey time. When they got to Kensington, Zaq used his iPhone to direct them to Campden Hill Road. Campden Hill Court itself was an imposing red brick mansion block. Jags turned into a road named Observatory Gardens and found a space to park.

'Wait here,' Zaq said, 'and let me know if Parm or anyone turns up.'

'Won't they've been nicked by now?'

'Hopefully, but if haven't been, they'll be on their way here right now. Just sit tight and call me if you see them.' Zaq got out of the car.

There was a security gate stopping anyone from entering the building grounds. It was only waist height and he would have jumped it – if not for the security cameras dotted around the building. Beside the gate was an intercom system, with buzzers for apartments one to twelve on this side of the building. Zaq pressed the button for apartment one.

No answer.

He pressed again. Still nothing.

This time he pressed the button and kept his finger on it. '*Come on, come on…*'

After what seemed like a minute but was probably only a few seconds, the speaker crackled to life. 'Yes?' It was a woman's voice.

'Rita?'

'Sorry, you've got the wrong flat.'

The intercom made her voice sound different but he was sure it was her. 'Rita, it's Zaq.' The hiss of static from the speaker told him she was still listening. 'Your brothers got Kasim.'

She hesitated – a moment too long – before saying, 'I don't know what you're talking about. You better leave.'

'He told them everything. They might be on their way here *right now*. You don't have much time.'

Another pause.

And then, finally, 'Where's Kasim?'

Zaq wasn't about to tell her he'd been murdered, not over the intercom. 'They grabbed him at the warehouse and took him to Hounslow. I saw them.'

'How? You were supposed to be at home.'

'I was. I had a mate watching the place.'

'Why?'

'To try and find Davinder. Look, that doesn't matter right now. We have to get you –'

'How do I know you're telling the truth, that this isn't a trick?'

'You just have to trust me.'

'I don't.'

'Kasim told them you're here. How d'you think I found out?'

'If he told *them*, how come *you* know too?'

'I was there. I followed them and I heard him tell them. Look, we don't have time for this.'

'You could be making this all up, so I'll let you in and then you'll take me back to my dad? Maybe Raj and Parm are out there with you too.'

'I'll explain everything once we leave but we have to get out of here *now*.'

'Sorry, I'm not going anywhere with you. I'm going to call the police.'

'And tell them what?'

'That I'm running away from a forced marriage. They'll help me, take me somewhere safe.'

'You better call them *right now* then.' If she didn't believe him, what could he do? 'If Raj and Parm get here first they ain't going to take you home, or let you go.' He hoped that spelt it out for her. When she didn't respond, he gave up. 'OK, have it your way. You're on your own. Kasim ain't coming back and if you don't want my help, ain't nothing else I can do. If you're going to call the cops, go ahead and do it. Good luck.'

He turned to leave. All he could do now was wait in the car with Jags to watch to see what happened. He'd gone two steps when he heard a buzz and the gate clicked open. He hurried back. 'What floor?'

'Lower ground.'

Zaq went through the gate and rushed to the main entrance, where she buzzed him straight in. Inside, he found the stairs and went down them two at a time. The lower ground floor hallway was dark. Apartment 1 was on the left. He pressed the bell and heard it chime somewhere inside, the sound muffled by the expensive door and thick walls.

He waited – tense, unable to keep still. *What was she doing?*

Then the door opened, but only a fraction. An eye and part of a face looked out through a narrow gap. There was a thick security chain across the opening. 'What're you doing? We've got to go.'

She was trying to look past him, into the hallway. 'Are you alone?'

'Yeah. Now open the door.'

'How do I know you won't just hand me over to my dad or my brothers?'

'If that's what I wanted, I could've just stayed at home and let them come get you themselves. We can talk about your dad later, but right now you need to open the door.' Still she hesitated. 'Listen,' Zaq said through gritted teeth, keeping his voice low. 'Kasim's *dead*.' He saw her eyes widen, her mouth drop open. '*They fucking killed him*. I saw them do it – and from what they said, they're going to do the same to you. They know where you are, they know where the money is, and they could be here any minute. Now open the goddamn door.'

She shut it in his face.

What the fuck? That was it. He had to go.

There was the sound of the chain rattling, the door opened – and he found himself face-to-face with Rita Brar.

She was wearing grey sweatpants and a grey hoodie and, even though she was frowning and worried, she still looked amazing. She didn't have any make-up on and, as far as Zaq was concerned, she didn't need any. There was just something fresh and natural about her. Her warm brown eyes were bright and intelligent. Her hair was tousled and she was biting her lower lip, both of which made her look vulnerable and sexy at the same time. Something vibrating in his jeans made him suddenly embarrassed – until he realised it was his phone.

He stepped into the flat, shut the door and answered the call.

'What the fuck you doing in there?' Jags said. '*They're here.*'

'Shit. Where are they?'

'They just drove past, probably looking for somewhere to park.'

'How many of them?'

'Just two by the looks of it. I think it was Parm and Chadha.'

Perhaps Jhutti and Prewal had been nicked and these two had gotten away or maybe something else had happened – Zaq simply didn't know. But the fact Parm and Chadha were here was bad enough.

'Hang on,' Jags said. 'They're walking up. Parm's on his way in but Chadha's going somewhere else.'

'All right. Stay there, we'll be out in a bit.' He hung up.

'Who was that?'

'Friend of mine, waiting outside.'

'You said you were on your *own*.'

'He's in a car, waiting to get us out of here. Or we can walk. Parm's here.'

'He can't get in. This place is really secure.'

'He's got Kasim's keys.'

She swore under her breath. 'What did they do to him? To Kasim?'

'Not now,' he said. 'Is there another way out of here? A fire exit or something?'

She had to think about it. 'I don't know.'

The flat was on the lower ground floor. 'What about a window we can get out of?'

'In the bedrooms.'

'Grab what you need and let's go.'

She ran into the lounge, swiped her mobile phone from the coffee table, then hurried back into the hall, jammed her feet into a pair of trainers and grabbed a black puffa jacket from a hook on the wall. Next she rushed into a large double bedroom and snatched up her handbag.

She was starting to go round the bed towards a nightstand on the far side, when Zaq said, 'That's enough. Let's go. *Now!*'

'I just need –'

He grabbed her arm. 'Leave it. Where's the window out?'

'Other end of the hall. Let me just get –'

'No time. Come on.' Zaq pulled her out of the room and along the hall, then stopped. 'You got keys for the front door?'

'Yes.' She rifled through her bag and pulled out a set of keys.

They went back to the front door. There were several high-security locks fitted to it. 'Lock them all from the inside. It won't stop him but it'll buy us some time.' Zaq put the thick security chain on too.

Then they hurried to the bedroom at the end of the hall. They crossed the room to the window, only to find it was locked. Flustered, Rita looked through the keys still in her hand for the right one.

Zaq heard something and turned his head to listen. There it was again, faint, but he recognised it – a key in a lock. 'He's at the door,' he whispered.

It would only take Parm a couple of minutes to find the right keys and open the locks. The security chain would take a little longer. He'd have to force it, probably by giving it a hefty kick and hoping anyone who heard would put it down to a door being slammed or something. That's what Zaq would do at any rate.

Rita found the key and got the window open. Cold night air blew in, chilling the sweat on Zaq's forehead. He helped Rita climb out then followed her and closed the window after them.

They were in a long, narrow private garden that ran along the side of the mansion block. The only illumination was the light spilling from the flats, otherwise the area was shrouded in shadow. Could they risk going out to where Jags was waiting? Was Chadha waiting around there somewhere in case they came out?

They heard a faint crash from inside the flat. Parm must have broken in. That didn't give them much time. He'd waste a minute or so searching the flat for Rita – but it wouldn't take him long to figure out she must've gone out a window.

'Come on, this way.' Zaq pulled Rita away and towards the far end of the garden where it met another street. He steered her off the path, away from any light and onto the grass, using the shadows of the trees and shrubbery for cover. They were nearing a flight of stone steps up to a gate when a bulky figure moved into view. '*Shit.*' Zaq recognised the bulky figure – it was Chadha. They stopped and he pulled Rita behind a tree.

'What do we do now?' she said.

Zaq was trying to think of something when he realised neither Parm nor Chadha knew *he* was there. As far as they were aware,

Rita was on her own. Could he use that…? It gave him an idea. 'You go up to the gate,' he told her. 'Let him see you, then run back down here past me.'

'What are *you* going to do?'

'I'll take him from behind as he comes past.'

'That's your plan?'

'You got a better one? Go on, hurry up.' He pushed her forward.

'Idiot,' she said but started for the gate.

Zaq watched from behind the tree. Chadha must have spotted her because he stopped and retreated behind the corner of the building. Rita climbed the steps to the gate and, as she went to open it, Chadha rushed out and tried to grab her. Rita was quicker. She turned and started back down into the garden. Chadha took the steps two at a time and caught up, grabbing her before she made it to where Zaq was waiting. *Shit.*

'*Kidaah, soniyeh*?' Chadha said, greeting Rita as he pulled her close, lifting her off her feet.

'Get off me!'

He clamped a big hand over her mouth, smothering what might have been a scream.

If Zaq went for him now, while he was facing this way, Chadha would see him coming and be ready. Last thing he wanted was to get into a drawn out fight which would prevent them escaping. What he needed was for Chadha to turn the other way. Fortunately, Rita was struggling hard, kicking and thrashing, making it difficult for Chadha to maintain his grip. In order to keep hold of her, he had to move with her – and as a result, got turned around.

Zaq seized his chance and moved.

Chadha had his face close to Rita's, as if he was sniffing or tasting her. '*Oi, hoy,*' he was saying, 'feels nice when you struggle. You move like that in bed?' He laughed. 'I'll find out soon enough. Me and Dev are going to have some fun with you... before you *disappear*.'

By the time Chadha realised someone was behind him, it was too late. Zaq leapt up onto his back and got his right arm around Chadha's neck. Grabbing the back of Chadha's head with his left hand and using it as leverage, he tightened his hold, cutting off oxygen to Chadha's brain. He kicked Rita out of the way and wrapped his legs around Chadha's waist, crossing his ankles in front. It was a near-perfect Rear Naked Choke.

Chadha tried to prise Zaq's arm from around his throat but the hold was locked, too strong and too tight. He tried to hit Zaq by punching up and back but he was unable to reach high enough to do any damage. Zaq pulled the choke tighter and felt Chadha start to panic. He spun right, then left, trying to shake Zaq off, but it was no use. The more he struggled, the weaker he would get and until he passed out.

In desperation, no doubt sensing his consciousness starting to dull, he ran backwards into the tree, but Zaq was ready for it and absorbed the impact without loosening his hold. Chadha tried again with less strength. Zaq could feel the fight draining out of him. His hands flapped uselessly at Zaq's arms, until finally his legs buckled and he fell to his knees then slumped onto his side, as if his bones had turned to rubber. Zaq kept the choke tight for a couple more seconds then slowly released it. He uncrossed his legs and shoved Chadha away from him.

'Is he dead?' Rita said, staring, open-mouthed.

'No, just unconscious.' Zaq got to his feet. 'Come on, let's go. He won't be out for long.' He pulled Rita along, hurried her up the steps and through the gate to the street. 'Which way?' he asked.

'I don't know.'

The nearest corner was to their left, so he took them that way.
'Where are we going?'

'Away from the flat. Then I'll get Jags to come pick us up.'

'*Jags?*'

'My mate, in the car.'

At the corner they had three options; straight ahead, left or
right. The road ahead of them was too long and straight and
so was the road going right. Looking left, Zaq saw a turning
a little way up. 'This way,' he said. When they took the turn,
Zaq checked the sign and saw they were on Pitt Street. 'Keep
going.' Zaq fished out his phone as they ran and called Jags.

'Where the hell are you?' Jags said.

'On Pitt Street, heading away from the flat.'

'How'd you get out?'

'Through a window but we went the other way from you.
Parm come out yet?'

'No. He must still be inside.'

Either that or he'd climbed out a window and found Chadha.
'Come get us.' Zaq said.

'I'm on my way.'

Pitt Street dog-legged right, then left and became a narrow
street called Dukes Lane. He trusted Jags would figure out they'd
carried on along it. They were halfway to the end of the lane
when a car turned into it behind them. It flashed its lights as
it approached and Zaq hoped that meant it was Jags and not
Parminder. They stepped back onto the thin strip of pavement
beside the road. Jags pulled up beside them and opened the
passenger door. Zaq let Rita into the back then got in after her
and pulled the door shut.

'Hi, you must be Rita. I'm Jags.'

'Save the introductions for later and get us out of here.'

Zaq slid down as far as he could in the back seat and told

Rita to do the same. 'Your brother and Chadha are still around. Last thing we need is for them to spot us.'

She didn't look happy but scrunched down all the same.

'What happened back there?' Jags asked. Zaq told him how they got out of the flat and then about Chadha in the garden. 'Bloody hell,' Jags said. 'He see you?'

'I didn't give him a chance.'

'You think they'll suspect it was you?'

'I bloody hope not.'

'You better watch your back all the same.'

Jags was right – Raj and Parm were already suspicious of him and knew he was talking to Rita. After tonight, they might well want to ask him some more questions – only this time he could be answering them at the business end of a knife.

CHAPTER THIRTY-TWO

Jags drove up Kensington Church Street towards Notting Hill Gate. In the back, Rita turned to Zaq.

'What happened to Kasim?'

'I told you...' Zaq said, not really wanting to talk about it, 'he's dead. They killed him.'

'Who did? How?'

'It doesn't matter?'

'It *does* to me.'

She had a right to know and she would find out eventually anyway. There was no real way to sugar coat it and no point trying. 'Parm cut his throat.'

Even in the shadows of the back seat, the shock on her face was plain to see. As the meaning of his words sank in, she had to look away and wipe at her eyes. They drove on in silence for a while and then she looked back at him and said, 'You saw it happen?'

'Yeah.'

'Why didn't you stop it?' There was an accusation there.

'I wanted to,' he said, 'and I feel like shit 'cause I didn't but there was nothing I could do. If I'd tried, I'd have ended up the same way, and Parm and Chadha would have you now.'

Was it a good enough reason? Or did it just sound like an excuse? Then Zaq had a question for Rita, something that had been bothering him since earlier. 'What the hell was he doing at the warehouse anyway?' As he asked it, he had a sudden realisation. 'Wait a minute, *that's why you called me*, ain't it, asking about the alarm? It wasn't for your dad, it was for him, so *he* could get in. Why, though?'

She looked away and didn't answer, so he tried to figure out a possible reason himself. 'I doubt it was for the heroin. What would you have done with it? It'd be too much hassle to shift. They've already seen what's on Davinder's phone and computer, so there wouldn't be any point going after them now. I already told you Davinder wasn't there, so it wasn't to find him. Only thing that leaves... is the *money*.' She looked out of the window. 'You've already got a hundred grand, ain't that enough?'

The fact Kasim had broken into the warehouse suggested it *wasn't*. Certain Kasim had to have been there for the money, he didn't bother pressing her any further about it. What difference did it make? Whatever he'd gone there for, he was dead now.

'Look...' Zaq said, in a gentler tone, 'I'm sorry about what happened to him, I really am, but... we still have to decide what we do next.' He hoped she was listening and carried on. 'Way I see it, you got two options. Either you go to your dad, give him the money and tell him what's happened, like we talked about, or you go to the police.'

She carried on looking out of the window. Just as Zaq was about to go over the choices again, she said, 'I can't do either of those.'

'Why not?'

She turned to face him. 'What do you think will happen if I

go to my dad or the police?'

'Your brothers'll get put away for a long time.'

She gave a bitter laugh. 'You really think my dad would turn them in?'

'We're talking about murder.'

'I *know*,' she snapped, still struggling to cope with it. 'We're also talking about *his sons*. I'll tell you what he'll do if I go to him – he'll take the money then he'll help cover up whatever they've done. After that they'll decide what to do about me – I'll know too much. If they think I might go to the police, what do you think they'll do to me?'

'Couldn't you use that to get what you want, in exchange for keeping quiet about it?'

'What about Kasim? Am I supposed to just let them get away with his murder? Besides, you think Raj and Parm would ever be happy, knowing I've got something like that on them? You think their deranged friends would be? It'd only be a matter of time before something happened to me... possibly something fatal.'

'Your dad would never let them do that.'

'They won't exactly go and ask his permission. They'll make sure it looks like an accident, something that won't be linked to them.'

'Then go to the police,' Zaq said.

'You honestly think I could be a witness against my own brothers? That my dad would let me? Or my family?'

'The police will protect you, put you somewhere safe.'

'For how long? I'd be looking over my shoulder the rest of my life.'

'If you don't get this sorted, you'll be doing that anyway.'

'But I'll have the *money*, and that will make things a whole lot easier. Your way, I'd have nothing. And even if Raj and Parm did get put away, my family – especially my dad – will hate me;

for going to the police, for sending my brothers to prison, for leaving home, for everything. They won't just leave it at that. They'll have everyone they know after me, all over the country, even abroad – and so will Raj and Parm. What do you think will happen when they find me? There won't be any forgiveness, any way back, not ever. That money is my only way out of all this.'

'What about Kasim? I thought you wanted them to pay for what they did to him?'

'Of course I do.' There was a flash of anger in the midst of her sorrow. 'But believe me, losing the money will hurt them more than you know.'

'Sorry to interrupt,' Jags said, 'but we're coming up to Shepherds Bush. Where are we going?'

'Take a right at the roundabout and head for the A40.' Zaq told him. It was the quickest route to Hanger Lane, where the money was, though he still wasn't sure what they were going to do with it.

'You saw what happened… to Kasim,' Rita said. 'Why don't you go the police?'

'I did. Well, I called Crimestoppers and they would've told the police.'

'Then how come Parm and Chadha still showed up at the flat?'

'I don't know. Maybe they left before the cops got there.'

'Did you give your name when you called?'

'No.'

'Will you go to the police and give a statement?'

'No.'

'Would you be a witness against them in court?'

'No.'

'Then why are you asking me to do things you won't even do yourself?'

He had no answer to that. He couldn't do himself what he was asking of her. It went against everything he'd learned growing up in Southall. If you had a problem, you sorted it out yourself or got help from your friends and family. You *never* went to the police. And in prison, where he'd seen people beaten, burnt and stabbed, he'd never grassed – *ever*. He'd done the next best thing, given the cops enough information to act on, without getting directly involved himself. He couldn't afford to, not with his record or with what the Brars had hanging over him. He was looking out for himself – why should he expect Rita to do any different?

'I can't just let you take the money and go,' he said. 'I have to find you for your dad, remember? And I don't want to go back to prison.'

Jags got them onto the A40 heading west past White City. It wasn't until they were nearing Savoy Circus that anyone spoke.

'What if I give *you* the hundred thousand to take to my dad?' Rita said. 'You can tell him about Raj and Parm, what they've done and why I won't be coming home.'

Zaq frowned. He didn't like the idea. Rita giving the money to her old man was one thing. If *he* did it, there was no way he'd be allowed to walk away knowing what he'd know about the Brars. 'I thought that money was your way out.'

'It is…' Her expression changed, as though she was thinking about something, then seemed to make up her mind. 'I haven't told you the whole truth,' she said. 'It was more than a hundred thousand I took from my brothers… a lot more.'

That didn't help the situation any. 'How much?'

'Enough that I can give you the hundred thousand for my dad and not worry about it. That would help you out as well, right?'

'I don't know… he ain't going to like hearing all that stuff from me – and I don't think I'm going to like being the one to tell him.'

'What if I made it worth your while? Both of you. Say… fifty thousand each?'

'You're joking?' Jags said from the driver's seat.

'That's a lot of money,' Zaq said.

'I'd still have enough left.'

'Yeah, you'd be fine, jetting off somewhere. How long do you think it'll be before your dad and your brothers decide I'm a liability and try to put me out of the picture?'

Rita thought about it briefly and then came back with another idea. 'All right,' she said, 'then you don't know anything. You just give the money to my dad and tell him I gave it to you to pass on. That's it. I can call him from somewhere afterwards and tell him the rest. He'll believe that I wouldn't have told it all to you.'

Zaq went over it in his head and then said, 'It don't sound too bad…' He could certainly pretend not to know anything and handing over the cash would be a convincing display of his honesty. The money would definitely make Mr Brar listen to what Rita had to say and probably get him to take a look in Raj and Parm's warehouse too. She could also give him the flannel about running away because of what her brothers were going to do her. 'There's just one problem though,' he said.

'What's that?'

'The money – it's at this storage place, right?'

'Yes.'

'Well, Parm and the others know where it is. They're probably on their way there right now.'

It didn't seem to worry her as much as he'd thought it would. 'We've got a head start on them.'

'Not enough of one. They could turn up while we're there.'

'There were only two of them.'

'Back there. We don't know if anyone's already at the storage place. We turn up there and get spotted, they'll be after me and Jags too. We'll all be screwed. Jags is only involved 'cause he's helping me out. I don't want to drop him in the shit.'

'I'm a big boy,' Jags said. 'I can take care of myself.'

'I'm keeping you out of this, if I can help it.'

'So, what do we do?' Rita said.

They needed the money for her plan to work. If they got it, Rita would be able to walk away, her dad would be a hundred grand happier, and even Zaq and Jags would come out with something to show for it. Raj, Parm and the others could go fuck themselves. Without the money though, all they had was hot air and Mr Brar wouldn't listen to a word of it.

'All right, let's go to the storage place,' Zaq said. 'We'll figure out what to do once we're there.' If the worst came to the worst and they couldn't get their hands on the money, at least he now had Rita. That meant there was always the option of dragging her back to her dad – kicking and screaming if need be.

They sped on towards Hanger Lane and Zaq allowed himself to lean back and close his eyes. He listened to the smooth roar of the engine and the music playing low on the stereo. He wondered if anyone was already there, waiting? If not, would they have enough time to go in and get the money? He opened his eyes and looked at Rita. 'This storage place... how do you get into it?'

'You need a security code to get in the building and a key for the actual unit.'

Zaq let out a laugh. 'Then they're screwed! Kasim told them where the place was and that they'd need a key, but he *never* said anything about a security code.'

Rita gave him a level look. 'If they searched the flat, they'll have found the code. Kasim had it written down.'

Zaq couldn't believe it. '*What?* You're f– No one ever tell him, *you never write that shit down?*'

Rita seemed a lot calmer. '*I* hired the unit and chose the code. He had trouble remembering it, so he wrote it down. He thought it'd be safe in the flat.'

'Well, he thought wrong, didn't he? Shit. OK, so they might've found the code… but they'd still need the *key* for the unit, right? And you've got that?'

Very slowly, she shook her head. 'It's back at the flat, in the night stand. Along with the code.'

'*Fucking hell…* Why didn't you take it?'

'You told me to leave it and dragged me out of there.'

'You didn't say anything about a key!'

'*You didn't give me a chance*. All you wanted to do was get out of there.'

'I didn't think you'd leave something as important as that behind. I thought anything like that would've been in your bag. You grabbed *that*. Shit. That means they've got the code and the key… so pretty soon they'll have the money too. All we can do is sit and watch them take it.' He couldn't believe it. Just when he thought they had an idea that might work, the rug had been pulled out from under them, thanks in part to his own haste and stupidity. Why the hell hadn't she mentioned the code or the key back at the flat? What a fuck-up.

They passed Gypsy Corner, heading towards Park Royal. 'So, what d'you want to do?' Jags said. 'Should I still turn off at Hanger Lane or carry on through the underpass?'

Zaq tried to think, calmly and rationally about what to do and fixed on something Rita had said – "*if*". If they searched the flat. There was always a chance they hadn't. 'Turn off at Hanger Lane.'

CHAPTER THIRTY-THREE

Rita directed them around the gyratory system to the exit for Alperton; it wasn't far to the 24-hour drive-thru McDonald's Kasim had told Parm about.

'Park in the McDonald's,' Zaq said to Jags, 'and find a spot we can see the storage place from.'

The parking spaces were fanned out in a circle around the building and Jags pulled into one that afforded them a good view. He parked facing away from it, towards the road so, although they had to watch through the rear window they had better cover.

The smell of french fries drifted into the car.

'It just me or is anyone else hungry?' Jags said.

'Stay put,' Zaq told him.

'All right. So what do we do now?'

'We keep watch. There's a chance they might not have found the code or the key.'

'How you figure that?' Jags said.

'Maybe they thought Rita took it with her and didn't bother to search for it. I mean, who'd leave something like that behind, right?' Rita ignored the comment. 'Or,' Zaq continued, 'after kicking the door off its chain and not finding Rita, maybe Parm didn't want to hang around in case someone had called the cops. Only way we'll know for sure is by watching the place.'

'For what?'

'For them. If they found the stuff, they'll come straight here to get the money. We see them move it, we can follow them, find out where they take it, maybe grab it to give to Rita's dad. If they haven't got the key, chances are they'll probably still come here. Chadha saw Rita, so they know she's running. First thing I'd do is come here to catch her moving the money. If they show up but don't go in, we'll know they ain't got the key, so we might be able to go back and get it ourselves.'

Jags didn't look entirely convinced. 'I guess we sit and wait then.' Rita had been listening but said nothing.

The engine ticked as it cooled and the whoosh of cars going by on the gyratory system sounded like surf breaking on a beach. Zaq wondered how the hell they'd ended up here, with him and Jags trying to help Rita get her hands on the money she'd stolen from her brothers? What he should've been doing was taking her somewhere safe until morning, when he could take her to her dad and be done with the whole mess. Instead, here he was, sitting outside a McDonalds, watching a self-storage building, looking to boost a load of drug money. Maybe he needed his head examined.

They sat quietly, each preoccupied with their own thoughts, music playing low. After a while, Rita turned to Zaq and said, in a faltering voice, 'When you were there, with Kasim... did they say anything about Davinder?'

Somewhere in the back of his mind, he'd been hoping she wouldn't ask about that. How was he supposed to tell her Davinder was dead, most probably murdered in the back of

Prewal's shop before being dismembered and dumped in the park? The answer was, he couldn't – and decided to hold off telling her, until later.

'No,' he said, feeling Jags' eyes on him in the mirror, 'they didn't.'

Rita spotted them first. 'They're here.'

They hunkered down in their seats until the Mercedes had passed by, then came up and watched through the rear window. Parm stopped in front of the gate to the storage facility. The place looked locked up tight and there were no lights on inside.

'Maybe they didn't find the code,' Jags said.

The big metal gate started to roll slowly open. 'Or maybe they did,' Zaq said. If they'd found the code, it meant they had the unit key as well.

When the gate was open enough, Parm drove through and to the main building. The gate rolled shut automatically. Parm and Chadha got out of the car and walked over to a set of double doors beside the loading bays. Parm jabbed a finger at a keypad on the wall. The doors slid open and fluorescent lights stuttered on as they went in. The doors closed behind them.

'What'll they do now they're in?' Zaq asked Rita.

'The security code will have turned off the alarm for the unit. It also turns on the power for the lifts.'

'All right, so they'll go up to the unit. Then what?'

'Then they open it with the key.'

'That's it? Guess all we can do is watch and see where they take it.'

'What about calling the cops?' Jags asked. 'I mean, they're going to come out with the money, right? We call the Old Bill and tell them there's a couple of Asian blokes acting suspiciously around a car, they'll probably send the anti-terrorist squad in, nick them right there, ask questions later.' He looked at Rita. 'Then you can call your dad and tell him they've been nabbed with a load of drug money and he can find the rest at their warehouse. He finds it and it backs up your story about them threatening you and everything.'

It wasn't a bad idea.

'No,' Rita said. 'We can't call the police.'

'*Why not*?' Zaq said. 'We ain't got the money – *they have*. The cops catch them with it, we don't have to worry about giving it to your dad – and the wouldn't be able to cover it up?'

'Calling the police won't do any good.'

'Why not?'

She took her time before answering. 'Because they won't bring the money out.'

'How the hell d'you know that?'

But she didn't say any more.

'There they are,' Zaq said, as Parm and Chadha came out of the double doors.

'They ain't carrying anything,' Jags said.

Zaq saw a flash of white out of the corner of his eye. He looked over and saw a white van pull up to the outer gate. 'That's Jhutti driving. What's he doing here? I thought he'd have been nicked back at the shop.'

'Fuck knows,' Jags said. 'Maybe they're waiting for him so they can put the money in the van.'

Someone must have given him the code beforehand as the gate started to roll open. He drove over to Parm and Chadha and climbed out. The three of them stood together and pretty soon it was obvious they were arguing, all angry hand gestures and aggressive body language.

'They don't look too happy,' Jags said, 'considering they just got their money back.'

After a couple of minutes, they got in their vehicles, Jhutti and Chadha riding together in the van. The Mercedes moved off first. Parm tapped in the security code at the gate, then screeched out and past them.

Zaq, Jags and Rita ducked in their seats. When they looked out again Jhutti and Chadha were also leaving. They ducked down again until the van had left too.

'What just happened?' Zaq asked Rita. She clearly knew more than she was telling. 'How did you know they wouldn't bring the money out? Why did they leave it there?'

She gave him a look as sharp as the edge of a cutthroat razor. 'They didn't leave it there. The reason they didn't take it is because *they didn't find it*. It wasn't there.'

Zaq glanced at Jags, who looked as confused as he was. 'What're you talking about? I thought you said the money was in there?'

'It is,' she said. 'Just not in the unit they checked.'

'What other unit could it be in?'

'The one I moved it to.'

It took a moment for what she'd said to sink in.

'*You moved it*? When?'

'The day after Kasim and I put it in there.'

'Why?'

'Because I didn't trust Kasim, not fully anyway. I'd only known him a few months, so not very well. We got on OK but, at the end of the day, he was a friend of my brothers – not even a friend really, more a business partner. We took the money from them together, but who's to say he wasn't just using me to get it, that he wouldn't have taken it all, first chance he got? I moved it as insurance, so he wouldn't leave me high and dry.'

'He obviously didn't know.'

Rita shook her head. 'I was the one who hired the unit, filled in the paperwork, got the code and the key. Only I didn't just hire *that* unit; I hired the one next to it too.'

Zaq told himself never to underestimate her.

'We took the money up there together and locked it away. He kept the key – it made him feel in charge – but I came back with a copy I'd already made and moved the money into the next unit. If he decided to ditch me and run, he'd have done it without the money.'

'What if he'd found out?'

'Then I'd know he'd been to the unit without me and that I couldn't trust him. I would've made him split the money there and then, and we would have gone our separate ways.'

'Why didn't you just do that to start off with?'

'We had to stay together for a while, until we got some things sorted out.'

She didn't lack confidence, that was for sure. 'So, you're saying the money's *still there*?'

'Yes, but in a different unit.'

'*Bloody hell*,' Jags said. 'That was a smart move.'

'I know. That's why I did it.'

'Please tell me you've got the key for this other unit,' Zaq said.

'Yes, I have.'

Thank fuck for that! Maybe they could see this plan of Rita's through, after all. 'As far as Parm and the others know, the money ain't here, so there's no reason for them to come back. Let's go over there and get it.'

'We can't,' Rita said.

'*Now* why not?'

'We just can't.'

'I thought the plan was to give your dad a hundred grand. Now you're saying we can't.' His frustration was making it difficult for him to maintain a reasonable tone.

'We'll give him some money,' Rita said, icy cool. 'We just can't give him any of *this* money.'

'What the hell are you on about?'

'Just what I said. We can't use this money.'

'Why not? And don't just tell me we can't – *why* can't we?'

Rita's mouth compressed into a tight thin line and there was a steely glint in her eyes. 'Because...' she said, her tone strained, 'it's all in foreign currency.'

Foreign...? So what? Maybe her brothers had changed it up for a drugs buy? 'We can still give it to your dad.'

'*No*.' She was emphatic. 'We can't. It has to stay here for now.'

It was obvious to Zaq that she was still holding something back and his patience had frayed to breaking point. 'If we can't use the money that's here, where the hell are we going to get a hundred grand to give to your dad?'

She gave him a level look. 'From my brothers' warehouse... the money they've got there. You said yourself, there's more than enough.'

'Are you mad? Kasim tried that and look where it got him. They've probably changed the locks by now, the alarm code too – and they've got a bloody gun there. I ain't risking getting killed, and neither is Jags. If you want to go and get it, be my guest.' Zaq was almost yelling by this point and immediately regretted losing his cool. 'Look...' he said, trying to be calmer and more reasonable, 'Why can't we just give him some of this foreign money?'

'It'll be too risky.'

'Why?'

Rita studied him for a long moment before she replied. 'Because, as soon as he sees it, he'll know where it's from... and he'll know how much more there is.'

Zaq felt himself frowning. 'How will he know? And how much more is there?'

'He'll know because it's been all over the news... and altogether, there's about *twelve million pounds*.'

CHAPTER THIRTY-FOUR

'Holy fuck,' Jags said.

Zaq was stunned. All he could manage was a feeble, 'What?'

'Twelve million pounds,' she repeated. 'Don't you watch the news?'

'What's that got to...?' His voice trailed off as the answer hit him. 'The *robbery*... at the *airport*?'

'Your brothers were involved?' Jags asked.

'It was all of them; they were all in on it together.'

'Wait,' Zaq said. 'The news said the robbers were a couple of white guys.'

'And who told them that?'

Zaq thought back to the newspaper articles he'd read and the reports on TV. 'The security guard, the one who was attacked during the robbery – he gave their descriptions.'

'And who was he? Do you remember his name?'

Zaq tried to recall. 'Something Butt?'

'*Kasim* Butt.'

There was a momentary silence as the relevance of the name sank in. 'You mean...' Jags started to say.

'Yes… Kasim was the guard transferring the money from the plane, the one who got beaten up and robbed.'

'Fuck…,' Zaq said. Should he have made the connection himself before now? No one had ever used Kasim's full name, only his first, that or they'd called him by some insult or other. One or two news reports might have mentioned it; there may even have been a grainy black and white photo of him, but Zaq doubted he could ever have put it all together from such scant information as that. The only time he'd seen Kasim in person, he was hanging naked from a meathook, being tortured and then killed. The last thing on Zaq's mind at the time had been if he'd ever seen the guy's picture anywhere.

'It was all his idea,' Rita told them. 'He'd transferred money between flights before.'

'Don't they use security companies for that?' Zaq asked. 'Armoured vans?'

'They do if the money's leaving the airport to go to a bank or a depot. But this wasn't. It was just coming off one flight and being taken across the airport to be put on another. The airport's one of the most secure places in the whole country and the security staff probably go through more checks than at any of the private firms.

'Kasim's been working there for over eight years and he's done a lot of transfers like that – not usually money though. They never really know what's in a consignment, but one time his manager let slip it was cash. Kasim made a note of the consignment code on the paperwork and after that he could tell whenever it was cash being moved. That's when he started thinking how easy it would be to take.

'He knew he'd immediately be suspected if there was a robbery and so he couldn't do it alone. He needed help. That's why he went to my brothers. They jumped at the opportunity and became his new best friends. They did whatever it took to keep him happy – they didn't want him to go to anyone else with his plan. That's how I met him and why my brothers let him take me out. They tried keeping their connection to him quiet, so they wouldn't be linked afterwards.'

Zaq rubbed his face. What the fuck were they mixed up in? How had his search for Rita got him and Jags involved with drugs, two murders and an armed robbery from one of the world's busiest airports? That wasn't even taking into account the arseholes from the Scotsman and the Hare & Hounds – where the hell did they fit into all this? He had a queasy feeling in his stomach. Apart from when he'd been sentenced to five years in prison and taken down, this had to be the worst few days of his life.

He sensed Jags and Rita waiting for him to say something. 'You're right about the money,' he said finally. 'We can't use it. In fact, I don't want to be anywhere near it.'

'What're we going to do with it, then?' Jags said.

'Leave it here.' Zaq held up a hand before either of them could argue. 'That lot have already searched this place and, far as they're concerned, it ain't here, so they won't be back. The money's safe where it is until we decide what the hell we're going to do.' He felt suddenly drained. 'Look, it's late and I'm knackered. Let's just go home, get some sleep and try to figure something out tomorrow.'

'Excuse me…' Rita said, 'but where exactly am I supposed to go? It's not like I can go back to the flat, and home is out of the question.'

Zaq hadn't thought that far ahead. 'What about your friend, Nina? Can't you stay with her?'

'No. She lives with her parents and they know my family. And I'd rather not get her involved any more than she already is.'

Zaq tried to think of somewhere else. There was no way she could stay at his place, not with the guys he –

'You can stay at mine,' Jags said. 'You can have the spare room. Should be safe enough, right?'

'Yeah,' Zaq said. 'It should be. No one knows you're helping me or where you live.' In fact, it was the perfect solution. Jags would be able to keep an eye on her too, make sure she didn't try and do a bunk. Now that they'd finally found her, the last thing he wanted was to lose her again – especially as, if they couldn't come up with a suitable plan, he'd have to take her back to her dad. 'You OK with that?' he asked her.

'I suppose so,' she said, and then to Jags, 'Thanks.'

Parm had turned right, towards the gyratory system, as had Jhutti and Chadha, so Zaq told Jags to go left, towards Alperton and Sudbury. They hadn't gone far when Zaq remembered something. 'Shit.'

'What?'

'The van – it's still over near the warehouse. I better go get it. I don't want it to get clamped or towed, and I definitely don't want to risk one of that lot spotting it.'

'I'll drop you off on the way.'

'Not too close, in case they're all back there. Anywhere nearby will do.'

As they drove, Zaq went over what he knew of the airport robbery. A flight had landed from South Africa with a shipment of banknotes in the hold, all different currencies. An airport security guard had met the plane on the tarmac, specifically to offload the consignment of money and transport it across the airport so it could be put on a connecting flight to New York. According to the reports, once the money was in the van and the security guard was getting into the vehicle, two white men in airport uniforms had appeared and held him up at gunpoint. They got in the van with him and forced him to drive across the airport, away from the main buildings and out of a gate used by maintenance staff. The empty van was later found burned out in a field near the airport, the security guard nearby, beaten unconscious. The severity of the beating meant the robbers were wanted for attempted murder as well as armed robbery.

'How did your brothers get into the airport and make it airside?' Zaq asked Rita.

She looked at him. 'They *didn't*. There were no two guys, white or otherwise. Kasim drove the van out of the airport himself. That was the easy bit. The hard part was what to do with it afterwards. That's what he needed my brothers for.'

'If he'd already stolen the money, why did he need their help?'

'To get away with it.' Light and shadow played across her face as the car passed under streetlight after streetlight. 'His story had to be convincing. Once the police were called, they'd check every CCTV camera around the airport to see where the van went. So he couldn't go to Southall or anywhere else and unload the money, then turn up in Hayes and say he'd been taken straight there. The police would know exactly where he'd been. That meant he couldn't take the money anywhere himself. He wouldn't have much time either, before the police started looking for the van. That's why he needed help.

'My brothers found a playing field, close to the airport but away from any main roads and CCTV cameras. Raj and Parm met him there. They had airport uniforms on to wear while they moved the money into another van.'

'What was the point of wearing uniforms *then*?'

'Something to do with fibres and forensics. Raj and Parm took the uniforms off after they moved the money and set them on fire along with the van. That way there would be some evidence to back up Kasim's story about two robbers but not enough to ID them. Then they had to beat him up, to make it look real.'

'From the news, it sounds like they almost killed him.'

'It had to be realistic. A black eye and a few bruises wouldn't have convinced anyone. I knew my brothers would really go for it and I told Kasim not to trust them, that he should watch out.'

'How did *you* know about it?'

'Kasim told me. I knew something was going on and that Kasim was a part of it. When he asked me out and my brothers didn't do anything to stop him, I knew I was right. It was so totally out of character for them. I said no, but then, more to piss off Raj and Parm than anything else, I agreed. He wouldn't tell me what they were up to at first but I managed to get it out of him eventually.'

'How?'

'How do you think?'

It took Zaq a second to figure out what she meant. 'You said you never –'

'It was only once and it didn't mean anything, not to me anyway. Afterwards though, he told me everything. When I found out what they were planning, I saw my chance. With that sort of money I could do what I wanted, go anywhere, start a new life.'

'With Davinder?' Zaq said.

Rita just looked at him.

'I saw the emails on his laptop. It's obvious there's still something going on between you.'

She let out a breath and some of the toughness seemed to leave her too. 'We were together for three years,' she said. 'I loved him – I still do. I couldn't just turn off my feelings and forget about him because my dad and my brothers told me to.'

'Nina told me what happened.'

Remembering their enforced separation brought the glimmer of tears to her eyes. 'They can't stop us being together. It's nothing to do with them, none of their business. If I want to be with Davinder, I will. It's my life, my choice. We can't do it here though – they'll never let us – that's why we decided to leave. We talked about it often enough but it always seemed like a pipe dream – until now. The money is our chance to make it happen. We'll be able to go wherever we want, do whatever we want, have a life together.'

How could he tell her it wasn't going to happen?

'So I told Kasim,' she continued, 'that my brothers were going to cut him out of their deal somehow. He didn't believe me at first, said they all needed each other and everything had been worked out and agreed. He told me their plan. I asked what would happen if they went too far when they were beating him up? He said they wouldn't – but it got him thinking. I told him, the robbery was all his idea, why split the whole lot with them? He was getting it out of the airport, taking all the risks, yet he was going to divide it equally with the others, which meant smaller shares for everyone. I told him, if *I* helped him, we could take it all and split it between us.'

'So you arranged to double cross your brothers? How did you actually do it?'

'Kasim told me where they were meeting and transferring the money. I got to the field well before and hid. I saw what they did to him; it was horrible. As soon as they left with the money, I called an ambulance for him, and followed my brothers.'

'You didn't stay and make sure he was OK?'

'And lose the money? The ambulance was on its way. What more could I have done there?' She must have read the look on his face. 'He knew what was going to happen, that they were going to beat him up. I stuck to the plan we'd worked out – otherwise it would have all been for nothing. I'd hired a car so they wouldn't recognise it and I followed them. They went to Twickenham and put the money in a lock-up garage. The plan was to leave it there until the heat had died down. The worst part was waiting for Kasim to get out of the hospital, in case my brothers decided to move it somewhere else. Kasim was pretty sure they wouldn't, it would be too risky.

'If the paramedics hadn't got to him when they did, he *could* have died. The doctors told him he was lucky to survive. That's what really convinced him I'd been right about my brothers, that they *had* tried to kill him and cut him out of their deal. He was so mad, he couldn't wait to get out of hospital and take the money from under their noses. That's when I hired the storage units and a van. As soon as he'd been questioned by the police and released from hospital we slipped over there at night and took it.'

'And he was going to split it with you?'

'He thought we were going to go away together, that we'd share it. I never said I would, but I let him believe it. Once we were in a position to split the money, I would've told him the truth.'

'You been together since last week, how come you didn't split it already and leave?'

'It's all foreign currency, remember?' she said. 'First we knew of it was from the news reports. That was another reason they had to leave the money where it was – so they could arrange to change it into pounds. It's not anything easy to use either, like Euros or dollars. It's other kinds, less common. And with the robbery all over the news, anyone with large amounts of those currencies will attract attention. Besides, if you want to exchange more than a couple of hundred pounds, you have to show ID. If our names kept showing up everywhere, the police would soon be looking for us.'

'What good is it then? What can you do with it?'

'We managed to change some, a little at a time, enough to last us a while.'

'That's why Kasim broke into the warehouse – for the cash I told you about?'

'Yes. We thought we could use some of that to tide us over. It'd be easier than having to keep changing those foreign notes. We just needed enough to hold on for a couple of weeks.'

'Why? What was happening then?'

'We were going to change the whole lot in one go. Kasim's cousin in Ilford knows some people that can do it. It was going to cost us, though – we were only going to get half the amount back in Sterling.'

'*Half?*' Jags said. 'It would've cost you six million pounds.'

'Six million we can *use* is better than twelve we *can't*.'

'Someone was going to make a hefty profit out of it,' Zaq said, 'especially if they could move that much cash.'

'The guys his cousin knows move large amounts of foreign currency for a living. They were going to combine it with all of that so it wouldn't be too obvious. Yes, they would have made a lot of money for not doing much at all but we would all have come out of it with something. It was the quickest and easiest way for us to sort it all out.

'My brothers were trying to put together a similar deal with people they know. I overheard them talking. It was only going to cost them *three* million, so they would've made nine out of it. That's why they're so desperate to get the money back. They had a date all worked out for the exchange. If they don't have the money, the deal will fall through and they'll be stuck with the foreign notes until they arrange something else. It's not that easy and it could cost them a lot more.'

'But why risk breaking into the warehouse? Couldn't you just have used your debit or credit cards for a while?'

'Are you serious? My brothers know which bank I'm with. They know people that work at my branch, and at others. They'll have someone checking my account for sure. Any activity on it, any transactions or withdrawals, they'll use the information to track me down.'

Zaq was about to say that was illegal, then realised how dumb he'd sound. Of course it was illegal – like that was going to stop her brothers doing it.

That explained the money and the warehouse but there was something else Zaq was curious about too. 'How did you manage to get that flat to hide out in? It couldn't have been cheap.'

'It belongs to Kasim's uncle, so it didn't cost anything.'

'Pretty swish.'

'His uncle's loaded, some sort of businessman. He lives in Pakistan but has property here and in America. Comes over in the summer. Kasim got the keys.'

'Sounds like you had it all worked out. If you'd had enough cash to see you through till the exchange, you might have got away with it. '

'If the money from the robbery had been in pounds then none of that would have mattered. But Kasim had no idea what currencies were in the consignment. All he knew was the code on the manifest meant it was a shipment of cash. It was just bad luck we ended up with a fortune in banknotes we couldn't spend.'

CHAPTER THIRTY-FIVE

Jags came off the A40 and drove through Yeading into Hayes. He pulled over halfway along Pump Lane to let Zaq out. 'What you going to do after you got the van?'

'It's almost 3.30. I'm going home to bed.'

'You want to come to mine? You can crash there.'

'No. It's Friday. I better turn up to work. After what happened tonight, if Raj or Parm come looking for me and I ain't showed up, they might suspect it's something to do with what went down tonight.'

'They might think that anyway.'

'Yeah, but if I don't show, it might just confirm it for them.' Zaq pushed the door open. 'Be careful when you get back to yours. Anything happens, call me. I'll come round tomorrow so we can work out what to do.'

Jags turned the car around and shot off. Feeling the cold even more after the warmth of the car, Zaq zipped up his jacket, shoved his hands in his pockets and started walking towards the industrial estate where the van was.

He managed to retrieve it without incident and drove back

to Southall. The Broadway was practically empty, with only the odd night bus sailing along unhindered. At the yard, Zaq parked on the service road, in the space beside the lorry. He got out and was locking the van when he sensed something wrong.

That was when he heard a low rumble, accompanied by a soft crunching sound. He looked round the back of the lorry and saw a large white van creeping up the service road, its headlights off. Whoever was driving must've thought they were being pretty sneaky doing that. In fact, they were being pretty dumb. The headlights would have dazzled him, made it hard for him to see anything. Instead, he could make out the van in the glow of the streetlight and recognised it as the one from the butcher's shop and the storage place.

It came to a stop, blocking the narrow road, preventing him from driving off. Jhutti and Chadha had been in it when it left the storage place. Zaq guessed it was them now. They must have been waiting for him. Why else would they be skulking around the back of the builders' yard at this time of night? They would have seen him come up the service road and park.

No way was he going anywhere in that van with them – he knew how that would end for him. He thought about making a run for it but discounted the idea. He was in no mood for a chase on foot; he'd do better saving his energy to fight, if that's what it was going to come down to. The streetlight behind him still wasn't working, and the one down the service road cast the lorry's shadow over him, which worked to his advantage.

Two figures got out of the van. They knew he was there but probably couldn't make him out, wrapped in shadows as he was. If the dickheads had kept their lights on, he'd have been lit up like a Christmas tree. He quickly scanned the ground for anything he could use as a weapon and caught sight of a discarded piece of two-by-four, about three feet long. He snatched it up and shifted into a fighting stance, left foot forward, the length of timber held out of sight, down by his right leg.

Tired as he was, his survival instincts had kicked in, sharpening his senses and giving him an extra surge of energy. His heart was beating faster and he recognised the familiar tingle of adrenalin entering his system, though he knew it wouldn't last long.

The larger of the two was Chadha, so the other had to be Jhutti.

It was Jhutti who spoke first. '*Bhen chaud*, where the fuck you been?'

Zaq was tempted to say '*With your mum,*' but didn't. Why start trouble if there was any chance he could talk his way out of this?

'We been looking for you.' They left the van doors open and started towards him. 'Think you been pissing about in stuff that don't concern you.'

'I can't help what you think.'

'Where's Rita?'

'How should I know? I ain't found her yet.'

'Is that right? See, we think you have. Someone helped her get away from us tonight.'

'*Get away...?* You mean, you found her? So why you asking me where she is?'

''Cause some *ma chaud* helped her get away, innit?'

'Must've been that Kasim she's with.'

'It weren't him, it was someone else.'

'They're together, ain't they? Who else could it have been?'

'It was someone else.' They were getting closer. Jhutti was doing the talking, drawing his attention, but Zaq kept them both in view. 'And the only other person we could think of was *you*.' Jhutti pointed at Zaq with something. Light caught an angled edge – was it a crowbar?

'You're joking, right?' Zaq glanced at Chadha and saw he was also carrying something – a large club hammer. *Shit*. He was glad he'd picked up a weapon of his own; looked like he'd need it.

'It look like we're fucking joking?' Jhutti snapped.

'I don't know, hard to tell in this light.'

'Well, we ain't. Get in the van and come with us so we can go have a chat.'

'You want to chat, do it here.'

'Nah, we want to go somewhere private.'

'Ain't no one around. This is private enough.'

They were almost within striking distance. One of them would probably attack first, distracting him, so the other could come at him from the opposite side. 'Get in, or we'll fucking make you.'

Zaq gripped the two-by-four tight. 'There is another option,' he said.

'What's that?'

'You can go fuck yourselves!'

He went for Chadha first, thrusting the length of wood straight out in front of him, into the bigger man's face. Chadha's attention had been focused on the exchange between Zaq and Jhutti so he didn't even see it coming. The jagged, splintered end of the two-by-four hit him in the mouth and nose, driving his head back. Zaq leapt forward and swung the wood like Sachin Tendulkar hitting a six. There was a sharp crack as it connected with Chadha's head and the wood split along its length. The impact sent shockwaves through Zaq's hands and arms. Chadha dropped on the spot.

Zaq threw a glance over his shoulder just in time to see a dark blur coming at him. No time to swing the two-by-four again, so he dropped it and pivoted to face Jhutti. The crowbar was already arcing down at him. He instinctively threw his left arm up to block it. Metal smashed into bone and pain lightninged through his arm. Jhutti swung the bar again. Zaq's fight training kicked in. He moved forward, inside the swing and blocked Jhutti's arm rather than the bar. The crowbar swung limply down and struck him on the shoulder but without the intended force. He took hold of Jhutti's wrist and pushed it out, away from him, so the crowbar flailed uselessly in the air. With his other hand, he punched Jhutti in the face, putting as much weight as he could into a mean right. The impact sounded like a kilo of mince hitting the floor.

He kept Jhutti off-balance, pulling him by his wrist, and hit him twice more. The first time, he felt cartilage pop in Jhutti's nose; the second, he thought he felt his teeth shift. Jhutti's legs buckled and he went to his knees. Zaq still had hold of his wrist and used it to yank him upright enough that he could drive a heel kick into his chest and send him sprawling.

Zaq bent to pick up the dropped crowbar. *'Motherfucker!'* came a shout from behind. Pain exploded across his back and right shoulder. He was thrown forward onto his hands and knees. The crowbar flew out of his hand and went clattering across the ground. Another blow slammed into his right hip, knocking him sideways. He didn't wait for a third and scrambled away across the rough concrete as fast as he could, then made it to his feet.

Chadha came at him with the club hammer. *'I'll fucking kill you, you cunt!'*

He pulled the hammer back, then swung it, the blow windmilling forward in a big arc. Zaq just managed to back out of the way. Chadha tried again and Zaq moved out of range a second time. The third time, Chadha swung the hammer at a different angle but his technique was the same and Zaq avoided it once more. Frustrated, Chadha rushed him, the hammer aimed at his head.

Only this time Zaq *didn't* retreat. Instead, he ducked under Chadha's raised arm and the hammer swung through empty air where he'd been. Its unchecked momentum threw Chadha completely off-balance, allowing Zaq to grab his forearm and drive it further forward and down, leaving his head up and unprotected. Zaq hit him repeatedly – short, sharp punches, until he was stunned. Then he rotated Chadha's arm back until it couldn't go any further, holding it straight up so his head was forced down. With his other hand, he grabbed hold of Chadha's hair and kneed him in the face until the hammer fell from his grasp. When Zaq pushed him away he stood swaying like a drunken tramp.

Zaq caught his breath for a second, then hit him with a left, a right uppercut, a left hook and a straight right. Chadha was out before he hit the ground.

Turning round, Zaq found Jhutti back on his feet, searching for something, his crowbar or some other weapon. He stepped back when he heard Zaq approach and brought his hands up in something like a fighter's posture. 'Dirty cunt, you took us by surprise.'

'Like two against one's fair.'

Zaq raised his own fists and moved forwards, testing, looking for an opening. He moved constantly, making himself a harder target, while Jhutti remained static and flat-footed. Zaq bounced forward and flicked out a left jab, nothing serious, more of a rangefinder. Jhutti flinched away from it. Zaq threw it again. Jhutti didn't try to counter. Instead, he charged forward and threw a big right that even a blind man could've seen coming. They circled each other. As an experiment Zaq threw a lazy left and let his arm drop, leaving his head exposed. Jhutti tried to take advantage with another big telegraphed right. Zaq hopped back out of the way. It confirmed what he'd thought; Jhutti favoured his right hand and stood square on when he threw a punch, so that he had to step forward each time to maintain his balance. He kept his hands up but only to chest height, which left his head undefended.

Time to finish it. Zaq bobbed forward, threw the lazy left again and let his arm drop. Jhutti saw the gap and launched his big punch. Zaq swatted it away so it sailed past his right shoulder. As Jhutti started to topple forward, Zaq stepped in with a straight right that Jhutti practically fell onto. The punch smashed him in the face and sent him staggering back, barely able to stay on his feet.

Zaq had a flashback to the night when Jhutti and Chadha had attacked him and Davinder. Anger welled up within him as he went for Jhutti again. This time he hit him with a solid left, then another, followed by a ramrod right. Jhutti lashed out with a wild right of his own. Zaq ducked under it without trouble and came up with a scything left hook that caught Jhutti flush on the temple. He teetered sideways, then his legs went from under him, and he crashed to the concrete.

After a second or two he stirred and tried to get up. Zaq grabbed him by the front of his jacket and pulled him to his knees. There was nothing but malice in Jhutti's mean little eyes. Zaq pulled back his fist like an archer drawing a bow, and put everything he had left into the punch – a pile-driving right that slammed Jhutti into the dirt, out cold.

Zaq straightened and sucked in deep lungfuls of cool night air. The last of the adrenalin drained out of him and he was left exhausted. His back and shoulder felt as if a brick wall had fallen on them and his hip and side hurt when he moved. He wasn't looking forward to the walk home.

Jhutti was on his back, making wet bubbling sounds as he breathed. Probably blood in his nose and mouth. Zaq used his foot to roll him onto his side so he wouldn't choke; pain flared in his side and hip as he did so. He hobbled over to look at Chadha. The big lump was still on the ground, moving and moaning. They were both still alive, which was probably more than they deserved.

Zaq left them and walked away. He thought about driving but their van was still blocking the way. He would've had to find the keys and move it before he could get his own van out and he didn't want to still be there when they came round.

The walk home took longer than usual. He wondered if Jhutti and Chadha would come after him, or if they'd go home and nurse their injuries instead? He thought he might've broken both their noses at the very least. It occurred to him that there could be someone waiting for him at the house too. He fucking hoped not – no way could he handle another fight now.

He shuffled along like an unwell pensioner, keeping his eyes and ears open, and eventually made it home without bumping into anyone else. He took some painkillers with a couple of glasses of water, then hauled himself up to his room. He knew he should stretch, to ease the pain and help prevent his muscles stiffening overnight, but *fuck it* – he was too knackered to bother. He left his clothes in a heap on the floor and collapsed into bed.

CHAPTER THIRTY-SIX

Zaq was woken by his phone vibrating. Keeping his eyes shut, he reached out his hand. It hurt to move. He had to pat around till he found the phone, then pulled it under the duvet and rejected the call. By then he was mostly awake.

Bollocks.

He tried going back to sleep but without success. Images from the previous night played in his head like a badly edited trailer. Kasim being tortured and killed. Blood, lots of blood, and chilli. Rita, standing in the hallway of the flat, scared but beautiful. He recalled flashes of news reports; two white men, with guns and northern accents. A security guard badly beaten. Twelve million pounds in foreign currency, stolen. Another news report; body parts in bin bags, Cranford Park, Davinder. Blood on a laptop bag.

And here he was, caught up in the middle of it all. What the hell was he going to do? He had better think of something soon, otherwise he might end up butchered and chopped into pieces too.

The darkness behind his eyelids was warm grey instead of

inky black. He eased them open and saw daylight at the edges of the curtains. Drawing his phone out from under the duvet, he checked the time. *Ten-thirty. Shit!* His phone had been on SILENT. There were three missed calls, all from the builder's yard. He'd have to make up some excuse. He called Sid.

'Sid? It's me, Zaq. You called?'

'*Arrey, haah. Thu haley sutha peya see?*'

'No, I been up for ages.'

'Then why you no here this morning?'

'I was out late, doing stuff for Mr Brar, so I took the morning off.'

'*Took off?* Who say you can take off? *Bhen chaud*, you fucking boss now?'

'You got a problem with it, take it up with him.' Zaq was counting on the fact Sid wouldn't go whining to the boss, especially as he knew Zaq was working on something for him.

'I send Ram with fucking deliveries again,' Sid said.

'So, what's the problem?'

'He no read bloody map, always getting lost and being the late.'

'Yeah, well, practise makes perfect. That it or was there anything else?'

'When you finish job for Brar *sahib*?'

'I don't know – couple of days maybe.'

'Couple of days? *Theri bhen di...*' Sid hung up.

Zaq called Jags next, to check everything was all right. 'You look outside? See if anyone's hanging about, watching the house, anything like that?'

'I didn't see no one – and I been checking a lot. This whole situation's got me well nervous, man.'

'Where's Rita?'

'Upstairs, having a shower. I'm was about to make us some

breakfast. You coming over?'

'I'll be there in a while.'

Zaq put his phone down. He tensed, ready for the pain he knew was coming, and rolled out of bed. His arm, back, shoulder, hip and thigh all ached deep inside, throbbing like a heavy bass-line. His arm was badly bruised from the crowbar blow, and his hands and knees were scraped from scrabbling on the ground. There was a deeper ache in his palms that he couldn't explain, until he realised it must've been from when he hit Chadha round the head with the two-by-four. The shockwaves from the impact had affected his hands. Still, it was better than if he'd been on the other end.

He was glad he'd taken painkillers before going to bed but could do with more now. He eased himself downstairs and into the kitchen. Fortunately, all his housemates had gone to work, so he was the only one there. He took two more ibuprofen, reflecting that he'd been popping the bloody things like Smarties the last few days.

Back in his room, he massaged his palms, made himself stretch and shadow-box, then took a long hot shower. The painkillers kicked in, the stretches had loosened him up and the heat of the water soaked into his bones, easing his aches. He started to feel a little better under the steaming spray and let his mind to drift over recent events.

Most important was they'd found Rita and had her safe at Jags'. She was his trump card. If there wasn't any other way out of the shit they were in then he would take her back to her old man. She'd never go along with it but he'd worry about that when the time came.

There were some things he still couldn't figure out though – like who were the guys that had jumped him outside the Scotsman and at the Hare & Hounds, and how were they involved? But, for the most part, he thought he knew what was going on now. He tried to put together a plan, some way to deal with the Brars and their mates, take care of the money, help Rita if he could, and still come out of the whole thing in one piece.

He was under the shower for a long time.

He took a slightly longer route to the builder's yard, figuring it would be safer than a more direct one and hoping the walk would do him some good. At least walking felt a little easier this morning.

The first thing he did was make sure Jhutti and Chadha weren't there, waiting for another try at him. He spotted the two-by-four lying on the ground close to the van, split along its length. Apart from that, there was no evidence of the fight. He didn't bother going in to see Sid; the manager would know he'd been there when he saw the van gone.

He took extra care as he drove to Jags', making sure no one was following him and parked well away from the house, across a park. No one could have tailed him without him knowing.

'What kept you?' Jags said. 'And why're you walking funny?'

Zaq stepped inside and shut the door. 'Jhutti and Chadha were waiting for me when I dropped the van at the yard last night.'

'Fuck! What happened?'

'They wanted me to go for a ride with them. I said no. They tried to make me. Where's Rita?'

She was sitting on a sofa with her legs pulled up under her. She had on the same tracksuit bottoms as the night before but a fresh T-shirt and tracksuit top that Jags must have lent her. The T-shirt was too long and the tracksuit top too big. They made her look like a little girl playing dress-up in her older brother's clothes. 'Are you all right?' she said, when she saw Zaq hobble in. 'What happened?'

He told her about his run-in with Jhutti and Chadha. 'I'd like to think they came off worst. I doubt I'll be so lucky next time.'

'You think they'll try again?'

'Soon as they can. They think it was me that helped you at the flat and that I know where you are – the money too. They ain't going to give up. They got twelve million reasons not to. If anything, they'll come at me harder and faster next time, won't give me a chance. We got to sort out what we're going to do.'

Rita nodded.

Jags brought Zaq a mug of tea. It was hot and strong, the way he liked it. 'I've been thinking –' Zaq said.

'So have I,' Rita cut in, ' and I want to do a deal. I'll give my brothers half the money to let Davinder go.'

Shit. Now what? She thought he was still alive and wanted to buy his freedom – before he met the same fate as Kasim. But he was already dead, cut up and disposed of. Zaq tried to stall as he figured how to break it to her. 'You think they'd settle for half?'

'They might. Six million's still a lot of money. I did all of this so me and Davinder could be together. That's all that matters. We'd still have more than enough to go away with. I have to try.'

Zaq took a breath. 'I'm sorry,' he said, 'you can't.'

'Why the hell not?'

He chewed his lip. He'd been putting it off but now he had to tell her the truth – she needed to know. He was aware of Jags watching him, waiting, knowing what was coming. There was no easy way to break it to her. Best he could do was tell it to her straight. 'Because your brothers have been lying. They ain't got Davinder... not any more.' She frowned, confused. 'They *did* mention him last night,' Zaq went on, 'and from what they said... I'm pretty sure he's dead.'

The news hit her like a slap. The colour drained out of her face. '*What?*' She was staring at him, eyes wide, not wanting to believe what he'd just told her. She shook her head. 'No… it's not true. *It can't be*. They can't have…'

'I'm sorry,' Zaq said quietly. 'I didn't know how to tell you. I was trying to wait for the right time.'

'*When the hell would've been the right time?*' she yelled. Tears brimmed in her eyes and spilled over, streaming down her face. She put her head in her hands and wept.

Zaq didn't know what to do. He thought about trying to console her but didn't know how and wasn't sure how she'd react, so he stayed where he was and let her cry it out. Jags put a box of tissues on the coffee table in front of her.

Zaq wondered what she had thought would happen if she stole twelve million pounds from her brothers? She knew what they were capable of. Had she really expected to just walk away scot free? That she would simply take her share of the money and disappear with Davinder? Could she really have been that naïve? If she had, reality was providing some very hard lessons to her.

He couldn't help thinking that everything that was happening was due, in part, to her actions – which had now drawn him and Jags in too. While he did have some sympathy for what she must be going through, it was tempered by a pressing desire to find a way out of the potentially lethal shit they were in.

He looked at Jags, who shrugged. They did the only thing they could – they sat and waited. Zaq hoped she wasn't going to cry forever.

She didn't.

It only felt like it.

When the first wave of grief eventually subsided and her

tears had slowed to a trickle, for the time being at least, she took a tissue and wiped her eyes. 'What happened?' she said. 'What did they do to him?' Instead of the pain or despair Zaq had expected to hear in her voice, there was an edge of steel.

'I sounded like they were questioning him about you when they killed him. They didn't mention his name but I don't think it was anyone else.'

'But if they didn't actually *say* it was *him*, they *could* have been talking about someone else?' She was clutching at straws.

'Maybe... but far as I know, they ain't kidnapped anyone else.'

'What exactly did they say?'

'It was while they were questioning Kasim... using a knife on him... One of them said something about not killing him too soon, *like the last time*. They'd obviously been questioning someone else and that's what had happened.'

Did... did they say *how*?' There was a tremor in her voice.

'Sounds like they cut an artery or something by mistake.' *Well, maybe not by mistake, just sooner than they meant to.*

Her eyes filled up and Zaq thought she was going to cry again, but she managed to hold back the tears. 'Was it my brothers?' she managed.

'Jhutti, Chadha... all of them were probably there.'

'What did they... do with him? Afterwards?'

Zaq shot a quick glance at Jags, who just raised his eyebrows and gave him a look that said *Rather you than me.* Zaq took a breath. 'A body was found in Cranford Park... an Asian male, about the same age as Davinder.'

'*No!* It can't be...'

Zaq wasn't sure who she was trying to convince. 'That's what I told myself... until I heard them talking last night.' Should he tell her the full extent of what they'd done to him? It was one thing to know her lover had been killed, something else to be told he'd been dismembered and dumped like a piece of rubbish. But she would find out eventually; it was all over the news. Once the body was identified it was likely Davinder's name and picture would be plastered everywhere too. If he kept it from her, it would only make it worse when she learned the truth. 'The body was cut up and dumped...'

'*No!*' Rita sobbed.

'Someone found part of it in the park. The police found the rest.'

Rita dropped her head and covered her eyes with a hand. Her breath came in short ragged gasps as she struggled to keep control... but failed.

'I'm sorry,' Zaq said. He looked away, uncomfortable watching her reaction to this latest terrible revelation, intruding on her grief.

It was some time before she spoke again. When she did, her voice was tipped with venom. 'I want my brothers to pay for what they've done,' she said. 'I want them *all* to pay for it.' Zaq looked at her. Her tears had gone, burned away by her white-hot desire for vengeance.

Jags made them all some tea. When Rita had regained her composure, she said, 'What are we going to do?'

'I was thinking about that,' Zaq told her, 'and I came up with a few ideas.' He gave her a level look. 'You might not like them though – but just hear me out. The first is, we give the money back to your brothers –'

'No way! Uh-unh. I'd rather set fire to it and watch it burn than give it back to them.'

'I thought you might say that. Second idea is, we leave it

somewhere and tell the cops where to find it.'

'What good does that do us? And what about me?' Rita said, frowning. 'I can't stick around after what's happened. I need that money to get away. And how does it deal with my brothers? Do they just get away with what they've done?'

'It's just an option. I didn't say we had to do it. And anyway, you can't keep the money. It's all over the news. Every cop in the country's looking for it. What would you do with it? You can't leave the country with it and the longer you have it, the more chance there is you'll get caught with it. Good luck explaining it away if you do. You'd be looking at conspiracy, accessory, handling stolen property, withholding information and anything else they can throw at you. High profile case like this, no chance you'd walk away without doing some time.'

'There's twelve million pounds... there must be something else we can do.'

'Like what? You said yourself, you can't change it at a bank or on the high street 'cause everyone's looking out for those currencies. There's Kasim's plan – you know the guys he was in contact with? Can you get in touch with them?'

'No.'

'Then that's no good.'

'What about you?' she said. 'Don't you know anyone that could do it?'

'No, and I ain't about to start asking around. I do that, it'll just bring us more trouble and we got enough of that as it is. Only way out of this mess, for all of us, means getting shot of that money.'

'I've lost the most important thing in my life... now you're asking me to give up the money too.'

'I don't see any other way. It's cost two lives already. I don't want any of us to be next.'

The last point hit a nerve and Rita's defiant attitude gave way to something more melancholy, tinged with loss and regret. She knew he was right.

'I'd love to keep some of the money too,' Jags said, 'but I got to agree with Zaq. It's too risky – and not just 'cause the cops are still looking for it. Your brothers ain't going to let up trying to get hold of it and neither will anyone else that finds out you've got it.'

'Fine,' she said. There was a renewed fire in her voice and in her eyes. 'We'll get rid of the money – but Raj, Parm and those other bastards have got to pay for what they've done. There's no way I'm going to just let them get away with it.'

'OK, so just giving the money back to the police isn't an option. It was just an idea anyway and like you said, it doesn't deal with your brothers. They'd still be after us, if only to see us all dead for losing them the money. Your dad sending me to prison would be the least of my worries then.'

'Well, if that's no good, what do we do?'

'I've got another idea…'

CHAPTER THIRTY-SEVEN

Zaq told them his idea and they discussed it for the next couple of hours, going over it again and again. By late afternoon, they still hadn't nailed down a way to implement it. While they were having a break for more tea and something to eat, Jags said, 'What I still can't figure out is, who those other guys are, the ones that jumped you on Monday and tried to grab Nina, Wednesday.'

'Neither can I,' Zaq said.

'You think they're after the money?'

'Maybe, but… if they knew about the money and Rita, they'd have known she ain't my girlfriend –'

'*Your what?*' Rita said.

He told her about the photo he'd dropped outside the Scotsman and the note that had been left on the van. 'They must've thought Nina was you the other night but they never mentioned the money, either time.'

'Well, if it ain't the money they're after, what is it?' Jags said.

'Can't be Rita, 'cause they didn't know who she was and if they grabbed Nina by mistake, that only leaves… *me.*'

'You? Why would they be after you? You sure you didn't recognise any of them?'

'I didn't get a look at them first time but...' Something had been bothering him ever since his run-in with the three guys at the Hare & Hounds. He hadn't been able to put his finger on what it was though. 'I think I might've seen one of them before somewhere, only I can't remember where.'

'They say anything? Mention any names?'

'No.' Zaq tried to recall anything he might have heard. 'One of them shouted something to his mate, outside the Hare & Hounds. Something weird. I think he was trying to warn him, sounded like, *mash* or *mesh* –' He stopped, as realisation finally hit him between the eyes. 'Fuck. It wasn't mash or mesh... it *was* a name. *Mahesh*.'

It took Jags a second to make the connection. '*Shit*. Mahesh Dutta!'

'Who's that?' Rita asked.

It was like the missing piece of a jigsaw falling into place, completing the picture. Zaq had seen the driver before, he just hadn't been able to place him... until now. Last time he'd seen the guy had been about six years ago, at his trial. 'The guy I went to prison for hitting...' he told Rita, 'the one who died. His name was Rahul Dutta. Mahesh is his brother.'

From the very outset, Mahesh Dutta had been furious that Zaq was only being tried for the lesser charge of manslaughter, rather than murder. He'd wanted Zaq put away for at least twenty or thirty years. When the judge had given him five, Mahesh Dutta had shouted his disgust from the gallery, and made his feelings clear outside the courtroom too. There wasn't anything Zaq could do about it.

He'd expected some kind of reprisals while he was inside, and he'd been right. Friends of Mahesh Dutta's, who were in prison, had attacked Zaq more than once – even tried to shank him. He'd managed to fight them off each time, though not without injuries on both sides.

After his released, he'd expected a visit from Mahesh and his mates, and he'd been ready for it. But a month had passed, then two, then three, and nothing had happened. Zaq had started to think perhaps nothing was going to happen, that maybe Dutta had finally come to terms with his brother's death and moved on. Five years was a long time, after all.

Not long enough though, it seemed. Now, almost ten months after Zaq had been released, here was Mahesh Dutta, seeking vengeance for his dead brother. He had tried on Monday and, when that hadn't worked, he'd gone for Nina, who he'd mistakenly believed to be Zaq's girlfriend. That hadn't worked either. *Dumb shit.*

Zaq wondered what the guy's next move might be... and suddenly sat bolt upright.

'What's the matter?' Jags said.

'I think I know who they're going to go for next.'

'Who?'

'Tariq.'

Zaq tried calling his younger brother right away but only got his voicemail. 'Tariq,' he said, leaving a message, 'I need to talk to you – it's urgent. Call me as soon as you get this.' He checked the time. Tariq was probably on his way home from work. 'Listen, I'm coming to the station. Wait for me there. I'll pick you up. Don't go anywhere. See you in a bit.' He hung up. 'I got to go.'

'You really think Mahesh'll go after him?' Jags asked.

'His brother's dead. Mine ain't. Who else you reckon he'd go for?'

'What if you run into Raj or Parm, or any of that lot?'

'I'll just have to chance it and hope I don't.'

'Want me to go with you?'

'No, stay here with Rita. Hopefully, I'll get to Tariq before anything happens.'

Zaq shot off back to Southall, only getting so far before he hit Friday rush hour traffic. The sluggish pace had him swearing and bashing his steering wheel. He eventually made it along the Broadway and up South Road. There was nowhere to park outside Southall station so he turned down a side street and pulled up onto the pavement outside a factory. He left the van there and hurried back, crossing the main road to the station, while still trying to get his brother on the phone again.

Could he have missed him? Had Tariq already come out of the station and got a bus or started walking home? Or could Dutta and his mates have grabbed him and bundled him into a car? Would they know what he looked like? Maybe Tariq was out after work, somewhere in town. He found it difficult to stand still and wait. *Hurry up and fucking call me, you idiot.* His eyes darted amongst the faces of people coming through the ticket barriers, searching for his brother amongst them.

Ten minutes later his phone rang. 'I just saw your message,' Tariq said. 'I'm just coming into Southall now. What's up?'

'I'm inside, near the ticket barriers. See you in a minute.'

The wave of commuters was funnelled through the barriers, into the ticket hall and out onto the street beyond. Zaq spotted his brother in their midst. He touched out with his Oyster card, came through the barriers and looked around before spotting Zaq.

Though they were roughly the same height, Tariq was slimmer, with the rangy build of a long-distance runner. His hair was longish and swept to one side. He was dressed in a suit and somehow managed to make it look both smart and casual at the same time. 'What's going on?' he said, pulling his headphones out.

'I'll tell you on the way home.'

'You didn't come to pick me up in that shitty van, did you?'

'No.'

'What else you come in then?'

'A different van. Still shitty though.'

'Great.'

They left the station. 'What's the rush?' Tariq said, as Zaq hurried him across the road, looking out for any of the guys he was trying to avoid. He took out his keys as they reached the van.

Tariq stopped to look at the van. 'It's worse than that old banger you normally drive.'

'Beats walking or waiting for the bus.' Zaq got in and pushed the passenger door open. 'Come on, jump in.'

'This thing's embarrassing. You could've just met me at home.'

'You're getting a lift, ain't you? Besides, I wanted to catch you before you got home.'

Tariq climbed in. Zaq started the engine and told him about Mahesh Dutta and the two attacks on him during the week.

'Shit. OK... but what's that got to do with me?'

'You're my brother. I think he might come after you next.'

'Oh, fucking great.'

'Look, I'll sort it out, but you need to be on the lookout for anyone suspicious, anyone approaching you on the street, guys waiting around in a car.'

'I don't believe this...'

'Neither can I. Coming after me is fair enough – I can deal

with that. But these guys'll go for anyone just to get to me. I had to warn you.'

'Thanks a lot.' He sounded anything but thankful.

'Now I know who it is, I'll take care of it. You just be careful until I do.' Zaq put the van in gear and turned it around.

'You ain't going to do anything stupid, are you? Something that could land you back inside?'

'Not if I can help it.'

'Five years was bad enough. I don't know what mum and dad will do if you get banged up again.'

Zaq's arrest, trial and sentencing had been hard on his parents. More so because he had always been a good kid, done OK at school and never really been in trouble. They'd been as proud as anything when he got his degree in Information Technology, even if he had only got a 2.2. He'd landed a decent job, got promoted and had just made the switch to a new company when that single fateful punch had brought everything crashing down.

The shock for his parents had been huge, and it had been painful to watch them deal with it. They had come to see him in prison but their visits hadn't done anyone much good. His mum would get overemotional and weep, while his dad would sit stoically and talk about nothing in particular. Zaq always ended up feeling bad afterwards, knowing he'd fucked things up and let them down. Even though they tried to hide their disappointment, it was always there, like a cloud casting a shadow over them. It had been something of a blessing when he'd been moved from London to a prison near Oxford and their visits had become less frequent.

His relationship with Tariq had suffered too. They had been pretty close before but time and distance had caused a rift between them and they'd drifted apart. His brother had visited regularly at first, twice a month, and would write too...

but after a while, the novelty wore off and having to come and see Zaq clearly became more of a chore. He soon seemed to resent sacrificing half his weekend to sit in a prison visiting room, almost as if he was having to do community service for a crime he'd had no part in. He never said anything, but Zaq could read between the lines.

As time passed they had less and less to talk about. Tariq was living his life on FAST FORWARD, while Zaq's was stuck on PAUSE. His world was contained within the walls of the prison, whereas Tariq's was ever expanding. The routine of prison life became boring to talk about, so Zaq let his brother do most of the talking, which meant their conversations became mostly one-sided. Half the time he didn't even know what the hell Tariq was on about; he didn't know the clubs, the people or any of the other stuff that filled his brother's life.

The times when Zaq was in solitary, he wasn't allowed any visitors at all. Tariq's visits became less frequent; once a month, then every other month, then once every few months. When Zaq was transferred to Oxford, the visits stopped altogether. By that time it was more than just the physical distance that separated them and, during the remainder of his time inside, the rift only grew wider and deeper. It was weird; they were still brothers – nothing could change that fact – but these days it felt more as though they were distant relatives, barely acquainted. They'd lost something they seemed unable to regain... and maybe never would.

The van moved slowly towards the Broadway. Zaq knew Tariq wasn't happy about the situation he'd been dumped in, but there wasn't much he could do about it. He was a big boy, he'd get over it. What Zaq *could* do something about was fixing things so there'd be no more threat to him or Tariq, or anyone else close to him. He *could* do it; the only thing he wasn't sure about just yet was *how* he was going to do it.

'Turn the radio on, if you want.' Zaq hoped some music might lift the mood and fill the silence between them. The radio was as cheap and basic as the van itself but Tariq turned it on and set it to KISS FM. The bass-heavy dance music was distorted by the cheap speakers but it beat listening to the noise of the van and the traffic outside.

'I hope no one I know sees me in this thing,' Tariq grumbled.

Zaq was hoping none of the people who were after him saw them either. The last thing he wanted was to run into the Brars or Jhutti and Chadha, and have Tariq get caught up in that shit too. 'Don't worry, you'll be home soon.'

CHAPTER THIRTY-EIGHT

It was dark by the time they got to the house Tariq shared with their parents and the streetlights were on. The three-bedroomed terraced houses were set back from wide pavements, behind front gardens, most of which had been turned into driveways. As a result, there were very few places to park on the road and Zaq paid particular attention to three cars parked near the house.

The first two, a Vauxhall and a Peugeot, were empty – but the third, a Lexus across the road, was occupied. He couldn't be sure if it was the same car from the Hare & Hounds and swore at himself for not having paid more attention the other night. There seemed to be two, maybe three people in it, which immediately put Zaq on edge.

He pulled over to the other side of the road, across his parents' driveway, and leaned forward so he could see past Tariq to the Lexus. Three figures got out.

Shit. Now what?

'Thanks for the lift.' Before Zaq could say anything or stop him, Tariq got out of the van and shut the door.

Fuck. If he drove off, they might grab Tariq. But if he waited until Tariq got inside, they might try and get him out of the van. There was only one thing for it...

He threw open his door, jumped out and raced after his brother. He bundled into Tariq and pushed him the rest of the way to the front door.

'*What the fuck're you doing?*'

'I need a piss.' Zaq said. 'Real bad. I'm desperate.' He looked over his shoulder and saw the three men now hurrying over. '*Come on.*'

'Can't you hold it, for fuck's sake?' Tariq got the door open.

Zaq shoved him in and slammed it shut. 'Thanks.' He bounded up the stairs but, instead of going to the bathroom, he went into the small bedroom at the front of the house, which was used as a study. He didn't turn on the light, but closed the door and leaned over the desk by the window to look out.

The three men were standing by the van, talking. Zaq recognised the one in the middle as the driver from the Hare & Hounds. Studying him now, he saw it was indeed Mahesh Dutta. The men split up and spread out. One moved away left along the pavement, one went right. Dutta took up position across the road, with a good view of the front door. They were waiting for him to come out. When he went to the van, they'd come at him from all three directions. What was he supposed to do now? He sat down to think.

He could duck out the back, jump the fence and leave that way – but that would mean leaving the three guys to try for Tariq again sometime. No, he had to draw them away from the house and deal with them somewhere else. As he thought about how to do it, he found he did need to take a piss after all.

When he came back from the bathroom and looked out of the window, they were still there. A sketchy idea came to him. He turned it around in his head and then decided it was what he'd do. He just hoped it would work.

He went downstairs and poked his head into the lounge. 'All right, mum?'

His mother was watching a Pakistani drama on TV. She was dressed in a pink *shalwaar kameez* with a black cardigan and had a blanket draped over her legs. She looked surprised to see him. 'Zaqir,' she said. There was a subtle shift in her features and her neutral expression became imbued with sadness and regret.

She was in her early fifties but seemed older. The last few years had etched lines in her face that hadn't been there before. Her nose was long and sharp and she wore her greying hair in a plait. She was relatively tall for a Pakistani woman and, though she had always been slender, she seemed to have put on weight recently. Every time she saw him she was reminded about the son who went to prison and a young man who had died. 'What's wrong with your face?' she asked him, frowning.

He gave her a reassuring smile. 'It's nothing.' Last thing he wanted to tell her was that he'd been in a fight. 'Sorry,' he said, 'I can't stay. I've got to go.'

His mother seemed to sigh inwardly, nodded and turned back to the TV.

His brother was sprawled across an armchair, one leg dangling over the armrest, busy on his phone.

Zaq tapped him on the leg. 'See you later.'

'Yeah, later,' Tariq said. He didn't even bother looking up.

At the front door, Zaq stopped to take a couple of deep breaths and go over what he was about to do. If it worked, he'd get past them but didn't know what would happen after that. He'd have to improvise. He took another breath, opened the door and stepped outside.

He crossed the driveway fast. Dutta saw him from across the road and whistled to the others. The van was straight ahead of him but Zaq knew he'd never open it and get in before they were on him so, instead, he angled away, heading to the right. Dutta hesitated when he saw Zaq wasn't going for the van. By then Zaq was out of the driveway, leaving the van behind.

The guy who'd been waiting away to the right was rushing forward. He pulled up short in surprise when he saw Zaq coming at him and, before he could decide what to do, Zaq hit him square in the face.

It was a short, sharp punch the guy wasn't expecting. It stunned him, so he didn't know what was happening. Zaq grabbed him by his jacket, kneed him in the balls and shoved him over a low brick wall separating two driveways. The guy hit the concrete on the other side with a grunt. Zaq didn't wait to see what the other two were doing – *he ran*.

'Get the car,' he heard someone shout behind him. He ran harder, doing his best to ignore the pain and discomfort every stride brought him. He'd put one down for the moment, another was chasing him; he didn't know about the third. If he could take them one at a time he might have a–

A sharp crack sounded and he felt something zip by his shoulder. *What the f –?* There was another crack and this time something whizzed past his head, like an angry wasp. A sudden realisation clenched his stomach in an icy grip. Someone had just *shot* at him. Dutta. It had to be. The crazy motherfucker had a *gun*. Zaq's brain wiped away any thought of his injuries and drove him to run with every fibre of his being.

He jinked left and right but most of all he concentrated on getting the fuck away. There was another crack and shards of brick exploded from the wall beside him. He ducked round the corner, using a wall for cover. Ahead of him were the gates to Spikes Bridge Park. Zaq sprinted for them and hurtled through the open pedestrian gate, just as another shot sounded. He didn't stop to think and took off across the grass to his left. It was a better option than carrying on along the lamp-lit path.

The park was wide and flat and dark. He was heading away from the running track and the children's play area, making a dash towards a dilapidated old building, the only real cover close enough to get to. It was close to the fences along the edge of the park, on the other side of which were the gardens of the houses that backed onto the open space.

He only stopped to catch his breath once he was in the deeper shadows provided by a tree beside the building. Bent over, hands on his knees, he sucked in lungfuls of night air. He was sweating and buzzing from the chemicals his brain was firing into his system.

The scanned the building; it was a complete wreck. It had been a youth centre once, when councils bothered to pay for such things. Now pigeons cooed from the exposed beams that overhung the walls all the way around. Zaq pressed close to the flaking wall and took a peek back towards the gates.

Two figures entered the park, clearly visible in the glow of the streetlights outside. They looked around, then walked further in, his view of them blocked by the bulk of the building. Behind Zaq a path ran around the edge of the park. Trouble was, if he made a break for it along the path, they'd see him and either come after him or Dutta would try and put a shot in his back. He didn't want to risk the second option – but he couldn't just stay where he was. They were bound to come over and take a look.

The building was boarded up tight, so he couldn't hide inside. There had to be some way he could use the place to his advantage… but how? If there had been just one guy after him, he might've been able to circle the building, keeping it between them so he wasn't seen and his pursuer would think he'd escaped somehow. But with two of them, they were bound to come around either side, catching him between them. Dutta had a gun – the other guy might be armed too – and they were both ready for him. Zaq started to get a sick feeling as he realised his chances of getting out of this were looking very slim.

He heard voices somewhere on the far side of the building, but couldn't make out what was being said. They grew louder as he listened, coming closer. In desperation, he looked around for a weapon. His eyes swept the ground, past the tree to the fence... and back again. He looked hard at the tree, then up at its branches...

He didn't have time to weigh it up, he just had to do it. He took a few steps back, focused, then ran at the tree. One step away from it, he jumped and, planting his right foot high on the trunk propelled himself even higher, so he was able to grab a branch. He hooked his right arm over it, then his left, and scrambled up the trunk until he could swing his right leg over too. From there he hauled himself into a sitting position; then he reached for the branch above and pulled himself up so he was standing. Keeping a hand on the higher branch for balance, he walked along the one he was on. It bent under his weight but he carried on regardless, until he stepped off onto the roof of the building.

The old timbers sagged under him and his stomach lurched, but the roof held his weight. He was surprised how much vegetation there was, mostly weeds. A lot of rubbish had been thrown up there too. Zaq got down on his belly and crawled to the edge, trying to spread his weight as best he could to ease the load on the roof. It didn't make him feel much safer. The smell of moss, damp and dirt filled his nose. He pushed some weeds apart and looked down.

'He must be round here somewhere,' a voice said. 'We'd have seen him otherwise. Come out, you *bhen chaud* bastard, and take what's coming to you!'

He couldn't see them yet but it had to be Dutta calling out. Was the guy for real? He couldn't fight Zaq man-to-man, so he'd brought a gun and now he expected Zaq to just come out and take a bullet? What an arsehole.

Zaq heard footsteps now. His mind and body hummed with nervous energy. He tried not to think about the gun. A figure edged around the corner to the right, holding a pistol straight out in front of him. Zaq watched Dutta emerge, sweeping his arm left and right, searching for his target. A moment later, a second figure came around the left corner. He also had something in his hand, a stick or bar of some kind.

Dutta lowered his arm. 'Shit. He can't have gone far. Did you see a door to this place?'

'No.'

The two of them came together directly below Zaq. How long before it dawned on them to look *up*? This might be his only chance. Clamping down his fear and moving with the utmost caution, he got his legs under him so he was crouching at the edge of the roof.

'Maybe he went off that way.' The guy with the stick pointed to the path going away from the building.

'This place wouldn't have covered him that far. We'd have seen him.' They took a step away from the building. 'Nah, he's round h–'

Zaq jumped.

Any fear or doubt he might've had was ripped away, replaced by a primal urge so powerful it was all he could do not to scream some kind of war cry. Time seemed to slow down and everything happened in slow motion. He landed on Dutta from behind, knees crashing into his back and shoulders, taking him to the ground, hard. Dutta had no chance to break his fall and his face and chest slammed onto the tarmac. The gun went clattering away. Zaq's weight drove all the air from his lungs so Dutta was left struggling for breath.

Though it seemed to happen slowly, in reality it only took a second or two and Zaq was off him and going for the other guy before he knew what had happened. Zaq grabbed him by the throat and wrist, turned and threw him over his hip, smashing the guy's head and shoulders into the ground. Then he twisted the stick out of his hand. It was smooth and weighted at one end; the lower half of a snooker cue. Zaq gripped it in both hands, his body trembling with rage, and brought the weighted end down on the guy's arms, torso and balls. When he was done he flung it away into the darkness.

Dutta was on his hands and knees, noisily wheezing for air and looking groggily around him. Zaq kicked his hands away, so he went down again. Sudden anger erupted within him and he kicked Dutta several times. 'Coming after me is one thing... but you go near my brother or come to my family's house ever again, *I'll fucking kill you.*'

Dutta's phone was ringing but he was in no condition to answer it. Zaq looked around for the gun and managed to find it nearby. He pulled the sleeve of his jacket down over his hand and picked it up. It was a small compact automatic. He shoved it in his jacket pocket, took a last look at the two men groaning on the ground and took off back towards the park gates.

The gun was a problem – someone might have reported the shots to the police. He decided to drop it down the first drain he passed.

The Lexus was parked right outside the gates; the front passenger door was open and the guy he'd heaved over the wall was leaning on the roof with his phone to his ear. Zaq reacted first and fastest. Pulling the gun, he covered the distance between them in three quick strides and slammed the butt right between the guy's eyes. Blood spurted from the gash and the phone flew from his hand, bouncing off the bonnet and into the road. Zaq hit him twice more. The guy's legs turned to rubber and he crumpled to the ground.

Zaq was about to leg it when he had an idea. He glanced around but didn't see anyone so, holding the gun with one sleeve, he used the other to wipe it down. Then, still holding the gun with his sleeve, he reached into the car and wedged it firmly under the front passenger seat, making sure it was jammed in good and tight. When he stood up there was a man, with a big German shepherd, watching him. The dog started to growl.

'*Kidaah*, Zaq?' the man said.

It took Zaq a second to recognise the guy as someone he and Jags had gone to school with. 'Fucking hell, Luds, you scared the shit out of me!'

'What's going on?'

'This twat and his friends just jumped me.'

Luds looked at the man lying in a heap beside the car. 'Looks like you took care of him OK.'

'Other two are laid out in the park,' Zaq said. 'Listen, I got to go – *but I wasn't here, right?*'

Luds nodded. 'I never saw you.'

'Cheers, Luds.' Zaq started to leave.

'If I see the other two…'

'Yeah?'

'Maybe I'll get Rambo here to take a dump on them.'

CHAPTER THIRTY-NINE

It wasn't until he was driving away from his parents' house, that the full impact of what had just happened hit Zaq. *Dutta had tried to kill him*. The crazy fucker had shot at him in the street, in the middle of Southall. Even though his brother's death had been an accident, he had come to commit premeditated, cold-blooded murder in revenge.

Zaq's knuckles were white on the steering wheel. He replayed the fight in his head, again and again, and each time he derived a savage satisfaction from it; giving Dutta a good kicking and beating his mate with his own snooker cue. It had helped to purge some of the tension in him. He was still too keyed up to drive all the way back to Jags' though and, as he was close to home anyway, he decided to head there instead. He'd text Jags when he got in.

He turned in to the cul-de-sac he'd parked in before and parallel parked between two other vehicles. He locked the van and started walking.

Leaving the cul-de-sac he turned right, searching the street ahead. Just as he was crossing over towards the house, he spotted the Mercedes parked further down the road. The doors opened and a couple of heavyset guys got out. Zaq picked up his pace. The two men crossed the road and intercepted him before he reached the house.

'Where the fuck you been?' Raj Brar said. 'We been wanting to talk to you.'

'You should've tried calling.'

'We wanted to talk to you in person,' Parm said. 'We didn't think you'd come if we just asked you.'

'That why you sent those two dickheads last night?'

'Maybe we underestimated you.'

'Yeah, maybe. What d'you want?'

'Like I said, we want to talk to you.'

'That's what Dumb and Dumber said, except they wanted to do their talking with a hammer and a crowbar.' Zaq saw movement, behind the Brars, away down the street. Two other figures had turned the corner and were coming towards them. If it was Jhutti and Chadha, he was fucked. There was no way he could take four of them, not now, not even if Jhutti and Chadha were injured. 'You want to talk? So talk.'

'Not here. Get in the car,' Parm said.

'I ain't going anywhere. You want to chat to me, do it here or leave it for another time.'

'Someone saw and heard something they shouldn't have last night.'

'OK, you've lost me already...'

'We chased whoever it was but they got away. Then they called the cops on us.'

'Why? What were you doing?'

'Didn't matter though. We managed to get everything cleared up, so there weren't nothing to see.' Parm was telling him what had happened, without actually telling him anything.

'That's great. I'm happy for you… still don't know what you're on about though.'

Parm was watching him intently. 'And someone helped Rita get away from the flat last night. We reckon it was you.'

'What flat? The fuck you talking about? If anyone helped her, it must've been Kasim. They're together, ain't they?'

'It weren't him. Only other person we can think of is you.'

'Why the fuck would I help her? You think I want to go back to prison? I don't even know where she is.'

'You been talking to her…'

'So? She don't trust me. She knows I'm working for your dad. But you managed to track her down, huh? To a flat, did you say?' Parm didn't respond. Raj just glowered at Zaq. 'Look, if you know where she is, you don't need my help anymore. Tell your old man so I can get back to driving deliveries. I can do without all this shit.'

The two men coming up the street were carrying bags. Zaq hoped there weren't weapons in them. That would be real bad news.

'Whoever helped Rita last night, jumped Chadha and laid him out. Maybe that was you.'

'Way he lumbers around, a four-year-old girl could've done it.'

'Yeah, but the thing is, every time something happens, we think of *you*. Why's that? We reckon you know more than you're saying. That's why we want to talk to you. So, get in the car.'

Zaq shook his head. 'It's late. Let's just call it a night.'

'One way or another,' Parm said, 'you're getting in that fucking car.' He pulled his jacket open. Zaq saw the grip of a handgun sticking out of the top of his jeans.

What the hell…?

The two guys approaching with their bags were close enough now for Zaq to recognise them. 'What if I say no?'

'Then I'll put a bullet in your leg and we'll drag you to the car.'

'Someone might hear it, call the cops. They could get your number plate.'

'I'll report it stolen. I can always get a new car. Now, let's go.'

Raj reached out to grab him but Zaq knocked his hand away.

The two new arrivals came up behind Raj and Parm. 'Everything all right here?' inquired the larger of the two. He set his bags down on the pavement.

Parm let his jacket fall back over the gun.

'What the fuck's it got to do with you?' Raj demanded, turning around.

'Keep talking like that and I'll fucking show you,' Manjit said. Raj and Parm were tall but the big Singh was a couple of inches taller.

'They want me to go for a drive,' Zaq said. 'And they ain't taking no for an answer.'

Bal put his bags down too. The tension between them all was palpable. But now Raj and Parm were outnumbered. Zaq watched Parm closely. If he went for the gun, Zaq was prepared to punch his lights out. He was pretty sure he could find the energy for that.

As it was, Parm just turned to Zaq and said, 'We'll be seeing you.' Then he looked at Manjit and Bal. 'You two better watch yourselves.'

'Or *what*?' Bal took a step toward Parm. He might have been short compared to the others but there was something distinctly menacing about the stocky plumber; he was as squat and powerful as a young rhino. 'What you going to do?'

Parm held his gaze for a second, then said to Raj, 'Come

on, let's go.'

Raj glared at Manjit a moment longer before breaking off and following his brother.

Zaq watched them go. 'I think he likes you,' he said to Manjit.

'They the fuckers that jumped you the other night?'

'No, that was some other fuckers. These jokers are Raj and Parm Brar.'

'I've heard about them. They're meant to be right dodgy.'

'Yeah? Well, they can go fuck themselves,' Bal said.

The Mercedes pulled away from the kerb. When it drew level, Zaq saw Raj and Parm glaring at them, their faces grim and hostile. Then Raj put his foot down and wheel-spun noisily away.

'What was the point of that?' Manjit said.

'Probably made him feel hard.'

'Fucking dickheads,' Bal said.

'You ain't mixed up with them are you?' Manjit asked. 'The shit they're into?'

Zaq shook his head. 'I'm doing something for their old man, but they've got an interest in it. That's what they wanted to talk to me about.'

'Don't look like they were talking too nice. Good job we turned up when we did.'

'Yeah, it is. Where you two coming from, anyway?'

Manjit picked up his bags and Zaq heard the clink of glass. 'It's Friday, man. We been to the offy, innit!'

CHAPTER FORTY

Zaq was surprised to find himself awake early the next morning. Surprised because he'd had a few drinks with Manjit, Bal and the others. The long cool Bacardi and Cokes had gone down a treat with the spicy *seekh kebabs*, tandoori chicken and other dishes they'd ordered from their favourite restaurant. The food and drink had made him feel better and the company had their bullshit taken his mind off his troubles – at least for a couple of hours. He felt better now he'd rested, his mind clearer and hopefully sharper. There was still some discomfort from his various injuries but not as bad as the day before. His arm hurt the worst, where he'd blocked the crowbar.

He lay in bed and thought about everything that had happened in the last week. It was a swirl of information in his head, too much to untangle and make sense of as a whole. Eventually, he got up and found a piece of paper – settling for the back of an A4 envelope – and a pen. He sat up in bed, using his pillow as a backrest and a book on HTML as a firm surface to write on.

The first thing he did was write down the names of everyone involved in what had been going on. Then he made a list of the places that were connected too. After that he began drawing lines connecting the people and places, creating a kind of chart. It was easier to see everything as a whole when he had it all laid out visually like this.

He studied it, trying not to let any feelings or emotions cloud his judgement. It was like looking at a puzzle with the pieces out of place. What he needed to do was move the elements around, try different variations, until he was able to fit them together into some kind of workable plan. He sat there for a long time, trying out possibility after possibility. He made notes, drew more lines, circles and doodles; crossed stuff out and started again. He went through it, over and over, making adjustments each time. Finally, he thought he had the outline of a plan that *might* just work.

It didn't look like much and wasn't easy to decipher from the marks and scribbles, so he laid it all out in a series of bullet points to make it clearer. He went over them several times, adding notes and making refinements, until finally he was satisfied. He put the book, pen and envelope down and stared at the ceiling.

After a while, he picked up the envelope and read through what he'd written one more time. It was definitely a long shot but it was the best he'd been able to come up with. There were still some details that needed to be worked out but, on the whole, he thought it might be possible.

He heard movement out on the landing and checked the time. It was just after eight thirty a.m. Even though it was Saturday, some of the guys would be getting ready to go to work. Zaq got up and pulled his rucksack down from the top of the cupboard. He stuffed in some clothes, the envelope with the notes he'd just made and a few other bits and pieces. Then he quickly got dressed. Someone came out of their room onto the landing and

Zaq opened his door to see who it was.

Manjit was just starting down the stairs. He was dressed in sweatshirt and jeans, both heavily stained with paint and plaster.

'Manj, you going to work?'

'I ain't going to a wedding dressed like this, am I?'

'Can you give me a lift?'

'How long you going to be?'

'I just need a quick wash. Give me five minutes.'

'I'll be in the kitchen.'

When Zaq got downstairs, he found Manjit finishing a mug of tea.

'Ready?' Manjit said. 'You want to grab something to eat?'

'I'll get something later.'

'Let's go, then.'

Zaq stopped him at the front door. 'Can you do me a favour?'

'What?'

'You loading anything into your van?'

'My tools. Why?'

'You going to put them in the back?'

'Yeah.'

'Can I get in the back as well?'

'What's wrong with the front?'

'Nothing. It's just those tossers from last night might be waiting for me and I'd rather they didn't see me leave.'

'All right. You want me to drop you at work?'

'No, just at the end of the street.'

Manjit sighed. 'I ain't even going to ask.'

Manjit's van was backed up to the front door. The rear of the Astravan partly hid the entrance of the house from anyone watching on the street. Manjit opened the back up and, while he grabbed his tools, Zaq crouched down and clambered in with his rucksack. Manjit put his things next to Zaq and slammed the door shut, then got behind the wheel and drove away. 'Should I be looking out for that silver Merc from last night?' he said, over his shoulder.

'Yeah, or a black one.'

'Make up your mind. Which is it?'

'Keep an eye out for one of those Nissan 4x4 trucks as well.'

'You know what? Forget it.'

Zaq told him where to stop. Manjit pulled over to the kerb and let him out. 'Cheers, Manj. I owe you one.'

'Don't worry about it. Just try and keep that ugly mug of yours out of trouble.'

'I'll try but I can't promise anything.'

Zaq ducked into the cul-de-sac as Manjit drove away. He hurried over to the van, got in and threw his rucksack onto the passenger seat. Once the engine was running, he took out his phone to make a call, all the while keeping watch on the road outside the close.

'What time is it?' Jags said, sounding like he'd been woken up.

'I don't know,' Zaq said, 'about quarter to nine, something like that.'

'It's still early, man.'

'What you doing?'

'Sleeping, what d'you think?'

'Everything all right?'

'Yeah, I was having a nice dream.'

'You know what I mean. Is everything all right there at the house?

'Yeah, as far as I know.'

'Where's Rita?'

'Still asleep, I think. Want me to go check?'

'No, it's OK. I'm coming over. Be there in a while.' If she was sleeping, he didn't want Jags to wake her – and if she'd done a runner during the night, he could wait until he got there to find out. 'There is something you can do though.'

'What's that?'

'Stick the kettle on.'

'Yeah…? What's the magic word?'

'*Motherfucker*,' Zaq said. 'See you in a bit.'

CHAPTER FORTY-ONE

'What's with the rucksack?' Jags asked, leading Zaq into the lounge.

'I need to crash here for a couple of days.'

Rita was there, sat on one of the sofas, dressed in jogging bottoms and an oversized hoodie.

'How come?'

Zaq filled them in on what had happened after he'd picked Tariq up, about the run in with Dutta and his guys.

'*Fuck*,' Jags said.

He also told them about Raj and Parm waiting for him at the house. 'That's why I need to stay here.'

'No shit? Rita's got the spare room, so it'll have to be the sofa.'

Zaq knew Jags had the third bedroom set up as an office. 'That's fine.'

'I was just about to make us breakfast. You want some?'

'Yeah, that'd be great.'

Jags made them *desi* scrambled eggs, with onions and chilli, along with toast and mugs of tea. 'What I don't get,' he said, when they were almost finished eating, 'is why you put the gun back in Dutta's car?'

'I weren't going to carry it around, had to get rid of it somewhere.'

'But why give it back to them?'

'They don't know it's there. They'll be driving around London with a concealed firearm. If they get stopped and searched...'

'They'll be screwed,' Jags said, with a grin. 'You going to call the cops and tell them?'

'Not yet. It might be something we can use later.'

'What d'you mean?'

'I think I might've figured a way out of all this for us. Let me get something from my bag and I'll tell you about it.' Zaq got the A4 envelope and smoothed it out on the table. 'OK, so this is what I've come up with...'

He went through his plan, bullet point by bullet point, clarifying the timeline with the aid of his roughly drawn chart. There were a couple of questions but mostly they listened without interrupting him. When he finished, Zaq wasn't sure if they were looking at him in amazement, or if they thought he was crazy.

'Can I be honest?' Rita said, breaking the silence. 'I think it sounds kind of dumb.'

'I got to agree,' Jags said. 'It just seems... well, a bit *amateurish*.'

'That's 'cause we are amateurs. You ever done anything like this before?'

'No.'

'Me neither.'

'You really think it can work?' Rita didn't sound convinced. 'It's all so dependent on the timing. If that's off, everything could go wrong.'

'We'll work it all out beforehand, make sure the timing's right.'

'It still sounds risky. Can't we think of something else?'

'Be my guest,' Zaq said. 'I've been over it and over it, and this is the best I could come up with. If you can think of anything better, I'll be all for it. We don't have a lot of time, though. Your brothers' lot are convinced I've been helping you and they're after me. I can't stay holed up here forever and if they get me, it won't be long before I tell them everything. Then they'll be straight round here for you and Jags.'

'I don't like the sound of that,' Jags said.

'What if I was to leave, now?' Rita said. 'You could tell them you don't know where I am.'

'They might believe that – after they've killed me. I'd rather not chance it. And, even if I manage to dodge your brothers, I don't tell your dad where you are, I'll end up back in prison. My idea might not be perfect and I accept that but there's a chance it could work. If you can come up with a better plan in the next hour or so, then great, but if you can't, we either go with mine or I won't have any choice but to take you home to your dad. Up to you.'

'How about I take the money and run?'

Zaq shook his head. 'I can't let you do that. Besides, how far you think you'd get? On your own, no one to trust, no one to help you, a load of stolen cash you can't use and your brothers hot on your heels? I don't know how we've ended up helping you but we have. You either want our help or you don't.'

It was Jags who eventually broke the strained silence between them. 'I can't think of anything else. If there's a chance it'll work, I guess we should go with Zaq's plan.'

'What about my *dad*?' Rita said. 'You haven't said how we're going to deal with him.'

'If it all works out, we'll decide what to tell him and go see him afterwards. With everything else that'll be going on, he'll be much more likely to believe it.'

'What if he still wants me to get married?'

'You really think he'll be worrying about a wedding if all this goes down?'

'Doesn't look like I have much choice, does it?' Rita said. 'I guess we go with your plan, no matter how dumb it seems.'

'Thanks for the confidence.'

'You sure this is the only way?' Jags asked. 'You'll be taking a hell of a risk.'

'I can't think of any other way to do it.'

'How do we make sure everyone shows up?'

'We've got to sort that out – and we also need to get a few things... here.' He passed the envelope across the table. 'I made a list at the bottom.'

Jags read it out. 'Two pre-pay mobile phones, a security timer switch, a small lamp with bulb and a palette knife. It ain't much.'

'Should be all we need. That and some luck.'

'A *shedload* of luck,' Jags said. 'When do we need all this?'

'Today. If we can get everything ready, we'll do it tomorrow.'

'Anything else we need apart from this lot?' Jags held up the envelope.

'Um, yes...' Rita was hesitant, but then said, 'Could you get me some underwear, please?'

Jags was momentarily lost for words. Zaq couldn't remember the last time he'd seen him blush, but he was doing so now. 'Sure,' he said, when he had his brain back in gear. 'Any kind in particular?'

'Just plain black will be fine. Let me give you my size.' She told him and Jags wrote it down.

'Anything else you want me to get?' he asked, turning to Zaq.

Zaq thought about saying he needed some underwear too, but didn't. 'No, but we have to get hold of some phone numbers. Rita'll have Raj and Parm's, but we still need Jhutti or Chadha's, and Prewal's too.'

'I should have Jhutti and Chadha's,' Rita said. 'Parm told me if ever I got hassled by anyone and couldn't get hold of him or Raj, I should call one of them.'

'Them looking out for you?'

'Hardly. Looking out their own reputation more like. Didn't want anyone thinking they could mess with me and get away with it – thought it'd make *them* look bad. They didn't give a shit about me, it was about them.'

Zaq nodded. 'That still leaves Prewal and we also need a number for Mahesh Dutta.'

'Even if we get their numbers, you just going to call them up and tell them what to do?' Jags said.

'Pretty much. But I'm not calling Dutta, *you* are. He could recognise my voice. He won't know yours.'

'What am I supposed to say?'

'We'll think of something.'

'Great.'

'What about the money?' Rita said.

'We'll get it tonight.' Zaq said.

'Are you sure we can't keep some? Even just a little?'

Zaq had already thought about it. 'How much were you thinking? It'd have to be a fair bit to make it worthwhile. A hundred grand? Two hundred? What you going to do with it? It's still hot and you'd have to change it somehow. You get nabbed with any of that cash, it'll link you to the robbery and everything else. I don't know about you but that's not a chance I'd want to take.'

'Fine,' Rita said. 'Get rid of it, then. Just so long as my brothers and their little gang don't get their hands on it.'

Zaq nodded and turned to Jags. 'You want to go get that stuff now?'

'*Me?*'

'I can't go. I'm trying to stay out of sight, remember? And we can hardly send Rita. Make sure you pay for everything in cash, OK? We don't want any of it traceable back to us.'

'Sorry if I snapped at you earlier,' Zaq said, after Jags had gone. 'I'm just a bit wound up with everything that's going on. I shouldn't have had a go at you though.'

'It's OK, I understand. None of this is normal for any of us... and what with you being attacked and all. I *am* worried about this plan of yours though. A lot of things have to happen the way you want for it to work. You really think they will?'

He shrugged. 'If we can get everything set up right then, yeah, why not?'

'That's a big *if*. I wish I was as confident as you.'

The truth was, he wasn't as confident as he was making out, but he couldn't tell her that. 'You might be, once things start falling into place.'

She gave him a half-hearted smile and looked at him for a moment, before saying, 'You're not what I expected.'

The comment surprised him. 'Why, what did you expect?'

'I don't know. I remember hearing my dad and my brothers talking about you, before you started working at the yard – about how you'd just got out of prison and what you were sent there for – and I thought you'd be like Jhutti and Chadha and the rest of Raj and Parm's friends, worse even.' She was looking at him as though trying to puzzle him out. 'But you're not like them at all, you're... *different*.'

'I'll take that as a compliment.'

'You don't seem the type to end up in prison.'

'I didn't think I was either. I never expected I'd end up there.'

'Does anyone?'

'I mean it didn't even seem like a possibility. I'd never been in trouble before. I had a decent job, a flat, a car – I was doing pretty well. And then it all just fell apart. One fight, one punch... and it changed everything. Getting arrested, and charged, and put on trial, it was a nightmare – only there was no waking up from it.'

'Nina told me it was an accident, that you were defending yourself.'

'You spoke to her?'

'Yes, last night.' She must have read the look on his face. 'Don't worry, I didn't tell her where I was.'

Zaq nodded. 'How is she?'

'Fine.'

'Anyway... Yeah, I was defending myself. I wasn't looking for a fight, I was trying to break up an argument. The guy hit me, I hit him. He fell down and died, had a medical condition no one knew about, not even him. He was the arsehole but I still got five years for it and now I'm starting again from scratch, working for your dad, trying to scrape my life back together, best I can. It ain't exactly how I imagined my life would go.'

'I guess it explains why you seem different, like you don't really belong there, at the builders' yard. You're not like the other guys.'

'Seeing as we're talking about first impressions... you're not exactly what I expected either.'

She raised an eyebrow. 'Why? What did you expect?'

'Honestly? A spoilt little rich girl, running away just to be rebellious.'

'Thanks. So, what do you think now?'

'Well, I don't think you ran away to be rebellious...'

'But you still think I'm a spoilt little rich girl?'

He paused, a little too long, then smiled and said, 'No, I don't think you're spoilt. But then, I don't really know anything about you.'

'What do you want to know?'

'What's your story? How did you end up in the middle of all *this*?'

'I took twelve million pounds from a bunch of criminals, two of whom happen to be my brothers.'

'I know *that*, but you didn't just wake up one morning and think, I know, I'm going to rip those guys off and go on the run. Has to have been more to it than that.'

A minute passed, and he was thinking maybe she didn't want to talk about it, when she said, 'I should have been a boy.'

The comment took Zaq by surprise.

'That's what it all boils down to,' Rita continued. 'My dad never wanted a daughter. All he ever wanted was sons. I was a disappointment to him from the moment I was born and that disappointment's been there pretty much my whole life.'

'That's a bit harsh, ain't it?'

'You think so? You should see how he looks at Raj and Parm, *his boys*. He's so proud of those two big, muscle bound idiots. He laughs and jokes with them. They're into the same guy stuff – drinking, fighting, money and cars – just like him. With them, he's a man amongst men. He sees *himself* in them. He doesn't see any of that in me. I'm just a *girl*. I suppose he loves me, in his way, but it's not the same, it never will be and the difference is huge.' It was clearly an emotional subject.

'You've got your mum though, right?'

She laughed at that. 'She's almost as bad as he is, with her old-fashioned attitudes. When she found out she was having me, a girl, she *cried* – can you believe that? They didn't celebrate my birth like they did with the boys. My dad blamed her for having me instead of another boy and I've been her responsibility ever since. Not exactly a great relationship. Don't get me wrong, I love my mum, but she's not someone I aspire to be like. She's never worked, never had any ambitions, just does whatever my dad tells her. She might be happy with that but it's not the kind of life I want. I want more than that.'

'You got it, ain't you? You seem pretty independent, you've got a job, and I'm guessing you went to uni, right?'

'Any independence I've got, I had to fight for. My mum and dad didn't think there was any need for me to go to university. What was the point if I was just going to get married? They said it would be a waste of time and money. So I had to work and pay my own way through university. I graduated with a first class degree, with honours, but were they happy? The first thing they said was, *OK, now you can get married.*'

'But you didn't?'

'I told them flat out – *no.* I wanted to get a job. We fought and argued about it. In the end, they only let me work when they found out how much I could earn. They said I could put the money towards my wedding.'

She was quiet for a moment, lost in her own thoughts. When she spoke again, her voice was more subdued, weighted with sadness. 'I met Davinder at uni. He was just a friend at first, one of our group, we all hung out together. I wasn't looking to get into a relationship or anything, I just wanted to concentrate on getting my degree.

'But there was just something about him. He made me laugh, he was smart, I could really talk to him. The more I got to know him, the more I liked him. Before I knew it, we were together and things just went from there.' Light shone from the tears her memories brought.

'We stayed together after uni. I started working near the airport and he had a job in Slough, so it was easy for us to still see each other. By that time we knew we wanted to marry each other and spend the rest of our lives together. The only problem was *my family*. I was just waiting for the right time to tell my dad... that's when my brothers found out and ruined everything.'

A tear escaped and trickled down her cheek. She wiped it away with a sleeve. 'And now...,' her voice caught, 'and now *he's gone*.' She put a hand over her eyes as the tears came in a rush.

It was a little while before she looked up and said, 'I'm sorry.'

'Don't be. I understand.'

'It wasn't worth it.'

'What?'

'The money – it wasn't worth his life. I only wanted it so we could be together, but now I've lost everything. It's all been for nothing. And no amount of money will ever make it right.' Her face dissolved into grief once more.

'I'm sorry.' He didn't know what else to say.

Eventually, she stopped crying and wiped the last of the tears from her face. 'I really hope this plan of yours is going to work,' she told him. 'Because the only thing I want now is for the bastards who killed him to *pay for it*.'

CHAPTER FORTY-TWO

Thinking Rita might want some space, Zaq took the breakfast dishes through to the kitchen to wash up. As he was putting the last mug onto the draining rack, his phone rang. It was work calling.

'What the bloody hell have you been doing?' demanded a heavy voice. It wasn't Sid.

'Mr Brar...?' Zaq said. Rita heard and looked over.

'*Well?* What have you been doing?'

'Looking for Rita, like you told me.' He could hear the sound of deep breathing at the other end.

'That is not what Parminder tells me. He said that you have been *helping* her, going against what I told you to do. *You want to go back to prison*? Is that it? Shall I tell Rajinder and Parminder to come here and call Hari to the office? Is that what you want? Because that is what's going to happen. You will have brought it upon yourself. Hari will suffer because of you, and you will go to prison for it.'

'No, *wait*... I almost had her, but Parminder scared her off.'

'*Kee?*'

'Didn't he tell you? *He found her.*' Mr Brar didn't say anything. 'He told me himself, he went round there – wherever it was – but she got away. He just went charging in, *of course* she was going to run off, and now he's trying to blame me to cover his own arse. I can *still* find her but I'm going to need a little more time now… '

'You have had long enough.'

'And if Parm hadn't gone barging in, I would've had her for you. Just give me a few more days, that's all.' Zaq looked at Rita, who was paying close attention to what he was saying. 'I haven't found her by then, you can do whatever you want. Prison will still be there.'

His heart raced as he waited for a response. What would he do if Mr Brar said no? Only thing he could think of was to tell him he'd have Rita there *today* and drag her straight over. He hated the idea, but if it came down to it, he'd have to do it. He just hoped it wouldn't come to that.

'You have until Wednesday. After that, you're going to prison.' He hung up.

'What did he say?' Rita wanted to know.

'I've got until Wednesday.' Zaq felt himself relax as relief washed over him.

'If we're going through with everything tomorrow…'

Zaq nodded. 'Yeah… and if it all goes the way we hope, it's all the time we'll need.'

'I miss anything exciting?' Jags asked, when he returned.

Zaq unpacked the mobile phones and told him about Mr Brar's call.

'*Damn*,' Jags said. 'Lucky you managed to squeeze a bit more time out of him.'

'I know.' Zaq plugged both the phones in to charge, then

said, 'Right, let's sort out what we still got to do. First thing we need are numbers for Prewal and Mahesh Dutta. We should get Dutta's first and contact him, in case we need time to convince him.'

'What're we going to say?' Jags said.

'Let's get a number for him first.'

'You know anything about him?'

'Not much. He had a shop in Acton somewhere, a newsagent's, I think.'

'That all you got?'

'Ain't like we were best friends.'

'You know where in Acton?'

'Name of the street began with 'A', Ask– something.'

Jags opened his laptop, typed Ask Road into Google and hit Search. 'It's all hits for some restaurant chain.' He tried Googlemaps next and got as far as the word Ask, when a list of possible locations showed up in a drop-down menu.

'That's it,' Zaq pointed at the screen. 'Right there, Askew Road.'

'Cool.' Jags clicked on the link and the map resolved itself to show an area of Acton. He opened another tab in his browser and did a search for the street name and 'newsagent', and a list of results appeared.

'There's only two that look right,' said Zaq, 'Let's try them.'

Before they made the call though, they spent half an hour working out what they would say to Mahesh Dutta to convince him to do what they wanted – without him knowing who they were. Zaq jotted down some notes to help Jags keep things straight, then handed Jags one of the new phones to call with, even though it was still charging.

Jags tried the first shop and asked for Mahesh Dutta. There was no one there by that name.

He called the second one and asked the same thing. This time he glanced at Zaq as he said, 'You know when he'll be back?' Then, 'Doesn't matter who I am, just tell him it's urgent. It's to do with what he was up to in Southall yesterday. If he don't call me back, he might get a visit from the police – *or worse*. You got that? Good.' Jags gave the number of the mobile he was using and hung up. 'It was just some guy working in the shop, but he knew Dutta.'

'What now?' Rita said.

Zaq shrugged. 'We wait for him to call back. With any luck, that guy'll be calling him right now. In the meantime, let's see if we can find a number for Prewal.' He pulled out the list of names and numbers Mr Brar had given him at the start of the week. On the back, along with his other notes, was; 'PREWAL AND SONS, BUTCHERS, HOUNSLOW.'

Jags did another quick search and found a phone number for the shop.

'I can call him,' Zaq said, 'he don't know my voice.' He was about to call on the second phone when the one Jags had used started ringing. 'It must be him,' Zaq said. 'No one else has got the number. Put him on speaker – and *here*...' he handed Jags the prompt sheet, 'don't forget what to tell him.'

Jags put the call on loudspeaker.

'Who's that?' a voice said.

'You Mahesh?'

'Yeah. What d'you want?' He sounded cocky and a bit too sure of himself.

'I want you to shut up and listen.' Before Dutta could argue, Jags went on, 'You were in Southall last night.'

'No, I –'

'*Don't lie*. We know it was you – and that you were waving a shooter about in the street, firing at some guy. *You were seen.*

Your car was seen. Weren't hard to find out who you were.'

'What do you want?' He didn't sound so cocky now.

'I want to know *who the fuck you think you are*, coming to Southall and blazing away all over the gaff, like you can do whatever the fuck you want and no one'll say nothing? You can't do that shit on someone else's turf without any come back on you. You think we're a bunch of pussies here, is that it? Think you're the only one with guns?'

'No. Look, I'm sorry,' Dutta said, worry now evident in his voice. 'I never meant –'

'I don't care what you meant,' Jags snapped, getting into his role. 'You need to be taught some *fucking manners*. How we going to do that? We could tell the cops who it was shooting up the street... but you'd just deny it and unless you're a complete fucking idiot, you'll have got rid of the piece anyway. So, the other thing we can do is send some people to pay you a visit, maybe petrol-bomb your shop, set fire to your car, break your arms and legs... something you won't forget in a hurry.'

'*Shit.* Look, wait, can't we just –'

'Or,' Jags said, 'you can *do something* for me and we'll call it quits.'

There was a long pause. 'What would I have to do?'

'The guy you were after –'

'*Zaq Khan*,' Dutta spat the name out like a curse. 'The motherfucker killed my –'

'I don't give a fuck,' Jags interrupted. 'What I care about is, that bastard owes *me* money, and he ain't paying up. I want him taught a lesson. You want to get him anyway, so it works out for both of us – only don't go waving a fucking *gun* around and don't kill him, else I won't get my money. Got that?'

Dutta didn't have to think long about it. 'OK, I'll do it. I'll get the cunt for you. Only thing is, I don't know where to find him.'

'*I do*,' Jags said. He gave Dutta the time and place Zaq had written down. 'Make sure you're there on time, otherwise you'll miss him.'

'I'll be there.'

Jags moved onto the final important note on the sheet. 'If anyone else turns up,' he said, 'or tries to get involved, tell them you're there to get my money for me. That's important. If they know you're there for me, no one'll fuck with you.'

'But I don't know who you are.'

Jags gave him the name Zaq had told him to use. 'Everyone knows who I am... and what happens to people that owe me, so they'll back off and leave you alone. Make sure you don't forget, else you'll end up in a whole load of shit you weren't expecting. You understand?'

'Yeah,' Dutta said.

'It's a deal then? You best not change your mind and back out either. Won't be no fucking second chances. We'll come for you.'

'I ain't changing my mind. I want that fucker even worse than you do. I'll be there.'

'Make sure you do him over good and proper.'

'I will, don't you worry.'

'All right. I'll be in touch after. Don't fuck it up.' He hit the button to end the call and looked at the others. 'How was that?'

'Good,' Zaq said, 'but what was that last bit – *make sure you do him over good and proper*?'

'I had to make it sound realistic.'

'Great, thanks a lot.'

'Right, my turn.' Zaq picked up the second of the new mobiles and keyed in the number for the butcher's shop. When the call was answered, he asked to speak to Subash.

'Hold on,' the guy said.

Zaq put the phone on speaker.

'Hello,' a new voice said.

'Subash?'

'Yeah, who's that?'

'You don't know me and I ain't giving you my name... I'm just calling to warn you.'

'About what?' Subash said, sounding irritated.

'Them guys you hang out with – Raj and Parm Brar, Gurps Chadha, Dev Jhutti – they're going to do you in.'

'What the fuck you talking about?'

'All I know is what I heard – and that was them talking about offing you.'

'*Bullshit.*' He tried to sound confident but there was an edge of fear in his voice.

'Raj and Jhutti said something about you being a *weak link*, a liability, you know too much – whatever that means. Parm agreed, said they should take care of you soon as possible. They decided on tomorrow.'

'How'd you hear all that?'

'I was in the next booth to them in the Red Lion. They didn't know I was there. I wasn't even going to call you – I don't want to get involved – but it was bothering me, knowing what they're going to do, so I'm warning you. But that's it, I ain't doing anything else.'

'Shit.' Prewal was definitely panicky now. 'Shit. *Shit.* You sure they weren't talking about someone else?'

'They said *your name*. Why the fuck d'you think I'm calling you?'

'Nah... I don't believe it.'

'Believe what you want. They're meeting at the Red Lion tomorrow, at 7.00, before coming to you. You want proof? Go see for yourself. That's it though, I've done my bit. You do whatever you want.'

Zaq hit the button, ending the call. 'Well?' he said to Jags and Rita. 'You think he bought it?'

'He sounded scared enough,' Jags said.

'How can you be sure he'll react the way you want?' Rita asked.

Zaq shrugged. 'What choice does he have? He can't exactly go to your brothers and ask them if they're planning to kill him. So what're his option? He either bricks it and hides out from them, or he goes to the Red Lion tomorrow to see if they turn up, which they will. Whichever one he does, suit us. Only way he could screw things up is if he goes straight to the cops but I doubt he will – he's too mixed up in everything that's going on. He'd drop himself in it along with everyone else.'

'What if he just legs it from that lot and leaves town or something?' Jags asked.

'Don't matter. Long as he doesn't go to the Old Bill before tomorrow night and everything else goes to plan, then come Monday, the cops will be looking for him anyway.'

CHAPTER FORTY-THREE

With Dutta and Prewal primed, there was nothing for Zaq, Jags and Rita to do until that night. They spent the rest of the day watching TV, eating and talking. Jags told Rita stories about him and Zaq growing up together and their school and college days, even managing to make her laugh, which was something she hadn't done since escaping from the flat. She told some too, horror stories about her parents ambushing her with prospective husbands.

They ordered a Thai takeaway for dinner and the mood remained light as they ate and chatted. After they cleared away, they watched some more TV, but by then the nerves had started to set in. At ten o'clock, they got ready to leave.

'How hard will it be to move it all?' Zaq asked Rita.

'Shouldn't be too hard. It's in twenty large holdalls.'

'How large?' Jags said. 'I don't know if I can fit twenty in the car.'

Rita used her hands to indicate rough dimensions. They were pretty big. Zaq shook his head. 'I'll have to take the van as well.' It was a risk, because of the chance he might be spotted, but there wasn't any other choice. 'I'll go the long way, Hillingdon, then Long Lane and the A40 to Hanger Lane. Less chance of bumping into anyone.'

'We might as well go the same way. Where's the van?'

'Not far.'

'Want me to drop you?'

'No, better if we go separately. I'll meet you there.'

It was 10:50 pm when Zaq reached the entrance to West London Storage. Jags' BMW was waiting near the gate. The passenger window slid down as Zaq pulled up alongside. Jags leaned towards him across the passenger seat. Rita was in the back.

'What kept you?'

'This thing can barely reach the speed limit,' Zaq said, 'let alone break it. Come on, let's do this.'

Jags drove forward and stopped next to a metal post with a keypad on it. He entered the six-digit PIN Rita gave him and the gate started to open. Zaq followed him through and across the car park. Jags parked in a dark, secluded spot, away from the building, while Zaq reversed up to one of the loading bays. Overhead security lights blazed on, lighting up the loading area and making Zaq feel far too visible.

They were all dressed in dark clothes. Rita was wearing a black hoodie Jags had lent her with her hair hidden under one of his baseball caps. Zaq and Jags each pulled on a pair of gloves. They went to the double doors beside the loading bays. Rita tapped her PIN into the numeric keypad and the doors slid open.

Inside, fluorescent ceiling lights blinked on. They crossed a wide cement floor to another set of double doors with the same kind of keypad. Rita entered her PIN again, allowing them to enter the main building. More fluorescents strobed on.

A long corridor stretched away in front of them, with blue doors at regular intervals on both sides, all the way along it. There was a line of flatbed trolleys against the wall to their left. To the right were two large freight lifts with folding metal doors.

'We need to go up to the second floor,' Rita said. 'You might want to get a couple of those trolleys.'

Zaq pulled open the door of one of the lifts and then the inner grille. He and Jags grabbed a trolley each and manoeuvred them into the lift. Rita hit the button for the second floor, and the lift jerked and started to rise, the sound loud in the otherwise silent building.

'I'll be glad when we're done with this bit,' Jags said. 'Handling all this stolen cash has got me nervous.'

'You and me both,' Zaq said.

Rita didn't comment. Maybe she was used to it by now.

They got out on the second floor and Zaq and Jags pulled the trolleys along, following Rita. Overhead lights flickered on, bathing the stark white walls in their harsh glare. The corridors were almost identical to the ground floor and seemed to have the same layout. It wasn't a place that made you want to hang around.

Rita led the way, turning right and then left, from one identical corridor into another.

'This place is like a maze,' Jags said. 'How d'you know where you're going?'

'The corridors are marked with letters,' she said. 'We got out of the lift on 'R' and now we're on 'S'.' She stopped at a door. 'This is it.'

Affixed to the blue door was a small disc at eye level, with the unit number – 233. The unit was secured with a heavy duty padlock.

'Parm and the others looked in there.' Rita indicated the door they had just passed. 'Unit 232.'

'You've got the key for this one though, right?' Zaq said.

'Yes, but you need to turn around, so I can get it.'

'Why?'

Rita just raised an eyebrow until he figured it out. 'Oh, right.' He and Jags turned to look away down the corridor. Zaq heard the sound of clothing being ruffled as Rita retrieved the key from wherever she had it on her person.

'OK,' she said. When they turned back, she was holding a key, which she used to open the lock.

'That it?' Jags said. 'Just one padlock?'

'There's the alarm system as well, remember? It got turned off when we entered the PIN to get in. If you try to open any other unit while you're in here, its alarm would go off. The lock's just the last bit of security.' She turned the handle and pulled open the door.

What was inside was a bit of an anti-climax after all the build up it had received in Zaq's mind. It wasn't like in the movies. There was no moment of awe at seeing piles of cash neatly stacked in a vault or anything like that. Instead, he saw a small cramped room with plain metal walls, lit by a single bulb hanging from the ceiling. Taking up nearly all of the bare concrete floor were twenty large black and grey holdalls stacked together. It wasn't what he'd imagined twelve million pounds would look like.

He pulled a holdall from the top of the stack to make sure it contained what it was supposed to. The weight of it surprised him – it was heavier than he'd expected – and it hit the floor with a thud. He pulled the zip open. Inside were two large shrink-wrapped blocks of banknotes.

'Well...?' Jags said. Zaq stepped back into the corridor so he could look in the bag. 'That's a shitload of cash! What is it though? Looks like play money. You ever notice how foreign notes never seem like real money? I mean – look at this.' Jags pressed the plastic down over one of the blocks. 'What's that supposed to be?'

Zaq leaned over his shoulder to take a look. 'Don't know, looks like a leopard or something.' He nudged Jags out of the way and knelt down for a closer look. He was just able to make out some of the lettering printed on the banknotes. 'The Reserve Bank of South Africa.'

'Are you two going to sit around looking at it all night, or are we actually going to move it?' Rita said.

'Yeah, right,' Zaq said. 'Come on, let's get going.' He zipped the bag up and started to lift it before deciding it would be easier to pull it across the floor. He got it into the corridor, then swung it up onto the trolley. Jags did the same with the second bag. It took them a few minutes to get all the bags loaded, ten on each trolley. When they were done, Rita closed and locked the door again.

They started back along the corridor, Jags in front pushing the first trolley, Zaq the one behind, with Rita walking beside him. He glanced at her and saw she was deep in thought. 'You still want to keep some?' he said.

She looked at him. 'Sorry?'

'The money,' he nodded at the bags. 'That what you're thinking about?'

She shook her head. 'I just want to be rid of it now. I thought it would solve everything but it hasn't; it's done the complete opposite. I wish I'd never found out about it. If I'd known about the drugs maybe I would have told the police, had my brothers locked up before they...' Her voice faltered for a second, then hardened as she continued, 'If doing what you say will get justice for Davinder, then the sooner we do it, the better.'

Jags reached the lift and pulled open the doors.

'You two wait here,' Zaq said. 'I'll go down, make sure the coast's clear. I'll let you know if everything's OK and you can bring the money down. If I don't call in five minutes, put the trolleys back in the unit and try and find another way out.'

'What about you?'

'Don't worry about me.' Zaq pulled the grille shut. 'Five minutes. Shut the door.'

Jags closed the outer door and Zaq pushed the button for the ground floor.

There was no reason for Parm or any of the others to have come back, but if they had, they would have recognised the van outside the loading bay. He didn't want to take any chances. It was better to have a look now, before they brought the money down and took it outside. He got out of the lift on the ground floor and walked to the first set of doors, only to find he couldn't open them. He phoned Jags.

'That was quick,' Jags said.

'I need the PIN for the doors.'

Jags asked Rita and relayed the information to him so he could punch it into the keypad. The doors opened and he walked through. He went to the outer doors and looked out. The van was right there. He could see Jags' car over in the far corner of the car park. It all looked clear. Zaq keyed in the PIN and went outside, the chill breeze swirling around him. He looked out past the gate to the road beyond but didn't see anything to concern him. Just in case though, he decided to stay where he was and have Jags bring the money down. All he'd have to do was manoeuvre the trolleys into the lift and then wheel them to the van. Zaq would help load the holdalls into the van. He phoned Jags and told him.

When he saw Jags pulling the first trolley out of the lift he went and opened the outer doors for him. 'Wait inside till we're done,' he told Rita. It was a quick job to load the money. When they were finished, they took the trolleys back inside and left them opposite the lifts and this time Rita came out with them.

'We'll drive out together,' Zaq said, 'but once we're through the gate, don't bother to wait. This heap's going to be even slower with a load. You know where we're going, so we'll meet there. Don't park too close. And Rita… stay out of sight.'

CHAPTER FORTY-FOUR

It was almost midnight when Zaq reversed into the driveway and turned off the engine. The trip from Hanger Lane had been a nervy one. Driving the clapped-out old van with twelve million quid's worth of stolen cash in the back hadn't made for a relaxing journey. Worse than that, it had suddenly struck him that he wasn't sure if the van was even road legal. Did it have an MOT? What about road tax? It hadn't crossed his mind before but now it did, adding an extra knot to the ones already twisting his stomach. It meant as well as making sure no one was following him, he'd also been looking out for the police.

He phoned Jags. 'Where are you?'

'On your left. Look…'

Zaq saw headlights flash up the road. 'I see you. Where's Rita?'

'In the back with a blanket.'

'Make sure she stays covered up.'

'She will. Shall I come over?'

'Yeah, and don't forget your gloves.'

A minute later Zaq saw him approaching on foot. He grabbed

his own gloves and got out of the van. 'Stay here while I go round the back and get inside.'

'You sure you can get in that way?'

'Yeah.'

Zaq moved off to the alley that ran between this house and its neighbour. A metal gate barred the entrance. When he was sure no one was around to see him, he stepped up onto the waist-high wall at the edge of the drive, then jumped and grabbed the top of the gate. He straightened his arms to push himself up, then swung one leg over, followed by the other, and dropped down on the other side.

He made his way along the dark alley until he came to the fence and the side gate that led into the back garden. It had a pretty standard Yale lock. He took out the metal palette knife Jags had bought and used it to spring the lock without much difficulty. It was surprising what you could pick up in prison. After that, getting into the house was easy. Once inside, he took a quick look round, turning on lights as he moved, then went and opened the front door.

Jags got out of the van, where he'd been sitting. 'What you turn the lights on for?'

'It'll be less suspicious, like we're meant to be here, dropping stuff off.'

'At this time of night?'

'You know what *desis* are like. Come on, let's get it done.'

They hefted the bags from the van into the stripped, bare hallway. When all twenty were piled inside, Zaq grabbed his rucksack and locked the van. 'Now we need to get it all upstairs,' he said, closing the front door.

'You think she's OK out there?'

'As long as she keeps her head down, she should be.'

'You don't think she'll do a bunk, do you?'

'Where would she go? We're probably her best chance of getting out of this mess. She'd have to be stupid to run, and that's one thing I don't think she is.'

Zaq boosted one of the holdalls onto his shoulder. It was unwieldy, and sagged in front and behind, but it was the easiest way to carry it up the stairs. Jags did the same. It took several minutes but then all the bags were upstairs and they'd both worked up a sweat. The effort brought back the pain from Zaq's various injuries and he wished he'd thought to take some more painkillers. He went downstairs and brought up his rucksack.

'What now?' Jags said.

'We need a ladder so we can get this lot up there.' He pointed straight up to the trapdoor into the loft.

'You're joking! You never said anything about going up into the loft before.'

'I'm saying it now. Kneel down and let me get on your shoulders.'

'What for?'

'So I can reach up and get that trapdoor open, see if there's one of those collapsible loft ladders.'

'Why can't I get on your shoulders?'

'Fine, if it'll make you happy. Just get a move on.'

Zaq knelt down and let Jags climb onto his shoulders. When he was seated, Zaq stood up, holding onto Jags' thighs.

'Balle, balle, balle!' Jags extended his arms and shook his shoulders like he was doing some *bhangra* moves.

'Stop messing about and open the hatch.'

Jags turned the latch and lowered the door. 'Safe, there's a ladder.'

He let it drop down through the opening. Zaq let Jags down, then made sure the ladder was fully extended and locked before climbing up.

In the loft, he found a light cord and pulled it. A single bulb lit up the space, casting plenty of shadows all around. He was standing on rough boards that had been laid down over the beams to create a usable floor. Towards the eaves at the rear, there were a couple of water tanks and lots of pipework. At the front were a load of old cardboard boxes, covered in a layer of black dust.

'Anything up there?' Jags called.

'Not much,' Zaq said. 'Start passing the bags up.'

Jags hoisted one of the bags onto his shoulder. 'How come I got to do all the heavy lifting?'

''Cause you're down there and so are the bags.'

'No wonder you shot up that ladder so fast.' He climbed the first few rungs, then leaned against the ladder for support and used both hands to push the bag up through the trapdoor.

Zaq grabbed it as it came up and pulled it the rest of the way. He swung it round onto the floor, where it landed with a bang that sounded like a gunshot in the confined space, especially at that time of night. He had to be more careful. Last thing they needed was any of the neighbours coming round to complain or investigate. Zaq lowered the next one more slowly, and felt the strain in his already aching muscles.

By the time he put down the last bag he had a light sweat on and was breathing heavily. 'Pass my rucksack up too?' he said and Jags threw it up to him.

He began moving the holdalls into the shadow of a roof joist. He lined up the first six, put the next six on top and another six on top of those. He opened a couple of the topmost bags and pulled the sides down so the shrink-wrapped blocks of cash were visible. Then he dragged over the last two holdalls and unzipped them. There were four large square blocks of cash. He tore the shrink-wrap off and let the banded bundles of cash tumble out onto the rough boards. There was no mistaking what they were.

'What you doing up there?'

'I'm almost done.' Zaq rummaged around in his rucksack and found the paperwork he'd taken from the warehouse in Hayes. He took it and shoved it inside one of the open bags on top of the pile. Then he grabbed his rucksack and clambered back down the ladder.

'Cool,' Jags said. 'Can we go?'

'One more thing – the *timer*.' Jags followed him into the main bedroom at the front of the house, where Zaq opened his rucksack again. He took out the small lamp Jags had got, the plug-in security timer and the lightbulb. He fixed the bulb into the lamp and plugged it into a power socket to test it. The light came on. *Good.* He unplugged the lamp and plugged in the security timer. Then he plugged the lamp into the timer. 'What time is it?'

'Just after 12:30.'

He set the timer so the lamp would come on at 6:40 p.m. and turn off at 6:50 p.m., and again from 7.00 p.m. to 7:10 p.m. He tested the timer to make sure it worked, then reset it. 'We're done. Let's go.'

Out on the landing, the ladder was still down. 'What about that?' Jags said.

'Leave it.'

'You sure?'

'Yeah.'

Zaq turned off all the lights upstairs and down. 'We'll go out the front door,' he said. 'You drive away first. I'll wait and make sure you ain't being followed. Go straight back to your place. And *be careful*.'

'You going to meet us back there?'

'Yeah, but I'm not going to drive through Southall. I'll go

back the long way. Anything happens, call me.'

Zaq opened the front door and Jags hurried out of the driveway. Zaq pulled the door shut and got in the van. The BMW's headlights came on and Jags pulled away from the kerb. He turned a corner and headed away along the side of the park.

Zaq waited a couple of minutes. Nothing happened. No cars started up and went after Jags. One or two vehicles drove by but none turned into the street Jags had taken. Satisfied Jags wasn't being tailed, Zaq started the van and pulled out. His eyes darted from mirror to road to mirror as he kept a look out in front and behind. He left Southall – and the further he got, the safer he felt.

It was after 1.00 a.m. when he got back to Jags'. Rita was on one of the sofas in the lounge.

'You want anything to drink?' Jags said. 'I was going to make some tea for Rita.'

'I could do with a beer after all that. And a couple of painkillers too.' Jags brought him a beer and a pack of ibuprofen. The beer went down a treat, the cold burning the back of his throat as he swallowed the pills.

'What we got left to do?'

'Not much,' Zaq said. 'Just make sure the phones are fully charged and then make the other calls in the afternoon before we head out. That's about it.'

'You seem pretty calm. Ain't you nervous?'

'I'm too tired. Ask me again tomorrow.'

'Well, I'm nervous,' Rita said. 'What happens if it doesn't work?'

'Then we'll have to think of something else – *fast*.'

CHAPTER FORTY-FIVE

Jags' sofa was comfortable enough but Zaq was unable to sleep. His mind was working overtime, imagining all the different ways things could go over the next twenty-four hours. He thought over each stage of the plan, the interactions involved, what could go wrong and how he would react. One thing he *did* know for sure – *he was going to get hurt*. The only question was, *how badly?*

He must have fallen asleep eventually because next thing he knew, he was surfacing from the depths of a dreamless sleep. It was 8:30 am. He'd slept for about six hours. He was comfortable under the duvet and stayed where he was, in no hurry to get up and face what the day ahead had in store.

It was another hour before he heard someone go into the bathroom upstairs. A short while later, Jags came down.

'Hope you ain't doing anything under that duvet you shouldn't be.' Jags went to the windows and pulled back the curtains. 'Know what I'm in the mood for?'

'I'm not sure I want to know.'

'*Aloo parathas.*'

'Sounds good to me. You know how to make them?'

'No.'

'That's a lot of use. Now you've mentioned them, I fancy some too. Maybe Rita knows how to make them.'

'We can't ask her. I'll do an omelette or something. You want some tea?'

'Yeah, OK. I'll go brush my teeth while you're making it. Can I borrow a towel?'

'Help yourself – you know where they are.'

Zaq went upstairs, washed and came back down. He folded the duvet and sheet and put them at one end of the sofa with the pillow, then sat down with Jags at the table to drink his tea. A few minutes later Rita came down and joined them.

Jags got up and made her a mug of tea and brought it over. 'Milk, no sugar, just how you like it.'

'Thanks.'

'Jags was wondering if you know how to make *aloo parathas*.' Zaq said.

He could feel Jags staring daggers at him. 'No, I wasn't. Well, I was – *just wondering*, that's all.'

'I can, actually,' Rita said, 'as long as you've got some potatoes and some *atta*.'

'Er, I have. It's for when my mum and dad come round. My mum makes *rotis*.'

'I don't mind making *parathas*,' Rita said. 'I'll have some too.'

'That'd be great.' Jags gave her a big smile, downed the last of his tea and stood up. 'Let me get the stuff together.' He was still smiling as he moved around behind her, but once she couldn't see him he scowled at Zaq, and mouthed the word *wanker* at him. 'Zaq can do any peeling and chopping you need done.'

'Thanks,' Rita said, looking at Zaq. 'Could you chop some onion and some chilli?'

'Sure.'

Jags got the *chapatti* flour and potatoes, along with the other ingredients needed for the *parathas* and put them on the worktop. Zaq was rinsing his mug in the sink.

'Why the fuck did you say I wanted them?' Jags said in a harsh whisper.

'You brought it up. Relax, you're getting them now, ain't you? Besides, she doesn't mind.'

Zaq started peeling the potatoes. Rita finished her tea and came over and put them on to boil. While he chopped the onions and chilli, she mixed the flour with some water to make the *atta* dough and let it rest. When the potatoes were done and had cooled down, she mixed the onion, chilli and spices in with them. Then she stuffed handfuls of the mixture into balls of the dough and rolled the parathas out. Jags' mum had even bought him a heavy cast iron *thava*, which Rita used to cook them. She slid the first one onto a plate and cut it into three so they could all try a piece.

'Man, that's so good,' Jags said.

Zaq nodded in agreement. The outside was slightly crispy, while the potato stuffing was soft and spicy.

'Shall I make some *masala* tea to go with them?' Jags said.

'Do you know how?'

'I think so... kind of.'

'Maybe I should do it,' Rita said.

She did. And that was good too.

Zaq and Jags had three *parathas* each, while Rita managed two. They were all nicely full afterwards. Since Zaq had done all the peeling and chopping, Jags ended up doing the dishes. Rita went up to shower and dress, and Zaq turned on the TV, surfing channels in search of something worth watching. He settled on a repeat of Only Fools and Horses.

Jags joined him. 'What now?' he said.

Zaq shrugged. 'We wait.'

It was easier said than done. Tension, apprehension and nerves were gnawing at his insides. The plan he'd come up with might've seemed fairly simple, but he knew there was plenty that could go wrong. He found himself going over all the variables yet again, not able to concentrate on the TV. After a while, he said, 'I'm going to go use the bag.'

He went up to the bathroom and changed into some workout gear he'd brought with him, then went back down and grabbed the key to the garage from the kitchen. He let himself out through the French doors and into the garden. In the garage, he put his phone on a shelf and ran on the treadmill for ten minutes to warm up, sprinting for the final minute. Afterwards, he stretched and then put on some wraps and a pair of bag mitts before going to work on the punchbag.

He spent the next half-hour hitting it with his fists, elbows, knees and feet, firing off blow after blow, striking imaginary opponents, throwing blocks and counters, practising for speed as well as power. At the end of thirty minutes, he was sweating hard but the physical activity had helped clear his head and calm his nerves. He finished the workout with a series of deep stretches, pulled his sweatshirt back on, and picked up his phone to make a call.

'What d'you want?' Parm Brar said.

'I don't know what you were on about the other night, but you wanted me to tell you if I found Rita, *before I told your dad* – that's why I'm calling.'

'Where is she?'

'Not so fast... we need to sort out a few things first.'

'Like what?'

'Like you and your mates coming after me, thinking I'm helping her or some shit.'

'All right, you tell us where she is, we get her, then we're OK.'

'No. I want to meet to clear everything up first – and I want those two goons of yours there as well, so they understand you guys made a mistake. What happened to them wasn't my fault... I was just defending myself, like anyone would've done in that situation.'

'They won't be happy about that.'

'Tough shit. You sort them out. I don't want be looking over my shoulder for those two arseholes after this is all done.'

'OK, fine.' The impatience was clear in Parminder's tone.

'And in case they think of coming after me anyway, later on, I want it made clear to them – next time I won't hold back.'

'All right, fine. Where do you want to meet?'

'Southall. The Red Lion, at seven. Be there on time if you want your sister.' Zaq hung up before Parm could respond.

He turned out the lights, locked the garage and went back to the house, where he took a long hot shower. Afterwards, he put on a T-shirt, jeans and a fresh sweatshirt, then joined Rita and Jags downstairs in the kitchen. Rita was helping Jags make a Greek salad for lunch, something light after their heavy breakfast. When it was ready, they sat down to eat.

'We still need to figure out a way to get Jhutti and Chadha there tonight,' Jags said.

'It's all sorted,' Zaq said. 'I made a call. They'll be there.' He checked the time. 'All we got to do now is wait till five-thirty.'

Time dragged at first, and Zaq could sense the other two getting edgier, though he was now strangely calm himself, resigned to the fact that whatever was going to happen would happen. Then time seemed to speed up and all of a sudden it was five-thirty. 'All right, let's go.'

'You sure we need to get there this early?' Jags said.

'I want us to be in place before any of the others turn up. We go later and run into them on the way, it could screw everything up. You know where you got to be, right?'

'Yeah. I'll find a good spot.'

'Not too close. You don't want to get caught up in it. Just near enough so you can see what's going on.' He turned to Rita. 'You're going to have to do the same as last night and stay out of sight. I know it'll be boring and uncomfortable but the only other option is you stay here and wait.'

'I'd probably pull my hair out if I had to do that.'

'Fine. Just stay in the back and keep your head down. Jags, soon as you make the last call, get the hell out of there. Don't wait to see what happens, just go. You got the phone?'

Jags held up one of the new pay-as-you-go mobiles.

'Good. Make sure you smash it up and dump the pieces when you're done.'

'I will.'

'That's it, then. Wish me luck.'

They clasped hands and Jags pulled him close into a hug. 'Try and be careful, man – you're ugly enough as it is.'

When Rita stepped forward, Zaq thought she was going to say something too and was totally unprepared for her to reach out and hug him as well. He felt himself flush, hot and bright as a light bulb, conscious of her body pressing against his. 'Thank you,' she said. 'I can't believe you're going to go through with this hare-brained scheme for me.'

He didn't know how to react, so stood there like a shop window dummy. 'Don't thank me yet,' he said. 'Let's see if it works first.'

CHAPTER FORTY-SIX

Zaq went the long way again via the A40 and approached Southall from the other direction. His eyes were constantly sweeping left and right. If he was spotted ahead of time and chased or grabbed, it could ruin everything. Even on a Sunday, the roads were jammed. Crawling along in traffic only made him more anxious – he just wanted to get to where he was going.

At last, he turned onto a road by Villiers High School, which ended at an entrance to the park. He drove to the end then turned the van round and pulled over. It was the weekend and there were no lights on in the school. It was a good spot to wait – out of the way but still close to where he would have to get to.

Tension and nerves coiled his stomach tight and made the van feel too enclosed. He thought he might be sick. He needed to do something, get some air. Making sure he had his own phone and the new pay-as-you-go, he got out of the van. The fresh air did help a little. He went into the park and did some shuttle runs back and forth in the dark. Then he started to shadow box, concentrating his mind on punches and kicks, knees and elbows, single shots and combinations. It helped to quell his nerves and ease the tension – not totally, but enough.

He was jogging up and down to stay loose and warm, when the pay-as-you-go phone rang. The time on the screen was 6:55 p.m.

'I think Dutta's just turned up,' Jags said. He and Rita were in the BMW, somewhere on the other side of the park. 'There's two cars, looks like three blokes in each.'

Zaq started towards the van. 'What're they doing?'

'They've pulled up outside the house.'

'They got out yet?'

'No, they're waiting. Six against one – you sure about this?'

'You know what to do, right? Just make the calls in the order we said and it should work out.' *Hopefully.* Zaq got in the van. 'Call me back when they're at the front door.' He started the engine and sat wringing the steering wheel with his hands as he waited. His mouth was dry and he wished he'd brought some water along. He was geared up now, ready, in the zone, his nerves suppressed by the adrenalin now rushing through his system. The phone rang again.

'The security timer did the trick,' Jags said. 'Soon as the light came on, they got out of their cars. They're going to the front door now.'

'I'm on my way. Make the next call as soon as I get there. I'm ditching this phone now. See you when it's all over.' Zaq stripped off the back of the phone and pulled out the battery and the SIM card. Leaning out of the door, he wedged them behind the front wheel then reversed over them. There was a satisfying crunch. He put the van in gear and drove over them once more, this time carrying straight on, racing to the end of the road and away.

When he was able to, he floored the accelerator, pushing the van to its rattling limit. A minute or so later he saw the junction he wanted up ahead. The house was just past it, on the right. He could make out figures in front of the property, on the pavement and in the driveway.

He pulled over opposite the house, angling the van so one wheel was on the pavement, giving the impression it had been parked in a hurry, that none of this had been planned. Jags had counted right – there were six of them. Two had noticed him stop and were watching to see what he'd do. When he just sat and watched what was going on, they turned back to concentrate on the house. Zaq checked the time. It was 7.10 p.m. The light in the upstairs window went out.

'WE KNOW YOU'RE IN THERE,' someone shouted. Zaq looked and saw a figure at the front door, hammering on it with his fist. 'COME OUT OR WE'LL COME IN AND GET YOU.' He seemed to be the leader, more agitated and worked up than any of the others. It had to be Dutta.

This was it – time for action.

Zaq's insides felt lighter than air, as if they were filled with helium and trying to float away. He got out of the van and crossed the road. As he approached, he checked to see if any of the guys were carrying weapons but didn't see any. That didn't necessarily mean they were unarmed, though he hoped that was the case. The group was so intent on the house, they didn't pay Zaq any attention as he slipped quietly between them, like one of their number moving forward for a better look. The fact it was dark helped.

Dutta was shouting through the letterbox, 'COME OUT, YOU CUNT.'

Zaq walked right up to him and tapped him on the shoulder.

'*What?*' Dutta swung round, full of anger and impatience. It took a second for him to realise who Zaq was. Then his eyes went wide. '*You–?*'

Zaq hit him. The punch bounced his head off the front door and into the path of a left hook that sent him toppling onto the driveway. Zaq spun round ready to fend off the others, but they just stood there, confused. Then the penny finally dropped.

'*It's him!*'

Zaq didn't wait for them He moved first and went for the nearest guy, who also happened to be the biggest, smashing an elbow into his face and shoving him flailing into the guy behind. They both went down in a heap. Zaq feinted toward the three still on their feet, who all jumped back.

Dutta was starting to get up off the ground. 'Come on, there's six of us – *let's take the fucker!*'

Zaq turned and kicked him in the ribs. Dutta yelled and fell flat again. The other two who'd gone down were on their feet again, so Zaq was facing five. Their advantage in numbers gave them the confidence to come at him, though no one was eager to be the first to trade blows. With Zaq occupied, Dutta managed to climb to his feet too, so five became six.

Jags would have made the first call as soon as he saw Zaq pull up in the van, which meant he only had to hold these guys off for a few of minutes – *he hoped*. 'What's the matter?' he goaded them. 'Six against one not good enough for you chicken-shit motherfuckers?'

'*Fuck you,*' Dutta said, his eyes blazing hatred. 'We got you now, you bastard.'

'So what the fuck you waiting for?'

Dutta sprang at him, the others following his lead.

As they rushed at him, a sudden surge of adrenalin turbo-charged his reactions and cranked his survival instincts up to maximum. Everything seemed to slow down, he saw his attackers with ultra-sharp clarity, his reflexes precisely attuned to the situation.

He fired a jab into the face of the guy in front of him, followed by a straight right that shunted him back. Zaq brought his fist back low, deliberately leaving himself open. It was a calculated move. The guys on either side of him saw a chance and went for it. As soon as they attacked though, he brought his guard up, high and tight. He was hit from the left and right but the blows landed mainly on his arms and shoulders.

The second he covered up, they all piled in, punching and kicking. It was like being back in the playground, getting *bundled*. Zaq took a lot of shots but fortunately, his defence was solid and, in their eagerness to batter him, his attackers mostly got in each other's way. So although he was subjected to a barrage of blows, none caused any real damage. Fists pummelled his back and arms but he managed to keep his head protected. He took a couple of whacks on the arm, where he'd blocked Jhutti's crowbar, which made him wince but other than that he was able to soak it up.

He'd been through sessions just like this in the prison gym – practising with his fellow fighters, defending against multiple attackers – because real life wasn't like in the ring. There was no such thing as chivalry or gentlemanly conduct, and if you thought a guy with his friends around was going to fight you one-on-one, you were going to get your head busted. He forced himself to control his breathing and stay as calm as he could in the circumstances. An old saying flashed into his head – *sometimes the best defence was a good offence.*

Psyching himself up to counter-attack, he shifted slightly to his right, crouched lower, then drove up and forward, straight at his assailants. The move caught them totally by surprise. Zaq led with his right elbow and caught a guy flush under the chin. It clapped his mouth shut with a clack and sent him tumbling away. Zaq instantly whipped the elbow round and smashed it into another guy's nose, the guy's hands flying to his face. He'd countered to the right; so now those on his left came at him. Punches caught him in the mouth and cheek before he got his arms up again to protect himself.

His attack had opened a gap on his right flank and he went for it, barging the guy closest to him out of the way so he stumbled into his friends, preventing them from blocking his way. He broke free but, once he was past them, instead of running, he stopped and turned back to face them. '*That all you got, you fucking pussies?*' he goaded.

He had to stay. He had to fight. It was part of the plan.

Dutta and the three who were still on their feet fanned out and came towards him. The two he'd elbowed in their faces didn't seem so keen anymore. One was holding his mouth, the other his nose.

The four coming at him were trying to surround him. That wouldn't be good. Zaq backed up against the low wall at the side of the drive, so none of them could get behind him. They formed a semi-circle in front of him instead.

He couldn't tell how long it had been since he'd arrived – was it minutes or seconds? It was hard to gauge time when your heart was thundering in your ears and your senses were in overdrive.

He had to keep these wankers right there in front of him. Four was OK; any fewer wouldn't be as convincing. He threw some punches, with no real intention of landing them, just to keep them on their toes. He fired off more shots, connecting with one or two to keep things believable, but not doing any real damage. It made Dutta and the others more confident and they started to close in on him, throwing more punches and kicks of their own.

'Got you now, you bastard,' one of them raged.

'You're going to fucking get it.'

'Have that.'

Zaq was hit several times and had to check himself, so he didn't retaliate too hard. It went against all his instincts and training but he made himself to stick to the plan. *How much longer though? Where the fuck were they? When did Jags make the fucking call?* Distracted by these thoughts, he was struck again. He had to concentrate.

Dutta caught him with a punch above the left eye. Zaq raised his arm to fend off another blow from that side but got hit from the right instead. He managed to block a kick coming at his balls – but it left him open to a punch that socked him in the jaw.

Fuck that.

Using both hands, he shoved one guy off his feet and slammed a right cross into another's face. Through the gap that opened, Zaq glimpsed headlights approaching at speed on the road and thought he could hear the sound of a big engine.

That had to be them. If it wasn't, he was about to make a huge mistake.

Dutta and another guy attacked Zaq at the same time, from either side. Instead of covering up, Zaq chose to block the punch from the guy on the right and threw a lazy left to counter, that he knew would leave him exposed on that side. Dutta would see the opening and go for it. That was what he wanted – and it was exactly what happened. He saw a blur of movement and tensed for impact.

Dutta's fist smashed into his cheek. Spots burst before Zaq's eyes. The blow jolted him to the right. The guy on that side saw his chance and attacked too. It took every ounce of Zaq's willpower for him to keep his hands down and let himself get hit. The punch caught him square in the face, followed by another to the side of the head. He tasted his own blood.

'*Got you now, you cunt,*' Dutta spat, and hit him again.

Zaq let his arms sag lower. Now the others, emboldened by what they saw, came rushing in, fists and feet flying. Through the noise of the attack, Zaq heard the squeal of brakes and the skid of tyres. A punch connected above his eye and Zaq decided now was the time to drop to his knees. He went down and let them hit him a few more times to make it look good, then slumped to the ground, where he immediately curled up tight and covered up as best he could. This was when he could suffer some real damage. A barrage of kicks came raining in. All he could do was soak them up as best he could. He barely heard the shout from the direction of the road. '*OI!*'

Dutta and the others carried on, oblivious.

'WHAT THE FUCK'S GOING ON?' another voice bellowed.

'*Fuck off,*' someone standing over Zaq yelled. It sounded like Dutta. 'Stay out of it.'

'*Fuck you.*' Zaq recognised Parminder Brar's voice. 'This is our fucking house.'

The kicks slowed, then stopped.

About fucking time. Zaq opened one eye a fraction, but all he could make out were boots and trainers surrounding him. Then he caught sight of two pairs of legs further away; Parminder and probably Raj with him. Further back, he saw Jhutti and Chadha approaching up the driveway.

Jags should have made the final two calls the second he saw the Brars turn up, then he was supposed to get out of there, so he and Rita wouldn't get caught up in what would happen.

Zaq lay still and concentrated on what was being said, fervently hoping Dutta would remember what he'd been told to say.

'I don't give a fuck whose house it is,' Dutta said. '*Kasim* sent us. We're here to get his money, so stay out of our fucking way.'

Yes, he'd remembered.

'What did you say? You're with *Kasim*?' It was Raj.

'Yeah, so butt out.'

'Maybe it was *these* fuckers the other night,' someone else said, maybe Chadha.

'Fucking *ma chauds…*'

Zaq heard running feet, then the meaty smack of a punch – and everything erupted into a confusion of noise and violence.

He might have smiled, if he hadn't been getting trampled and buffeted there on the ground, in the midst of the brawl. He stayed where he was, covered up, protecting himself as much as he could.

Response times for this sort of thing were supposed to be fast; he hoped it was true. The fighting seemed to go on for ages. Someone tripped over him and went down. Kicks came flying in, hitting him as well as the other guy. Then it all moved away, toward the middle of the drive.

That was when he heard it, what he'd been waiting for – the sound of more vehicles pulling up sharply. He'd expected sirens but there weren't any. Seconds later, there came the shouted warning: 'STOP! ARMED POLICE! GET YOUR HANDS IN THE AIR – NOW!'

CHAPTER FORTY-SEVEN

The command was repeated until the fighting stopped. Zaq lay still but peeked out to see several cars in the middle of the road, some with flashing blue lights on their roofs, others in their radiator grilles. They'd come in quietly, so as to catch everyone before they made a run for it. There were a lot of armed cops, pointing a lot of guns. Dutta's group and the Brars' were all standing with their hands in the air.

'MOVE AWAY FROM EACH OTHER AND GET DOWN ON YOUR KNEES, ALL OF YOU. *NOW!*'

'What's going on?' Parm said. 'This is our house. We were just defending it from these fuckers.'

'DOWN ON YOUR KNEES!'

Parm kissed his teeth but did as he was told. The others did the same.

'NOW, FACE DOWN ON THE GROUND, ARMS STRAIGHT OUT, EITHER SIDE. *MOVE!*'

The men did as they were told. Zaq saw several cops come around the vehicles and edge into the driveway, guns trained on the men lying there.

'STAY DOWN! DON'T MOVE!'

Two cops were coming straight towards him. Zaq closed his eyes and let himself go limp. He heard their boots on the concrete next to him.

'You,' said one. 'On your stomach, hands behind your head.' Zaq stayed slumped on his side. Something hard dug into him, a boot or a gun barrel, he wasn't sure which. 'I think he's injured. Maybe he's the victim the call was about.'

'All right, stay with him till the medics get here. If he comes round, get what you can out of him.'

'Right, Skip.' He felt a hand on his shoulder. 'Can you hear me?' the cop said. 'Where are you hurt?'

Zaq just groaned.

'Can you tell me where you're hurt?'

Zaq let out another groan and croaked, 'All over.'

'OK, just sit tight, paramedics are on their way. Do you remember what happened?'

Zaq didn't answer straight away, but then said, 'Fucking jumped me.'

'Do you know who it was?'

'Guys… breaking into… the house.'

'What were you doing here?'

'Driving… past.'

'All right. There'll be someone here to look at you soon.'

Zaq responded with a grunt. Now the policeman knew he was conscious, Zaq moved a little, to get a view of what was going on in the driveway. The cop helped him into a sitting position, his back against the wall.

He stayed with Zaq, keeping an eye on him. He had a machine gun held across his chest, barrel pointing up in the air. Zaq put on a pained expression and acted like he was injured a lot worse than he actually was.

The Brar and Dutta groups were being patted down and handcuffed by regular uniformed police, while the armed officers covered them with their guns. Once they'd been searched and cuffed, they were hauled into sitting positions.

A uniformed cop with an air of authority and a lot of silver on his uniform strode into the driveway and came over to where Zaq and his minder were. 'Is this the victim?' he said. 'The one we got the call about?'

'I think so, sir,' the cop said. 'He's pretty beat up. Seems to have sustained some injuries. We won't know how bad until the paramedics have checked him out.'

'They're standing by at the RVP. I'll have them come up as soon as the scene's secure.'

Another armed officer came over. Taller and broader than the senior officer he had a bristly red beard and sergeant's stripes on his arms. 'Inspector,' he said, addressing his superior. 'No sign of any firearms on any of them, not so far.'

Jags' first call, made as soon as he saw Zaq arrive at the house, had been to Parminder Brar, to tell him some people were trying to break into his house, on Park Avenue. When the Brars showed up, Jags would have made the next call straight away. That one was a 999 call to the police, to report a man being attacked at the house and someone wielding a gun. *That* was what had brought the armed response units to the scene.

'All right, sergeant,' the inspector said, 'I'll have some of my men search the vehicles. Can we let the ambulance up now, get this one seen to?'

'Yes, sir, should be all right. The suspects are all secured.'

'How about the fire brigade?'

'*Fire brigade*, sir?'

'Someone reported seeing smoke and possibly flames, coming from the house.'

That had been Jags' third and final call.

The sergeant frowned. 'I didn't notice anything, sir. I suppose they better come up and take a look though.'

'I'll pass the word for them to come through. We'll run PNC checks on this lot. Once that's done, we'll get some transport to take them away. At the very least they can be charged with affray and assault. All right, carry on.' The inspector left.

'Stay with him,' the sergeant said to the cop with Zaq.

One of the regular uniforms came over and squatted in front of Zaq. 'You look like you got the worst of it.' Zaq grunted in agreement. The uniform pulled out a notebook and pen. 'What's your name?'

'Zaq Khan.'

'*Zaq* – that your given name?'

'Zaqir.'

'Can you spell that?'

He did. Then the officer asked him for his date of birth and address. Zaq gave them to him.

'Can you tell me what happened? What you were doing here?'

'I was just driving past.'

'Where's your vehicle?'

'The van, outside on the road.' Zaq nodded in the direction of the van and didn't have to pretend it hurt to do so.

'If you were driving past, why did you stop?'

'Some guys were trying to break in.'

'What made you think they were trying to break in?'

''Cause it ain't their house.'

'How did you know that?'

''Cause it belongs to those two over there.' Zaq nodded in the general direction of the others. 'The two big sods that look alike.'

'You know them?'

'Not really. I work for their old man.'

'You know their names?'

'Parminder and Rajinder Brar.'

'And what is it you do for their father?'

'I'm a delivery driver. I deliver building supplies.'

'How do you know this house belongs to them?'

'I been here before, dropping stuff off.'

'OK, so you were driving past and saw some people outside the house. What happened then?'

'I saw what was going on and turned around and came back.'

'Why didn't you call the police?'

Zaq gave a shrug and put on a wince. 'I thought it was just kids messing about. I was just going to tell them to piss off. Next thing I know, they jumped me.'

'Looks like your good deed's cost you a bit of a beating. I'd say Rajinder and Parminder over there owe you one.'

'Tell them that.'

'Do you remember what happened next?'

'Not really. I was too busy getting the shit kicked out of me.'

'Do you remember seeing anyone with a weapon?'

'I don't know.'

'Did you see a gun?'

'I didn't see much of anything.'

The cop nodded and put his notebook away. 'Do you have the keys to your van?'

'In my pocket.'

'We'll need them. We going to have to search it.'

Zaq pulled the key's from his pocket and handed them over. 'You might not need them. I think I left it unlocked.'

'I'll take them just the same,' The uniform got to his feet, nodded to the armed officer and went off toward the road.

Zaq saw the ambulance pull up, lights flashing. Zaq hadn't

heard a siren. Then he noticed there were no other cars going past. The cops must have closed the roads. He hoped Jags and Rita had made it away in time. A fire engine stopped behind the ambulance and the street was lit up by red and blue lights, like an outdoor rave in full swing. Zaq saw people watching from their doorways and through windows. It was quite a show.

The ambulance crew were beckoned over by the armed cop with Zaq. He relayed what Zaq had told him to them. While he was doing that, several firemen came up the driveway and talked with the sergeant, who seemed to be in charge while the Inspector was off doing whatever he was doing. Once the paramedics had been briefed, they knelt down beside Zaq and began to examine him. They asked him questions and pressed, prodded and poked him to assess his injuries.

While they did that, Zaq tried to keep tabs on what was going on around him. The sergeant turned to look at the men cuffed and seated in the driveway. 'Which one of you said this was your house?'

'I did,' Parm said.

'You got the keys to it?'

'Why?'

'So we can take a look inside.'

'Don't you need a warrant for that?'

The sergeant looked down at him. 'Someone reported seeing smoke and flames from inside and these gentlemen,' he indicated the firemen, 'have to go in and take a look, make sure everything's OK. I'm sure you don't want your house to burn down, so it's up to you – you can give us the keys or they can smash their way in.'

Parm looked at the sergeant. 'You can have the keys, only one of your lot's already got them, took them to search my motor, the black Merc, over there.'

The sergeant sent one of his men to retrieve the keys. When he returned with them, the sergeant told him to accompany the firemen into the house and take a look around.

'SARGE!' came a shout from over by the vehicles. 'We've got something.'

The sergeant went to see. A minute later he called another firearms officers over. Then the inspector re-appeared and went to talk with the sergeant as well. There was a detectable buzz in the air.

'Right,' the sergeant called to some of the regular officers nearby. 'Have this vehicle cordoned off and get SOCO down here right away.' He stalked back into the driveway. 'Which one of you is Mahesh Dutta?'

'Me,' Dutta said.

'That's your name, is it?' Raj said, so everyone could hear. 'We ain't going to fucking forget it.'

'You,' the sergeant gave him a hard stare, 'shut it.' He turned back to Dutta. 'And you,' he pointed at him, 'you're under arrest.'

'What for?'

'Assault, affray... and possession of a concealed firearm.'

'*Firearm*? What the fuck you talking about?'

The sergeant called over one of the uniforms. 'This one's nicked for the weapon. Read him his rights and move him away from the others. Then separate the rest of them, don't let them talk to each other – and see what's keeping the transport.'

The paramedics finished examining Zaq. As far as they could tell, nothing seemed to be broken, although he had multiple cuts and abrasions, with areas of tenderness and some swelling. To be safe, they wanted to take him to hospital for some X-rays and further checks, to rule out concussion or any internal injuries. One of them went back to the ambulance to get a stretcher.

Dutta, who was being formally arrested, was still protesting his innocence and looking thoroughly confused. Zaq wondered how long it would take him to figure out who must have put the gun there.

'*Skipper.*' This time the call came from the other direction, from the front door of the house. It was the armed officer who'd gone in with the fire crew. 'You better come take a look at this.'

'What's going on?' Parm called out. 'Is there a fire in there, or what?'

The sergeant ignored him as he strode past and disappeared inside with the officer. A few minutes later, the Inspector appeared and hurried up the driveway to the house too. The sergeant met him at the door and they exchanged a few quick words before going inside. Zaq felt his heart beat faster.

Parm frowned and looked at his brother. Raj shrugged.

As the paramedic brought up the stretcher, Zaq saw the fire crew come trudging out of the house.

'What's going on in there?' Parm called to them.

None of them responded. They looked at Parm as they passed and exchanged comments amongst themselves.

Parm kissed his teeth, loudly. 'Yeah, *fuck you* too.'

'Can you get up?' The paramedic with Zaq asked.

'I don't know,' Zaq said.

'OK, take it easy. We'll get you on the stretcher.'

While they were manoeuvring it onto place, the three policemen came out of the house. They seemed barely able to contain themselves. 'What's going on?' Zaq asked the cop with him, even though he had a much better idea of what was happening than anyone else.

'I don't know.'

'Carry on, sergeant,' the inspector said and started back toward the road. 'I'll let the powers that be know.'

'Yes, sir.' The sergeant turned to the uniform with him. 'Stay here until we get the house sealed off. No one goes in or out without my say-so. Going to be a busy night for the SOCOs when they get here.'

Zaq was put onto the stretcher and had a blanket placed over him. He watched as the sergeant approached Parminder and said, 'This is your house, right?'

'Yeah,' Parm said. 'Me and my brother's.'

'Which one's your brother?' Parm nodded at Raj. 'In that case,' the sergeant said, 'You're both under arrest.'

'*What the fuck for*? We was just defending the place from those cunts. They're the ones that were trying to break in. You should be nicking them.'

'You might have a point, there. But don't worry, we'll be talking to all of you. In the meantime, you're under arrest on suspicion of armed robbery –'

'What the fuck...?'

'– and handling the proceeds of said robbery.'

Everyone stopped what they were doing to listen, including the paramedics who were wheeling Zaq towards the ambulance.

'You do not have to say anything,' the sergeant went on, 'but it may harm your defence if you fail to mention, when questioned, something which you later rely on in court, and anything you do say may be given in evidence.'

'You've made some sort of mistake,' Parm said.

'Only mistake here,' the sergeant said, 'is you deciding to have a fight right outside the place you've got twelve million quid stashed.'

Parm frowned, confused.

'What the fuck's he talking about?' Jhutti said. 'The *money's in there*?'

'It *can't* be.'

'It's there all right,' the sergeant said. 'Looks like all of it too.'

'*Ma di lun*, you've had it the whole time,' Jhutti said. 'You trying to rip us off, you dirty fucking bastards!'

'*Kasim* must've put it there,' Parm said.

'Like fuck.'

'Who's *Kasim*?' the sergeant said. 'On second thoughts, never mind. We'll find out later.' He turned to a uniformed officer. 'Nick the lot of them.'

CHAPTER FORTY-EIGHT

Zaq wasn't placed under arrest but was accompanied by a police officer in the ambulance. Two more uniforms followed them to Ealing Hospital in a patrol car. When they reached A&E, Zaq was taken to a secure room reserved for police use and, while he waited to be seen by a doctor, had to go over his story once again for the two cops who'd come by car. They asked a lot of questions about his relationship with the Brars and Dutta.

'Did you know one of the men who attacked you was Mahesh Dutta, the brother of the man whose manslaughter you were convicted of?'

'No, I didn't.'

'We also have police reports that say you were assaulted on two separate occasions earlier this week. Do you know who it was that attacked you on either of those occasions?'

'It was dark both times. I didn't get a look at them.'

'Twice in one week... you're either very unlucky or someone's out to get you. Any idea who might want to do that?'

'No,' Zaq said, then, 'You don't think...?'

'I don't think anything,' the cop said. 'But we'll be having a serious talk with Mr Dutta.'

Finally, a doctor came and checked him over. He'd been lucky. Despite the amount of punishment he'd taken, he didn't have any serious injuries; a few bruised ribs, some lumps and bumps and an assortment of cuts and bruises. The doctor did note, however, that some of Zaq's injuries were older than that night.

'I've had a bad week,' Zaq told him.

A nurse cleaned up his cuts and scrapes and gave him a couple of ibuprofen for the pain and swelling. He had to have some X-rays, as a precaution, to rule out any head, facial or internal injuries. The X-ray results showed there was nothing to worry about and he was discharged – only to be taken to Ealing police station.

He'd expected to be detained, maybe even arrested, so it didn't come as a shock. He was calm and polite with the police officers, unlike the others who'd been nicked at the house on Park Avenue. Bandaged and patched up as he was, the cops were pretty decent to him. He was taken to an interview room and given a cup of tea and some biscuits before being questioned. Then he was left in the interview room while the detectives went to verify the information he'd given them.

He tried to get some sleep but couldn't get comfortable on the chairs and thought, perversely, that he might've been more comfortable in a cell, where at least he could have lain down. The painkillers also started to wear off, allowing pain to creep it way back into his body.

After and hour or so the detectives returned, offered him more tea and went over his entire story again. Fortunately, he knew it well and stuck to it. Everything must have checked out; it would've looked as though he got caught up in the whole thing purely by chance. He wasn't charged with anything but was told he'd probably need to answer more questions at a later date. He was free to go.

One of the detectives looked at the state he was in and had a couple of patrol officers drop him home. He went straight to the kitchen and took some painkillers. The time on the microwave said 04.35. He felt drained. He dragged himself up to his room, undressed, drew the curtains and crawled into bed.

When he eventually woke up, he was pretty sure he what it felt like to be a tenderised steak. Even the *thought* of moving hurt. It was dark in his room and not just because the curtains were drawn; proper night-time dark. What time was it? He lay for a while, wondering, and then heard voices and movement downstairs. Finally, moving as slowly and carefully as he could, he reached for his phone. He'd been punched and kicked so much that any movement at all caused him some degree of pain. His body felt like it had aged thirty years in one night.

He checked the time on his phone. It was almost 6.00 in the evening. He'd slept on and off for over twelve hours.

He'd set the phone to silent and saw there were several missed calls. Half were from Sid at the yard, probably wanting to know where he was; the rest were from Jags, probably wanting to know the same thing. He lay as still as he could and called Jags.

'*Where the hell you been*?' Jags wanted to know. 'We've been sitting here worrying about you since last night.'

'Shit, I should've called. Cops let me go about half four this morning, dropped me home. I was so knackered I went straight to sleep. Sorry.'

'We didn't have a clue what happened. How you doing?'

'I been better. Feel like shit but the doctor said I'll be OK.'

'You get hurt bad?'

'As opposed to good? Couple of bruised ribs, a few lumps

and bumps, some cuts and bruises.'

'Man, you've sure taken some licks over the last week. You seen the news? The story's all over the place – cops arresting people for the Heathrow robbery, recovering the money. Suspects from Southall. Firearms at the scene. It's a huge story. Looks like your dumbass plan might just have worked.'

Zaq cracked a smile, staring at the ceiling. 'News mention anything about Dutta and that lot?'

'Not yet.'

'What about Davinder?'

'No. Why would they mention him?'

'Might be too soon for that. I took some paperwork from the Brars' warehouse and stuck it in with the money. Once the cops find it, they're bound to go search the place and they'll find a lot more than they bargained for, including some of Davinder's stuff. Soon as they get an ID on the body, it'll link Rita's brothers to him and his murder. You can bet it'll make the news then.'

'*Damn*, those guys are in some deep shit.'

'Right where they belong.'

'What you doing now? I'll come over and pick you up. We can all have a couple of drinks to celebrate.'

'It's still early days. We don't know how things are going to pan out.' Zaq shifted position and pain flared in several places at once. 'I need to shower and change. Give me about an hour.'

'It's going to take you that long to get ready?'

'It's not like I can move very fast.'

'What the fuck?' Bal said, when Zaq came into the lounge. 'Looks like you got your *bond* whipped again.'

'I didn't think you could look worse than before,' Lax said, 'but you do.'

'That's it. You definitely need some help, man,' Bal said. 'You ain't handling shit on your own. Tell me who they are and I'll go with you, make sure they don't fuck you up anymore.'

'Thanks, but it's been taken care of,' Zaq said.

'Weren't them two *phudis* from the other night, was it?'

'Don't worry, they won't be hassling me anymore.'

'I wasn't worried. Just saying, I don't mind kicking the shit out of a few people.'

'Thanks but it's all right.' Zaq's phone rang. It was Jags, calling to say he was outside. 'I'm going out for a while.'

'You sure you can?' Bal said. 'You're moving around like an old granny.'

'I'll be OK.'

'Try not to get beat up again. Don't look like you can take any more.'

Zaq left the house, made his way gingerly to the kerb and eased himself into the passenger seat of Jags' BMW.

'Man, you look terrible,' Jags said.

'Don't you start. How's Rita?'

'Pretty good, considering everything that's happened. She's been better since the news broke about the arrests last night. She's worried about you, wants to see how you are. She can't believe the plan worked either.'

When Rita saw him, her hands went to her mouth. 'Oh-my-God.'

'Don't worry,' Zaq said, 'it looks a lot worse than it is.' He made it to a sofa and lowered himself onto it. 'Doctors checked me out at the hospital, said I'll be OK. All this'll fade in a week or so.' He waved a hand at his injured face. 'The ribs will take a bit longer, but I'll be fine.'

'What happened? We left when you said we should, so we didn't see any of it.'

'Went just like we hoped. Jags' 999 call about me getting beaten up and someone waving a gun around got the cops there quick time. Loads of them too, armed, pointing their guns at everyone. We all got searched and then they looked in the cars, found the gun under Dutta's seat.'

'What did he say?' Jags said.

'What d'you think? He denied knowing anything about it – but it was in his car, under his seat. They find any prints on it, they'll be his. I only ever handled the thing with my sleeve.'

'The fire brigade turn up too?'

'Yeah, they had to because of the fire you reported. Even though there was no sign of one when they got there, they still went in to check it out just in case – and must've found the money in the loft. You should've seen the cops' faces when they realised what it was, like Christmas come early for them. Then they nicked everybody.'

'What about you?'

'I think they gave me the benefit of the doubt,' Zaq said. He told them how he'd been taken to the hospital with a police escort, then transferred to the police station, where he'd been questioned for a few hours. 'They made me go over and over what happened, and then they let me go.'

'You should've called,' Jags said.

'I know. Couple of cops dropped me home and I was so tired I just fell into bed and conked out.'

'Well, you're here now and in one piece – just about. Let's have a drink to celebrate.'

'Actually, I could do with something to eat. I haven't had anything proper since yesterday.'

'Sure, let's all order something.'

Jags got some takeaway menus and they settled on Chinese. Zaq had a beer while waiting for the food to turn up, so did

Jags; Rita opted for a glass of wine.

'What happens now?' she said.

'We'll have to wait and see,' Zaq told her, 'though I'm pretty sure your brothers are screwed.'

'*Good*. Serves them right. There wasn't any mention of Davinder on the news though.'

'The cops will have found the paperwork from the warehouse, might even have searched the place already and found all the stuff there, along with some of Davinder's things I left around. They'll only be able to make the link once they've ID'd his body and I don't know if they have yet.'

A shadow to passed over Rita's face. 'But the warehouse isn't registered to them, is it?'

'No. They'll be looking for Prewal for that – but the paperwork being with the money at your brothers' place connects them to it somehow and you can bet the cops'll be taking a real close look at it all.'

'What if they just deny any knowledge of it. That's why they put it in Prewal's name in the first place, isn't it?'

'The paperwork being with the money will make that difficult – and once the Old Bill get their hands on Prewal, he'll probably confirm it's all theirs.'

'What if he doesn't?'

'And take all the blame himself? For the drugs, the cash, involvement in the robbery – and for Davinder's murder? He'd be looking at a real *long* stretch inside for all that. You really think he'll keep his mouth shut and go down for it – especially if there's any chance for him to wriggle out of it by grassing on the others? Besides, if he believes what we told him about them – that they were going to kill him – it'll make it a lot easier for him to turn on them.

'Even if he doesn't, once the cops start digging, there'll be all sorts of DNA and forensic stuff to tie your brothers to the murder.'

Rita thought about it. 'I hope you're right,' she said. 'What about Kasim?'

'The police are already looking for someone called Kasim. Won't take them long to figure out it must be the same Kasim who was robbed at the airport. Then they'll want to know where he is and, once they find out about Davinder, it won't be much of a stretch to think they might've done the same to him.

'Anyone investigating Prewal finds out about the call they got Thursday night in connection with the shop, will take that report a lot more seriously. I don't know how Parm and those guys managed to cover it up then but the cops will take a lot harder look at it now.'

Rita bit her lip. 'Looking for Kasim will lead them to me.'

'Just stick to the story we worked out. He was a friend of your brothers, that's all. You don't know anything about the robbery. You found out about the drugs. Your brothers and their mates threatened you. Kasim warned you they were going to get you in trouble with your dad, so you ran away. Tell the cops you were going to be forced to get married – it's against the law. They might even have a word with your dad about it, warn him against it.'

Rita nodded.

'Police will probably want to talk to me again, about Davinder. My number'll be on his phone and I was the last person with him before he disappeared.'

'What will you tell them?'

'Not much. I already said I was attacked somewhere else that night. If I change my story now, I'll just drop myself in it. I'll just say I met him for a drink and that's the last I saw of him.' He had an idea. 'Maybe I can say there was a white van

435

parked near his house with a couple of guys in it. Might add another nail to their coffin.'

So far, their plan seemed to be working, like a neatly constructed web, with Raj, Parm, Jhutti, Chadha and Prewal all caught right in the middle of it, along with Dutta's bunch too.

'What about Dutta and his guys?' Jags asked.

'I don't think I'll have to worry about him for a while. He's in the shit way over his head.'

'With a little help from us.'

'Yeah,' Zaq said. 'The gun alone could get him five years. On top of that, he's dropped himself and his mates right in the middle of the whole robbery scenario. From what he said to Rita's brothers, it seems like he knew all about the money and was there at the house to take it.'

'He said what we told him to?'

'Pretty much word for word. You should've seen Raj and Parm's reactions – they went completely apeshit.'

'What if he turns round and says he didn't know anything about it?'

'Who's going to buy that? You really think anyone's going to believe he was breaking into a house, with twelve million quid inside, 'cause he got a mysterious phone call telling him to do it? I seriously doubt it.'

'He could tell them he was there after *you*.'

'That won't do him any good. He'll be admitting he was there to attack me – and he had a gun. That's all sorts of additional charges, right there. Plus, there are the other two attacks on me during the week. He's got motive and was definitely in the area on Monday, maybe even looking for me Tuesday too. They already said they're going to talk to him about it.'

'So he's screwed whatever he says? That's him and his little posse taken care of then.'

'There's still my dad,' Rita reminded them.

'We'll go see him tomorrow,' Zaq said.

'What am I going to tell him?'

'Exactly the same thing you're going to tell the cops – only with a few little extras.'

It got late and Jags had drunk too much to drive. 'Forget going home,' he told Zaq, 'just stay the night. I'll take the sofa, you have my room – you've earned it. I'll put some fresh sheets on for you.'

Zaq agreed.

'That's settled then,' Jags said. 'We might as well have another drink. Same again?'

CHAPTER FORTY-NINE

Next morning they all watched the breakfast news on TV. The arrests in connection with the Heathrow robbery was the main story on every channel.

Zaq popped a couple of ibuprofen and took a long hot shower. His body was still a mass of aches, all stuck together. There wasn't a lot he could do about it. The best course of action was simply to take it easy and let himself heal. His injured ribs meant that even stretching and exercising were out of the question. He dressed in the same clothes he'd worn the previous evening, then made a phone call.

'Hello, Brar Building Supplies,' a heavily accented voice answered.

'All right, Sid? It's me, Zaq.'

'*Theri bhen di...* Where you are? Why you no come to work yesterday?'

'I was busy.'

'Busy *da bucha...* You taking piss. I not bloody happy with you.'

'Mr Brar there today?'

'*Haah*, Brar *sahib hega*. He very angry yesterday, asking for you. Maybe you not have job today.' He didn't sound too concerned.

'Tell him I'm coming in to see him? I'll be there in a while.'

'*Meh thuada* secretary –'

Zaq hung up.

'You want me to drop you guys at the yard?' Jags said, when they were ready to go.

Rita was dressed in her own clothes again, which had been washed and dried. She'd put on some makeup, using what she had in her handbag; a little eye shadow, some blusher and a bit of lipstick. As far as Zaq was concerned, she looked great.

'No,' he told Jags, 'but you can take us to Park Avenue to see if the van's still there.'

'What for?'

'So we can drive it to the yard.'

'Why, when I can drop you there?'

'Us getting out of your car might raise questions and the last thing we need right now is anyone wondering who you might be and how you're involved in all this. It's better if me and Rita just turn up in the van.'

'All right,' Jags said. 'I suppose you're right. You sure you can drive?'

'It ain't far. I'll manage.'

'Park Avenue it is then.'

The house was still cordoned off with police tape. There were several police cars parked outside and uniformed officers were stationed on the pavement and by the front door. The van was where Zaq had left it, though the police had moved it off the pavement and parked it straight. They had returned the keys to him when he left the police station.

'No way I can work today,' Zaq told Jags when they'd all gotten out of the car. 'I might come back to yours afterwards, if that's OK?'

'If things don't work out, I might come too,' Rita said.

'You're both more than welcome, anytime.' Jags said. 'I hope it does work out for you though.'

'Thanks, Jags, that's sweet of you,' she said, and hugged him.

He wasn't expecting it but clearly enjoyed it all the same. 'You need anything, just call me,' he said, when she broke away. 'In the meantime, I'll keep my fingers crossed for you.' He told Zaq he'd see him later, then got in the car, gave them a wave and drove away.

Rita turned to Zaq, with a serious look. 'I want to thank you, too,' she said, 'for everything you've done. You took a big risk to help me. I'm not sure I deserve it but I really appreciate it, more than you know.'

'It's OK,' he said, slightly embarrassed by her gratitude and the way she was looking at him. 'Don't worry about it.'

'I hope you feel better soon... your ribs and everything.'

'Thanks – me too.'

She hesitated, as if she wanted to say something else but didn't know how. Then she leaned forward, rising up on her toes, and kissed him on the cheek. For the briefest instant he forgot about all his pain and discomfort as he felt a little burst of warmth inside, like a firework exploding in his chest. He looked at her in surprise.

'I didn't think I should hug you, in case it hurt.' She smiled at him.

He smiled back. 'That's OK,' he said. 'You sure you should've done that out here, though? Someone could've seen.'

'I might not get another chance.'

* * *

It was only a short drive from Park Avenue to Brar Building Supplies. Zaq parked on the pavement in front of the shop and led Rita in through the main entrance. The guys in the shop had seen the van pull up and Rita get out with him. He could see the questions on their faces but none of them said a word. They knew something was going on and that Zaq had been doing a special job for Mr Brar. This had to be connected to it. Why else would he show up, battered and bruised, and lead a girl through the shop? If any of them recognised the boss's daughter, it only added to their puzzlement.

Zaq lifted the hinged section of the counter, and ushered Rita through. Jeet, the shop supervisor, was sitting on his stool behind the counter. 'Mr Brar upstairs?' Zaq asked. Jeet nodded. Zaq punched in the security code and pulled the door open. 'This way,' he said. Once they were through, he gestured to the right.

'I know,' Rita said. 'I have been here before.'

They went up the stairs to the door with Mr Brar's name on it. Zaq knocked three times.

'*Haah? Ajaah.*'

Zaq went in first.

Mr Brar was seated at his desk, a brooding figure with a lot on his mind – none of it good. His eyes narrowed when he saw Zaq and his face clouded with the promise of thunder. '*Where the bloody hell* –?' He didn't finish. His expression changed, the storm clouds parting, when he saw who else was there. '*Rita...?*' he said.

'Hi, Dad.'

CHAPTER FIFTY

'Where have you been?' Mr Brar got up from his chair.

'Staying with a friend,' Rita was calm and composed.

Her father's face screwed up with disgust. 'This *Muslim* boy?'

'No, dad, it was nothing like that.' She and Zaq were still by the door.

'Your brothers told me –'

'They *lied*... about everything.'

The muscles around Mr Brar's eyes and mouth tightened. His eyes shifted to Zaq. '*Thu jaa,*' he said, dismissing him.

'No,' Rita said, 'I want him to stay. He's the only one who's helped me. I wouldn't be here if it wasn't for him... and he knows everything anyway.'

Mr Brar looked at him again. 'Shut the door.' Zaq did as he said. '*Bejah.*'

Zaq and Rita sat down in the chairs facing the desk. Mr Brar sat back down too. 'If you weren't with this boy, who were you with?'

'A friend.'

'What *friend*?'

'I don't want to get her involved in any of this. I said I'd keep her out of it.'

The fact she referred to this imaginary friend as a *her* seemed to placate her dad a little.

'Why did you run away?'

'This arranged marriage you're trying to force me into is one reason –'

'You *should* be married by now.'

'Then I should be allowed to choose who I want to marry.'

'We have found a suitable boy for you.'

'How do you know he's suitable for me? I don't even know him.'

'I am your father. I know. I have seen him and he is from a good family.'

'You like him so much, you marry him.'

Mr Brar's eyes flashed with anger. Zaq could sense the thunder building behind them.

Bloody hell, this wasn't how it was supposed to go. She was going to have a fight with her old man before they did anything they'd come here to do. Zaq cleared his throat in an effort to remind her to stay on track with the story they had worked out, hoping she got the hint.

Maybe she did, maybe she didn't – but she changed subject anyway. 'That was *one* reason,' she said. 'The other was Raj, Parm and their friends. You have no idea what they've been doing.'

'Oh, I know now,' Mr Brar said, redirecting his anger and venting it. '*Everybody* bloody knows now.'

'You don't know everything though.'

Her dad glared across the desk at her, clearly not liking that his daughter was pointing out his own ignorance to him.

'This is what they didn't tell you but it's probably all going to come out soon, so you should know. The guy I'm supposed to have run away with, *Kasim*, he was the security guard who got robbed at the airport. He was working with Raj and Parm. They knew each other way before *they introduced him to me*. They were all in it together. But after the robbery, Kasim took the money and ran. Raj and Parm wanted it back. They were going to tell you I was seeing him anyway, because they wanted me out of the way for another reason.'

'What other reason?'

'I'm getting to that. Kasim warned me and helped me get away but that's the last I saw of him. I had no idea they were involved in the robbery and only found out about it afterwards. Raj and Parm told you I was with Kasim because they *knew* if they told you that, you'd have people looking for me *and him* and they made sure they'd be first to know if anyone found him.'

'It's true,' Zaq said. 'They wanted me to tell them whatever I found out *before* I told you.'

Mr Brar forehead creased into a frown. He was having some trouble processing this new information.

'Raj and Parm obviously managed to get the money back somehow,' Rita continued, 'but what's happened to Kasim? What have they done to him? He's missing according to the news. I doubt they just let him go. The police are going to find out, dad, sooner or later. You need to be prepared.'

'For *what*?'

'I think you know.'

Mr Brar's expression hardened.

'The other reason they wanted me out of the way - and what I was most scared about – is because I found out about something they're involved in, something they didn't want me to tell you, or anyone else about. Their friends threatened to rape and kill me if I said anything.'

Mr Brar's whole body tensed, rage carving its way into his features. '*Who said this to you?*'

Rita hesitated, acting as though she was scared to even say their names. Eventually, she did; 'Sukh Jhutti and Gurps Chadha.'

'*Bhen chaudeya...*' Mr Brar was breathing so heavily Zaq half expected to see flames coming from his nostrils. He looked as though he wanted to smash something too. Zaq was glad there was a desk between them. 'What are they involved in?' Mr Brar demanded. 'Why would they let their *friends* threaten you in such a manner?'

'They're dealing drugs, dad. Heroin, and I don't know what else. And not just a little bit – a *lot*.'

Mr Brar was clearly struggling to take in these new revelations, especially so soon after finding out that his sons were behind the Heathrow robbery and now possibly a murder too. 'You should have come to me.'

'I couldn't. They said not to tell anyone. I was scared. They were watching me all the time. If they thought I was going to tell you or the police, those guys would have taken me away and Raj and Parm would've told you I ran off with Kasim. That's why they were pushing you to get me married, so I'd be out of the way. They must've thought if I was married and moved away, I'd be too preoccupied to worry about what they were doing and let it drop. I couldn't take it any more. That's the other reason I left.'

It was the story they'd worked out together. It stuck fairly close to the truth, with slight deviations and omissions to ensure they both came out of it OK. And he had to hand it to her – she was doing a good job, even managing to make her voice tremble in the right places.

'I'm only telling you all this now because Raj and Parm have

445

been arrested and so have Jhutti and Chadha. I didn't go to the police but it's only a matter of time now before they find out about the drugs anyway.'

'Why?'

'The police will be looking for any evidence to do with the robbery, it won't be long before they find out about the warehouse Raj and Parm have got in Hayes. That's where they keep their drugs and money. Once the police go there and search it, they'll find everything. They might even be searching it right now.'

Mr Brar listened, silent and unmoving, but Zaq could sense his mood from the tautness of his body and the flat glare of his eyes.

'There's more,' Rita said.

'What else?' her dad managed, in a strained voice.

'When I left, they were scared I might go to the police, so they *did kidnap Davinder*, to make sure I'd keep my mouth shut.'

'But they told me...' He didn't finish as he realised it didn't matter what they'd told him. It now seemed as though everything they'd told him had been a pack of lies.

'He hasn't been seen since.' Rita's voice broke.

This time, Zaq knew, it was genuine. He saw tears roll down her cheeks. Mr Brar was smouldering like a volcano about to erupt. He was having to deal with a whole new ton of shit, on top of what had already been piled on him. The robbery itself probably wasn't so bad as far as he was concerned – there was a kind of Robin Hood quality to getting away with a good haul, if no one got seriously hurt – but there was nothing good about dealing heroin on an industrial scale, or with kidnap and murder.

Mr Brar was staring into the middle distance, his mind working over what they'd told him. Then he focused on his daughter again and said, 'Is there anything else?'

She shook her head.

He looked at her for a long moment before saying, 'Then go home.'

'But… Raj, Parm and the others…'

'Don't you worry about them. No one is going to touch you. *I* will make sure of that.'

'What about the marriage and everything you –'

'You think I have time to worry about any marriage *now*?' His voice was louder and harsher than he must have intended, because he took a moment to compose himself before continuing. 'Your brothers will drag our family name through the mud. You think anyone will want to marry you now? Everyone will think we are nothing but a bunch of criminals. If all this is true, your *kuthae kaminae* brothers will be going to prison for a long time. You can forget about any marriage for the time being. I have other things to deal with. I need to talk to the solicitor about what can be done. Go home and explain to your mother. *Just tell her what you have to*. I will be home when I can. How did you get here?'

'I drove her,' Zaq said.

'Then you will take her home.'

Zaq started to get up and winced at a sudden shooting pain in his ribs. Mr Brar seemed to take in his beaten-up appearance for the first time. 'You were at the house when Raj and Parm were arrested?'

'Yeah.'

'What were you doing there?'

'I was driving past, on my way to meet them at the Red Lion.'

'Why were you meeting them?'

'To straighten some things out. They got it in their heads I was trying to help Rita get away – that's what they told you too.

They managed to find out where she was – but so did someone else. Seems it must've been those other guys, the ones they had the fight with. They were looking for her too because they'd heard she was with Kasim and they were after the money too.'

'How did they hear that?' Mr Brar said.

'The rumour Raj and Parm started. They didn't know anyone else was after Rita and they just assumed it was me. They sent Jhutti and Chadha after me. When that didn't work, Raj and Parm tried to kidnap me as well, even pulled a gun on me. I was lucky a couple of my friends showed up and stopped it, otherwise they might've done the same thing to me they've probably done to Kasim and Davinder.' Mr Brar didn't like what he was alluding to but Zaq continued before he could say anything, 'I didn't know what was really going on or what Raj and Parm were going to do, so I talked to Rita on the phone, to see if we could work out some sort of deal with them.'

'Deal? What deal?'

'If they told you the truth – that there'd never been anything going on between Rita and Kasim – and they laid off pressuring you to get her married, she'd come home and promise not to say a word about what they were doing. I was on my way to the Red Lion to put that to them and also to explain I wasn't helping her like they thought.'

'But you didn't get to the pub?'

'No. I saw those other guys at their house. Looked like they were trying to break in. I knew it was Raj and Parm's place – you sent me there yourself – so I stopped to ask what the hell they were doing? Then they jumped me. Next thing I know, I'm coming round on the floor and the paramedics are treating me. Someone must have called Raj and Parm, 'cause they were there too.'

'You knew nothing about the money?'

'Not a thing.'

'And the drugs at this warehouse?'

'No. Why would I?'

Mr Brar stared at him. Finally, he said, '*Jaa*, take Rita home.'

Zaq turned to leave, then looked back at his boss. 'What about after that?'

'*Kee*?'

'What should I do once I've dropped Rita? The doctor said I've got some cracked ribs, that I should rest for a few days.'

'Then go home. Take some days off.'

'Will I still get paid?'

'*Haah, haah*,' Mr Brar said, unable to keep the annoyance from his voice.

'Thanks,' Zaq said.

He and Rita walked out of the office, leaving her dad to brood over the mess he had to deal with.

CHAPTER FIFTY-ONE

'You really think he believed all that?' Rita said when they were in the van.

'Seemed like it.'

'I feel kind of bad for my mum and dad and how they're going to cope with Raj and Parm going to prison.'

'Yeah, my parents had a hard time with it when I got sent down too. What your brothers will be up for is in a whole different league as well.'

'But they deserve it, for what they've done.'

Traffic through Southall was heavy, as usual. They talked about what Rita was going to do next. She would have to see if she still had a job after disappearing for a fortnight without any word. She'd also need to help her parents deal with the fallout once the police released her brothers' identities to the media and the public.

Although they didn't discuss it, there was also the matter of Davinder's death and how she would have to come to terms with it.

When they eventually reached Norwood Green, Rita directed

him to a large house with a big driveway, that overlooked the green itself.

'You going to be all right with your mum?'

Rita nodded. 'She might be a bit angry but she'll be glad I'm home. She'll worry what my dad will say but I'll tell her I've already spoken to him. She'll be relieved about that. Happy as I am about Raj and Parm getting arrested, I'm not really looking forward to explaining it to my mum... the things they've done. She won't take it well.'

She put her hand on the door handle, ready to open it, then turned back. 'You know, you should give Nina a call sometime. She was asking about you.'

'Really?'

'Yes. I think you made an impression on her – don't ask me why.' She said it deadpan but Zaq thought he saw a twinkle in her eye.

'She's obviously very intelligent,' he said.

'That's one explanation.' Now she did smile. 'You should call her, seriously.'

'What about the whole religion thing?'

'What religion thing?'

'You know – me being Muslim.'

'You are? Can't say I noticed.'

It was his turn to smile.

'We're not talking marriage or anything,' Rita said. 'She seems to like you... and I get the feeling you like her too. She's a grown up and thankfully, her family are *nothing* like mine. You should call her.'

'OK, I will.'

'Good. And thanks again, for everything you've done. I mean, look at the state of you; you went through all that for me.'

'I did it for me too.'

She put her hand on top of his, discreetly, and gave it a gentle squeeze. 'I really appreciate it, I want you to know that.' She withdrew her hand. 'I better go,' she said and opened the door. 'Maybe we'll see each other around.'

'Yeah, maybe we will.'

'How'd it go?' Jags asked when Zaq got to his place.

'Good. He bought it, just like we hoped. It all fits together and, when the police turn up the gear at the warehouse, it'll make everything we told him look like it was the truth.'

'How'd he take it?'

'Put it this way – I'm glad Rita was there. She's the only reason he kept a lid on it. Would've been a different story if I'd told him all that shit on my own.'

'He say anything about your part in it?'

'Yeah, asked me why I was at the house. I gave him the story. I don't think he'll suspect anything. The police report'll have me down as the victim. Raj and Parm saw me getting battered too, so even they'll say the same. It'll look like I was trying to protect their property, plus I made it clear they had nothing to do with beating me up. Looks like it's all going to work out.'

'I can't believe it,' Jags said, shaking his head and smiling. 'Where's Rita now?'

'Her old man told me to drop her off at home.'

'She going to be all right?'

'Yeah, I think so.'

'What about the arranged marriage and all that stuff?'

'No chance of that happening now, not with all the other shit that's going on. The old man said so himself.'

'Sorted. What about you? What you going to do now?'

'Sweet F.A. I managed to get the rest of the week off work – *paid* as well.'

'Wow, ain't you lucky? Talking of pay, that reminds me... Wait here, I'll be back in a minute.' Zaq heard him go upstairs, move around a bit and then come down again. 'I almost forgot about this.' He placed a package on the coffee table and pushed it toward Zaq. 'Here, it's for you.'

'What is it?'

'Open it and see.'

It was roughly the size of a house brick and looked like a large brown envelope wrapped around whatever was inside. It weighed about the same as a brick too. Zaq unrolled the package and examined the contents.

'What the fuck is this?'

'What's it look like?'

What it looked like was a fat wad of fifty-pound notes. 'Where d'you get it?'

'Don't get mad, OK...?'

'Tell me.'

'From Raj and Parm's warehouse, the night we were there having a look round.'

'What the –? *When*?'

'While you were upstairs, checking out the office.'

'I thought I told you not to take anything.'

Jags shrugged. 'It was just lying there. How were they going to know who took it?'

'*Bloody hell.*' Zaq looked at the bundle. 'How much is here?'

'That's about thirty grand.'

Zaq stared at it. 'What am I supposed to do with it?'

'Whatever the fuck you want. What you worried about? The rest of the money's going to be impounded by the cops. No one's going to miss what you got there. Besides, you ask me, you *earned* it. I mean, what else you got to show for all the shit you been through?'

Zaq had to admit he had a point, and when looked at that way it wasn't hard for him to agree. 'All right, but we should split it.'

'I already have. That's your half.'

'My *half*? That means you took –'

'Yep, sixty grand. I would've taken more but it was all I could fit in my jacket.'

Zaq recalled how Jags had carried his jacket out of the warehouse, all bundled up. 'You said it was covered with cement dust.'

'It was. I shook most of it off, then used it to carry the money.'

'You sneaky sod.' Zaq said, though unable to keep the smile from his face. 'You know what this calls for, don't you?'

'Let me guess. You want me to stick the kettle on, make some tea?'

'*Fuck tea*,' Zaq said. 'Let's go down the pub.'

ACKNOWLEDGEMENTS

This book took a long time to write and I've had the help and support of a great many people during the writing of it.

I'd like to thank Mary Flanagan, novelist and creative writing tutor at Birkbeck, University of London, who encouraged me to take a first stab at writing a novel, even though I wasn't sure that I was ready to. Her feedback and advice, along with that of the Creative Writing class I was part of, helped me to shape the first few of chapters and get the ball rolling.

I owe huge thanks to the Crime Writers' Association for awarding me their Debut Dagger, which was an enormous and totally unexpected surprise but one that gave me a tremendous boost along with the confidence to continue working on this story.

A massive thank you also to my agent, Jane Gregory, and all her team, especially Stephanie and Mary, who helped edit and improve the book and make it better than it would otherwise have been.

I am very grateful to Arts Council England for awarding me Grants for the Arts funding which allowed me time to concentrate fully on writing and completing the book.

For help in the early stages of writing, I would like to thank Romi Anwar and Meena Ladwa.

I am especially indebted to both Soop Sibia and Harvey Raihal, not just for reading early material and giving their feedback, but also for being there when needed and for being such excellent mates throughout the years – cheers guys. I'd also like to express my gratitude to Steve and Rob Brown, for all their help with this project – but even more importantly, for their friendship and all the laughter it's entailed.

I've been very fortunate to have had the support and encouragement of a great many wonderful friends and colleagues over the years, not just in the writing of this novel but throughout my life in general. I truly appreciate my good fortune in this and am immensely grateful to each and every one of you. This book would probably still have been written, regardless – but it would have been a lot harder and I would've been a much grumpier, more miserable sod without you all, so thank you.

Amer Anwar
London
2017

ABOUT THE AUTHOR

Amer Anwar grew up in West London. He has worked as a warehouse assistant, a comic book lettering artist, a driver for emergency doctors and a chalet rep in the French Alps, before eventually settling into a career as a creative artworker and graphic designer and spending over a decade producing artwork, mainly for the home entertainment industry. He holds an MA in Creative Writing from Birkbeck, University of London. Western Fringes is his first novel and was the winner of the prestigious Crime Writers' Association Debut Dagger Award.

Sign up to the free newsletter to receive news about forthcoming books, signings, events and offers, at;
www.ameranwar.com

Or link via social media at:
Twitter: @ameranwar
Facebook: www.facebook.com/ameranwar.author